**Alison Bruce** is the author of two non-fiction crime books. This is the first Gary Goodhew novel.

Alison lives in Cambridgeshire with her husband Jacen, and their two children.

# CAMBRIDGE BLUE

Alison Bruce

Robinson • London

Constable & Robinson Ltd
3 The Lanchesters
162 Fulham Palace Road
London W6 9ER
www.constablerobinson.com

First published in the UK by Constable,
an imprint of Constable & Robinson Ltd, 2008

This paperback edition published by Robinson,
an imprint of Constable & Robinson Ltd, 2010

First US edition published by SohoConstable,
an imprint of Soho Press Inc., 2009

This paperback edition published by SohoConstable,
an imprint of Soho Press Inc., 2010

Soho Press, Inc.
853 Broadway
New York, NY 10003
www.sohopress.com

A copy of the British Library Cataloguing in Publication Data is available from the
British Library

UK ISBN: 978-1-84901-264-5

US ISBN: 978-1-56947-877-6
US Library of Congress number: 2008028447

Typeset by TW Typesetting, Plymouth, Devon
Printed and bound in the EU

1 3 5 7 9 10 8 6 4 2

*For Jacen, Mum,*
*Natalie, Lana and Dean*

# PROLOGUE

Jackie Moran opened her eyes and stared up at the underside of her duvet – pulling it over her head was the last thing she remembered doing the previous night. One of her pillows now lay cocooned alongside her; the only sign that she'd moved in her sleep.

Unless someone else had put it there.

The faint orange glow of her night light leached through the edges of the duvet. She guessed it was still some time before dawn.

Motionless, she watched the graduated shades of ochre and grey, trying to persuade herself that there was no movement on the other side of the covers, but she was scared to look out, sure that someone would be waiting for her if she did. She listened, but the more she strained to hear, the more she was convinced that someone was breathing quietly in time with her. She held her breath and listened. Nothing.

She waited until the sound of her heart palpitations filled her ears, then began to breathe again.

Jackie moved slowly, turning her wrist just enough to see the fluorescent glow of her watch face. The trick would be to do it without disturbing the bedding. 4 a.m.

It was no surprise; every night without sleeping pills went this way. The same fear and paranoia. The same cold sweat that drenched her neck and breasts. The same feeling that her world was flat and she was sliding ever closer to the edge.

She shut her eyes and willed herself to sleep, counting her heartbeats and trying to ignore the familiar uneasy feeling that hovered above her, realizing that, today, it had become far more intense.

\* \* \*

1

She woke again at 6 a.m. with her hair tousled and tangled as though she'd tossed her head from side to side in her sleep. Her duvet lay on the floor. She couldn't remember what she'd dreamt; she refused to dwell on her nocturnal self-torture.

By 6.30 a.m., Jackie Moran had been out of bed for a full half-hour. She still wore her nightshirt; grey and thigh-length with the words 'Personal Trainer' across the front in pink lettering. She had been amused by the thought that she could one day be fit enough to work in a gym.

Her cottage originally had two bedrooms, but she had decided to have the second refitted as a bathroom. She kept the first floor heated throughout the night – it was one of her luxuries in life, allowing her to pad around with bare legs and feet. Pulling on her jeans and thick socks was always the last thing she did before going down to the cold downstairs.

She made up the bed, drew open the curtains, then crossed the small landing between the bedroom and bathroom. She called downstairs to her Border collie, 'Bridy, walk in five minutes.' She turned a blind eye to her dog spending nights on the settee.

In the sitting room, Bridy uncurled herself and slid on to the stone floor. She dutifully took her place at the bottom of the stairs and waited for her mistress.

Jackie's clean underwear was drying in an orderly left-to-right queue on top of the radiator. They had come from the same home-shopping catalogue as her nightshirt. It was only the second time she had worn them, and already she could see that the quality wasn't great.

She ran the basin's hot tap until the water steamed, then dropped the polished plug into place and left the basin to fill. She pulled off her nightshirt, folding it as she made her way, naked, back to the bedroom to leave it under her pillow. Jackie glanced at herself in the dressing-table mirror; she had no objections to her figure. She had long since accepted that it was her lot to be boy-like rather than womanly. Perhaps she would have paused longer if there had been anyone to see her naked. There wasn't.

Dressed in her ski jacket and jeans, Jackie opened the cottage's side door on to the Fen Ditton morning and checked the weather for the first time. Not that it mattered: barring a change of boots for floods or unexpected snowfall, there was no British weather that would prevent her from taking Bridy on her morning walk.

A damp chill hung in the air. She put Bridy on the lead, and the dog trailed at her heels, grey muzzle close to her left hand.

This was the village at its best; fresh with a new morning and blissfully few people. Not that she disliked people, but they were likely to be a distraction, and she needed space to think.

Bridy paused to snuffle in the verge. Jackie rattled the choke chain and made a clicking noise with her tongue against the roof of her mouth. 'Not yet, Bridy.'

Bridy responded with a sneeze, then continued to trot alongside her.

Jackie cast a concerned eye over the war memorial. A delinquent had defaced the 'Lest We Forget' by changing the 'L' to a 'B'. The press had inevitably jumped to the defence of the youth. The *Cambridge News* had done a survey of local schools and reported a 'commendable knowledge of the two World Wars amongst local teenagers'.

Words are cheap.

Mr Mills at the post office had actually done something about it. He had campaigned for a custodial sentence, which had apparently scared the lad witless in the process.

She walked past the post office, its windows polished and paintwork immaculate; she had a great deal of respect for Mr Mills and his determination to care for the village. The idea of standing up in public like that was impossibly daunting and she'd been glad when the press's brief interest had died.

She checked herself. Wasn't she suddenly sounding middle-aged? The point of her whole routine had been to make her daily life more efficient, but she could now see it had merely caused her to become set in her ways. She was touring the village complaining about other people, when perhaps she should look at her own life with the same critical eye.

Jackie wasn't about to dwell on all the things she'd once thought she would be able to accomplish by the age of thirty. She didn't need to list them to know that she'd ticked none of the boxes, and with only one month to go they were most likely to remain unrealized. But was this it, then?

3

Damn, what if it was?

At the Plough public house, the road curved to the right with a tractor-width mud track diverging to the left. She let Bridy off the lead and followed this trail in the direction of the river path, walking between the tyre tracks on the raised strip of stones and divots.

Once clear of the pub and its family gardens, she enjoyed her favourite view of the village: the mercurial Cam flowed on her left, grey and swift today; like cold, molten metal.

On her right, beyond the paddock, stood a telegraph pole fanning out cables to the surrounding houses. Villages were still supposed to be places of community, even if the neighbours didn't know one another anymore. For the umpteenth time in her adult life, Jackie wondered how different it would have been if her mother had lived; the cottage could have been less of a comfort and more of a joy.

She diverted her attention away from the houses to where, in the paddock itself, a grey and a roan wore matching royal-blue head collars and New Zealand rugs. The grey raised his head and watched the pair of them pass. Jackie paused to pat Bridy.

It started to drizzle, the tiny rain droplets making silent dimples in the river, adding to the waters flowing through from Cambridge and out towards Ely, and eventually the Wash.

Two eight-oared boats nosed around the bend ahead, pulling upstream, rowing back to the college boathouses. They came and went in seconds, each man puffing warm white breath and breaking the peace with grunts of coordinated exertion. The oars skimmed and creaked past Jackie and she knew that they were concentrating far too much to notice the figure she had just glimpsed, standing in the shadows.

The man waited in the drizzle, a quarter of a mile further along the banks of the Cam, leaning on the fence that ran beside the footpath, sheltering under the bare branches of the overhanging trees.

As far as she knew, she was the only one who'd ever noticed him. The first time she'd passed him, she thought he looked strange, standing alone under a tree. He looked like a labourer waiting for the team van. Except there was no road; and she happened to know he had his own van.

That had been three weeks ago, when she'd heard him trying to start it as she walked back home. It had taken several disruptive attempts before the van's starter motor stopped rasping like a distressed saw and reluctantly allowed the engine to fire. It had driven past her as it whined and pinked its way back out of the village, puffing oil-tinged blue smoke from its exhaust.

She'd written the registration number on her memo board, where it had stayed until she'd overwritten it with the date of her dental appointment.

She was less than 100 yards from him when he glanced at her. Today he had his black woollen hat tugged tight over his cropped ginger hair. In fact, all his clothes were dark and, somehow, that made him loom larger on her path ahead.

She turned to Bridy; it gave her an excuse to look away. Bridy snuffled in the hedgerow, interested in the smells drawn out by the rain.

'Come on, Bridy.' Her voice sounded unnaturally bright, brittle even. 'It's too cold to stop.'

Britain, she decided, had become a country full of women looking for rapists and muggers down every alley, and she wasn't about to become the next victim of a nation's raging paranoia. But goose-bumps still rose on her neck and scuttled up on to her face. Suddenly she wanted to turn round and go home.

He stared at her as she approached; he'd never made eye contact before but, she reminded herself, he'd never done her any harm before either. His face glowed moon-white, punctured by dark, dilated bullet holes for eyes and nostrils exuding short blasts of steam.

She ignored the way her heart was thumping as though it wanted to escape her chest. Besides, she was not prepared to change her routine for anyone.

Jackie forced herself to keep walking, even though every instinct told her to turn and run. She drew deep breaths, hoping they'd calm her, but the harsh chill in the air only felt like an in-draught of terror. Her muscles seemed to have atrophied. Her head felt giddy and all she could think was *run, run, run.* She thought it until she was too close to change course.

She passed within two feet of him and heard a sharp crackle of movement from the hedgerow. She didn't turn to face him, but the first wave of fear arrived even before she felt his hands at her throat.

5

It paralysed her. Sucked her inside herself to a place where her body was no longer her own and where her last seconds would be torn from her as easily as tearing paper. His grip was ferocious, compassionless, crushing her windpipe, making the pain scream in her ears and silencing the rest of her world.

She saw Bridy, just a tumble of black and white. Then a second wave washed over Jackie, but this time it was adrenalin that surged through her. And Bridy rushed again, barking and buffeting his shins.

'Shut up,' he snarled, and lashed out with his boot. Bridy was faster and dodged the kick. His grip slipped, and Jackie threw herself sideways, grabbing at the undergrowth; anything for escape. She tried to roll away, but he lunged at her legs, grabbing her at the knees, pulling her back to the ground. One hand reached up and his fingers grabbed the belt buckle on her jeans; he hauled himself on top of her, working his way up her body. His face drew closer to hers, his breath hot. She had no room to manoeuvre now, and for one long moment it seemed that neither of them moved. His weight pressed down on her, chest to breast, pelvis to pelvis, pushing her legs apart. With one free hand he reached downwards, and she expected to feel his fingers tugging at the zip on her jeans, but instead he felt for something in his own back pocket.

Bridy renewed her barking, just as Jackie saw the knife in his hand. He lashed out his leg once more. This time the dog launched herself, grabbing the hem of the man's trousers between her teeth. She pulled hard. He extended his foot and attempted another kick. 'Fuck off,' he yelled, but Bridy held tight and growled as she yanked at his outstretched leg.

The knife sprang from his fingers, landing silently in the long grass. As he reached to grab it, Jackie wriggled one arm free, slipped her hand into her jacket pocket and grabbed for Bridy's collar and lead.

Still on the ground, the man hauled himself towards the knife, heaving the weight of Bridy along with him. His fingertips brushed the handle, but he was still not close enough to take hold of it. She knew that if he reached it, he would finish the job.

The choke chain still ran in a loop and, with one movement, Jackie hooked it over his head. His reaction was delayed: it seemed several seconds before his body jerked, then he let go of her and his hands shot up to his own throat.

She dragged on the lead and he pulled it back towards him, slackening the chain momentarily. *It's him or me. Him or me.*

His eyes were still wild, but now they bulged with fear. Jackie kicked out. One leg, then the other, pulled free of him and the hard toes of her boots drove into his abdomen and chest. He hung on to the metal links of the lead, but she refused to release her grip. Then her knee connected with his jaw, cracking against the bone and sending his teeth into his tongue.

Finally she found the foothold she sought and pushed hard on his sternum. Her body flexed rigid and she pulled the lead tight until the links slipped out of his fingers and the chain had all but disappeared into an engorged welt around his purpling neck.

Bridy let go first, but by then the man was dead.

Jackie Moran retreated. Standing with her back in the hawthorn, she stared down at the body. Two questions screamed at her. *Who? Why?*

Bridy looked up at her, waiting for her to decide what to do next.

Something bright caught her eye. She stepped past Bridy and looked down at it. It was the knife, its blade poking up at the angle of a shark's fin. She knelt beside it; it was a kitchen knife, not an everyday folding pocket kind that some men carried.

Jackie picked it up, holding it with the tip of its blade between her forefinger and thumb, before taking it by the handle and testing its sharpness. It would have been an efficient murder weapon. She stroked the flat of the steel. This man had deliberately brought it with him to use on her. She wasn't surprised when a familiar nausea began to stir inside her. This had been no random attack. This had been the lingering and diseased fingers of the past clawing at her just when she'd dared to think about the future.

The edge of the water was about eight feet away. Heavy tufts of grass topped the bank, and from there she knew that the eroded sides dropped sharply into the deep river just beyond. She threw the knife and watched it disappear below the ripples.

She could have handed it over to the police, of course, but she pictured the familiar doubtful expression, and that look it turned into: part pity, part disgust. She closed her eyes and when she reopened them, she couldn't locate the spot where the knife had sunk.

The riverbank remained deserted, and she guessed a body could be buffeted some distance before it was eventually discovered. Then she shook her head, not fully believing what she had just done.

She rolled him over to the water, reminding herself of a single truth: it was now too late to look for help.

He slipped in head first, making a wave of water which slopped back against the bank. He descended gradually, turning slowly from man to a ghostly shadow to nothingness.

Jackie stepped back from the edge and reached out for the warmth of Bridy. She rubbed the soft fur at the base of Bridy's ear. 'Good girl, we're safe now,' she whispered shakily. 'It's all over.' But in her own voice she heard the unmistakable sound of a lie.

# ONE

Rolfe Street was only a short walk from the heart of Cambridge, but it was a perpetual backwater, seeing no accidental visitors and few daytime inhabitants.

A lone man stood on the pavement waiting to speak to Lorna Spence: the same woman who was spying on him from her first-floor window. So far he'd knocked twice, but she had no intention of letting him know she was at home.

She stood behind a carefully placed ruck in the curtains. She knew he couldn't see her but, even so, she kept perfectly still in case he glanced up and caught the flicker of her shadow.

Lorna Spence had gone to bed wearing nothing but yesterday's knickers, and that was all she wore now as she studied the top of his head.

He took a few short steps towards the door, and then a few towards the street. Again he ran his hand in an impatient foray through his hair, completing the gesture by clasping it across the back of his neck. He drew closer to the door, leaning in towards it and listening. His hand, still on his neck, massaged the rigid muscles which locked the top of his spine.

He was obviously stressed.

She imagined him swearing under his breath. He took a step back and his gaze shot up to her window, boring into the gap between the curtains. He seemed to stare straight into her face, but she didn't blink.

A tingling feeling sprang across her bare skin, racing in waves across her shoulders and trickling across her small, freckled breasts. Only her chest moved, rising and falling ever quicker; trying to keep pace with her heartbeat.

Lorna waited for him to knock again, but instead he stepped away and out of sight of her little spyhole. She moved closer to the gap and crept around until she had a view of the closed end of the cul-de-sac. She soon located him again. He stood on the edge of the kerb with his hands on his hips.

'Go away. Go on, get in your car and drive away,' she whispered down to him.

His attention had settled on the rows of parked vehicles flanking each side of the road. She knew he wouldn't recognize any of them.

Then he left, walking briskly towards his own car at the end of the street. He'd accepted what she already knew: that he had no reason to believe she was at home.

She waited. He started the engine and let the postman pass without cross-examination. Then he pulled away and drove out of sight. But she still waited, watching the road until she'd counted to one hundred and was sure he wouldn't return.

And then she exhaled with a long puff. Her heartbeat gradually slowed and her pulse steadied.

The letterbox creaked as it opened and there was an echoing snap as it shut. The junk mail made a heavy thud as it hit the hallway's tiled floor. She leant over the handrail and checked, in case an unexpected letter looked tempting enough for a dash downstairs.

A large holiday brochure lay face down, obscuring any other post that may have been underneath. A photo of a caravan park and the words 'Family Entertainment' jumped out at her through the clear plastic envelope.

'Why me?' she groaned. Last week the mail had been sit-in baths and stair-lifts. What a waste of time.

Her dressing table was a wide antique pine chest of drawers with a reproduction pine mirror on top. She only owned the mirror and the battery clock next to it. It was 8.35 a.m. and she was going to be late for work.

In the circumstances, late would be a good thing. But not too late, she couldn't afford trouble at the office as well. She padded into the bathroom, pulled off her knickers and threw them into the corner with the rest of the week's laundry. She ran the hot tap until the water flowed warm, and meanwhile damped down her short, ash-blonde hair, working her fingers through the feathered strands at the back so they lay close to the nape of the neck.

She dressed quickly and chose Warm Mocha lipstick. She ran it back and forth across her lips, then dabbed it on to her cheekbones, rubbing it in to give the approximation of blusher. That would do.

She checked her reflection, aware that the skim of freckles across each cheek and a lucky gap between her two front teeth gave her face more character than any layer of make-up.

She grabbed her bag and hurried downstairs. As she reached the bottom stair, she could see other letters buried under the brochure.

Five pairs of her shoes were lined up beside the door; in two-inch heels she made five foot five. Just.

She reached for the post, slipping her feet into her highest shoes as she turned the envelopes over. There were four. She flicked through them. Mobile phone bill, bank statement, credit card bill. Then the fourth. White, A5, and emblazoned with an advert for a bank loan. But it was the addressee's name which caught her eye. Miss H. Sellars.

Lorna frowned. A chill tickled her scalp, then vanished. How strange, she thought. She shook her head and smiled. What an amazing coincidence. She suddenly wondered whether the holiday brochure was similarly addressed. She slid it from under the other post.

The black print on the white label jumped out at her. Instant fear washed the smile from her lips. She recoiled and the post scattered, tumbling from her fingers on to the floor. The corner of the clear envelope hit the mat, bounced and landed, slapping down flat on its face.

She opened the front door and hurried away down the street. Behind her, the hall tiles stayed cold, rebuffing the unanswered ring of the telephone upstairs.

11

# TWO

The punting station was quiet. A few ducks paddled on the river but the punts were stationary, and tightly moored to one another.

Most of the buildings around the cobbled quayside square had been converted into cafés and restaurants. Some had flats above; luxury apartments with romantic views of the river and discreet street-level entrances. One of these doors, however, bore a chrome plaque which read 'The Excelsior Clinic'.

As Lorna crossed the quayside, she was already forty-five minutes late for work. The wind blowing along The Backs made it too cold to sit outside, but tables and umbrellas cluttered the pavement. No doubt trying to entice people inside. Lorna knocked over a chair as she hurried through. It clattered on to its side, then clattered again as she paused to haul it back on to its feet.

The outer door was unlocked and Lorna hurried up the steps to where a woman with a prematurely grey, middle-aged haircut sat behind the reception desk. She wore half-moon glasses and her blouse was buttoned up to the top.

Lorna slapped her hand on the oak counter-top. 'Morning. Are you from the agency?'

The woman nodded and introduced herself as Faith Carver. That figured: nothing more glamorous would fit.

Lorna smiled, reached over and shook her hand. 'I'm Lorna. I do the accounts through there.' She pointed at the frosted-glass panel behind Faith's chair.

'Oh, good. I have lots of messages for you.'

Lorna swung up the hinged end of the reception counter and slid back the glass partition which led to her office. She worked alone in a twelve-foot-square space that contained two desks, two phones, two chairs and one kettle. 'Give me a minute to sort myself out and I'll be with you. Tea or coffee?'

'Not for me, thanks. I'll wait until eleven.'

The corner of Lorna's mouth flickered with the hint of an ironic smile. That made a change; a temp with a work ethic.

Though Faith remained on her side of the open door, Lorna chatted to her as she organized her morning drink. 'When I first worked here, I thought Excelsior sounded like a brand of condom. After a while, I realized how appropriate it was too.' Lorna stole a quick glance at Faith's ring finger and saw that she wore a wedding band. 'This business is all about sex,' she added.

Faith raised an eyebrow. 'Is it?'

'Yup. I've been here two years and nearly every treatment that we perform is cosmetic. The dental department does caps and whitening, the eye clinic does laser treatment so people can chuck out their glasses, and that's nothing compared to the surgery lot. Have you heard of Botox?'

Faith shrugged. 'I've heard the name.' She sounded vague.

'It costs three hundred and fifty quid for a ten-minute session. And for that, Mr Moran injects them, paralysing their facial muscles with shots of purified botulism. It's nearly all women, and they roll out of here feeling like sex kittens.'

Faith picked up a notepad and tore off the top sheet. 'Dr Moran is one of your messages.'

'It's Mr, not Dr,' Lorna corrected and carried on cheerfully, 'I think there's nothing like tossing money around to boost a woman's libido.' Mr Moran's schedule lay on the top of her in-tray. She checked it: no cancellations. She ran her finger down the list, making a rough total of the bills to be issued. Almost £12,000. 'Same tomorrow, too. Twelve grand for one day's work.'

Faith shook her head. 'I don't think I need to know all of this.'

Lorna paused. 'I'm sorry, I didn't mean to sound indiscreet, but I find it fascinating. Besides, you work here now. And I'm not saying he doesn't deserve his success. He often works ten-hour days so he can see people who travel up from London after work. And everyone says he's very good.'

She looked across at her post tray, stacked deep from a single delivery. Her job included issuing neat bills in crisp, tamper-proof envelopes and banking the personal cheques which, in his case, arrived by return of post. No one kept Mr Moran waiting for payment, not when his diary was full two months ahead, and trustworthy consultants were so hard to find. 'Very, very good,' she added.

Faith nodded. 'Don't mind me, I just have some old-fashioned views and I'm sure they don't count for anything in the world of business.'

They each turned back to their respective desks. Faith's note was written in her own style of shorthand, with names and single words separated by commas. 'Dr Moran, moran, redhd.'

Lorna frowned, rolled her chair towards Faith and passed the note back to her. 'What does it mean?'

Faith glanced at it and explained, stressing that '*Mr* Moran rang twice. Wanted to know where you were and said you had to ring the second you arrived.'

Lorna cut in. 'What did he say?'

'Just that. And then a nurse stopped by.'

'Victoria?' It was a redundant question since Victoria was the only person in the building who looked remotely nurse-like.

'Again, I don't know. To be honest, she was pretty rude. She looked rather out of sorts when I said you weren't in. Swore several times, in fact.'

'A slim redhead?'

Faith nodded. 'Skinny and rude.'

'She's all right, she just gets stressed and makes a drama out of things. So, what did she want?'

'I'm sorry, I have no idea.'

Lorna didn't respond immediately to any of the messages. Instead, she raised invoices until she stopped for an early break at 10.30 a.m.. She closed the door between herself and reception, had two cups of coffee and a packet of salt and vinegar crisps, then composed a two-word text on her mobile. 'Miss you.'

Her phone bleeped twice almost immediately. 'Where are you?'

'Here.'

She put her mobile to one side and positioned herself with her fingers poised over the keyboard and an alert gaze fixed to the centre of her screen. She estimated he'd be in before she'd counted to thirty. She'd reached twenty-seven when she heard the office door opening.

She didn't turn, but she could imagine he still looked as stressed as he had earlier from her bedroom window. 'Good morning,' she said brightly.

'Where were you?' His words were clipped, tight with the anger he was trying to keep screwed up in a ball of reason.

'Sorry I was late in.' She spun slowly in her seat and gave him an easy smile. 'I overslept.'

'I called by your flat this morning and you weren't there.'

She kept the smile going, warming her face with it and letting her eyes glow. 'Today?' she queried. She saw stubbornness in his gaze. 'I just told you, I overslept.'

'You would have heard me,' he insisted.

'I didn't. Perhaps I was in the shower?' She tilted her head to one side and stayed patient.

'You weren't there,' he insisted.

'Where was I then?' She suddenly glared at him.

He glared back. 'That's what I want to know, Lorna.'

'Where are you accusing me of being? Are you saying I was off screwing another man?'

'Keep your voice down.'

'Are you?'

'Just tell me where you were.'

'And if I was with a friend? Isn't that OK? Do you suddenly have a right to dictate what I do in my own time?'

'Of course not.'

'So you think I was with someone else?'

'Lorna.' He reached out to grab her arm, but she squirmed away from him. Finally, she heard the first note of defeat in his voice. 'Please stop.'

'OK, I'll tell you. I was there when you called and I saw you from my window.'

He looked doubtful.

'You parked at the end of the road and the postman walked by just before you drove away.'

'Then why—'

15

'Because you were checking up on me again. I was at home. Alone. And I'm not going to keep pandering to your jealousy.' She reached forward and took his hand, then whispered, 'I love you, Richard, but I won't go on like this.'

At twelve, Lorna took lunch, glad to have a break from looking through her post tray. It reminded her of the mail scattered on her front door mat; she was desperate to rush home and open it. She needed to know if she would find a note inside. Or a threat, even. She pressed her tongue against the gap in her teeth for luck, and slipped out past the receptionist.

# THREE

The previous week's bank holiday had motivated a surge of tourists to descend on the city, and now, although busier than in April, the streets were comparatively quiet again. The shops bustled, but the tills were slow.

Alice Moran was just over five feet eight, and slender; at thirty-nine she possessed a mix of maturity and girlishness. Her skin was tinted with a hint of winter tan and she wore well-polished sunglasses.

She held a large paper carrier from one of the better dress shops; it contained a pair of size-ten suede trousers and a coordinating rust-coloured blouse. The fact that they were almost identical to the ones which she was wearing hadn't deterred her. Trousers suited her they were practical and sat better on her narrow and slightly angular frame.

She had used the morning in a deliberately unproductive fashion, having decided she had been pushing herself a little too hard lately. She knew, from experience, that it didn't take a great deal of effort to achieve results, and continuing to spend time perfecting the filing would do nothing more than turn her into another Richard. God forbid.

Besides, when she became too fussy, she knew it took the fun out of working alongside her brother. She liked to think that he enjoyed being supported, rather than managed.

Alice was now approaching the last of the shops. A few yards ahead, the Round Church was busy trying to entice the older tourists with brass-rubbing and tea event. Probably served in flowered china and accompanied by a sugar-sprinkled slice of Victoria sandwich. Would that be the highlight of her own day in another thirty years, she wondered?

Suddenly she wasn't looking forward to the end of her free morning and, although she knew she'd feel guilty if she arrived any later, she pushed her sunglasses up on to her head and slipped in through the nearest doorway. The shop was full of old-fashioned, glass cases displaying pipes and tobacco and model cars. A big boy's nostalgia emporium.

A globe caught her eye; it was football-sized and stood in the window, displayed against a fanned-out selection of postcards depicting the golden age of steam. Bet they didn't know it was a golden age when they were actually in it, she thought idly.

She touched the globe's surface, her fingers brushing across Europe. She was about to look closer, wondering whether she'd managed to find the Pyrenees by feel alone, when in the street just outside, a familiar figure caught her eye.

The figure wore black, as she always did, and walked quickly – any faster would have been a jog. It was Lorna, her colleague and her brother's girlfriend. She looked preoccupied, her expression slightly manic: somewhere between mild ecstasy and bubbling hysteria. She passed the window without spotting Alice.

And, as if just the act of her walking past had dragged a change of mood along in its wake, Alice felt reluctant to go to the Excelsior Clinic. But she had the instinct to find Richard. She could always sense when he needed her.

# FOUR

Alice took the stairs and, as she reached the top of the first flight, she heard footsteps coming towards her. They were leather-soled shoes which skimmed the steps as they hurried down. She knew by sound alone, that they belonged to her brother. He rounded the corner, pulling himself quickly towards the handrail to save himself from careering into her.

'I'm sorry!' He was holding his car keys and mobile phone, and trying to keep moving while still bundling himself into his jacket.

She smiled. 'In a rush?'

'Yes, I need to catch up with Lorna. She's not answering her mobile.'

'She's already gone.'

'I know. I wanted to have lunch with her.'

'No, no, I saw her. She's already in Sidney Street.'

He stopped in his tracks and scowled. 'Oh fuck.'

Alice touched his arm. 'Will I do?'

He smiled and it made him look boyish, almost as young as Lorna, in fact. 'Anything to avoid work?' he quipped.

She narrowed her eyes in mock annoyance. 'Do you really begrudge me my morning off?' They walked back down the stairs side by side. Alice, in her heels was only an inch shorter than her brother. She saw their reflection in the mirror-panelled foyer wall and wondered whether they might have been mistaken for twins, if he didn't look at least eight years younger, instead of nearly two.

'No. You'll do.'

'Thanks,' she said sarcastically. He held the outer door open for her, and as she glanced into his face, she saw he really didn't look as good as she had first thought. Perhaps the interior lighting had been overflattering, or maybe the May daylight was just a bit too honest.

She gave him a smile, but it was a sad one. She felt sorry for the stress he was under: bad events certainly took their toll on him. 'Are you snowed under still?'

'I'm fine.' He glanced at her and seemed to know that she was worried. 'It's not that, Alice. It's . . .' He paused. 'Come on, I'll tell you over lunch.'

They walked back the same way she'd only just come, heading towards the centre of the city. 'I don't mind where we go; I've just been in town. Here will do,' she added, hopefully, as they passed the last of the restaurants.

Alice spied the globe in the shop window ahead again, and then the sign outside the Round Church; God help Richard's frame of mind if he were to try taking her for lunch in there. But instead, he took a right up Trinity Street and led them past the entrances to the colleges.

'I don't need the tourist route, Richard,' she protested.

They marched shoulder to shoulder, their strides matching.

'I do. I think it's good to remember what a beautiful place we live in,' he replied. 'How lucky we are.' Yet he passed Trinity without even a glance through the ancient gate, towards the perfect green of the quadrangle lawns beyond.

She knew they were both lucky to live there. She always looked. Even now, with Richard walking ever faster, she stole a glance at the small statue of King Henry, and the chair leg he held in the place of a sceptre. What sort of man brandished a chair leg? Hadn't the university establishment realized that leaving it in place was mocking the monarch? 'I don't need the tourist bit today is what I meant. Where are we going exactly?'

'By the river.'

Of course, he wanted to look at the water.

Neither of them spoke again until they reached the Anchor pub. Alice chose a table with a clear view of the mill pond, while Richard went to the bar and returned with two half pints of IPA.

Alice was looking at the river, and Richard settled into the opposite seat and watched it too. It snaked towards them through the flat of the water meadow, in the distance, a scattered herd of cows grazed, up to their hocks in rich spring grass.

'Do cows get laminitis?'

Alice shook her head. 'Never heard of that. It's probably only an equine illness.'

'Just as well.'

The water slipped through the sluice gates, calmer and more refined as it tiptoed up The Backs, probably so as not to disturb the scholars.

Alice was the first to look away from the river. 'Remember when we were children? We all loved the water, but you most of all.'

Richard sipped his beer.

'And if you cried, Mother would say, "Let him see some water," and if we were indoors, she'd run the tap and you'd settle down straight away.'

He let her finish the anecdote, though she'd told it many times before. It gave him extra time to put off talking about the present. Those were his best childhood memories anyway; the later ones were rarely so fond.

His eyes flickered and made him refocus on the present. Alice was staring at him, not unkindly, just tolerantly, as if she'd been doing so for some time. Waiting for him to answer something. He tried to remember hearing a question. No, but he could guess what she was expecting, and he wanted to tell her anyway. Or at least, he *thought* he would feel better if he did.

'Do you think Lorna's too young for me?' he began.

Alice smiled. 'Well, the age gap's the same as it's always been. Are you suddenly thinking of marrying her or something?'

'No. Should I?'

'Haven't a clue. Do you want to get married?'

Richard screwed up his face. 'Sometimes I do, but I'm not sure enough. But then again, I don't want to lose her.'

'And you think you will?'

'She wasn't at home when I dropped by this morning.'

'So?'

'That means she didn't go home last night. But she didn't stay with me either.'

'Perhaps she was up early. Don't start making assumptions. You can't expect to know every move a person makes, that would be unreasonable. You know that, don't you?'

'Uh-huh.'

'Ask her where she was, then. But in a nice way.'

'I did.'

'And?'

'She said she was in the shower, but . . .'

Alice leant across the table. 'Richard, look at me. You can't let yourself start to get possessive. You know that's when it starts going wrong.'

Richard nodded dumbly. Finally, he whispered, 'You're her friend . . .' His words trailed away, but Alice could guess the rest of the question.

'OK,' she replied, 'I'll have a chat with her, but I'm sure you're worrying over nothing. You always feel she's loyal to you, don't you?'

'Yes, but . . .'

Alice reached over and squeezed his hand. He seemed like a little boy again, but that gave her a feeling of relief rather than concern. 'You're feeling jealous again, aren't you?'

He squeezed her hand in return. 'I know it's stupid, but yes, I am.'

# FIVE

Lorna never made it home. Three times her mobile rang, and each time she saw Richard's mobile number appear on the display. When it rang for a fourth time, she expected it would be him again, but this time the name 'Victoria' flashed up. Lorna was still tempted not to answer, but she knew how some people were like bills: sooner or later, they had to be paid off.

She flipped open the handset and held it to her ear. 'What?'

Lorna wasn't surprised when there followed two or three seconds without reply. She could picture Victoria, alone, at a table or standing in a corridor, cigarette in one hand, mobile in the other, smelling of cosmetics and letting a languid smile settle on her lips before even thinking about opening them to speak.

Victoria's voice was mellow. 'I'd love to take a vacation in your brain – just empty space and the luxury of being the centre of the universe for two whole weeks.'

Lorna didn't rise to it, and pitched her reply mid-distance between matter of fact and uninterested. 'What do you want?'

'An answer.'

This was the conversation she knew she already needed to have with Victoria, and despite avoiding her for a week or more, she felt relieved it was finally here. 'I'm not leaving.'

That was easy.

'Then I'll speak to Richard.'

'That's fine, because I've told him everything.' Lorna put a chirpy note into her voice, hoping it might hide the bluff.

'Even about your latest plan? I doubt it somehow.'

Lorna frowned. 'I have no idea what you're talking about.'

23

'That's funny, because a murdered baby wouldn't slip *my* mind.' Sardonic as ever.

Lorna's intake of breath was both sharp and audible. It wasn't Victoria knowing about little David that was frightening – after all, they'd both read the same pages. Even though the case was now over twenty years old, they both saw the potential in a document that turned it from 'natural causes' into 'wilful murder'. It was the mention of him in relation to recent events that made her gasp since she'd suddenly realized that one malicious moment from Victoria could destroy everything.

Victoria added another of her long pauses. When she spoke again, Lorna guessed it was intended to make her squirm even more; though, in fact, it had the opposite effect. 'Or doesn't he believe it was murder?'

Victoria hadn't exactly got the wrong end of the stick, but she was clearly poking it around until she could be sure which was the right end. Lorna was determined not to give anything else away. They'd both recognized the initial vulnerability in her voice; now Lorna was careful to maintain an air of panic. 'I don't know. We should discuss this.'

'Talking to you never works.'

'Hold on, let me think. Look, Victoria, I can come up with an answer that will work for both of us. I know I can, but just give me a little time.'

'By tonight, Lorna, or I'll tell them everything. Today is the last day where I get screwed around by you.'

After that phone call, Lorna changed direction. She wandered into the city centre, casting an unenthusiastic eye towards the shop windows. At least she knew there was no rush to reach home. But beyond that, she had no idea what to do next. After almost ten minutes of deliberation, she made two calls. She was pleased when her first was answered with 'Hi, Lorna.' At least her number was still stored in his phone's memory.

'Are you around later? I need cheering up,' she said.

Then she phoned Richard's mobile to apologize for missing his calls, and found him in a state of post-jealousy calmness. She offered to work late to make up for her late arrival, but instead he offered to buy her lunch. When she hesitated, he added, 'And dessert. Alice is here too.'

24

She laughed. 'Good.'

'Dessert or Alice?'

'Both.' She strode out towards the Anchor pub, her mind never leaving the dilemma of Victoria's ultimatum.

Richard waved when he saw her. She waved back, momentarily wondering whether he really did love her enough to forgive everything. However, it wasn't worth the risk.

Alice held out a large glass of white wine. 'You look like you need this.'

After the second glass, Lorna began to see the possibility of a compromise: a version of the truth she could tell Richard, as well as the opportunity to make Victoria leave her alone. Jackie was the key. Perhaps, with a little help and a little luck, she wouldn't face losing him.

By the third, she saw that it was just a question of juggling her plans for the evening, and keeping the right people on her side.

# SIX

DI Marks reached the top of the stairs and headed down the corridor, towards his office. He was reviewing the statement he'd just made to the local paper, turning it over again in his head. It preoccupied him, though no one would have known because he had always found it so easy to remain expressionless.

For example, he knew that his fifteen-year-old daughter, Emily, currently had a crush on a lad called Pip. Pip was taking his GCSEs and liked The Kooks, ice hockey and skateboarding. Marks imagined that Pip would have shoulder-length wavy hair, chewed nails and a total vocabulary of about two dozen varying grunts.

Meanwhile, his wife swapped flirty emails with a builder called Gordon, who lived near Inverness and claimed to share her interest in daisy growing. Marks didn't take it too seriously, and was pretty confident that his wife didn't either.

But the point was no one suspected that he knew, and whether it was really a skill, or just his natural demeanour, it was something he'd often found useful when dealing with both his detectives and his suspects.

This evening, he'd used it as a mask for his concern. He'd left the team finishing a three-hour stint in the city centre, handing out leaflets and reminding women that most of the recent spate of rapes had occurred between 5 and 8 p.m. As though they needed reminding. He was sure that every office worker within fifty miles was fully aware that any one of them might become the next target and, unless a swift arrest followed, there would undoubtedly be a 'next target'. Forensics had managed to isolate a sample of the attacker's DNA and Marks had made a statement to the press using words like 'confident', 'imminent' and 'positive identification', thankful that they couldn't read the helplessness he really felt. Yes, he was certain that they would catch the man, but without a stroke of luck, he doubted that it would happen before they had the details of at least one more traumatized woman added to their files.

He walked into his office, flicked the light switch and spotted a manila envelope left squarely in the centre of his otherwise empty desk. He drew a sharp breath of recognition and his memory flashed back three months to the first time this had happened. Despite the official line, he found himself hoping that this might provide the same sort of luck that had helped close their last serious case.

Initially, he didn't touch the envelope. He hooked his jacket over the hat stand, walked around the desk and lowered himself slowly into his chair. He paused for several seconds, tapping the desk in indecision, as he considered calling a SOCO down to open it, letting them fingerprint it pending an investigation. Then he considered the next victim and slid it closer. He'd look first, then decide.

He tore open one end of the envelope, and tipped its contents onto the desk. The first item to slip out was a toothbrush in a clear plastic bag, the second was a single page of white A4. It had been folded in half, just as before, and he could see the shadow of print showing through from the other side of the sheet. In his top drawer he kept a pack of sterile gloves, and he slipped a pair over his hands before touching the paper. He smoothed it open on the desk.

The text was brief, and to the point. 'This toothbrush belongs to Ian Knott, 205 York Road, Cambridge, and will be a DNA match for the Airport Rapist.'

He smiled; he liked the note-maker's use of the words 'will be', and he also liked the way they thus crushed his pessimism. Next, he found his own evidence bag and scooped up the envelope and its contents.

He realized that the notes had to stop before they began to undermine the official investigation. He stopped smiling with the knowledge that the culprit must be one of his own team. For all their front and initiative, they'd be sacrificing their own job if they didn't watch out.

There wasn't one he wanted to lose, but Marks thought about each of his detectives in turn, silently listing them from the longest-serving to the latest to finish his probation. Only the final name stood out.

DC Gary Goodhew: the departmental enigma. The twenty-five-year-old who had reached detective faster than anyone else Marks knew.

Goodhew had been at Parkside for six months. Marks had informed the team that their new colleague was a high-flying, privately educated graduate with a First in Maths. He had immediately realized that what he'd intended as a build-up sounded more like a warning, and Goodhew was thus met with a very chilly reception.

It had only lasted until about lunchtime on day one. By the afternoon, DC Charles had offered him a place on the pool team and PC Kelly Wilkes was referring to Goodhew's slightly unkempt appearance as that 'just out of bed' look.

The word 'fit' had been bandied round the canteen a fair bit too. In many ways, Goodhew came across as just an average bloke: his features a little too sharp, his hair a nondescript brown and he was slim-built with no discernible accent. But somehow the composite wasn't average at all. Maybe it was his personality that did it: laid-back but serious, intuitive, but seemingly unaware of his own appeal. Private enough to be intriguing.

Just as well that Goodhew had remained apparently unaware of the frisson that crackled through the corridors within a couple of days of his arrival. Marks thought it more likely that the young detective was under the delusion that the female staff were consistently that helpful, but there were also days when Marks suspected that he got better results when he asked Goodhew to ask someone to do something than even when he asked them himself.

By contrast, DC Kincaide was the peacock of the department, mentally and physically smart, but surrounded by an air of fraught ambition and a whiff of insecurity. He still wasn't too warm towards the new arrival. Marks liked the idea of pairing them up sometime soon, figuring that it would give them both an opportunity to develop.

He turned the evidence bag over, and the toothbrush left a wet streak on the inside of the plastic. Kincaide, at least, wasn't in the market for sending anonymous tip-offs; he liked his efforts publicly rewarded at every point.

Goodhew was considerably less simple to assess. From Marks' point of view, the contradictions he noticed were what defined Goodhew and, more frustratingly, left him feeling that he had grasped only a superficial understanding of him. He knew DC Kincaide had diverted his initial opinion from: 'He's got a degree in Maths, so he must be a geek', to 'Women like him, he must be gay.' DI Marks wasn't at all sure how to categorize his new DC, but he was confident that he wouldn't be able to do it in a single word.

# SEVEN

DC Gary Goodhew had been off duty for forty-five minutes, spending at least half of them walking away from the centre of town. He was slightly later than planned, but he still allowed himself time to stop halfway across the railway bridge. There was a chill in the air, but he didn't hurry. He rested his elbows on the painted steel and watched Cambridge station for several minutes. He wasn't looking for anything in particular, more like everything in general. A single-engined plane curved through the sky, turning away as it left the airport in its wake.

Somewhere below it, he knew there would be an arrest shortly. Marks would have the envelope by now, and soon the streets recently scarred by the Airport Rapist could begin to heal. Goodhew drew in a therapeutic lungful of air; his head had cleared and everything smelt fresher now. He started to walk again. He reached the traffic lights and had to wait for a bike to pass so he could cross the road. The cyclist was a young woman, about his own age. She freewheeled towards him for a few yards, then rang her bell and called out with a spontaneous 'Hi'.

'Hi,' he smiled, and she laughed and pedalled on.

It took him another ten minutes before the Rock pub came into sight, and he heard it almost as soon as he saw it; it wasn't the sort of venue to book a band incapable of entertaining any passing pedestrians. Tonight it was The Vibes, plus guest saxophone player. The Vibes were four craggy guys, each with more miles on the clock than Keith Richards, but it was the guest saxophone player that he'd really come to watch.

He pushed the outer door. It tremored with their version of

'Misirlou', the alto sax doing the whole Dick Dale thing, and opened wide enough for him to fall into the hot churn of bodies, noise and alcohol partying enthusiastically in the same confined space.

He expected to only see two familiar faces: his colleague Mel and the older woman he was planning to meet. Of course Mel was easy to spot, standing centre stage like that, but she was too lost in her solo to notice him. At least that gave him a moment where he could observe her without making her feel self-conscious. Most distinctive was her hair, bright red and back-combed into spiky tufts; maybe she intended to add the impression of robustness to her slight build, or maybe she just liked it like that. And her dress sense for tonight was tomboy meets Debbie Harry: a look she toned down for work, of course, but even so, she offered a touch of sparkle to the dusty Admin department of Parkside police station. In a way, it was amazing they'd even given her the job, except that her efficiency was just like her sax playing – pretty damned hot.

Someone called out his name, and snapped him out of his reverie. He recognized the voice immediately, and began to turn towards it before he had time to consider stepping further into the pub and pretending he hadn't heard. DC Michael Kincaide was leaning with one elbow on the bar and one foot resting on the rail beneath it. As usual, he wore a suit, and the effect was a pose à la Catalogue Man, which was actually how he looked most of the time.

Kincaide shouted over the noise: 'It's my local, what's *your* excuse?'

'I'm meeting someone.'

'Not jailbait from Admin, I hope?'

'Mel? No. I'm meeting someone else.'

'Good, cos her fella's over there, and I don't think he likes all the attention she's getting. I think it's the way she blows on that instrument.' Kincaide looked pleased with his joke.

It took Goodhew no effort to look indifferent as a reply as he scanned the pub again. This time saw her. 'And there she is,' he said loudly, for Kincaide's benefit, and walked over to join his grandmother. She sat further into the pub, in front of the raised area where the band was performing but, typically, just to the left of centre.

'I bought you a pint,' she announced and took a sip from her own half of lager.

Tonight she wore black slacks and a turquoise lambswool sweater and, with her usual style, she managed to look as though she'd just returned from a day at the salon, as ever cheating her real age by at least fifteen years. Goodhew had inherited her distinctive green eyes and, in turn, she'd pinched her smile from Doris Day.

'Did you do it?' she asked.

He kept his voice level and his expression inanimate. 'Marks should get it tonight. I left it on his desk.'

'No one saw you?'

'I don't think so, although I can't be sure I guess . . .'

'Who was that guy at the bar?'

'DC Kincaide.'

'Ah.'

'Ah?'

'And he grates on you?'

'Just a bit.'

'You've never mentioned it.'

'He seems to have a good reputation, and I don't feel I've worked with him long enough to justify feeling any differently. So I keep my feelings to myself.'

'But I could tell.'

'You know me.'

'You're not as good at lying as you think you are. In fact, you're the wrong person to try leading a double life. You really ought to stop now, Gary.'

'We'll see,' he said and turned his attention back to the band.

His grandmother waited until the next gap between numbers before she spoke again. 'She's nothing like Claire.'

There was no edge to her voice and he knew that stirring up trouble wasn't her way, so he just shrugged. 'I'm only here to watch her play.'

She touched his arm. 'I didn't mean that in a negative way, just that you obviously don't have a type.'

'I know,' he replied. And it was a fair point. Claire was like the clichéd Scandinavian blonde, despite having been born and bred in Derbyshire. They had met in their first week at university, and they'd found themselves bowled over by the kind of hit-you-in-the-face, all-encompassing love that exists in movies. Until he met

Claire, Goodhew had assumed real-life romance could never be that intense, but for three subsequent years they had been inseparable, inhabiting each other's lives with an intensity that never soured into claustrophobia or boredom. But, ultimately, they reached a mutual understanding that it wasn't a relationship that would translate into their adult lives: it was more like a three-year-long holiday romance.

He couldn't imagine loving anyone more than he'd loved Claire, but the hard truth was that, in the end, whatever they felt for each other wasn't enough.

She had ambitions to be an architect in London, while his dream was to be a police detective here, in what she called the 'museum city of Cambridge'. OK, they might have overcome the geographical obstacles, but he guessed their post-university lives were destined to follow increasingly divergent trajectories. Their split was one of those rare amicable break-ups: term finished and so did they. But that didn't mean it didn't hurt.

Three years on, and he thought about her infrequently now, but on those occasions she still glowed, basking in Color By Deluxe while every girl he'd met before her had long since faded into grainy black and white.

His grandmother was right: Mel wasn't Claire but, more importantly, Mel wasn't monochrome either.

Kincaide drained his glass, then leant his elbow on the bar while he waited to be served again. He noticed Goodhew was still sitting with the same woman who was sixty if she was a day, and it wasn't just the age difference that made them seem an odd couple; Goodhew was perpetually under-groomed while she'd clearly been high maintenance her whole life.

As the barmaid handed some change to the man standing next to him, Kincaide waved his glass in her direction and demanded 'Foster's'.

He felt his mobile vibrating in his pocket, and though he had no intention of answering it, he took it out anyway, just to see who was calling. His pint arrived as the caller display announced 'DI Marks', which probably meant there'd be nothing stronger than coffee for him for the rest of the night.

Marks just wanted the two of them, Kincaide and Goodhew, back at the station, and was therefore pleased to learn that a single phone call had found them both.

Kincaide pushed his way towards Goodhew thinking, This is absolutely great. He didn't want to be thrown together with some enthusiastic new kid anyway, but being his taxi service back to town irritated him even more. No doubt the journey would be filled with inane conversation when all Kincaide really wanted to do was wind down for the night.

'Marks wants us back in,' Kincaide announced to Goodhew, with a glance at the woman who seemed intent on only listening to the music.

'Now?'

'No, next Tuesday. Yes, right now, if that's not too much trouble.'

Mel was still playing as Goodhew mouthed 'Goodbye' to her. She didn't smile back, which was fair enough considering she was halfway through the Stray Cats' 'Wild Saxophone'. But it may also have been because her boyfriend Toby was sitting two tables away and looking more taut than the top E on the guitarist's Gretsch.

Goodhew said little on the way back to town, having glanced across to the driver's side and weighed up his colleague's mood. Kincaide had never-out-of-place black hair and perfect grooming, and he could do neat with less difficulty than Goodhew managed to do marginally unkempt. For every pair of jeans Goodhew owned, he guessed Kincaide had at least two suits. Kincaide's current lack of humour didn't bother him, but nor did it motivate him to make any unnecessary conversation.

They were inside Parkside station and heading towards Marks' office before Goodhew spoke again, 'Why does Marks want us in?'

'Dunno what it's about. He doesn't seem to want to see anyone else, just us.'

'So it's going to be something either really interesting or incredibly dull.'

Kincaide shot him a sideways glance. 'What makes you say that? Have you got wind of some new development, or are you just going on that "average jobs take most people" theory?'

'B,' Goodhew fibbed. 'Anyway, I haven't been here long enough to get roped into anything above mundane, have I?'

'We'll see.'

Goodhew paused and let Kincaide walk through the doorway of DI Marks' office first. The room never changed: an empty, undersized desk that faced the door and stood island-like, with enough space to walk around it on either side, the spare chairs in a slightly different shade of olive to the filing cabinet, the water-cooler beside the window. On sunny days he could see it sparkling from his own window and it looked turquoise, the way a lagoon looks from twenty thousand feet. The room smelt of sweet lilac air freshener intermingling with the stale whiff of tobacco rising from Marks' jacket.

A dying bluebottle buzzed in the window, the latest victim of an odourless fly killer hanging from the room's only picture hook.

Today one of the three spare chairs was heaped with documents, and a cardboard crate lay half full beside it on the floor. Marks sat at his desk with a pile of other papers on his lap, his head bowed. Something he spotted made him tut and shake his head.

Goodhew and Kincaide waited and, after a few seconds, Goodhew began to wish they'd announced their arrival so he cleared his throat. 'We're here, sir.'

'My deduction skills aren't quite that poor yet, Gary. Sit!' Marks instructed.

Goodhew wondered whether his boss had ever trained as a dog handler. Probably not a good time to ask. A half-smile reached his lips but he pushed it away.

Marks put the papers on his desk, looked up at Goodhew, then nodded at the free chair. 'I said, sit down.'

Kincaide had already taken the chair to the side of the desk, so Goodhew settled into the second one, which was directly facing the inspector.

'How many weeks has this rape investigation been running?' Marks looked irritated. Kincaide glanced at Goodhew but neither of them spoke. That was just as well, as it turned out to be a rhetorical question. 'Eleven weeks tomorrow.' He patted the pile of papers he'd moved to the desk. 'Do you know what all this paperwork is?'

Kincaide looked blank and Goodhew did his best to follow suit.

'The case notes for the rape investigation – our last major investigation.' He emphasized the word 'last' and spotted Kincaide stiffen. 'Yes, that's right, two rapes near Cambridge airport, and this evening we've brought a suspect in for questioning.' He took a quick breath and his expression settled back into its usual beady-eyed mask: the one that read much and revealed little. The very same expression that caused habitual discomfort around the station.

'You're familiar with the case, I take it?' As they'd both been working full-time on it, they were definitely facing another rhetorical question. 'I thought we all were fully informed, and yet tonight I received another anonymous tip-off. An envelope was hand-delivered to my desk, yep, this desk here, and it contained a letter addressed to me and a toothbrush. This guy was so accurate last time that I have every confidence that the DNA from that same brush will match the rapist's DNA, so we've already brought the suspect in. He's an Ian Knott, by the way.' He glanced from one to the other as if hoping for a glimmer of recognition. 'I'm about to suggest to him that he might like to allow a mouth swab to be taken, just to eliminate him.'

'He'll say no,' Kincaide pointed out.

Goodhew spoke at last. 'Not necessarily.' They both looked at him. 'Tell him that no DNA has been recovered from the victims so far, but that we may get lucky if there's another attack. He'll know that refusing will look suspicious, and may decide to risk the possibility that you're telling the truth. We know he understands how to be careful, and he may even think he's not going to do it again – they often do genuinely believe that, don't they?'

Marks didn't reply, but studied the top report on the pile. Goodhew and Kincaide waited for him to speak.

'Michael,' he said finally, 'I'd like you to accompany me while I question Mr Knott. You go down now and make sure the interview room's ready and that we have all the necessary kit.'

'Kit?'

'Like chairs for starters,' Marks muttered drily. 'Just use your initiative and I'll be with you in a few minutes.'

If Kincaide was surprised to be dispatched so abruptly, he didn't show it. However, just before he closed the door, he heard Marks announce that Goodhew had drawn the short straw. So it was as Goodhew had predicted: Kincaide had bagged 'the something really interesting' while Goodhew was about to receive 'the something incredibly dull'.

Marks watched Kincaide leave, then spent the next few seconds quietly scratching his ear.

'When's my birthday, Gary?'

The question seemed odd but the junior officer answered without hesitation. 'July 14th, sir.'

'You're very open about your ability to do that.'

'Do what, sir? Remember dates?'

'Find things out. What is it, a talent or an obsession – or something else?'

Goodhew shrugged. 'I didn't know it was anything special, I suppose I just have a good memory.'

'Bollocks,' Marks grunted, but without any hint of anger in his voice.

Silence.

Each stared at the other with a kind of respectful curiosity. Marks strummed the desk and looked like he was trying to read Goodhew's thoughts.

He then took a breath and addressed his junior. 'If I were speaking to the person behind these tip-offs, the first thing I'd want to know is where they get their information and, secondly, why they can't come to me directly. Perhaps they break the law to retrieve the evidence – so if I condoned that, not only would it be inadmissible evidence, but they could lose their job over it.'

'If they *had* a job,' Goodhew pointed out.

'But why am I asking you all of this?' Marks' eyes shone, though Goodhew couldn't decide whether he was looking at a gleam of anger or a glint of encouragement.

'No idea,' he replied evenly.

'Because I have a sneaking feeling that you're taking the piss, Goodhew. That's why.'

Goodhew raised an eyebrow. 'Not at all, sir.'

Marks rapped the desk several times with a sharp tap-tap-tap of his index finger, using the sound like a gavel to ensure he had Goodhew's full attention.

Which he did.

'These two tip-offs have both occurred in the three months since you arrived here.'

Goodhew's eyes widened. 'I had no idea, sir. But I suppose new people start work here all the time, so it was bound to coincide with someone new. Just circumstantial evidence then, I guess. Sir.'

'Don't be smart, son. It is just as well that circumstantial is all I have. I'm now going over the files to see what we missed, and to find out why someone with either an unusual talent or an obsession with uncovering information, managed to hone in on that obscure group of men called "recently divorced, sociopathic wife-beaters who can only get a hard-on when they have sex under the flight path of jets taking off from a commercial airfield". I can see how obvious all that is, now it is pointed out to me. To think the rest of us thought we were cleverly scrutinizing simple things like sex offenders, plane spotters and disgruntled ex-airport staff.'

Goodhew eyed his boss with concern. 'I sense this is frustrating you, sir.'

The phone rang and Marks mouthed, 'Piss off, Gary,' as he lifted the receiver to his ear. His voice kept its usual unemotional tone, and he spoke for about thirty seconds.

He replaced the handset and continued. 'Well, in this particular case, I don't care too much how we caught him, assuming we've got the right guy. I'm just relieved we did so before it happened again. I'm not saying the end always justifies the means, but in this case, it's a job well done. Now, back to that short straw I mentioned. One of the victims states that the last person she spoke to before she was attacked was a man who sleeps rough and who she thinks is called Ratty. He usually hangs round the shops during the daytime. The name mean anything to you?'

Goodhew nodded. 'And you want me to get a statement from him?'

'Just a confirmation of time and place of his recent whereabouts, if he can. But he's made himself scarce and I'm guessing you'd love to spend some time hunting for him.'

'You can't tell me we're seriously relying on any statement he provides?'

'Absolutely correct, we're not. Just call it belt-and-braces stuff, and don't moan, because I'm sure you'll turn it into something interesting. It's late now, so I suggest you start first thing in the morning. In fact, just so there's no ambiguity, I'm insisting that you leave it until then and, right now, go home.' Marks stood up and

Goodhew followed suit. 'And the next time there's a major investigation, I would like to think we could at least attempt to solve it faster than by depending on an anonymous envelope, eh?'

'Let's hope so,' Goodhew agreed cheerfully as he followed his superior from the room and down the stairs.

Marks waited until they were on the half landing to suddenly stop and turn to face him. The move was so abrupt; Goodhew almost piled into him and would have apologized had Marks not cut in first.

'No, Gary, it's more than hope so. I don't want it to ever happen again, and if it does, I will root out the individual responsible and see that he's thrown on the scrapheap – no matter how promising his career might seem.' And it didn't take an expert to identify the diamond hardness in the inspector's eyes.

Goodhew didn't really believe that Marks knew anything whatsoever about the source of the anonymous letters, but he was curious as to why and how his boss had achieved such an accurate stab in the dark. Perhaps he would ask him sometime. But then again, perhaps not. Some things were best left well alone, especially if, as his grandmother suspected, he didn't have the makings of a plausible liar.

# EIGHT

Lorna loved the feeling of midnight: one day completed and the clocks restarting at zero for the next. Twenty-five minutes had passed since Cambridge had travelled through that magic moment and, even so, she still felt the buzz of opportunity that came with a fresh day.

They'd arranged to meet on the Victoria Avenue Bridge, which in itself was unusual, but Lorna chose to take it as a sign that her own enthusiasm for night-time walks had finally sounded tempting enough to put to the test. And it was a good evening for it; so still, with patches of fog staining the air and hanging between the bridge and the tree-lined paths leading into the heart of the city. The moon glowed just enough, like its dimmer switch had been turned to minimum. The city itself was hushed.

Lorna leant on the balustrade and tried to see her reflection in the water below, but it was too wide to look directly downwards, so instead she contented herself with gazing at the rippling reflection of the white walls and blue gables of a boathouse further downstream. Her freckled skin looked creamy against the grey stone of the bridge, and behind her, the streetlamps dropped pools of light on the railings and verges. She held the pose and listened. She guessed that she was already being watched, that two keen eyes were studying her through the mistiness.

Within minutes, she heard approaching footsteps. They stopped beside her, and she only turned her head when she felt another arm slide alongside her own on the balustrade.

'Why here?' Lorna asked.

'I liked the idea.'

'You're strange sometimes.'

'Yes, a bit chilly, I guess. Any goosebumps yet? Let me feel.' Lorna gave a bemused smile as the hand rubbed up and down the back of her arm. 'No, you're still nice and warm. Shame, because I brought us drinks.' For the first time, Lorna noticed the two insulated beakers resting on top of the wall. 'Coffee?'

Lorna removed the lid and blew into the cup before sipping. 'It's Irish coffee,' she observed.

'Is it all right?'

'Absolutely.' It must have been poured a while earlier because it had cooled to the point where it was easy to drink. She gulped a third of it immediately before becoming conscious of being closely watched. 'I like a good swallow,' she whispered, then giggled.

Her remark went without comment. She pretended then to be apologetic, even though a suppressed smile twitched at the corners of her mouth. 'You don't approve of my double entendres, do you?' she asked.

'I think they're more habit than cleverness. Or perhaps it's your way of showing me how outgoing you are; say something daring and I'll think you're confident. Is that it?'

Lorna refused to rise to this dig, and instead just snorted. 'Impressing you isn't something I've ever felt I needed to do. Perhaps I'm only trying to bring you out of your shell. Has that ever occurred to you?' Then she reminded herself that she hadn't come out here for an evening of gentle bickering. 'Come on, let's walk.'

They strolled on towards the city with the common on their left and the roadway on their right, their two figures becoming synchronized again. Through habit, they both noticed the same things at the same time: a taxi in the distance driving from left to right, three students cycling from right to left, the echo of a bell chiming a late half past to the sleeping denizens of Cambridge.

They were halfway to the next road junction before there was any response to Lorna's comment. 'No, I don't think you could bring me out of my shell, actually.'

'I thought we'd finished with that conversation.'

'I don't think sex is ever far from your mind, is it?'

'You don't let things drop, do you?' Lorna sounded huffy. 'Nothing wrong with a strong libido, is there?' she continued and

41

then cheered up when she saw that she was being smirked at. 'You're funny,' she decided.

'First strange, now funny?'

Lorna sucked on her drink and shrugged.

The railings that kept them from drifting on to the common ran away from them, like a black-painted railroad track, curving left on to Maid's Causeway, before taking them towards their destination. Lorna's fingers followed the route, skimming along the horizontal poles and rising and falling at each Victorian dome-topped post.

'Do you know what I want to know?'

'What it's like to have no inhibitions?' Lorna suggested.

'Interesting, but no.' Her companion had stopped walking, and Lorna guessed that they would soon arrive at the real point of the conversation. 'I want to know exactly what you know about David.'

They were quite alone, but Lorna whispered anyway. The little nods and sounds of encouragement she received spurred her into more detail than she had planned. Earlier in the day, hearing David's name like that might have startled her, but not now. Now she repeated it with familiarity, as though he'd always been part of their conversations. Her words only dried up when she realized she was no longer being listened to. 'And that's it,' she concluded.

'I see.' It was said in a way that told Lorna that this part of the conversation was over. Her companion leant on the railings and Lorna did the same, aware that the mood between them had become subdued. They both gazed back the way they'd come, towards the far end of the common. There was nothing visible, bar the faint glow of the boathouses and restaurants on the other side of the Cam. Nothing discernible, at least. They were alone together and still close enough for their elbows to touch. Her companion broke the silence first.

'Finish your coffee and I'll show you something.'

Lorna finished the dregs of her coffee, then took the pen that was being held out to her. 'So what am I supposed to do with this?'

The marshy land between them and the river lay motionless, as though it held its breath.

'I want you to write "I'm like Emma" on each palm.'

'I'm like Emma?' Lorna's eyebrows twitched upwards. It seemed like nonsense, but she guessed it wouldn't hurt to play along.

'Yes, go on. It's clever, I promise.'

Lorna wrote in Biro on her left palm, the blue ink looking black under the thick light from the sulphurous streetlamp. She used capitals and the letters stretched across, from the heel of her hand to half an inch short of her middle finger.

'Like that?' She held out her hand.

'That's it. Now the same on the other one.'

Lorna gave a short, nervous laugh. 'These things always catch me out, so even when you get to the punchline, you'll have to explain it.' In truth, she hated looking stupid, and didn't want to take part at all. But the atmosphere between them was curiously fragile; it made more sense to go along with this and avoid anything nastier. She wrote slowly on the other palm in jerky lower case. 'This isn't so good, it looks like a four-year-old's written it.' She forced a grin.

'No, that's fine.'

'Now what?'

They were facing on to Midsummer Common with their backs to the non-existent 1 a.m. traffic. 'I love it here when it's quiet and, once the weather's warmer, that's only at night. And in the summer it's never quiet – the fair's here, then the circus and all those hippies camping out.'

'So what about this writing?'

'Hold on.'

Lorna squirmed like a child. 'Can we go now?'

'No, please, let's stay here for a minute or two.'

Lorna peered at the ground on the other side of the railings. 'We're standing right next to a load of rubbish sacks. And I'm getting cold.' She sounded sulky.

'I said you'd get goosebumps, didn't I?'

'Clever you.' Lorna sniffed. 'And when are you going to explain this?' She waved her hand, palm upwards. 'Why are you smiling? Have I missed something funny?'

'I guess so.'

Lorna reran her last sentence in her head, realizing she'd slurred it, and for some reason 'have-I-missed' had coalesced into a single word. She straightened and turned her back to rest against the railings. She gazed in the direction of the Four Lamps roundabout and tried to work out what felt wrong. It couldn't be just cold, fog and tiredness that were making her suddenly disorientated. She wanted to go home but her feet wouldn't move.

Instead of walking away, she stood fixed in the same spot, a look of mild bewilderment dawning on her face. 'I feel ill,' she muttered, but her companion never even replied. Lorna wanted to repeat herself, but was overtaken by the feeling that her brain could no longer connect with her mouth.

She felt giddy and needed to steady herself. Her left hand moved, it rose from her side and drifted back towards the top rail. And like the slow topple of a felled redwood, the rest of her followed, staggering back, the railing all that stopped her from hitting the ground.

It was then that she had a moment of clarity, an instant where she knew how and why she'd been drugged, and the enormity of her fatal miscalculation. She tried to reach out, to beg for her life. She managed to gasp, 'I'm sorry,' just as two hands flew forward and, with a single push to the sternum, sent her toppling over the railings and on to the pile of rubbish.

She landed on her back in a crumpled heap, almost parallel to the footpath, with her head nearest the ground and her hair trailing in the mud. The other figure squatted and they stared at each other from either side of the bottom rung.

Lorna heard the words hissed at her: 'Do you know why?'

She knew, but she couldn't reply. She attempted to nod instead, but her head wobbled through an uncontrolled arc and her arms and legs twitched with a life of their own. Lorna tried to stay conscious, guessing she'd been overdosed and hoping that she would be found before it killed her. To stand a chance now, she just needed to be left for dead.

But no one was going anywhere. Lorna watched as first a plastic carrier bag, then a length of string, were brought out of a pocket. A little more consciousness suddenly returned; her eyes widened and her breath came like the little huff children use to steam up windows. A pair of hands reached through the railings and dragged the plastic bag over the top of Lorna's head, like a swimming cap.

Lorna's heart was beating so loudly that she barely heard the words spoken to her, the words that were merely intended to add to her suffering. Then the bag was pulled over her face and she felt the string being knotted at her throat.

Inside her head she was screaming out, *Oh, God help me.* She breathed in and the bag was sucked into her mouth, then out again as she exhaled. *I'm sorry.* On her second breath, she knew the supply of air was already used up. Her chest rose and fell, burning with the effort. *Please no more.* Her heart beat louder. *Please, please.* Then, eventually, it stopped.

# NINE

Goodhew woke at 5.25 a.m. and hoped that the early bird really would catch the worm. He had no desire to spend more time than necessary trailing around the back streets and squats of Cambridge, hunting for the elusive Ratty.

He was pissed off with Marks, and too familiar with Ratty's activities to believe that the mission he'd been sent on was any more useful than being sent to stores for the clerk's long stand.

Ratty was about five-five in height and somewhere between twenty-five and forty – Goodhew guessed nearer twenty-five, despite the pock-marked skin, receding hair and sunken eyes that argued older. Ratty had once boasted that he'd been on the stage as a child, and then attempted to prove the point by belting out the first lines of 'Unchained Melody'. It wasn't a bad performance, but his liquorice-stump remnants of teeth hadn't done him any favours; in the end he'd merely been cautioned for disturbing the peace.

From time to time, he vanished completely, and on the first few occasions his acquaintances had assumed he lay rotting somewhere after a fix too far. But he'd always reappear and, assuming the role of an oracle for the city's nightlife, he would proclaim to have witnessed virtually every major event that appeared on the police station's radar. Often his information was remarkably accurate, but Goodhew guessed that Ratty was no more than a top-class eavesdropper, sucking up drunken gossip the way some of his down-and-out cronies hoarded newspapers or carrier bags.

OK, so in this case it was the rape victim who had identified someone resembling Ratty, but with the DNA match and the victim's statement, Ratty – if found and if cooperative – would still

46

be pretty redundant; he just wasn't the kind of witness that juries trusted.

Goodhew's face tingled in the cold air; clear spring nights sucked the warmth from the flat open streets and left early-morning Cambridge encased in a frosty shell. He wiggled his nose, trying to restore the circulation there, hoping it would stop running. It didn't, so he dabbed at it with the only square of clean tissue he could find in his jacket pocket.

The 6 a.m. sun stretched gradually over the rooftops and touched the second storeys of the locked shops and cafés. At ground level, however, there was still no hint of dawn as he walked down the grey slab passageway of Bradwell's Court towards the coach station: the master bedroom for the city's down-and-outs.

He kept to the centre of the pedestrian walkway, equidistant from the doorways on either side. Only the newsagent at the far end would reveal any official activity this early; all other signs of life came from the homeless.

No one occupied the blankets heaped at the entrance to East Anglia Pet Supplies on his left this morning, but on his right, a blue nylon sleeping bag in the portico of the discount book store stirred and groaned. The black-and-tan terrier curled beside it scratched, turned over, then resettled itself against its master's stomach. Even with the occupant's head buried under the covers, Goodhew knew it wasn't Ratty. Too tall for a start. The man and his dog were the only ones camped out in Bradwell's Court itself.

Goodhew came out the other side to find the bus bays empty, apart from the end space, where the first London coach of the day still waited for non-existent passengers, its engine idling.

Logically, Goodhew should have turned right, past the first bus, and walked a circuit back to the shopping centre, via the smaller, edge-of-town stores. He glanced out, past the coach station and over Christ's Piece, where tree-lined paths crossed the common land and late daffodils sprouted. The sun had melted the frost and the grass stood bright and dewy in the growing daylight.

It was a much more appealing prospect than poking at cardboard boxes behind office outbuildings. He could check for sleepers on the park benches. He never understood how anyone could survive outside when the day's warmth evaporated from the Fens, and he expected each curled-up body to have died in the night, frozen to its draughty slatted bed.

But from where he stood, each bench appeared unoccupied, and he decided to check the public toilets instead before walking further.

They were housed in an old red-brick square block with individual cubicles along each side, and had been recently refurbished with a range of gadgets, including cisterns that automatically flushed upon the opening of the doors, and soap and water dispensers that squirted and sprayed without any actual physical contact. It would only take a few more such advances in technology, and bums wouldn't even be touching seats.

Goodhew checked the doors one by one and found that none were occupied, they were obviously too compact for even the dispossessed to spend the night in. It was as he turned the final corner that he finally found him.

Ratty stood, tilted back, with his shoulder blades against the outside wall. He was smoking a roll-up, holding it between index finger and thumb as it sat in the centre of the tunnel made by his other curled-over fingers. Goodhew almost felt that Ratty was waiting for him, perhaps resigned to being tracked down and choosing to get it over with.

Even when Goodhew spoke, Ratty continued to stare vacantly across Christ's Piece and Goodhew quickly deduced that he hadn't emerged from the cooperative side of his sleeping bag that morning. 'Did you know I was looking for you, Rat?'

Ratty spoke slowly, his voice rasping like bone against bone. ''Course I did.'

*Yeah, of course*, thought Goodhew. 'OK,' he said, then paused, waiting for Ratty to turn his head and look at him. He didn't. 'We have a witness who saw you.'

Ratty blew out a thin plume of smoke. 'Oh yeah, doing what?'

'Nothing, really, but you were out near the airfield. My guess is that you were heading for that lake off Coldhams Lane when she walked past. A few minutes later she was assaulted. Did you hear about it?'

This time Ratty looked directly at Goodhew. 'We've all heard about the Airport Rapist.'

'Did you see a man following her?'

Ratty shook his head.

'That's not an answer, Rat.'

'Why not?'

'Because you have your code. When you mean no, you say no – shaking your head is merely avoiding the question.'

Ratty shook his head again. 'You think you're smart, don't you? Well, you are, too. Lucky-fucking-you, that's all I say. I'll tell you about it, Gary.' He had emphasized the 'Gary' and then stopped speaking which, word-wise, was more economical than saying *I know stuff you don't know*. Goodhew waited, almost hypnotized by this macabre spectre trying to stare him out.

Despite Ratty's stillness, his eyes were dark and hollow, and he seemed even less substantial than he'd been the last time they'd met: he'd always been a shell of a man, but now the walls were thinner. Sooner or later, the drugs inevitably took their toll, and Goodhew could see that Ratty now viewed the real world from the other end of an ever-extending tunnel.

Ratty ground the half-inch butt of his cigarette between his finger-tips until it flaked to the ground. 'I'm not talking to you. Right now, I'm *nothing*, and when things go bad that's the best thing to be.' He fanned out his nicotined fingers. 'Trouble is like poison. You go near it and you get infected.'

'That's deep.'

'What, coming from someone like me who's never been out of it?'

'That's not what I meant.'

'Well, there's trouble and there's trouble. I always have some, but only my own. And I know all about other people's, but there's a line.' He turned his face away and scraped his thumbnail down the wall by his shoulder. 'Can't see it, can you? But it's there, trust me. On one side is me, and what's mine, and over there is other people's shit. What I don't do is anything that takes me over *there*. I can see what's going on, but I don't visit, if you get my drift.'

'You don't get involved?'

'People get possessive about trouble, so they only want help on their own terms. And if they don't want it fixed, getting in the middle of it is dangerous, even if it looks safe. That's another problem: it can seem like nothing, but then—' He walked his fingers from his side of the line to the other, then rubbed his hand across the wall in a small circle. 'The line's gone and you're fucked.'

Ratty pushed himself away from the wall, swinging his skinny body round until he faced Goodhew squarely. 'So I look, but I don't touch. I don't let it seep over me.'

He didn't seem high, he emanated nothing but stale tobacco and paranoia. 'Touch it and it *stains* you, Gary. Remember that.'

Getting Ratty to make a statement was clearly not something to look forward to. Goodhew wondered if he could persuade Marks to drop the whole idea; this was unlikely to be the witness to swing a court case in any direction it wasn't already headed. He sighed, but Ratty didn't seem to notice.

What path had the younger version of Ratty stumbled down to end up in such a bleak cul-de-sac? Goodhew looked away from him, and the first person he saw was a distant cyclist, standing up out of the saddle, pedalling furiously towards him. He saw a flash of orange swing from behind his back and realized it was the paper boy from the bus station. The kid was short; he'd noticed him on other mornings, struggling with his sack and the high seat of his adult bike. Had that been Ratty once, striving to get somewhere in life?

Ratty was still talking, but Goodhew ceased to listen. The boy's sack swung wildly as his shoulders swayed from left to right in an effort to move faster still. He was about a hundred yards away and his face burnt red from under his mop of blond hair. His mouth was moving. Shouting something, or just gulping air?

Goodhew made a single instinctive step in the cyclist's direction, hairs rising on the back of his neck: he knew something was wrong.

At fifty yards, he heard the breathy squawk of the boy's voice, all the words but one mangled to nothing in the gap between them. 'Quick!' was the one word he recognised.

At twenty yards, the boy became more clear. 'There's a body.'

He lurched to a halt next to Goodhew, wobbled as his foot reached for the pavement. Goodhew grabbed his arm as he toppled from his bike and held the boy upright until he'd disentangled his other foot from the frame. It clattered to the ground and lay with the back wheel spinning in the weak sunshine.

Sweat pinned a veil of hair flat across his forehead, while the rest stuck up at all angles. He waved his hand back excitedly in the direction he'd come, clinging to Goodhew's jacket with the other hand as he fought to catch his breath. 'I recognise you, you're police, aren't you? Up there,' he gasped. 'Up there, on Midsummer Common.'

'Where exactly?'

'This end.'

'Hang on.' Goodhew spun round to see Ratty retreating back towards the city centre. 'I need a statement,' he called after him.

Ratty turned and walked back several steps. 'I don't know anything,' he shouted.

Goodhew turned his attention back to the boy, whose right arm was still partly raised in the act of pointing. The most obvious sign of distress was his trembling hands; beyond that he didn't look too bad. Goodhew peered into his face: not quite ready to pass out from shock, he decided. 'Can you show me yourself?' he asked gently.

The boy shut his eyes for a moment, then nodded. 'I touched her,' he whispered.

Goodhew righted the bike and they walked with it between them. 'Don't worry, we'll get it sorted out.'

He quickly radioed in to the station.

'They're sending a car, want us to meet them there.'

'I heard.'

Goodhew nodded. 'Sorry, of course you did. What's your name?'

'Matt. Matt Lilley. I do the papers on Maids Causeway.'

They walked quickly towards the end of Christ's Piece, where the aptly named Short Street would take them through to Maids Causeway and the southern boundary of Midsummer Common. Goodhew's stomach churned uneasily. 'So tell me what happened.'

'It's bin day, isn't it? And there're sacks outside most of the houses. I'd done the houses near the traffic lights, and noticed there was rubbish over on the other side of the road, beyond the railings – you know, on the grass. I didn't think anything at the time. It was only afterwards when I remembered they were there. So I did the houses on that side, too, then I went back to the lights to cross over and do the houses down Brunswick – you know, the ones that face the Common.' Goodhew noticed Matt's left hand resting on the saddle of his bike: how the fingers gripped the narrow front, and a smear of sweat from his palm had stained the brown leather a liquorice black. 'I don't usually cross just there, but one of the houses had an extra paper I'd missed, so I went back and crossed at the lights, 'cos that's, you know, where I ended up. There weren't any cars and I just rode across, and so I was looking straight on, right where the pile of rubbish was. That's when I wondered which house it all came from. It was a big pile of sacks, and it wasn't really light by then, but I saw her straight away.'

They both knew that the terrace now on their right was the last visual obstruction to their view of Midsummer Common. Goodhew turned to look at Matt and, for the first time, he saw tears well in the boy's eyes, and horror sweep across his face as he fought against the indignity of crying.

Goodhew laid his hand gently on the lad's shoulder. 'How old are you, Matt?'

The boy's voice trembled. 'Thirteen, and I've never seen a dead person.'

The corner of the last house loomed, and then the first glimpse of the black metal railings surrounding Midsummer Common slid into view.

'How did you know she was dead?'

'I touched her hand. It felt cold – not like a person.'

'Did you recognize her?' Goodhew asked quietly.

Matt shook his head and whispered, 'No, her head's in a bag.'

# TEN

As he turned the final corner, Goodhew had no need to ask Matt to point out the body. It was rubbish day, after all, and a bright-blue dustcart stood with its wheels up on the pavement, and an orange warning light blinking from the roof. Three dustmen, two men and a woman, stood in a huddle at the spot Matt had described. A fourth had returned to the cab of their lorry, and Goodhew could see his free arm waving as he shouted into his radio.

'I'm from Cambridge CID. Don't touch anything,' he shouted and hurried forward, but Matt slowed. 'Can I go now?' he asked. Fear filled his eyes and he looked more like a ten-year-old than a teenager.

'Not yet.' Goodhew pressed the flat of his hand between Matt's shoulder blades and kept him walking. 'You won't need to see the body again, but I do need your help. Is that OK?' He gave an encouraging smile and Matt nodded.

The fourth dustman dropped back down from the cab and joined the others. Goodhew stopped a few feet short of the group, and he beckoned the dustwoman over.

'This is Matt. He found the body and he's a bit upset. Can you stay here with him until another patrol arrives in a few minutes?'

'Do the maternal bit, you mean?' The woman scowled and straightened her reflective waistcoat.

Goodhew shrugged. 'I just think women are more versatile.'

He guessed he'd just appeared very sexist, and dustmen were probably now known as waste-management operatives, especially since one of them was female.

He sighed and approached the corpse. Sirens wailed in the distance.

Strictly speaking, the dead body wasn't quite on the ground. She lay heaped on top of a makeshift bed of at least a dozen black plastic rubbish sacks piled on the other side of the railings. Two more had been dumped on top of her, covering her torso in some attempt at concealment.

Some of the sacks were split, with their innards strewn on the grass. A bloodied meat wrapper lay beside the main pile, obviously pilfered by a fox or cat during the night, and now rested directly beneath her outstretched hand.

Her head was furthest from Goodhew, and concealed in a plastic carrier bag, just as Matt had described, but Goodhew was relieved to find it still attached to the rest of the body. The bag was black and tied at the neck with a length of ribbon-width black cotton. Goodhew leant over the top railing to get as close as he could without actually stepping on the grass. He could see that someone had poked a sizable hole in the bag with their fingers so that air had entered and lifted it away from the dead girl's face.

He held the railing with one hand for support, and gently touched the plastic with the other, thus expelling the air so that the bag sank back against the woman's face. Vein-chased swollen eyes now stared out, and blue lips, drawn back to expose creamy teeth, her tongue still pressed hard against the prominent gap between the middle two.

Goodhew suddenly thought of the stuffed fox, mounted on the wall in his local pub, all bulgy-eyed and grinning. He suddenly caught a whiff of the meat wrapper, its slick of dried blood releasing the sweet smell of decay.

He averted his gaze and it fell on to the woman's palm. There, he read the words 'I'm like Emma', or perhaps it was 'I like Emma'. Either way it seemed odd, and it definitely looked more like 'I'm', not just 'I'.

The sirens were getting closer now, and he wondered which of his colleagues was on the way. DI Marks, he hoped.

Two police cars came into sight, and he spotted a couple of people inside the first, and two further officers in the marked car which followed. Both sirens trailed off as the lead vehicle swung across the road and parked beside the dustcart. Goodhew waited until the engine died before looking that way again.

DI Marks stepped on to the pavement and the dustmen moved

aside to let him through. His companion was Kincaide, who paused to lock up and then followed.

Goodhew greeted them sombrely.

'Morning, Gary,' Marks grunted.

Too-cool-for-school Kincaide managed a nod.

Marks said nothing further, but their silent communication must have included a line where Kincaide said, 'I'll talk to the boy,' because he changed direction and headed over to young Matt.

Goodhew turned back to face the body and DI Marks now came and stood at his shoulder, studying the corpse for a long, silent minute. 'She didn't die in her sleep, that's for sure. Who made the hole in the bag?'

'One of the dustmen.' Goodhew pointed to the driver of the dustcart, back in his cab smoking a roll-up. 'Him, I think. He said he just wanted to be sure she was dead, but I think it was maybe a case of morbid curiosity. Marks nodded. 'What else?'

'The kid over there found her. His name's Matt Lilley, claims he's thirteen, but I bet he's only about ten.' He watched as Kincaide relieved the dustwoman of her charge and took the boy to sit in the relative calm of the patrol car. 'He's quite shaken, but he seems like a good kid, and at least *he* worked out she was dead without ripping open the bag.'

Goodhew hadn't meant to sound sarcastic, though that was how it came out. He smiled.

Marks didn't. 'What else?' he repeated.

Goodhew turned back to study the body. 'Her hand has something written on it. From here it looks like "I'm like Emma". I couldn't check the other palm, though, without moving her. She's dressed all in black, so that could mean something.'

'Like witchcraft?' Marks asked drily.

'No,' Goodhew snorted. 'Like camouflage amongst all these black sacks.'

Marks smiled a little. 'Good point.' He called across to one of the uniformed officers. 'Right, we need the area sealed off immediately, and that includes all footpaths leading on to the common. This will be a nightmare, especially as rush-hour will be kicking off any time now.' He turned back to Goodhew. 'And you can have the pleasure of viewing the post-mortem.'

Goodhew wasn't sure whether looking pleased and saying 'Thanks' was entirely the appropriate response, so he followed Marks back to his car without any further comment.

# ELEVEN

Goodhew later drove DI Marks to Addenbrooke's Hospital. He already had questions to ask his superior, but Marks was preoccupied with making notes on the murder scene. Goodhew had made his own before they left the station, and he knew that the post-mortem would shortly take them from a passing acquaintance with the woman to a most intimate relationship.

He chose the most direct route, and was surprised when Marks glanced up and directed him down the next right-hand turn. 'Then pull over in the lay-by this side of the lights.'

The car stopped outside the Big Teas Café, and Marks had opened his door even before Goodhew had a chance to cut the engine. 'Come on,' he said, 'there'll be at least half an hour before the pathologist is ready for us.'

The café was deserted, but as soon as the door rattled, a skinny guy with grey hair and a grease-splattered apron emerged from the kitchen. Marks ordered a mug of tea and a bacon sandwich and sat at a table near the door. Goodhew decided to order the same, and joined him.

'Let's see if you're still good at keeping your dinner down.'

'Breakfast actually, sir. Any idea who the corpse might be?'

'Female, twenties, that's all I know too. What about the lad who found her?'

'Poor kid, he's really shocked. Kincaide arranged for someone to pick up his mum so he's got company while he makes his statement. He's only ten, and he shouldn't even be doing a paper round, but he lied to get himself the job. He was even worried his boss would get in trouble. But, despite his age, he gave very clear descriptions of the route he took, and the times it took too. Hopefully the details will still stack up when it's all written down.

'What did you notice about the crime scene?'

Despite having seen the body itself close up, Goodhew began instead by describing its location in relation to the road. 'Assuming it doesn't turn out to be a bizarre suicide, then I'd also think this is a premeditated attack.'

'Why?' Marks asked sharply.

'The attacker was in possession of both a carrier bag and something to tie it with.'

Marks tutted and opened his mouth to speak, but Goodhew continued to explain. 'I know, sir. On their own, those factors don't mean much, but it occurred to me that there are plenty of more secluded locations where the body could have been left, yet there she was, right by the footpath where the first passer-by was likely to find her. But that was not likely to be dawn or soon after; even vehicle headlights would have had trouble picking her out.'

Marks was frowning. 'I still don't . . .' he began.

Goodhew raised a hand and carried on talking. 'She would have been particularly hard to spot before dawn, even though she was in the open, because she was mostly concealed and wearing black amongst all those black sacks.'

'I spotted that fact myself, believe it or not.'

Goodhew ignored the sarcasm. 'Well, I checked around, and all the nearby houses had similar sacks waiting outside, so I asked the dustmen whether the spot where the body was found was a regular place for rubbish to accumulate. They said this was the first time it had ever happened, which makes me think someone shuffled them there ready for her.'

Marks' eyes were now closed and his head made a small rocking motion, back and forth, in a slow rhythm.

Goodhew kept quiet, realizing that interrupting the inspector at such moments was never a good idea.

Finally Marks raised his eyebrows, which had the simultaneous effect of heaving his eyelids open. He inhaled a long, slow breath through his narrow nostrils. 'Assuming it is murder – and, for the record, I think it is – I will want you on the investigating team. I'd be pleased for you to take more of a role than in previous cases because I think you're ready now but . . .' he paused to pick his words. 'I'd like you to work closely with someone more experienced, just so you're not unnecessarily exposed if you find yourself in unfamiliar territory. I hope you get on OK with Michael Kincaide?'

'Fine,' Goodhew fibbed and promised himself it would be.

'Well, I'd like to pair you with him, but I'll have a word with him first as he's probably feeling a little put out because you're here right now and he's not. But then I would rather he was sick of me than sick during the autopsy.'

Marks checked his watch, stood up, drained his mug, and clunked it back down on the table. 'He'll be at the station still, with that boy Matt. By the way, did you find Ratty?'

'Yes.'

'And?'

'Says he knows nothing.'

'And you've got that in a statement?'

'No, I was sidetracked with this business. Do you really think it's still necessary?'

'Absolutely. Is that a problem for you?'

'No, it's fine,' Goodhew fibbed again.

Within five minutes, they crossed from the edge of leafy pre-war suburbia to the sprawling sixties development of Addenbrooke's Hospital. Goodhew took the perimeter road around the campus. Two parking bays were reserved for pathology and both stood empty.

'Pull in here. We'll wait until Sykes shows up, there's no point in us hanging around inside.' Marks unclipped his seatbelt and shifted round in his seat so his head rested against the window.

Sometimes Goodhew wished he could spend just five minutes inside his boss's head. But then, on second thoughts, it might be – like Ratty had said – healthier to stay on your own side of the line. And therefore leave Marks on his.

# TWELVE

The laboratory reminded Goodhew of a showpiece commercial kitchen. Stainless steel appliances hummed, keeping the meat chilled and the cutlery sterilized. The sinks gleamed and the work surfaces were perforated with holes that allowed water and juices to drain from the carcasses. Implements, including knives, scalpels and a small tenon saw, were sorted by type then size, waiting for use.

The room was almost square, with a single door over to one corner. It had a window, too, but only in the partition wall between it and a small viewing gallery. Lighting, bright and white, blazed down from flush panels in the ceiling; confirming that plenty of people got more attention when they were dead than they ever did in life, although Goodhew was sure that didn't apply to this particular corpse. Even in the aftermath of her squalid death, she held on to neatness. Strands of her hair still held the shape of their last cut, and not one of her short nails was chipped or broken.

Goodhew felt like a school kid on the first day of a new term; the surroundings were familiar, but his senses were heightened. He knew his way around, but he'd forgotten the detail; the dry air, the disinfectant that never quite covered up the rusty smell of blood, and the toe-tag on the body that was always filled in with black ink from a fountain pen.

The girl hadn't been beautiful, but she wasn't ugly in any way either. She had a roundish face and features that were in proportion but unremarkable. Her hair was slightly longer than a bob, and layered, as if anything more feminine might not have suited her. She was boyish rather than womanly and that applied to her body, too: her breasts were small and her hips narrow, and the overall effect was more like parallel lines than an hourglass, but attractive nevertheless.

She'd taken care of herself too. Her complexion was flawless, and all over her body her skin appeared blemish-free – even on her feet it was smooth and unchafed. Her legs and underarms were hairless with no sign of regrowth, and her bikini line had been waxed to leave just a half-inch strip of pubic hair.

Sykes's first job had been to remove the victim's clothes and personal effects. And, of course, the ripped black plastic bag that had ended up looking like a grotesque balaclava.

She now lay on the examination table, naked with blue-marbled skin stretched over the stiff tissue underneath. The only hint of colour was in her lower legs, where the flesh had turned a deep purplish-red. Later, Sykes would open her up and the trapped blood would leak, like a side of beef oozing on a butcher's block.

Goodhew pushed this food analogy from his mind. Luckily, nothing about Anthony Sykes reminded him of a chef. The pathologist was no more than five six, aged around forty, slim – probably lighter than most teenage girls of that height. He didn't look capable of manoeuvring a large carcass of any kind but, in reality, he was remarkably skilful at lifting and turning the lifeless corpse.

Two anglepoise-style brackets projected downwards from the ceiling. On one, a camcorder was mounted, and on the other, a rectangular lamp which would act as a floodlight for illuminating Sykes's close-up work.

When he spoke, it was slowly and clearly for the benefit of the recording, but in a tone which didn't alter when he turned to address Marks or Goodhew.

'Body 8926. Unidentified female.' He wheeled a side trolley into shot, on which was a collection of clear plastic bags, each one sealed and labelled. He took them one by one and held them up to the camera. 'Already removed and bagged are: item 8926-01 black leather left shoe, size four, item 8926-02 black leather right shoe, size four, item 8926-03 black skirt, item 8926-04 black bra, item 8926-05 black T-shirt, item 8926-06 black roll-neck woollen sweater, item 8926-07 hallmarked gold ring, item 8926-08 gold earring set with small white stone removed from left ear and item 8926-09 matching earring removed from the right ear. Each of these items was found on the body. These were the only items discovered at the scene—'

'No knickers?' interrupted Marks.

'These were the only items discovered at the scene, but in isolation this does not indicate sexual assault.'

Sykes pushed the trolley to one side and turned to the body.

'Body 8926. Unidentified female, early to mid-twenties, Caucasian. Height 156 centimetres, weight 112 pounds. External examination of the body . . .' Sykes paused to position himself at her ankles.

Goodhew guessed it was just procedure, but he wondered why Sykes always started at the feet, especially when, in this case at least, the more interesting information was obviously concentrated at the other end.

Sykes inspected the soles, then spread the toes, checking the skin between. He pointed to the dark colouring of the feet and ankles. 'That's not bruising.'

'It's post-mortem lividity,' Goodhew replied.

'Sorry, I forget who knows what.' Sykes took samples from under each of the toenails. 'The feet are both of normal development and they show no visible signs of injury.'

And so he continued, inch by inch, up towards her armpits, then down her arm to her fingers, where he again took samples from under her nails.

He pointed to a small bruise in the middle of her upper left arm. 'The contusion here appears to be recent and, while it is only small, there is a similar mark on the other arm, possibly consistent with an assailant gripping her and leaving thumbprints.' He lifted each arm and examined it. 'On both arms there are a number of smaller contusions to the rear of the limb. These are, in my opinion, bruises made by fingertip pressure. The distance between the thumb and finger marks, and the clarity of them, suggest a person with largish hands and a strong grip. There are no other signs of soft-tissue damage to the arms or hands.'

'No defence wounds, you mean?' Goodhew queried.

'Exactly,' Sykes replied.

Marks was also keen to get down to the key detail. 'What about her head and neck?'

'Yes, well, I'm coming to that next.' Sykes pulled the inspection light in closer and scrutinized the puckered skin around the victim's throat. 'Already bagged are items 8926-10 and 8926-11, a black carrier bag and a length of black bias binding.' He felt up and down her windpipe, pressing gently with his finger and thumb. 'The marks around the neck could imply strangulation, but with the majority of manual strangulations the use of excessive force causes damage in the larynx area. At first examination, neither the thyroid cartilage nor the hyoid bone feels damaged, and a more likely use of the bias binding seems to have been to secure the bag, and therefore cause asphyxiation.'

Marks interrupted. 'Is the ribbon itself significant?'

'You mean, rather than use rope or tights, for example? It's bias binding, used in needlework I believe, so not what most people would normally carry about their person. Of course, we don't know that this tape wasn't the victim's own. As you know, many sexual murders involve strangulation, but this stuff isn't intrinsically strong . . . well, who knows? Let's just say that, on face value, it doesn't tell us much. What is more interesting, of course, is the fact that, whether strangled or suffocated, the victim did not appear to struggle, so . . .'

Marks finished the sentence for him: '. . . she may well have known her attacker.'

'Or been drugged,' Goodhew added.

'Or already been unconscious,' Sykes finished. He paused for a few seconds, making sure their attention reverted to the corpse. He then took a series of swabs from her mouth and nose, ears and eyes. 'Suffocation,' he muttered, almost to himself. After that, he plucked a few hairs from her head, identifying each by its precise location on her scalp.

Without asking for assistance, he rolled the corpse over on to its belly. It was a practised move that left her symmetrically arranged. Her mouth was partially open and Goodhew had to remind himself that nothing would come dribbling out past her swollen lips; even her tongue would now be powder dry.

'Time to find out about her private life,' Sykes announced in a matter-of-fact voice. He flicked a switch on the inspection light and a second bulb lit up.

'What's that for?' Goodhew asked.

'It's a Wood's lamp, fluorescent, used to identify the presence of semen,' Sykes explained, before producing a fresh clutch of cotton buds and swabbing the entrance to her anus. Then he reached to his array of sterilized equipment, selected a speculum and obtained internal swabs. 'You haven't seen one before then?'

Goodhew shook his head.

Sykes rolled her on to her back again. 'We're more likely to pick up something around the vagina.' He parted her legs and swung the light lower, inspecting her labia and clitoris. 'Bingo, likely presence of semen.' He switched back to the normal light and reverted to studying her skin, working his way up the inside of her legs. 'A few minor contusions on each inner thigh, some recent, some less so,' he reported.

He took more swabs and examined the vagina and perineal skin for injuries. With a small metal comb from his instrument tray, he combed through her pubic hair and collected the loose ones, then plucked several further hairs for comparison.

Goodhew's gaze wandered back to the instrument tray. The scalpels, saws and drill were lined up ready on the cold stainless steel. Their turn had almost come.

He knew what was coming next, and knew it didn't bother him. Or, at least, it never had in the past. He saw it merely as an evidence collection process, a key tool for helping the victim and the victim's relatives.

So far, Goodhew had attended few post-mortems, only during training and, like now, simply for the experience. He had never seen a body dissected that was so close to his own age. Perhaps she had been one of the girls he had seen lounging on Parker's Piece just a few days earlier. He glanced at the corpse and looked away again, then stared at the clock, concentrating on the second hand slowly stepping around the dial and waiting for his sense of detachment to return.

Then he heard Marks speaking to him. 'Gary?'

'Sir?'

'I said, any questions before we go for the internal?'

'Sorry. No.'

'Everything all right?'

'Fine.'

Marks nodded to Sykes. 'Let's get on with it, then.'

Sykes picked up a scalpel. Goodhew always found the first cut the hardest to watch, and so pinned his attention on the soft skin near the girl's right shoulder. He needed to know whether he could handle this. His stomach tightened with apprehension.

With firm pressure Sykes made the blade break the skin and drew it across the top of the chest, dipping in the middle to make the cut form a low wide V, like the neckline of a ball gown. The skin parted like silently ripping silk.

He made a second incision, slitting her from the base of the V straight down to her pubic bone.

He then reached back to his instrument tray; his next job was to cut through ribs and cartilage and remove the heart and lungs.

Blood began making a metallic plink-plink-plink as drops hit the stainless steel drip trays.

The first waves of smell reached Goodhew's nostrils and the food analogy wafted back, with an uninvited suggestion of uncooked pork casserole. Soon Sykes would be cutting deeper and unleashing the thick invasive odour of flesh, faeces and stomach contents, so it really wasn't the time for planning dinner.

After a few seconds of deliberately thinking about nothing, Goodhew relaxed again; the scene wasn't repulsing him. He felt the same as he always had: they needed to know who she was and the cause and time of death, and he was in just the right place to gather that kind of information.

# THIRTEEN

From the corner of his eye, Goodhew caught sight of their reflections in the viewing-gallery window. He was in the centre, flanked by DI Marks and Anthony Sykes. Twice Goodhew glanced up, half-expecting to see three other people instead of the same three reflections staring in at the body. However, after an hour, he sensed someone really was watching, and looked up to find Kincaide peering in from the other side of the glass.

Kincaide mouthed something and pointed at Marks.

Goodhew touched his superior's arm. 'Sir, Kincaide's arrived.'

'Better see what he wants.'

Sykes looked up, too. 'There's an intercom button next to the window. Turn it on and we'll be able to hear him.'

Goodhew clicked the plastic on-off switch and slid the volume control up to halfway. He guessed this had been considered modern technology, somewhere back in the eighties.

Kincaide cleared his throat and his short cough came out as a tinny crackle from the single speaker mounted above the booth. 'Your phone's off so I decided to come in and find you. We think her name may be Lorna Spence.'

It was funny how just having a name made a difference. All four of them turned their attention to the corpse's face: it was an automatic reaction to hearing her name. Lorna Spence. Oval face. Wide mouth. Freckled skin. Hazel eyes. Feathered hair.

It was a bit like a dot-to-dot game, where the name joined them up. It was the missing feature, the thing they'd needed to complete the picture.

'How do you know?' Marks asked.

'Lucky teeth.' Kincaide half-smiled and Goodhew guessed he was enjoying his moment of keeping everyone hanging in an expectant pause.

'Lucky what?' Marks asked. 'Teeth?'

Kincaide tapped his own. 'A space between your two front teeth is supposed to be lucky, sir. I expect kids are told that to stop them picking on the gappy ones.' He knew just how many seconds Marks would tolerate the suspense and waited until the inspector drew an irritated breath. 'The station received a call from a consultant at the Excelsior Clinic on Magdalene Street. One of their staff, Lorna Spence, is missing from work. She's twenty-three, five two with short highlighted hair and a gap between her teeth. The station couldn't get hold of you, so they contacted me because I'd seen the body. I thought it sounded likely, so I came straight over.'

'Have you found an address for her?'

'21 Rolfe Street. It's in the centre, about five minutes' walk from the Excelsior.'

'Yes, yes, I know where it is.' Marks turned back to Sykes. 'We're almost done?'

'Another half-hour at most.'

Then he turned to Goodhew. 'Take that gown off and go along with Kincaide to the Excelsior.' He gave a quick nod in the direction of the body. 'If it still looks likely that she's this Lorna Spence, call me and I'll get someone over to the girl's house as soon as possible. See if you can find out anyone who knows her, and if anyone lives with her. Don't forget to keep it in the present tense as it still may be the wrong woman.'

Goodhew discarded his gown in the first laundry bin he found. He came across Kincaide waiting for him in the corridor leading to the main hospital exit. 'Do you know this Excelsior Clinic?' he asked.

'Only by reputation,' Kincaide muttered. 'It does cosmetic work, I gather. It was set up originally by several specialists, and does eye surgery and dental work along with the usual stuff.'

'The usual stuff?'

'You know, boob jobs, nose jobs, tattoo removal, skin treatments that stretch away wrinkles and shot-blast faces to keep fifty-somethings looking like forty-somethings because forty-somethings are busy trying to look like thirty-year-old Barbies.'

'You don't approve, then?'

Kincaide flashed him a lopsided smile, accompanied by a short snort. 'I'm sure it's the sort of shit that my wife Janice would rather spend money on than use to pay the household bills. But there you go, just not my scene.'

It took them about twenty minutes to reach Magdalene Street. They used the small car park belonging to the Excelsior Clinic, which had eight staff spaces and eight more for visitors. Four of the staff slots had been assigned eight-by-three plaques with two lines of dark-blue letters on a light-grey background. The top line said 'Reserved For' and the second line gave the occupant's name. Goodhew took a quick look at each: R. Moran, A. Moran, D. Shan and P. Norgren. Two Mercedes, one green, one silver, a new 'S' type Jag and a Saab convertible. 'These must be the consultants, I guess. Which one rang it in?'

'Guy called Richard Moran.'

Dark-green Mercedes saloon. This year's model, he noted. 'In person?'

'Seems so. That's what I heard, anyway. I don't know how long she's been missing.'

A paved footpath led from the car park and continued through a narrow walkway between two buildings. They stepped out from the alley intervening into Magdalene Street.

Goodhew knew the thoroughfare well: it ran from Magdalene College, where leaning Tudor cottages hung over the congested street, down a shallow slope towards the pedestrianized city centre, finishing at Magdalene Bridge amid a knot of pavement cafés.

They now paused at the heart of the coffee shops and restaurants. A stiff breeze threatened rain. It rustled napkins and lifted menus but, even so, the tables were all filled with couples composing postcards, lunchtime meetings of diaries and Danish pastries, and coffee drinkers seated alone with thick books and slow thirsts.

They slipped between the tables and found the entrance to the Excelsior Clinic. There, they buzzed the intercom and heard the door being released. Inside, the walls, ceiling and light fittings were all plain white. Kincaide was about to press the lift button, but Goodhew took to the stairs and he reluctantly followed.

'It's a bit clinical,' Kincaide quipped.

The landing door opened into a foyer, where the all-white theme continued. Here it was toned down with a beige sofa and an oak floor, complete with matching coffee table and reception desk. Apart from being female, the receptionist was about as far removed from the stereotype of her role as Goodhew could imagine. Her fringeless hair – a lack-lustre brown – had been dragged back and pinned at the nape of her neck. Her make-up stopped at her temples, leaving her exposed forehead bare of everything except the two deep frown furrows which dug permanent tramlines between her eyebrows. Hardly a good advertisement for cosmetic surgery.

And worse still, she didn't smile. But perhaps that was just because she had already realized they were police.

Goodhew spoke. 'We're here to see Mr Moran.'

She pushed back her chair and stood up. 'He's with a client at the moment. I'll let him know you're here, but I expect he'll be about ten minutes, if that's all right.' She lifted the hinged end of the counter and waved them through. 'Alice Moran is in the office, but that will be the best place for you to wait.'

She omitted the words 'out of sight' from the end of the sentence, but they both got her drift. Once they were both through, she slid back the opaque panel which separated her area from the room behind. 'Alice, it's the police,' she announced.

Goodhew and Kincaide entered the main office and heard the door slide shut behind them. The room was small with two desks, one heaped with papers, the other bare. Another door, on the opposite side of the room, stood ajar, with an electric fan positioned near it, presumably with the aim of dragging fresh air in from the corridor beyond, even though the temperature was already fairly low.

'Alice' sat at the untidy desk, adding up a list of figures with a desk calculator which whirred and churned out tally roll each time she hit the + key. Adding figures was clearly her forte, as the spewing list stretched to three feet and looked to be growing at several inches per minute. Her gaze flashed up to them, then back to her list. 'One minute, please.'

It was more an instruction than a request.

The woman looked in her early or mid-thirties. She wore a white man's shirt folded back to the elbows and chocolate-brown trousers.

Her hair was short and her footwear sturdy and, by rights, she should have resembled a male manual worker but, in reality, the effect was wholly feminine.

A tiny amethyst pendant on a fine gold chain sparkled in the hollow of skin exposed by the unbuttoned neck of the shirt. It was her only item of jewellery.

Here was a woman whose appearance implied great understatement, since she knew she could let her bone structure do the hard work for her. High cheekbones and a delicate jawline gave her a face that would turn from above average to striking as the years progressed. She sat upright, making the most of being five eight.

The calculator gave an extra judder as she finished adding, whereupon she copied the final figure from the display, then put her pen to one side. 'Sorry to keep you, but I was right at the end.' She stood and shook hands with both of them. 'I'm Alice, Richard Moran's sister. I work here part-time. Thanks for coming.'

Kincaide did the talking. 'I'm DC Kincaide, and this is DC Goodhew. We understand your brother is concerned about one of the staff. Lorna Spence?'

Alice nodded. 'It's probably nothing, but we can't get hold of her.' She screwed up her nose and looked apologetic. 'Richard panics,' she added.

A year planner was pinned to the wall above the coffee station. Goodhew wandered over to inspect it. 'How long has she been missing?' he asked.

'She didn't turn up this morning, or even phone in.'

'One day?' spluttered Kincaide 'You mean she was in yesterday? That's not *missing*; it's throwing a sickie.'

Goodhew continued to read the holiday chart.

'I told you,' Alice sighed. 'Richard panics.'

'I am not panicking, I'm concerned,' snapped an unseen man's voice. They all looked towards the open door, and it was obvious that the voice belonged to Alice's brother. Richard Moran was taut and angular, his bone structure like his sister's, but with less flesh to cover it. He was clean-cut and clean-shaven. He even had her skin colour and the same dark hair. Otherwise, he was dressed in chinos and an open-necked linen shirt, and they looked close enough in age to have been twins.

He closed the door behind him and stabbed the on-off switch to kill the fan. 'Why do we need this bloody thing in here, Alice? We're running the air-conditioning and yet you make this place like an ice house.' He held a pen in his hand and twiddled it between his fingers, and although he was, in effect, standing still, he shifted his weight from foot to foot with an agitated rocking motion.

Kincaide suggested he sat down, just as Goodhew opened his mouth to do the same. Instead of taking the spare chair, Moran perched awkwardly on the edge of his sister's desk.

Kincaide spoke in an even, unhurried voice. 'Lorna was due at work this morning at what time?'

'She usually gets in between eight-thirty and nine.'

'Why are you so concerned that you decided to report her as a missing person at only eleven? By then she was less than three hours late.'

'I . . . um . . .' His voice was tight with nervousness. He coughed to clear his throat and started again. 'When I couldn't get hold of her on the phone, I popped round to her flat. Then I heard word that you'd found a woman's body, though I don't have any reason to think it's her. I suppose Alice is right, and I am panicking, but the radio said she was all in black. Lorna always wears black.'

'So do lots of women,' Goodhew pointed out. 'Do you happen to have a photograph?'

Richard nodded. 'Hang on.'

But Alice was already flicking through a small sheaf of papers that she'd taken from her handbag. 'I've got one here.'

She slid a colour six-by-four print across the desk; Goodhew picked it up and held it midway between himself and Kincaide. Three people leaning across a restaurant table for the benefit of the camera: Richard, Alice and this morning's corpse. 'I'm very sorry, but this appears to be the woman we found earlier today.'

There was a moment of nothingness, no reaction from either of them. It was just a second, but it seemed to last longer.

Then Alice gasped, and her hand shot up to her mouth to suppress the sound. Richard gave a grunt, like all the air had been thumped from him. Then he pressed his face into both his hands, as if suddenly desperate for privacy. His shoulders rose and fell as he drew heavy breaths.

Kincaide looked at Goodhew, raising his hand in a 'wait' signal. Goodhew nodded and they silently waited.

# FOURTEEN

The rest of the day passed slowly. It seemed like a huge contradiction: one person had killed, another had been killed, and yet there was no fast track past the everyday snags. No one filled out forms any faster, or made walking quicker, and the pavements never grew shorter. So, while each point of the investigation was important, the lines that joined the dots were the same old, same old.

Goodhew had accompanied Richard Moran to the morgue. Alice had waited there with her brother and, from time to time took his hand. Richard stayed composed, but Goodhew detected a greater restraint in Alice herself. It didn't mean she was less concerned, of course; in fact, he guessed the difference between them had taken many years, possibly a lifetime, to forge.

When Richard reached out for his sister's hand, it seemed to be an automatic movement, almost a reflex. And just as his facial muscles seemed accustomed to running through a gamut of expressions from doubt to fear, so hers ranged only from completely expressionless to a look designed to urge him to hold it in. Clearly she wasn't the heart-on-the-sleeve type.

And the silence maintained had been heavy. Without any doubt, they all knew that the identification would be positive, and the certainty of that meant that Lorna Spence's flat was already being searched. But talking about it as a *fait accompli* seemed like wishing her dead. Even though she was.

Goodhew turned his thoughts to Lorna's flat. Kincaide would be there already, methodically working his way through her things.

Goodhew himself wished he could be in both places at once. He wanted the chance to absorb the feel of her there before her death fully settled in a dusty layer. It often struck him that the last breaths of a life stayed in the deceased's home long after leaving the body. And, although in his conscious mind he knew it was illogical to assign human attributes to buildings and inanimate objects, his subconscious had never quite been able to let go of the idea that some places waited for a familiar footstep or scent or routine, and that the last remnants of the person were only lost when the feeling of abandonment eventually set in.

So he wondered what Kincaide was uncovering there, but he also knew that he wanted to be present, here, when Richard and Alice looked down at Lorna's face and made the leap from being told she was dead to actually absorbing the reality. He knew that was the moment when spontaneous emotional responses often illuminated both the deceased and their nearest and dearest better than bright lights or an inquisition.

Eventually, they were called in to view the body, and afterwards Goodhew wondered what he'd really learnt from this. Alice stood further away, as if three extra feet of floor space would be enough to leave her detatched. Her spine was poker-straight and her arms were crossed, Morticia-style. The only change the imminent peeling back of the sheet produced was the subtle movement of Alice's right thumb, which flexed until it was pinching the soft flesh of her upper arm. She fixed her stare somewhere beyond the sheet, still covering Lorna, and resolutely refused to make eye contact with either of the men.

Richard reacted differently. At first, he seemed unable to stand still and kept rubbing his palms against his thighs, but when he nodded that he was ready for the sheet to be lifted, he drew in one deep breath, then managed to stop fidgeting.

His eyes bulged, as if the conflict between not wanting to look and having a duty to, was threatening to make them explode. He swallowed, but didn't look away from her as he spoke. 'It doesn't really look like Lorna,' he said.

Goodhew looked at Lorna too. 'But it is?'

'I can touch her, can't I? It is all right?'

'Of course.'

Richard ran two fingertips across the top of her cheek, as if wiping away a tear.

73

'We had plans,' he said.

'What kind of plans?'

Richard didn't answer, but instead turned to face his sister. 'We had plans, Alice.'

'I know,' she whispered. He reached out to her and she wrapped him in a tight embrace. 'I'm so sorry,' she murmured.

And the whole time, Goodhew never saw her look anywhere apart from the blank wall on the opposite side of the room. He didn't ask about the plans; sometime later would do for that.

Goodhew hadn't waited for another instruction from the station; instead, he'd just cleared off to Lorna's flat. He walked there; the late-afternoon traffic was already thickening, and driving would save him no time. But, more than that, he wanted to lose himself in Cambridge for a few minutes, to snatch a breath of fresh air and remind himself how the city outside the laboratory really smelt. He aimed to step into her flat with a clear set of senses, and thus a chance of snatching a last metaphorical glimpse of her.

The sun was out this afternoon and he realized that it was the first time since seeing Lorna's body on Midsummer Common that he'd been aware of anything unconnected with her. He could reach her flat with a brisk ten-minute walk along the edge of the pedestrianized shopping streets. As he passed the *Cambridge News* kiosk on the corner of Sidney Street and Petty Cury, the billboard announced 'Latest on Midsummer Common Murder'. People walked along with the late edition under their arms or protruding from their bags. Soon her name would be announced, and shortly after that the whole city would be on first-name terms with her.

A few minutes later, he turned from the busy shops in Bridge Street, down Rolfe Place and towards Rolfe Street beyond. No one followed and, ahead of him, the pavements were empty. He could see two marked cars parked in the middle of an atypically empty row of parking spaces. Meanwhile, a lone uniformed officer stood in a doorway. Goodhew knew that every activity would be closely watched from one neighbouring house or another, but he was glad that her home hadn't yet descended into a general gawping ground.

It was the type of street where the terraces had originally been functionally unglamorous, but now existed in a new incarnation of desirable and fashionable city living. Few had not been 'moderniz-ed', the term which currently implied adding period features alongside state-of-the-art gadgetry.

Lorna's flat appeared to have once served as the living accommo-dation over a shop. The shop itself looked like it had ceased trading somewhere back in the 1970s, when aluminium window frames and stone cladding or pebble dashing were still options of modernization that left one's neighbours on speaking terms. OK, so the conversion from shop to ground-floor flat had escaped any onslaught on the brickwork, but the metal replacement windows with brown-glossed windowsills were a dead giveaway, and now it stood forlornly empty with a faded 'For Sale' board in the window. By contrast, Lorna's front door was solid wood: not one of those pseudo-traditional knock-offs but, the real McCoy; the two-inch-thick type made half an inch thicker by a century of gloss paint, and still with the original stained-glass panel set in the top.

He was now close enough to recognize that the constable standing in the doorway was Kelly Wilkes. She smiled in greeting, stepping forward and to one side as he came within a few feet of her.

'Who's here?' he asked.

'Just a couple of forensics guys and Kincaide.'

'He's the only one?'

'Uh-huh. DI Marks was here earlier, but left Kincaide and DC Charles to finish off. Then, about twenty minutes ago, Charles said he was off too. I think they've pretty much finished.'

'That's fast going,' he commented as he stepped through the door. 'Must be a small flat.'

The hall had a floor laid with the familiar year-dot dark-red tiles, interspersed with black and white diamonds, and a few in cobalt blue for contrast. Four pairs of shoes had been bagged and left at the bottom of the stairs, which, beneath the protective plastic laid down by the forensics team, were carpeted. He ascended the centre of the flight, carefully avoiding touching either wall. Above him, the landing was partially visible, the banisters blocked in behind hardboard panels, but still low enough for someone to look over them to find out who was approaching. On this occasion, no one did.

A single unlit bulb, decorated with hand-painted swirls, hung from an overhead light fitting, and if that counted as an artistic touch, it was the only one. Immediately beside the top step stood a small dark-wood table. Goodhew's attention settled on it for a moment before being diverted by the sound of Kincaide's voice. But he had looked just long enough to see that the post contained nothing more than a few advertising brochures.

Kincaide stood close to the top of the stairs. 'That stuff was on the mat when we arrived, so at least we know she left before the post came.'

Goodhew looked past him into the flat itself, noticing that the curtains were drawn shut and the lights were on. 'How's it going?'

Kincaide shrugged. 'Just about wrapping it up. There's not much left to do here.'

The living room was a reasonable size, and furnished with a few well-chosen items, mainly in pine. Both the chest of drawers and the bookcase looked like they'd been bought from local antique dealers, and the soft furnishings from a shop which specialized in neither cheap nor cheerful. Somehow he knew they weren't Lorna's own. By contrast, the television, mirror and a frame containing dried flowers had all arrived on a much more modest budget and looked pack-up-and-go convenient. One remote control, two pens, and a box of tissues were the most clutter she'd left lying around. Perhaps she'd been hooked on those sell-your-home shows which preach depersonalizing your living space – anyhow, it wasn't hard to see why the police search hadn't taken long.

Kincaide had now moved on, and Goodhew found him adding Lorna's bedding to the inventory of items being removed.

'I guess she rented?'

'Guess so,' Kincaide grunted. 'Haven't got that far yet, but who can afford to buy a place here, in the centre?' He glanced up, raised an eyebrow, and added pointedly, 'Don't even know who can afford to even rent in this town; you'd have to be lucky enough to have it in the family.'

Goodhew ignored the personal dig. 'Nice bed.' It was a king-size, with an asymmetric headboard composed of wrought-iron gothic scrolls. Nice wasn't the right word for it; more like quirky with a touch of the Gaudi-esque.

'You serious?' Kincaide looked from Goodhew to the bed and back again, clearly unsure whether he was being had.

'Absolutely.'

'Really? I think it looks tacky, like some shitty art college project.' Kincaide couldn't wipe the grimace of distaste from his face, in fact he made no attempt to. 'It looks dodgy to me. Pervy in fact. And hideous.'

Kincaide wandered off again, but Goodhew stayed behind to study the curves of the metal, trying to see it the same way Kincaide obviously had. He found himself pulling that same expression, but still didn't understand what there was not to like.

Finally, he walked over to the window and lifted the curtain briefly, then dropped it again. He turned back and ran his fingers along the topmost curve of the bedhead, then crossed the room and began opening and closing the wardrobe. There was nothing left inside, no essence of Lorna's presence left for him to disturb.

Kincaide, meanwhile, was in the kitchen, leaning on the worktop and sending a text with some fast and ambidextrous thumb activity. 'Hang on,' he grunted to his younger colleague.

Goodhew flipped open an overhead cupboard, where he found the crockery. Apart from two mugs, the contents were all clearly from a standard issue everything-proof set. The taller mug was cream-coloured with the word 'Chocolate' curling across it, the other was brightly painted with the name 'Lorna'. Not very revealing. He let the door snap shut.

Kincaide glanced up. 'I've already done the cupboards.'

Goodhew took the hint and left the next one alone. 'What about that calendar?'

'Oh, yeah. Nothing much on it, but it can go with the other paperwork. There's a box of it I've just moved to the top of the stairs.'

The calendar was the type with one square per day but no picture; it had come courtesy of Staples Office Supplies. The current month had only one entry, 'Hair – 12.00' on the 16th. If that was a good example of a month's activity, 'nothing much' really would be an accurate description. Goodhew unhooked it from the wall and turned forward the pages from the back. When it came to their calendars, people were either flip and keep, or rip and bin, and he was pleased to see that Lorna had been with him on this one.

'Oh boy,' he sighed. Either her life was depressingly uneventful or she recorded her more interesting activities elsewhere.

He had turned right back to the start of the year before any entry caught his attention: 9th January – 'Bryn to MOT car'. Goodhew read this just as Kincaide dropped his mobile back into his pocket.

'Seen something?'

Goodhew frowned. 'Don't know, really. Did she have a car?'

Kincaide took the calendar, 'I saw that too and checked with the others at the Excelsior, but they say no. She sold it apparently.'

Goodhew followed Kincaide out of the kitchen, and watched him drop the calendar into the document crate.

And later, as he walked towards home, he reminded himself that there could be numerous people called Bryn in this area. More than just the Bryn O'Brien who'd sat nearest the paint cupboard in primary school. He was the class practical joker, whom Gary couldn't even remember speaking to, but had secretly admired. Bryn had made light of education, never buckling under the weight of expectation, always doing just enough to get by.

When Gary's mother had switched him to a private school at the end of Year 6, he'd found himself reeling from the shock of going from the top of his state school class to being considered mediocre among his new peers. And, for the first couple of years, he gave Bryn credit for helping him through. Mentally he'd kept Bryn alongside him, imagining how Bryn would navigate the narrow ledge that was bottom of the class.

But the real Bryn was someone he knew next to nothing about. And the chances were it was a different Bryn, except that as he'd read that entry in the calendar, his memory had conjured up a single item of O'Brien family trivia: Bryn's father had been a mechanic. And, when he factored that in, he knew that the odds narrowed dramatically.

The decision he therefore made, as he walked home, was a simple one: he would track down Bryn O'Brien. With any luck, he'd be meeting someone on first-name terms with Lorna.

# FIFTEEN

Goodhew walked across Parker's Piece towards home, a one-bedroomed, rooftop flat in Park Terrace. The building had once been a four-storey townhouse, but since the 1990s, the basement and first three floors had been converted into office space, so the only remaining living accommodation was Goodhew's. He glanced up to his window, then walked down the short garden path and unlocked the heavy front door. It closed behind him with a solid and purposeful click, the sound always reminding him he now had the place to himself.

He took the stairs two at a time and, on reaching the final landing, opened a second door, which led directly into his flat. He paused, and despite instincts telling him that nothing had been disturbed, he let his eyes make their routine three-second sweep of the room. His scrutiny began at the far end, checking for three reassuring things: undisturbed bookshelves, his bedroom door still closed, and his beloved Bel Ami jukebox unplugged and unharmed. All OK. Finally, he made sure that his pile of papers still lay on top of the closed case of his laptop. He concluded that nothing had been moved, which gave him his cue to unwind one more turn.

He frowned, finding his own habit of double-checking things annoying, and acknowledging that it wasn't far from bordering on compulsive. But, hell, everyone had their personal foibles, and it wasn't like he wasted much time on it.

He changed into jeans and a t-shirt, poured a glass of orange juice, and set his jukebox on free-play. The mechanism clicked and whirred before making its selection and dropping the single on to the deck. The arm swooped, giving the stylus a bumpy landing on the run-in strip. The 45 crackled, then broke into the opening bars of Chuck Berry's 'School Days'. How apt.

Gary slid his Sony Notebook from one of the bottom book-shelves, pressed the power button and, as he waited for it to boot up, flipped open the Yellow Pages and flicked towards 'Car Repairs'. He had expected he'd need to use search engines for electoral rolls and credit checks, and possibly even a visit to Friends Reunited, but the Notebook was not even in the running – by the time it had fully loaded Windows, Gary had already drawn a blue box around the name 'O'Brien and Sons' with his Biro.

He checked his watch. Ten past seven. He rang the number. No reply. No surprise there then. But it was within easy walking distance, just across Parker's Piece and then a few streets further on, behind the swimming pool. His curiosity had been stirred and he decided to go there in any case. He waited for Chuck Berry to finish, then pulled the plug from the wall socket and left his flat again.

Gary saw Parker's Piece as the no man's land between two distinctly different parts of the city. He lived on the historic side, the tourist trap brimming with distinctive buildings and enough magnetism to draw people from, literally, all over the world. The other side was certainly poorer and less distinctive, with a criss-cross of any-town backstreets and a surfeit of struggling or vacant premises. Personally, he had no preference for either area, knowing that, like backstage and front of house, neither could function with-out the other.

He had no idea what to expect now from a visit to a locked workshop, probably nothing more than a sign saying 'Closed', and another indicating the phone number that he'd already tried. He walked on anyway.

Bryn O'Brien had heard the phone ringing; in fact it was impossible to miss the sound of the extension which made an outside bell jangle up under the eaves of the garage. But he made no move to answer it.

He was sitting within reach of it too, and knew, without looking, that the handset was resting on the bench, less than two feet from his left shoulder. Only one item lay between it and himself: a face-down copy of the *Cambridge News*.

He stayed where he was, sunk into the improvised battered vinyl settee that had once been the bench seat of a '62 low-line Ford Consul. He still wore his maroon overalls, and his steel-toed working boots were planted squarely on the concrete floor. Bryn had short blond hair and blue eyes, made brighter by the smudges of grease that he'd smeared on to his face during the day. One palm rested on each knee, and the first two knuckles of his right hand were grazed, pink circles left by a sudden departure of skin.

In front of him, his current project was elevated to full height on the ramps. It was another Mark II Ford, but this time a Zodiac, the fully equipped and subtly modified version of its deceased cousin. Bryn stared up at its underside, where he'd replaced the 2.5 litre straight six with a rebuild V6, and at the twin exhausts, each branching into two, their four chrome tailpipes protruding from beneath the bumper. The car was a clean black underneath, with low-profile tyres on Wolfrace wheels, wider than the originals had been.

He knew he'd created a retro-custom of a yet more retro car. There had even been a phase when he'd been tempted to trade it in for a PT Cruiser, but then he realized that could suck him into a scene full of all-too-earnest enthusiasts, so he'd decided to stick with the little beast he'd already created. And he'd been glad of it, especially at moments like these. He slid down in the seat and tilted his head back, still watching his car through part-closed eyes. It had the same effect as unwinding in a hot bath; his thoughts floated at their own speed, taking their own routes and pulling others along with them. Bryn wasn't a deep thinker, and he never had been. More than that, he was conscious of a distrust of contemplation and where it might lead. He wanted to release two particular thoughts, and he hated the way they now seemed to be linked, and kept coming back, hand in hand, to bother him.

He gazed up towards his car and almost let these thoughts go. If a face hadn't suddenly appeared in the small window in the workshop's concertina door, he might have succeeded. But probably not . . .

Gary found O'Brien's straight away. It was one of those places that he'd never really noticed, but equally knew he'd seen it countless times before. It was brick-built with navy-blue steel doors and an apex roof covered in something which looked suspiciously like corrugated asbestos. There was no 'Closed' sign, just one with a name and telephone number, and a second board at one corner which read 'No Smoking'. Underneath it there was a collection of stubbed-out cigarette ends; Gary wasn't sure whether that was a good sign or a bad one.

The workshop had all its other windows high up on the side walls, near to the roof, so that only the six-by-nine Perspex pane in the door was within reach. He cupped his hands and tried to peer inside, but the evening sunlight and scratches made it cloudy, and he knew that wiping it would make no difference. He tried anyway, ever the optimist.

He kept his face close to the aperture for longer the second time, and shapes gradually began to pick themselves out. Enough weak daylight made it through the windows for him to see the roof of a white van, and a second car raised up on a ramp. In one of the lighter patches, he spotted a year planner and then, further across, the familiar red crate-like shape of a Snap-On tool kit.

Then he thought he saw movement and, illogically, pulled back slightly. When he looked again, a figure was approaching the door. Gary stepped to one side and waited.

Gary knew, as soon as the door clanked open, that he'd found his former classmate. It was a funny thing; if he'd been asked to describe Bryn before seeing him, he might well have replied, 'I can't remember.' In truth, he had a vague recollection of fair hair, a slight build, and perpetually scuffed shoes – hardly the stuff of a positive ID. But, confronted with the man himself, a whole barrelload of details flooded back: the eyebrows that always looked slightly raised, the single piercing in the right lobe, now unoccupied, the head tilted in interest or defiance, depending on interpretation, and the serious set of the mouth which accompanied it.

The slight built had been replaced by broad shoulders, but the boots were still scuffed, and it was soon evident that he still had that habit of either pushing his hands into his pockets or leaning against something whenever he began to speak. Today it was pockets, Gary noticed. The teachers used to have a field day pulling him up on that habit each time they were busy pulling him up on something else – which had been often.

'We're closed,' he announced.

'I know.' Gary took a moment to continue. Despite convincing himself that the odds of finding the right Bryn were quite good, he'd only actually visualized meeting the wrong one; now he knew he was about to hear something completely unrehearsed coming out of his mouth.

He decided to steer clear of Lorna Spence. 'I went to school with you,' he began. How inane did that sound? 'At Chesterton Primary.'

'Congratulations.' Bryn raised one eyebrow very slightly but didn't smile.

Gary had recognized Bryn, partly because he knew who he was looking for. Bryn, on the other hand, clearly didn't have a clue who this was.

'I'm Gary Goodhew, you probably don't remember . . .' He left his words to trail off.

Bryn shrugged. 'Remember the name. What's up?'

Gary nodded towards the workshop beyond. 'I need to ask you something, but not out here.'

'I'm just leaving.'

'Five minutes.'

Gary saw Bryn hesitate before he glanced back into the workshop, then he slid the door closed.

'Five minutes,' Gary repeated.

Bryn gave in. 'OK, I've got time for a quick drink. The Salisbury's just round the corner.'

They walked in silence for the first hundred yards, and Gary wondered how he should approach the subject. Lorna Spence may have just used Bryn to repair her car and, if so, what next? Yet Gary was well aware that anything he now found out should form part of an official statement, not a friendly chat over a pint.

Bryn broke the silence first. 'By the way, I'm not up for a school reunion, if that's what you're here about. Not my thing at all.' He said it in an easy way, the way Gary remembered, as though the answer didn't really matter, except that his eyes flickered as they watched for the reply, and it was clear to Gary that the answer he gave was actually very important.

Gary deflected the question. 'Maybe you need to hit thirty before you start getting nostalgic.'

The Salisbury Arms stood on the other side of the road. Bryn darted across in front of a car, leaving Gary trailing a few yards behind. He figured, however, there was no need to hurry, and reached the bar just as Bryn was being given change for his pint of lager. Gary ordered a Stella, and followed Bryn to the table he'd selected at the far end of the room.

The pub was genuinely traditional, not just styled to look that way. The beams and old floors had really aged with the building, rather than arriving there as prefabricated panels. Bryn sat on a long bench, his back to the end wall, while Gary chose a square chair that looked like it belonged in a dining room. The table itself had been converted from a treadle sewing machine, and the word 'Singer' was curled into the metal footplate.

'Ever see anyone from school?' he began.

Bryn shook his head. 'I remember you, though.'

'Really?'

'Yeah, I thought your sister was cute. Then you left and we were told you'd both got scholarships to some private school.'

Gary smiled: funny how such rumours turned the truth into something else. Funny, too, how Bryn remembered his sister. 'Debbie probably was cute,' he conceded, 'but I think she was only ten at the time.' They both paused to drink. 'I'm with the police now,' he added, with no change of tone.

'Ah.' It was said with neither surprise nor alarm, but just as a recogniton of a matter of fact. 'I see.'

'Do you know a Lorna Spence?' Gary continued quietly.

'A little, I think.'

'You think?'

Bryn rubbed imaginary sweat from his forehead with the flat of his right hand, further smudging the greasy streaks that already marked the exposed skin right up into his hairline. Gary noted the raw patches on Bryn's knuckles, and wondered what object he'd hit.

Bryn thought for a few seconds, then answered Gary's question with one of his own. 'Do you mean "Do I know her", or do you mean "Did I know her"?'

'What makes you think she's dead?'

Bryn dropped his hand on to the tabletop, covering a Guinness beer mat with his palm, then spread his fingers out like he was trying to come up with five good reasons. He managed two. 'You lot found a woman's body this morning, right?'

Gary just nodded.

'It's been on the radio all day. Then you start to search a flat in Rolfe Street. Know how many flats there are down there?'

Gary didn't know, but he hadn't noticed many, that was for sure. 'It's mostly houses, isn't it?'

'Maybe there's more, but I can only recall *two* flats, Lorna's and the empty one underneath. So when you turn up asking if I know her, what else am I going to think?'

'Can you tell me when you last saw her?' Gary asked, wondering whether there was a record for the number of times someone could keep answering a question with another question.

'Am I making a statement or is this an informal chat?'

Gary decided to level with him, and with no question at the end of it. Letting people talk was a more accurate way of weighing them up than showering them with continual questions. 'I spotted your name on Lorna's calendar, where she planned for you to MOT her car back in January. I guessed that there might not be too many Bryns in the area, so I thought I'd check out whether it was you. I'm part of the investigation team, so you will certainly be asked to make a statement, but for now I'm just trying to get some of the groundwork done.'

'Yeah, well, you always were good at homework.' Bryn drained the rest of his pint. 'OK, hang on a minute,' he added, and headed towards the Gents.

Gary watched him go, deciding nothing about him gave the impression of a man ill at ease, and yet Gary couldn't help wondering whether Bryn was planning to head out of a back door.

He went to the bar for another couple of pints, and hoped he wouldn't end up drinking them alone.

Bryn washed his hands, carefully squirting a large pool of liquid soap into his palm and taking time to work it between each of his fingers. Gradually, some of the oil stains began to shift, but he wasn't fully conscious of what he was doing, most of his thoughts were focusing on Goodhew.

Gary Goodhew.

That was a name from the past, and it was true that at first he hadn't recognized his old classmate. But once the name had connected with the face, memories had rushed into his head. And he'd been surprised, not by the number – so far there had only been a few – but by the clarity.

Suddenly he could picture the whole class. Like the bulk of the kids there, he had gone on to Chesterton Secondary School, but there had been others who had disappeared at the end of that same year. He'd subsequently forgotten they'd ever existed – until now. Suddenly he remembered Karen Jarvis and her frizzy hair, her book bag perforated with holes from a pair of compasses.

Steve 'Stench' Manning, who didn't actually smell, but just looked like he did.

Jon Wu, with the skinny legs and scraped knees, who wasn't that bright but created masterpieces from papier mâché and poster paint.

And Gary Goodhew.

Goodhew's desk had stood at right angles to the window. He'd mixed with everyone and no one, friendly enough, but seemed to spend most of his time staring through the glass. Who knew what he had found so absorbing out there in the car park, a few trees and a fence, but even so, he never missed a trick. When Mr Mosley threw him a question, Goodhew never failed to pluck the right answer from thin air and throw it right back.

And if he'd matured into an extension of that junior self, he wouldn't be missing much now, that was for sure.

Bryn dried his hands and took a deep breath before reaching for the door handle.

For someone who claimed he didn't like to think too deeply, he currently had a great deal on his mind. He knew that saying nothing wasn't an option but, then again, he could see that saying too much might be dangerous. Just enough is what he now had to aim for. Precisely enough, at least until he'd had time to think.

Gary didn't read anything significant into Bryn's return to their table, but was pleased about it nonetheless. He wanted their conversation to start up pretty much where it had left off, so for that reason, he made sure to speak first. 'You said you *thought* you knew Lorna Spence a little. I don't understand what exactly you meant by that.'

He saw that Bryn had relaxed somewhat: he leant back in his seat, his posture seeming more open and his eye contact steady. As he answered, his speech was neither rushed nor overly hesitant. 'She brought her car in one day. It was a Rover, I remember. She'd been parked up further down our road, and now it wouldn't start. The alternator was on the blink, but it was a bit of a Friday car . . .'

Bryn paused there, and Gary knew he was looking appropriately blank.

'A lemon. A dog. A car turned out quick 'cos everyone wants to knock off for the weekend. You know, one that keeps throwing up so many niggly faults that you think the whole machine must be a bit suspect.'

Gary nodded; he'd already got it at 'lemon'.

'Well, she came in a few times after that. I think it suited her because we're so close to the town centre. Like I said, the car had mostly minor problems, but a couple of times we ended up having a drink afterwards. In here, actually.'

'Her idea, or yours?'

Bryn screwed up his face, like he'd been asked a disproportionately difficult question. 'Can't remember.' He looked at Gary as if waiting to be told whether or not that was a reasonable answer.

'Fair enough,' Gary replied.

'I remember she asked if I fancied a game of pool, and we ended up in Mickey Flynn's on Mill Road.'

'Is that the American place?'

'Yeah, that's it.'

'And what then?'

'That happened a couple of times, too. She was funny – easy company. We saw each other a few times, but it wasn't ever planned. She'd turn up and, if I was free, we'd spend a couple of hours together.'

'Just as friends?'

Bryn smiled apologetically, like he'd just been caught with his fingers in a metaphorical jar of biscuits, then he shifted his expression rapidly towards neutral. 'Sure,' he replied.

'OK.' Gary meant it as in *OK, if that's how you want to tell it*, and he could see that that was what Bryn realized he meant. However, they both pretended he'd intended it the other way. 'So when did you last see her?'

'About the time she wrote me on her calendar, I guess. I MOT'd the car, and then she said she planned to sell it. Never saw her after that.'

'Did she ever mention friends, or seem lonely or unhappy? You know where she lived, so what else do you know?'

'She mentioned people from work, said she had something going with her boss, but we never got into that. I think it might have been one of those on-off things. She never seemed like one of those women that can't handle being on their own, and she certainly didn't seem like she wanted to settle down soon. I run a mile from those types.'

'Sounds like you knew her more than a *little*.'

That stalled Bryn, opening a route to somewhere he evidently had no plan to go. No matter, it could wait. Whatever composure he'd regained began to freewheel away. He slammed on the brakes and his earlier hesitancy reappeared. Gary knew that the productive part of the conversation was as good as over now.

'Look,' Bryn said finally, 'maybe that's how it seems, but she was one of those people . . . you know, you see them a few times and really feel you're on the same wavelength, then suddenly you realize they've learnt plenty about you, but you know bugger all about them. So I don't know if I knew her much at all. I never had any romantic interest in her, if that's what you're wondering. But I thought she was really genuine and sweet. And I liked her.'

Gary's gaze wandered towards the windows, and settled on the sulphurous light pooling down from a streetlamp. He left his instincts to summarize the conversation and decided that what little he'd heard had been the truth, but he doubted it was the whole truth, and was equally dubious that it had been nothing but.

# SIXTEEN

Gary Goodhew left the Salisbury Arms at a few minutes before nine. The air was clear and still; it had hushed away the usual blur of background sounds, pushing its stillness between cars and pedestrians, leaving everyone to move in their own pool of solitude. He cut through the back alleys behind the houses, deliberately keeping his distance from any pockets of activity, heightening his feeling of isolation.

Even the sky had backed away, retracting the stars until they were just minute dots in the heavens.

The flatness of East Anglia kept the horizon low and the sky vast. When Goodhew had been about seven, his grandfather had told him to look at the ceiling, then to lie on the carpet and do the same. Goodhew knew that most things became smaller when you moved away from them, but when he lay down and looked up, the ceiling seemed to have grown. His grandfather had said that Cambridge was lying on the carpet, and the sky was there to remind it that it was only a tiny corner of the world. Beyond that, Goodhew couldn't remember the exact purpose of the conversation, but he never failed to notice the sky.

By the time he was crossing Parker's Piece, his thoughts had gravitated back to Lorna Spence. He was on the far side from Parkside station and from here, he could see that the light was off in Marks' office. He'd spent most of the afternoon and early evening away from his boss, and therefore away from the latest thinking regarding the case. He'd been away with Richard Moran for the identification and at Lorna's flat, but neither task had given him any insight into the direction their thoughts would be moving back at the station. He probably wouldn't know until morning.

He guessed that Bryn had stepped beyond the boundaries of a mechanic–customer relationship. Too early to read much into it though, since Bryn's reluctance to talk about it may have stemmed from one of several sources, like the desire for privacy or a simple aversion to the police. There'd be time for that kind of detail when Bryn made his official statement.

Goodhew felt wide awake, his mind buzzing too much to face the confines of his flat. Without any definite plan, he realized that he was drifting, in an arc, away from the straight line taking him to his front door and left towards the city centre. He began to think about talking to Richard Moran, and wondered whether he could get away with visiting him at this late hour. He tried to remind himself that it wasn't exactly his place to be the first to know everything, except that his obsession for knowing was what had pulled him into the job in the first place, and he fully recognized the shortcoming and enjoyed giving in to it.

Goodhew glanced at his watch. He knew, before he checked, that it was around ten past nine, but he just wanted to convince himself that it really wasn't too late. Nine o'clock was the end of kiddies' bedtimes, the watershed where adult TV began, and the soaps mostly ended. News didn't air until ten; oh yes, it was early enough.

He'd already checked out Moran's home address and had immediately been able to pinpoint the house itself. It was the left-hand half of a towering six-storey semi which stood next to a church, and enjoyed a rare, elevated position looking down on Chesterton Lane and from there towards the Cam.

It involved a short walk through the town and out the other side, past the Excelsior Clinic itself, then across the river and right at the next junction. He kept to the main routes now, walking with purpose, keen to reach the house as quickly as possible.

He ignored the arguments against this visit, only beginning to consider it might be a bad idea in the moments between ringing the doorbell and seeing a shadow approaching it on the other side of the glass. He hadn't even decided what excuse to use for his visit, trusting himself to come up with something appropriate when the need arose.

It didn't.

Richard let him in without question, clearly having already got the hang of understanding that he'd now lost his entitlement to privacy. Had Goodhew been asked for a snap judgement, 'resignation personified' would have been how he summed up Moran; he looked hollowed out and punch-drunk, still standing but just waiting for the killer blow.

But once he was inside, the light got better, and when Goodhew saw the man face-on, he knew that punch-drunk wasn't the appropriate phrase. Stoned more like. Yes, he looked out of it, broken even, but there was an unnatural energy in his stare.

Whatever. He looked like shit.

Goodhew opened his mouth to speak, but Moran got in first. 'More questions? I'm glad, because I've got some for you, too. Plenty, actually.'

Goodhew followed him into the room immediately next to the front door. It was what makeover shows describe as 'lacking an identity': a study cum library, or TV room cum lounge. Or, equally, a goods-in cum charity collection point. It all depended on which corner you studied, but it had none of the pretentiousness evident in the Excelsior Clinic and looked to Goodhew like any ordinary student flat.

Richard sat at one end of a settee facing the door. Goodhew chose to sit at the other end. The house was silent and, although a steady stream of headlights passed the window, nothing disturbed the stillness with anything louder than a low hum.

'You said you had plenty to ask?'

Richard nodded. 'I'm glad you came. I thought I wouldn't be able to speak to anyone this late, but I knew I wouldn't sleep either – not with so many unanswered questions.'

Goodhew knew the feeling. 'And these are regarding things that have come to mind since you gave your statement?'

'Partially. In fact, I'd say they've been on my mind all along, but earlier I didn't stop long enough to distil them into clear questions. But now I have. Firstly, I want to know why suspicion is falling on us.'

'Us?'

'Me, then. Me in particular.'

'You shouldn't assume it is, just—'

'Yes, yes.' Richard made a dismissive gesture. 'You would say that, wouldn't you? What makes you think Lorna wasn't snatched by a stranger, or by some passing acquaintance?'

Sometimes it was useful to be able to call up a stock answer to such a question, because half the time, it was what a witness or victim expected to be told in any case, which in itself brought a feeling of calm. 'Mr Moran, we are still only in the first hours of our investigation and nothing has been ruled out yet . . .' One look at Richard's sour expression told Goodhew that he'd misjudged it, but he plugged on with a second attempt. 'There are many routine questions that we need to ask, and they aren't intended to make you feel that you yourself are under any unreasonable suspicion, but obviously it's important that we can construct an accurate picture of Lorna's habits and her relationships.'

Richard's sceptical expression hadn't diluted, and Goodhew could sense that he wasn't within a thousand miles of achieving the cathartic effect he'd hoped for. The silence hung awkwardly during a long pause.

'Do you think I'm a dullard?'

Dullard? Goodhew found the word quaint, but had no trouble not smiling, especially since Richard's mouth looked like it was stuffed with lemons. 'No, of course not. What makes you think I'm not being straight with you?'

Richard's eyes were still glassy, but they'd steadied enough to scrutinize Goodhew keenly. 'It's the problem of conventionality, I think. You people ask all the standard questions, to which I've been making all the standard replies, so then you come back with all the standard responses. Now I have questions myself, which I can't ask without making it clear that I've been giving you a misleading picture. Do you see?'

'In theory.'

'And?'

Goodhew felt a surge of good luck sweep over him; now he had the chance to catch up on everything that had already been said and, probably, better it. He feigned a sigh and hoped he sounded cautious. 'Any discrepancies need to be corrected as soon as possible, and therefore you may need to make a new statement – you understand that, don't you?'

Richard nodded. 'I just wanted to keep my privacy.'

'But you were in a relationship with her?'

'Oh, yes. That part's true.'

'What's not, then?'

'Nothing's untrue, I just put some spin on it.' He made a little snorting noise that was probably meant to be a laugh. It didn't work, but did succeed in demonstrating what he looked like while toppling out of his fragile comfort zone – naked, and without hope of being thrown even the smallest pair of briefs.

Goodhew just waited.

Richard licked his lips, then finally committed himself with his opening gambit. 'I was out of my depth with Lorna.'

Goodhew waited some more, then Richard's words began to flow in earnest.

'Obviously I was in a relationship with her. On the face of it, I don't suppose we seemed at all compatible – there was an age gap of over ten years, and our backgrounds were quite different. We didn't even look very well suited. But those are very outdated notions, and neither of us took them as valid reasons for . . .' He drew a deep and weary breath and then let it out noisily, like it was steam forcing itself through a faulty valve, 'Not pursuing each other.'

Without warning, he rose and walked towards the window, stopping just before it. He stared downwards and Goodhew couldn't tell whether it was at the traffic passing outside or at the square work station which occupied the floor space immediately in front of the bay. Then his hand reached out, with narrow fingers extended, the tips touching an item which lay out of Goodhew's view in the open top of a container marginally larger than a shoebox.

He carried the box back with him, and Goodhew now saw that it contained a variety of books and magazines. *Men Are From Mars, Women Are From Venus* lay on top, and it must have been its cover that Richard had been stroking. 'These are Lorna's,' he explained. 'She would sit in here, often just where you are, and read them. Never for long, just brief snatches of books or magazines. She had a short attention span, and needed constant diversions, new things to do or to read. New people, too.'

Goodhew sensed that Richard was close to making his point.

'She was lovely . . . please, that's one thing I don't want you to misunderstand. She was warm and caring and never set out to hurt me. I know that. And she wasn't unfaithful, not in her own eyes.' Richard delved back into the box, lifting out a chunky handful of paperbacks. Mostly books that fell into the category of Popular Psychology. Goodhew spotted one called *On Kissing* and another entitled *Toxic Parents*. Richard dumped them on the cushion in-between them and carried on digging through the box. Goodhew flipped over *When Your Lover Is a Liar*, which promised 'practical strategies to stop them before they ruin your life'. He then picked up the other books and shuffled it in between them.

Richard seemed too preoccupied to notice. Finally he pulled his hand out again, and with it a bundle of seven or eight glossy magazines which he spread out on the settee. 'These are the sort of things she would normally read.'

Goodhew studied them. He was no expert on magazines and really had no idea what insight was supposed to be jumping out at him. Two of them were aimed at men: lad mags, but certainly not top shelf. Middle shelf or thereabouts. The other five were women's magazines, and he could see instantly that they were aimed at the younger end of the market; single independent girls, the so-called ladettes. Whatever Richard was showing him, he wasn't getting it.

'I was out of my depth here, because this is what she embraced. Sexual freedom was part of who she was; she never wanted monogamy and told me so from the start. And, like a mug, I thought she'd change her mind, or wasn't really serious, or . . . God, I don't know, perhaps I thought I could handle it.' He flicked the mags sharply with the back of his hand, making a brittle crack. 'Promiscuity is a fashion now, a must-experiment necessity. I've read these articles, but find them sick and vacuous.' Blotchy red patches had begun rising around his throat, like he'd swallowed his discomfort, just to have it break out through the skin. His voice quietened as he hit his stride. 'It's society going down the tube, by turning decent women into whores.'

Goodhew guessed the word 'whores' wasn't one that Richard often used. Of course, he didn't know for sure, but he noticed the way the word dried up on Richard's lips, the way his mini-tirade vaporized as he registered what he'd just said.

'Sorry,' Richard muttered.

'It's fine,' Goodhew replied. 'So Lorna saw other men?'

'No, I don't think so, but she insisted she could if she wanted to. And that she would at some point, and would tell me when she did.

That's bad enough – no, actually, I think it's worse. On one hand she told me she loved me, and I know she did, but on the other . . .' He paused and gnawed his bottom lip.

There was something about Richard that reminded Goodhew of a teenage boy talking about his first romance. He should have been sitting on a tubular steel and canvas chair with his feet hooked round the legs as he leant over an old wooden desk scraping something like 'LS 4 RM' into its hinged lid with his pair of school compasses.

'If she never followed it up, perhaps it was only the fantasy of the notion that attracted her.'

'She was pretty insecure. I told myself she only did it to keep control, but I was getting to the end of my tether. I wanted it to be just a phase, something she'd abandon when she realized we were stable. We'd only been together since last December, but I couldn't stand the thought of being without her.'

'That's not long.'

'No, it's not. It's been strange, true, like time since I met her has moved at the wrong speed. Alice says I rushed into it, but it never *felt* like rushing.'

'And you met through work?'

'She started with us last summer, first of all as a temp, then we gave her a permanent contract.'

'She came through an agency?'

'Yes. Sort of. She was friendly with Victoria Nugent, who works for the dentist in the same building. Lorna came in to meet her for lunch on several occasions and, in the process, started talking to Alice.' He paused and smiled affectionately. 'My sister was constantly frustrated with the temps we were sent, as they often lacked basic written English skills and struggled to balance figures. When she found out that Lorna was job-hunting, she suggested that she register with the agency we use, then hired her.' Richard nodded towards the ceiling. 'Ask her yourself.'

That threw Goodhew. 'Alice is here?'

'She lives here, I thought you knew. We've always lived together.'

'Always?'

For the first time since meeting him, Goodhew saw genuine amusement reach all the way up to Richard's eyes. But it didn't add warmth to his face; in fact it dropped the temperature to well below bitterly cold. 'Lorna and I were very close,' he continued. 'The point I'm trying to make is that Lorna could have been out walking on her own. It doesn't follow that she had to be meeting someone she knew.'

'No?'

'No, not at all. Sometimes she just liked to be alone. She would go off for hours on end.'

'Even at midnight?'

'Yep.'

'She said that?'

'No, I made it up.' He sounded deliberately sarcastic, but the words had come out too fast. A defensive reflex, perhaps.

'Sorry, what I mean is, did you ever see her taking one of these solitary walks?'

'It wasn't an excuse.'

'Excuse?'

Richard's eyes narrowed and he looked away without replying.

Goodhew nodded. 'What happens when you reach the end of your tether, Richard? She told you she went walking alone, and you wanted to believe her, but you had to be wondering how open she was really keeping your relationship.'

Richard continued to look away, and when he next spoke he sounded distinctly pissed off. 'You've just twisted it right around. She was faithful to me,' he gasped, then stopped. The next couple of minutes ticked by and Goodhew watched him try to shut down the emotions that were suddenly clamouring to escape. Richard blinked, and then swallowed. He tried breathing deeply. He pressed his hands over his mouth in an attempt to curb the quivering of his lips.

Goodhew cringed. He hadn't foreseen this, and didn't know how to handle it either. He willed Richard to hold it together. Fat chance, though; here was a man unravelling before his eyes. It wasn't a systematic unravelling either; more like a moth-eaten sweater falling apart in many places all at once.

A voice came from the doorway. 'Leave him.' He hadn't noticed any movement, but looked round to find Alice glaring at him, one hand resting on each side of the door frame. Her hair was brushed straight down from a centre parting, and she was fully dressed in a pale-stone trouser suit. Apart from eyeliner under her lower lashes, her anger had drained all the other colour from her face. For someone so thin, she made an excellent job of filling the doorway, and Goodhew found himself on his feet, reacting to her words like a naughty Labrador caught with its nose in the shopping.

Her head tilted sharply, directing him out into the hall. She removed one arm to let him pass. 'Go,' she hissed.

He was happy to oblige; a swift retreat seemed like an all-round healthy idea.

He wondered whether there was anything appropriate he should say to her, but before he'd seriously begun considering this question, Alice had joined her brother on the settee. She sat very close to him, and Richard leant forward, burying his head into the crook of his sister's neck. Her chin now rested in his hair and her arms curled him in towards her, like a protecting shawl over his shoulders.

She continued to glare at Goodhew, who mouthed the word 'Sorry' before turning away.

Each step he took echoed loudly on the hardwood floor, advertising both his intrusion and his retreat.

Finally, from behind him, Richard let out a whimper as the last of his self-control fractured. By the time Goodhew opened the front door, the man's hysteria was in full flow. It didn't sound attractive: altogether too much snot, dribble and wailing.

Goodhew didn't look back at the house; he was too busy thinking about his conversation with Richard. It had been interesting, bizarre and not quite the laid-back, low-key chat that he'd had in mind.

Perhaps it was just his sixth sense, but he guessed that Marks would not be impressed.

# SEVENTEEN

Goodhew walked home the long way, alongside the river until he reached the footbridge that crossed above the gentle gushing of the small weir. A houseboat was moored below; one window was lit and in it, he could see the silhouette of a woman and the book she read. The water barely moved, almost inviting him to dive in, but he knew that stillness was deceptive. It was a thought which stayed with him as he entered the long corridor of unlit trees crossing Jesus Green and leading towards the spot where he'd first set eye on Lorna's body.

There was no breeze, just the darkness of unmoving shadows. This would have been a more secluded place to commit murder. His gaze wandered over the grass beyond the trees; he seemed to be alone, but even so found it hard to believe that no one was watching him.

He had felt strangely unsettled since leaving Richard Moran's house, dwelling on Richard's idea that Lorna had been murdered by a stranger. It was possible, of course, but then there still needed to be a reason why Lorna would have chosen to be alone near Midsummer Common in the early hours, especially on a foggy night when someone could be waiting just out of sight.

Like Alice waiting out in the hall.

He tried to imagine the relationship that Lorna and Richard had had, and wondered whether Alice had always been there, either trying to suck Lorna into their claustrophobic clique, or leaving her shut out of it. He wondered what Richard and Alice were like when alone altogether. He'd only seen them three times in twenty-four hours, but they already reminded him of the two halves of a pantomime pony. Next, he wanted to know who would play the front half.

Goodhew was pleased when he reached the end of the footpath, and he now kept to the road, with the common on his left. At almost the eleven o'clock position, he could see the ripple of the blue-and-white police tape cordoning off the southernmost corner. In the time it took to draw alongside the crime scene, only two cars had passed, but neither driver seemed to notice him. There were no other pedestrians either.

So much for thinking this junction would be less deserted; when this area of Cambridge slept, it was virtually comatose.

He crossed the road, then stopped to look back at the taped-off section. Even without fog, it remained a dark corner, falling outside the nearest pools of lamplight and absorbing any natural light into its thick, deep grass. In daylight, he had found it impossible to believe that no one had witnessed Lorna's death, and that the killer hadn't taken an enormous chance. At night, though, it seemed a very different place, and he now left it with a more open mind. And glad, too, that he'd taken the detour to see for himself.

Within another ten minutes, he'd reached home and, apart from the new message light blinking on his phone, everything looked the same. He allowed it to blink a dozen times or more, wondering if he was about to hear DI Marks demanding an immediate call-back. Goodhew considered not listening to it at all; if ignorance really was bliss, then he could enjoy a decent few hours' sleep without having to plan a conversation with his boss.

He sighed, then pressed 'Play'. Might as well know what he was up against.

But the voice that spoke wasn't Marks', it was his grandmother's. 'Gary, I'd like to have a chat with you, so I'll ring you later. But perhaps, if it's not too late when you get in, you could ring me instead. I've come to a decision and it's time I put you in the picture.'

He checked his watch and decided it was too late to call back, then he rang anyway; they were both night owls, after all.

She had caller display on her phone, and answered with typical directness. 'Can you meet me tomorrow?' she asked.

'After work?'

'Yes, latish, if that suits you.'

'It would actually. There's a new case—'

'Yes, I saw the papers. I hoped you'd be working on it.'

'But I don't know exactly when I'll be free.'

'Doesn't matter. I'm having a late dinner at the Felix. Call my mobile once you're on your way, and I'll make sure I'm home for you.'

'What's going on?'

'Nothing to worry about, I promise.' She hesitated. 'It was just that, when we were at the Rock the other day, I suddenly realized how much you've grown up . . .'

'And?'

'I'll tell you tomorrow. It's too complicated for a phone call.'

'You can't just tell me half the story!'

'I haven't told you any particular fraction of anything, actually.'

'Now I'll be kept awake trying to guess.'

'Well, then, that's better than lying awake thinking about your work. In any case, you'll never guess.'

Goodhew went to bed still curious. But as he drifted into sleep, his thoughts ended up back with Lorna Spence and his own unofficial visits to Bryn and Richard. There would be a team briefing session first thing; updating Marks beforehand was his best chance of avoiding greater fallout later. In the end, he was too tired to feel anything but philosophical, happy just to make an early start and think what to do about Marks then.

# EIGHTEEN

Goodhew was up and dressed again before it was fully light. DI Marks usually arrived around 8 a.m., therefore Goodhew decided to turn up at the station half an hour before that.

It was another clear but chilly morning as he made a quick and jacketless trip across Parker's Piece to the swimming pool. He knew that over an hour of swimming would leave him better able to withstand the cold than an extra layer of clothes.

He found he had the pool to himself, which wasn't unusual for very early mornings. Most days he barely noticed the other swimmers in any case, but today he particularly appreciated the silence. He soon fell into a rhythm based on his regular breathing and his hands constantly plunging into the water, punctuated every twenty strokes by the turn and glide he made at the end of each length. Maybe it was this easy rhythm that made him crack a full one hundred lengths fifteen minutes faster than usual. He stepped from the water and paused at the pool's edge, burying his face in his towel just long enough for the chlorine sting to fade from his eyes. He felt like he'd made such good time because he'd woken totally focused, and that was how he intended to tackle the rest of the day. He slung his towel over his shoulder and headed for the changing rooms, reflecting that it was either that, or he'd just miscounted.

It was 7.25 a.m. when he walked through the car park at the rear of the station. He was pleased, but equally not surprised, to notice the absence of Marks' Mazda. The car park itself was almost full, but quiet still, too early for members of the general public to be scrapping over each of the three visitors' spaces, and too late for the upheaval signalling early morning shift changes.

Goodhew glanced through the closest windows as he approached the double doors. As always, he paid particular attention to the three coat hooks visible through the window directly to his left. Today, however, this was just out of habit, as he expected them to be empty. Mel, he knew, always wore one of four jackets to work, a red cut-off parka with a grey fur-edged hood on the coldest days, through to a bleached denim jacket on the warmest, with either her brown bomber jacket or her knee-length red trench coat taking care of the temperatures in between. Now hanging on the middle hook was her red mac: an early start for someone not due in until 9 a.m., and especially early compared to her normal clockwork-precison arrival at three minutes to.

Mel's cubby-hole of a desk was buried too deep inside the building to be seen from outside, and Goodhew was happy to put his single-mindedness on hold for a few minutes, just to say good morning.

She wasn't at her desk, he discovered, but he hovered for a few minutes anyway. He doubted she'd left her coat behind the night before; also, her purse sat next to the telephone, and two empty polystyrene cups lay in the bin, post-cleaning lady and therefore post-8 p.m. the previous evening. In addition, her chair wasn't tucked neatly away either, but marooned halfway between the desk and where he now stood. He tucked it back under the desk.

He guessed he must have heard Mel before he actually saw her, though he wasn't aware of any sound, just had an instinct to turn around.

'Hi,' he said.

She wore a baggy jumper with sleeves hanging loose down to her knuckles, but even with her hand closed, he could see it was clutching a screwed-up ball of tissues.

'Hi,' she mumbled, and she did a funny up-down thing with the corners of her mouth – the one people do when they wish they could flash a signboard saying 'Imagine I'm smiling back at you.'

'Doing overtime?' he enquired.

'No.' The way she said it left no opening for further conversation. 'What's up?' She looked up at him enquiringly, and he saw that, although her eyes weren't red, she'd obviously been crying.

'That's what I should be asking you. You look upset.'

102

'No wonder you made detective.' She pulled her chair back out from the desk and dropped on to it with her full weight, the gas-lift letting the seat bounce down by an inch before it recovered. She threw the ball of tissues into the bin. 'Looking crap and feeling crap, it's always a winning combination. Thanks for pointing it out.'

'You look nice, just upset.' He smiled. 'I mean, you don't look crap, even if you feel it.'

She studied his face for a while, in silence, then spoke. 'I'm messing up, and I'm making choices that are meant to bail me out, and it's only once I've made them that I see I've fucked up again.'

'It can't be that bad, can it?'

Mel was still staring at him. 'Fuck-up on top of fuck-up, that's me, Gary.' With no warning, a new flood of tears rose and teetered, defying gravity to stay put until she finally managed to blink them away.

To him, the 'If you need to talk' offer always sounded like a line, but he said it anyway, and then wasn't surprised when she shook her head.

'I don't think so. I've decided I'm not making any more choices. My new plan is to stick where I am, as my anti-fuck-up strategy. But thanks for the offer.'

He started to say something else, but she stopped him, her voice suddenly firmer. 'If you don't mind, Gary, I don't want to talk to you any more right now.'

Perhaps he showed some surprise because she added, in further explanation, 'You always make me feel so transparent.'

And whatever he'd expected her to say, it wasn't that.

'Like you're not there?' he queried.

'No, not like that.' She looked impatient then. 'Transparent,' she repeated.

She looked at him as if thus saying it a second time would make it clear. But he wasn't just missing the point, it was invisible: no pun intended.

'Is that good, or bad?' he asked.

'Completely shit.'

'Oh.' He took a deep breath. 'I'm sorry, but it's not deliberate.'

She pressed one eyelid closed with her right thumb, determined to poke away anything resembling another tear. Her voice had an edge to it now. 'Even if you were trying to do it, you probably couldn't, so there's no point feeling sorry, is there?'

He was lost now. No point saying no, just to be agreeable, but he could also see that asking her to explain what she meant wasn't going to help either. He raised both hands from his sides and then dropped them again, a kind of pointless penguin-thinking-about-flying type gesture. 'OK, then.' He stood still for an awkward moment, then tried for a belated but dignified exit. 'I'll leave you to it.'

She nodded and he turned away, but her voice followed him and caught him when he'd barely taken his third step. 'When I see you . . . around, I mean . . . you make me feel uncomfortable,' she said.

He turned to look at her. 'Sorry.'

'It's not your fault, but I thought you should know.' She bit her bottom lip, then she added, 'Sorry.' too.

'OK,' he mumbled, then inexplicably, and without any trace of sarcasm, added, 'Thanks.' He felt pretty dumb.

He took the stairs to the third floor to wait for Marks, wondering as he climbed the steps when Mel had noticed his interest. How long had she been aware that he watched her arriving at work and leaving in the evening? And did she know he'd been disappointed when she started wearing an engagement ring?

Her boyfriend was called Toby Doyle, and he had two speeding convictions and one caution for being involved in a late-night disturbance. Apart from that, he'd never been in trouble, but his father and older brothers were well known for lashing out. Goodhew thought she deserved someone better, but kept telling himself it was none of his business. But he still watched the way she walked, loved the sound of her laugh, and made flimsy excuses to come and stand at her desk with his small talk.

He wondered when exactly he'd become that creepy guy from the third floor. As the whole picture sank in, pretty dumb escalated to really, *really* dumb. People never saw you in the same way as you saw yourself; he'd never seen himself as stalker material, but now he knew.

Up on the third, Kincaide was already seated at one of the desks, and spoke before Goodhew had even registered his presence. 'You're in early.'

'So are you,' he replied, and was pleased to have someone to take his thoughts away from his encounter with Mel. 'What's dragged you out of bed at this hour?'

Kincaide rolled his eyes. 'Don't ask.'

He wondered if that meant trouble at home but, considering Kincaide's well-known reticence where his marriage was concerned, he didn't ask. Goodhew reminded himself of what was higher on the agenda.

'Actually,' he began, 'I've been meaning to have a word.'

'Oh?'

Goodhew hesitated and the words suddenly clogged inside his brain. In the end he just held out his hand, and said, 'I'm pleased we're working together.'

Kincaide shrugged. 'Sure. Me too.'

'I just wanted you to know.'

'Good.' Kincaide's handshake was brief and hard, but he smiled. 'So why are *you* here so soon?'

'Oh, I need to see Marks. Think I might get a bollocking.' He then explained his visits to Bryn O'Brien and Richard Moran.

Kincaide tried to look as if giving a positive response, but couldn't quite pull it off without wincing. 'I'd just tell him about this O'Brien guy – maybe you'll get Brownie points for finding him – then shut up about the Morans and hope they don't mention it either.'

Goodhew shook his head. 'No, I'll just get it over with. Like some coffee?'

'No, thanks.' Kincaide pointed over behind Goodhew. 'Marks just walked past.'

Goodhew reached Marks' office doorway before the inspector had even reached his chair. He sat down, but didn't invite Goodhew to do the same.

'If you have a minute, sir, I'd like a word.'

'I'm sure you would.' Marks tilted his head and raised his right brow, making one eye look oddly bigger then the other. It wasn't his best look, but Goodhew guessed it wasn't done for appeal. 'And I'd like a few with you, too,' he added.

Goodhew waited.

'Get yourself a chair,' Marks barked, 'then sit in it.'

Goodhew did what he was told, reaching for the nearest chair, which stood against the wall. He began speaking straight away, before sitting, hoping to pre-empt some of the conversation. 'I saw Lorna Spence's calendar, and noticed she'd booked her car in for an MOT with someone called Bryn . . .' He paused mid-sentence.

Marks pointed at the carpet in front of his desk. 'Don't talk, just sit.' Marks then picked up his Parker ballpoint and jabbed the button into his desk blotter a couple of times, making the pen retract and reappear noisily.

When he was ready, Marks spoke. 'I suppose there was nothing worthwhile on at the cinema last night?'

'Sorry?'

'Alice Moran rang to complain about your visit, and I must say that wandering around chit-chatting to witnesses is not how I expect you to find yourself an evening's entertainment.'

'Oh.'

'Yes, "oh" indeed. Think I wouldn't find out? Remember, I'm supposed to be coordinating this investigation, so I don't expect to arrive at work on day two to find I've been wheeled into kept-in-the-dark-corner. I want a full explanation, then I don't want it to happen again. All right?'

Goodhew nodded. 'Right.'

'Now, then, start talking.'

An hour later, Marks held a briefing session, perching on the edge of a table with a pile of papers beside him. He scanned the faces of his team, noted some semi-vacant expressions, and hoped it was just because they'd emptied their minds in readiness for this meeting. There weren't enough of them to go round without having to compensate for any dunces on the team. Everyone would become stretched too far without more manpower.

Goodhew had arrived early with notebook and pen, and was now filling a page with a doodle resembling a spider juggling hoops. Marks thought it would be more appropriate to see him doodling a hangman's noose, considering the lucky escape he'd just had. It was fortunate for the young detective that they were so short-staffed; it made dropping him an impossibility.

Kincaide looked unusually distracted: wide awake, of course, but his gaze periodically wandering towards the floor.

Marks hated meetings that dragged on, and kept his own direct and fast-paced; he reckoned the sooner they were all active again, the better. He cleared his throat and waited to ensure everyone's full attention, and only started to speak when Kincaide's focus floated back up from the carpet. 'At the moment, this is the full team and, as you can see, we are very thin on the ground. As a result, this will mean two things. Firstly, you will have too much to do.'

Someone murmured, 'There's a surprise.'

He ignored the comment. 'And secondly, you'll be expected to handle elements of this investigation that many of you will not have had experience in dealing with in the past.' He tapped his temple. 'None of you are thick, because if you were, you wouldn't be here, so use your eyes and ears and, most of all, your common sense. Now, down to business.'

On top of his pile of papers lay a ten-by-eight photograph, face down. He turned round it to face the assembled group. It was a scene-of-crime shot of Lorna Spence. 'Preliminary information points to a time of death between 10 p.m. on Monday night and 2 a.m. yesterday morning. As you can see, there is a ligature around her neck – this was used to secure the carrier bag. The cause of death has been confirmed as asphyxiation, not strangulation.

'However, there is no sign of defence wounds on her, or of any injury which may have incapacitated her. Nor evidence of any attempt by Lorna to free herself, so we are waiting for toxicology tests to determine whether any substances were taken or administered previously. We will not have the results of those until tomorrow, at the earliest.

'The same with the swabs. The victim was fully clothed, except for any knickers. We do not know whether these were removed, or absent from the outset. There are no visible signs of sexual assault, only some old bruising around the inner thigh region, but nothing else that's more recent in that area. Both her upper arms show some bruising, and this seems to be consistent with being gripped by someone facing her, while both parties were standing upright. Obviously there are detailed shots of all such injuries.'

He turned over the next photo and held it up, too. 'This is a close-up of her left hand. The same thing was written on both palms. It appears just to say "I'm like Emma", or it could possibly be part of a longer message. The same person probably wrote both, and the characters are noticeably better formed on the left palm. Since Lorna was right-handed, the current theory is that she wrote this herself.

'Why, and what it means, we have yet to discover, but I need to know of any connections she had with someone of the name Emma.'

The next photo was a studio shot of Lorna when alive. 'This is the photo that will be released to the press. To fill you in, Lorna Spence turned twenty-three on 6th February. She was five two, single, working as an administrator for the Excelsior Clinic. So far, no relatives have been traced.'

Marks scanned the room. No one looked at all vacant now. Good.

He then added the salient points he'd recently gleaned from Goodhew and assigned various tasks to the team. Goodhew was, as usual, pretty damned unreadable, but Marks had noticed his interest peak as Bryn O'Brien's name was mentioned. He quickly assigned O'Brien's interview to Kincaide, then informed Goodhew that he would be spending the day studying Lorna's phone bills and bank statements.

Goodhew opened his mouth to speak, but Marks raised his hand in a halting motion. 'Is there something you don't understand, Gary? Perhaps the idea of sitting in the office and not moving at will is a bit alien to you?'

Goodhew shut his mouth again, and strummed his fingers on his knee a couple of times, probably in frustration.

Marks remained silent, letting the room settle, then dismissed the team. 'My mobile will be switched on.' He paused, making sure he had Goodhew's full attention. 'I need to know *every* development. Understood?'

Goodhew nodded. The other officers filed past him. He could hear them breaking into conversation once they hit the corridor outside.

Marks glanced at his subordinate's notepad. The spider doodle had progressed, and some of the hoops it juggled now contained names. He saw 'Excelsior', 'Richard Moran' and 'Bryn O'Brien' written in neat capitals. The other hoops remained blank.

The spider's body had 'Lorna' written clearly in the middle.

# NINETEEN

Goodhew wasn't the only one to think that a pre-emptive strike might be the best way forward.

Bryn had unlocked the garage at 8 a.m. that morning, but after forty-five minutes, he already found he had done nothing so far but fight the urge to bunk off. On one hand, with his father taking a month off to do some decorating, and only himself to answer to, it was never going to be an escape of Ferris Bueller-style proportions, but on the other hand . . .

He thought it over carefully.

On the other hand, there would be no joy in hanging around here, waiting for the inevitable visit from the law. He could see how that would go, probably with the unsubtle arrival of two uniforms in a marked car, generating enough local gossip to knock the business back further than a couple of days' skiving ever would. Better, then, for them to catch up with him somewhere away from work.

Or, better still, for him to do the catching. And that was when he relocked the workshop and began walking towards Parkside police station.

He pulled a pack of Benson & Hedges from his pocket, and lit up without breaking his stride. One packet usually lasted him all week; three per day wasn't much of a habit. But this wasn't 'most weeks' and, as he came within sight of the station, he was using the remains of the first cigarette to light his second.

He left two messages at the front desk of the station that morning, both times accompanied with his mobile number. After each visit, he stepped out into the fresh air and lit up again. After the second time, he made up his mind to sit it out, and found a spot on the edge of the park that boasted both a bench and a convenient bin.

In the end, he had no idea how long he remained there, his elbows resting on his knees. He lit each new cigarette from the last but, instead of putting any of them to his mouth, he spent the time watching the ash growing in length, then falling on to the path.

He thought constantly about Lorna. He wondered how much he needed to say, and how much he'd be able to leave out, and whether he was pulling the lid on a can of worms. The Gary Goodhew he'd known from primary school had been quick-witted, logical and intuitive, in retrospect. It was a worrying combination. Bryn was realistic; he wasn't going to be driving the conversation, but he held on to the idea that it was safest to take a ride with someone you knew.

He finally decided against lighting another cigarette as he pinched the current one dead between the tips of his forefinger and thumb. He was about to toss the butt into the bin when he looked up and, for the first time, realized he was being watched.

Gary was no more than fifteen feet away. 'I noticed you came in twice, so I thought you might still be out here somewhere,' he said.

Bryn nodded. 'That figures.' He threw the butt at the bin then, and for the first time, missed. It bounced on to the ground right in front of Gary, who retrieved it and dropped it in safely.

'DC Kincaide is looking for you at the moment and, meanwhile, I'm supposed to be doing something else. What's up?'

Bryn laced his fingers, then loosened them again when he realized it might look like he was praying. 'There's a thing . . . a coincidence, I suppose. It was at the back of my mind when I saw you yesterday, then I thought about it overnight. It's probably nothing, but I wanted to point it out – you can check, can't you?'

Gary glanced back at the police station, then at Bryn again. 'Sure. But whatever you tell me, you'll need to repeat to someone else, just to keep everything straight. It can't be unofficial, you understand, don't you?'

Again Bryn nodded, but Gary still looked hesitant. Finally, he sat down and also rested his elbows on his knees. Bryn realized that it was just one of those body-language mirroring techniques, designed to put him at ease, but it did make him feel more comfortable in any case. They were both now facing forward. For his part, Bryn stared at the kerb across the road; it was the most mundane focus for his attention, and he knew that was what he needed as he deliberately exposed himself to police scrutiny. Sticking his neck out like this really went against the grain, so much so that, even when he started talking, he still took the long way round.

'I think it was back in December when I first met Lorna, maybe the end of November. Well, not long before Christmas anyway. And, like I told you last night, we went out a couple of times to the pool hall on Mill Road. I was in there one night having a game and a drink with Colin, this bloke I knew. He used to do odd jobs and he'd done a bit of cash in hand for me, a couple of services and a few bits, just helping me catch up with stuff. Well, Lorna turned up with a mate of hers, and we ended up playing doubles.'

'Mate, as in another woman?'

'Yeah, yeah. Lorna told me she worked with her, a girl called Victoria.'

'Victoria Nugent?' Gary still uttered it as a question, even though he clearly knew the answer.

'Yes.' Bryn then paused a beat. He should have guessed that Victoria might already be in the picture, and the thought only made him more sure that this conversation was a good idea. 'I partnered her, Victoria, and we had a laugh. Have you met her?'

Gary shook his head. 'Not yet.'

'Feisty and flirty. We had quite a few to drink that night, all of us, that is, and Lorna spent as much time chatting to Colin as I did to Victoria, which was the first odd thing.'

'Why?'

'Well, to be honest, Colin wasn't a nice bloke – I mean, especially from a half-sophisticated woman's point of view; he looked bad, smelt bad and was a bit of a scrounger. But they got on fine.'

'Unless Lorna was just put out by you flirting with her mate?'

Bryn twisted around, leaning on the back rest for the first time, and eyed Gary with what he hoped looked like mild amusement. He waited for Gary to do the body-mirroring thing before he replied. 'Trust me, as far as her friend Victoria went, Lorna was just not the jealous type. And, as I said before, there was nothing going on between us, anyway.'

'Well, then, what?'

'Yeah, well, according to Colin, they met again. He even reckoned he was "on a promise". I thought he was having me on, but he was adamant.'

'But we're talking some months ago, right?'

'Yeah, January.' Bryn could almost hear the tick-tick-tick as his bombshell counted down. 'Colin's dead.'

Only Gary's eyes showed an instant response. The pupils dilated and his stare made Bryn feel pinned down. 'And what was Colin's last name?' he asked.

'Willis.' Bryn's throat tightened as he spoke. No wave of relief followed; he felt no burden lifting after this revelation. But what had he expected, anyway? After all, his conscience was far from clear.

'You'll need to make a statement,' Gary told him.

Bryn just nodded, as he felt himself making a nauseating slide towards centre stage. It was for Lorna, he told himself. But, as he walked towards Parkside police station, shoulder to shoulder with his old classmate, he couldn't help wondering how deep he was about to get buried.

# TWENTY

Marks still looked pissed off. But even if there was no mood change apparent to the naked eye, Goodhew was certain his boss would have mellowed during the day.

Marks repeated the essence of Goodhew's request back at him. 'So, you've left Kincaide with this O'Brien guy, and now you want to follow up this Colin Willis lead?'

'Absolutely.' Goodhew plonked a bulging folder on to the desk. 'I thought it would be a good idea to go through this stuff, just as a start. If there's a connection to Lorna Spence—'

'What happened to her bank statements and phone bills? You're not gallivanting off on anything else until they're properly done.'

'They are.' Goodhew slid out a thin plastic wallet from inside the front flap of the larger folder. 'And there's not much to know. She used her bank account for paying bills and drawing cash, but for little else. Her bills were mostly on direct debit and, aside from rent, rates, heating etc., she used just one credit card and one store card. She doesn't appear to have been the type to bother about keeping paperwork, so we don't have a complete set of household or mobile bills.'

He eyed his boss hopefully. 'Without the detail, there's not much to say, but I've requested a full set of both, as well as all calls relating to her office extension, a list of the incoming calls on her private numbers, and copies of her credit card statements.'

'Nothing else?'

'Not yet, no.'

Marks held out his hand. 'Leave that with me, and you'd better hope I don't find something you've missed.' Goodhew felt sure he had spotted an encouraging gleam in Marks' eye. 'So, how are you proposing to look for a connection to Colin Willis?'

'Aside from the file here? Maybe she mentioned him to someone at the Excelsior Clinic.'

'And while you're at it, I suppose you could find out whether she ever mentioned Bryn O'Brien to them.' Marks leant back in his chair and surveyed Goodhew through narrowed eyes. He tapped his temples as he thought. 'And you may as well speak to Victoria Nugent, since, after all her name's popped up a couple of times now. And if anything else does crop up, you'll be burrowing into that while you're there, I suppose?'

'Something like that.'

'Why do you think I sent you off to trawl through Lorna Spence's paperwork?'

'Because—'

'Because I thought it was time you grasped the idea that I need to know where you are and exactly what you're doing. I thought you'd be bored to death for a few hours, then you'd come back in happy enough for *me* to direct *you*. Instead of that, you bounce in here, bright-eyed and bushy-tailed like some frigging Disney bunny, then tell me you've got your whole day already planned out. Look at my face – doesn't this look like a scowl to you?'

Goodhew tried to appear apologetic. 'I assumed that was concentration, sir.' Marks gave him a poisonous look in return. OK, so he hadn't mellowed much after all. 'I could promised to focus on the Colin Willis link and nothing else?' he suggested hopefully.

Marks leant forward again and splayed his hands out in front of him on the desk. Maybe to stop his fingers from tapping with irritation. Or maybe this time he really was concentrating. 'All right,' he sighed, 'but I still want regular communication, and don't decide to go running off at obscure tangents without checking with me first.'

# TWENTY-ONE

Old habits die hard, or so they say. Goodhew's favourite quiet spot at Parkside police station had always been the spare desk on the third floor, in the corner nearest his home. In the days when file servers and hubs had looked like extras from sci-fi sets, the original layout of the building had been modified to accommodate an air-conditioned IT room, thus eating into the open-plan office space and leaving an almost useless little cul-de-sac where a redundant desk had been shunted, out of the way.

Rather than pulling up a chair, Goodhew sat on the desk itself. He leant his back against the wall and faced the window.

It was ten to two.

He opened Colin Willis' file and glanced at the first few documents, hoping to find the one that would suck him easily into this unfamiliar case. He already knew the bare facts: partially decomposed body dragged from the Cam, no missing person report, ligature still around throat, victim's car abandoned, death suspected to be debt or drugs related. No leads. No further progress.

His gaze wandered back to the window and was drawn towards the Avery, the pub on the far side of Parker's Piece.

That's when he admitted that old habits die hard. Mel was standing there, indistinguishable and Lowry-like in the distance, but he knew her. She was with Toby. Even from that distance he could tell that their body language wasn't good.

Get over it, he told himself, and looked back down to the file, flicking through it until he felt the gloss of photographic paper. With renewed interest, he slid out a clutch of prints. The first showed the water and the puffed-up clothes covering the torso.

It looked like a Guy overstuffed and ready for a bonfire on 5th November.

He glanced through the window again. They were closer to him now. Mel was heading back to work, or trying to, but Toby stood in her path. Goodhew saw her speak, she pointed to her watch, then attempted to side-step him. He blocked her. She stopped and spoke again. Toby reacted instantly, the flats of his hands flew up, connecting with her shoulders so she involuntarily took a couple of quick steps back.

Goodhew found himself on his feet, the photographs making a cracking noise as one edge of the pile hit the floor.

Mel pushed past Toby and, although he reached towards her, he made no attempt to grab her. He appeared to be shouting. He stood facing the police station, And Goodhew was ready to move if Toby did, but in the end it was Mel who hurried back alone.

Toby continued to shout something, but she didn't acknowledge him. She was about to cross the road directly in front of the station when she looked up at Goodhew. He had to be standing three or four feet back from the glass, yet he *knew* she could see him. Her stare was defiant, like she was demanding that he back off, telling him to interfere at his peril. He didn't move for the first seconds, fixed to the spot by increasing discomfort. She glanced to her left, checking for traffic.

He stared down at the splay of photographs, now lying at his feet, and fixed his attention on the least pleasant shot of Colin Willis' unnaturally pale skin stretched across his bloated corpse. The last body Goodhew had seen recovered from water had been dead for over a year, deliberately weighed down and wedged beneath an abandoned jetty on the Ouse. Flesh kept under water for that length of time reacts to form a soapy substance called adipocere. It stinks, worse than any normal decaying matter. Willis had been nowhere near that far gone, but Goodhew let memories of the stench of the other corpse seep back into his mind.

It was more than enough to jar him to action.

He bent on one knee to gather up the photos, and once he had them back on the desk he started again.

The cause of Willis' death had been strangulation: a dog's chrome choke chain, still lodged around the throat, had exerted sufficient pressure on the windpipe to crush it. No one seemed to have missed

Willis, and therefore identification might have taken longer if Mill Road's community beat officer, PC McKendrick, hadn't recognized him from one of the morgue shots.

On the scale of parasites and predators, Willis had been somewhere between house mites and head lice: a persistent but manageable irritation. He'd been a dabbler; he'd dabbled with handling stolen goods and with selling cannabis, and when money became short he'd even dabbled with work. Once or twice, he'd tested the water by offering the police tip-offs but, despite his bold talk, Willis knew very little, and was taken into people's confidence even less.

An exact date of death had never been determined but, according to the pathologist, the body had been left submerged for several weeks. Willis' landlord hadn't received rent for all of February, not in itself unusual, but he'd stuck to his routine of weekly visits to every tenant who owed him money and had not seen Willis since the first Friday in February.

On the 21st of that month, the residents of Fen Ditton had reported an abandoned vehicle, and on the 26th, the untaxed and inaccurately registered van had been impounded. It was only proved to be Willis' after his DNA was matched to the DNA found in the pick-your-own snot collection Willis had been accumulating in the driver's side door pocket. This narrowed the time of Willis' disappearance and death down to weeks two and three of February.

Goodhew searched the file for any connection to Lorna Spence, or even any mention of Bryn O'Brien, but, much like the investigation itself, he drew a blank. The popular theory among the investigating team was that Willis had pissed someone off badly. Amazing the results a couple of centuries of police expertise can produce.

It turned out that Colin Willis had no friends or relatives pushing for answers, and it was clear that the killing had been considered a one-off. The perpetrator was assumed to be someone busy committing other offences: the type of criminal that would either get grassed up at some point, or drop himself in it when committing another unrelated crime. Therefore the case remained open and active. But clearly not *that* open and not *that* active.

Once Goodhew was sure that there was nothing in the file to affect his immediate plans, he turned his attention to his first visit of the day: Richard Moran.

# TWENTY-TWO

Twenty minutes later, Goodhew left Parkside station for the short walk towards the city centre and another visit to Moran's home.

Faith Carver, the Excelsior Clinic's stern-faced receptionist, had informed Goodhew that Mr Moran had not been into work all day, and had cancelled his imminent appointments.

Goodhew decided not to phone ahead to the house, but to take his chances on finding Richard at home. As he approached the front door, two scenarios flashed into his mind: one where Alice was also home and he might struggle to speak to Richard privately, and the other where Alice was out and he was faced with dealing with Richard alone. As he waited for the door to open, he tried to imagine how he would deal with Richard's histrionics if they kicked off again while the two of them were by themselves.

Goodhew checked his thinking: histrionics maybe wasn't the right word. It hadn't felt like watching a display of over-acting; there had been nothing false about the amount of emotion that had poured out, perhaps just its cause. Richard Moran possibly felt sorry for himself, and elements of the relationship had clearly troubled him, but did he really seem genuinely upset at Lorna's death? Goodhew had no answer to that.

The door swung wide, and it was Richard himself who held it open. Today he wore a suit. White cuffs, collar, and a small triangle behind his tie were all that showed of his shirt. It looked cleaner and better pressed than any new shirt Goodhew had ever seen.

Goodhew imagined Moran making meticulous efforts with his appearance, perhaps now determined to keep control of the façade he put up between himself and the world. Did he know he'd failed?

And failed dismally, at that. He looked brittle, like he was suffering the human equivalent of metal fatigue, and the next breath of bad news would make him crumble. He'd certainly been crying, and not sleeping much.

Richard mumbled something about an office, then headed upstairs and Goodhew assumed he was supposed to follow. Neither of them spoke until Richard opened the door to a room at the rear of the second floor and motioned for Goodhew to go in.

'Have a seat,' he said flatly.

The room was large and square, and the most true-to-life depiction of the Cluedo library that he could imagine. Bookshelves ran along two facing walls, packed mostly with sets of matching leather-bound volumes. The major item of furniture was a large oak desk positioned ninety degrees to the window. Its surface was bare, apart from an ornate letter opener lying near one edge. Goodhew didn't bother trying to spot the lead pipe, but thought he'd keep one ear open for revolving bookcases and secret panels, just in case.

Richard sat down at his desk, leaving Goodhew to occupy a low-slung Chesterfield-style armchair on the other side of it. Goodhew's line of vision was now somewhere level with the middle of Richard's chest, therefore not ideal for questioning; it made Goodhew feel he was supposed to raise a hand and wait for permission to speak, but he left his hands where they were and waded in regardless.

'Does the name Emma mean anything to you?'

Richard was leaning forward with his weight resting on his elbows and his hands interlaced at the fingers. He stared into his palms. 'Because of that writing?' He shook his head. 'No.' There was no sign he wasn't telling the truth but he still looked nervous.

'She never mentioned anyone with a similar name? Maybe Emily or Gemma?'

'No, never.'

'And there's no one connected with yourself and not Lorna, a patient perhaps?'

'I've already been asked about all this, and I've been right through my files. There's nothing. I asked Alice, too, but her friends and contacts are mostly the same as mine, so she couldn't suggest anything either.'

Goodhew changed tack. 'Has your sister ever been married?'

'No.' Richard unclasped his fingers and leant back in his chair, a gesture perhaps designed to exude relaxation. Perhaps he didn't realize that the fingers of his right hand were now tightly gripping the edge of the desk, as if to stop it sliding away from him. 'If she had ever been serious about anyone, she'd still be with them; that's the sort of woman she is. I remember my father describing her first encounter as an aberration, and that was soon the end of that.' He raised his head, jutting his chin out, as if daring Goodhew to comment. Goodhew, however, said nothing, and one corner of Moran's mouth began to tremble.

'Parental pressure,' Richard added, as though just those two words provided a fully comprehensive explanation for all such failed relationships in the Moran family.

'What sort of pressure?'

Richard blinked twice. 'The same sort I'd have been under when I was seeing Lorna, if they'd been alive.'

'Which is?'

Richard was gripping the desk with both hands now. 'It doesn't really matter now, does it?'

'I'd still like to know.'

'My father decided Alice was precocious, and so he kept us isolated from other families. Their rules seem ineffectual now, but when you're a child, they seem omnipotent, and you don't realize they're only human like the rest of us.

'This room was my father's study. He was a well-known figure in his day, the umpteenth generation of Moran doctors, but the first to make his mark in treating the wealthy of Cambridge. He achieved success through his determination rather than by any exceptional medical skill. Not the type to take any prisoners, as they say. I found him a terrifying man, and if I'd done something wrong, he would summon me in here and I'd have to sit in your chair, right there, and wait silently until he was ready to speak to me. Now I'm the one behind the desk, fancy that.'

If Richard was enjoying his position on the throne, it didn't show.

'So you've lived here all your life?'

'Yes. I even took my degree at Cambridge. We all grew up here and inherited the house last year when he died. Alice and I are very attached to the place.'

120

Goodhew empathized with the sentiment, although he wasn't sure he'd want to live with his own sister – but then, he only had one bedroom.

'Besides, I'm not . . .' Richard stopped.

'Go on.'

Whatever Moran had almost said was now firmly shut away again.

'You were about to say something,' Goodhew pushed.

'It was nothing.'

'It won't hurt to say it anyway.'

'No, I was just rambling – I keep doing that. Then, mid-sentence, I flash back to the way she looked at the hospital. Everything's become so insignificant since she died. I feel so naïve, plodding along, thinking we were going somewhere together. I should have known.'

'That she was going to die?'

'That things would go wrong. Do you really think that anyone's life progresses on the up and up?' Richard finally released his double grip on the desk. 'You'll find out for yourself, just when you least expect it.' He punched one fist into the other palm. 'Fair enough, you don't see it coming the first time, but once you realize that's what life's about, it's naïve not to expect it.'

Goodhew raised his eyebrows. 'That's your philosophy on life then?'

'Absolutely.'

'Based on?'

'Everything – from the first time I was stamped on in the playground onwards.'

Ah, the Chicken-Licken school of positive thinking. No wonder Richard was a nervous wreck.

Goodhew tried another change of direction. 'Did Lorna have a dog?'

'A dog?' Richard repeated. His eyes flickered, his focus darting away and up, as if hunting for paw prints on the ceiling. 'Maybe as a child, but I have no idea.' He kept his voice level and dragged his attention back to Goodhew. 'Why do you ask?' He sounded genuinely baffled.

'We have a possible lead; some dog hairs. They could be nothing, though.' He managed to stop himself from punctuating the sentence with 'Excuse the pun.'

'Do you know any more? What colour of dog, or breed?'

'At this stage we just need to know of any dogs she might have come into contact with.'

'I certainly don't know of any.'

'Did she talk about anyone she knew owning a dog?'

'Not that I remember.'

'No one at the clinic?'

'No. *Still* no.' Now he was starting to sound irritated, but every time Goodhew had seen him, Richard had hovered permanently in the uneasy zone: uncomfortable, anxious or distressed. Goodhew couldn't read him well enough to identify which behavioural signs counted for anything. Not yet, at least.

Deciding it was time to leave, he stood up and extended his hand. 'I'm sorry if I seemed at all tactless when I visited you last night.'

They shook hands. Richard's grip was firm. 'Thank you.'

'And I'm sorry for your loss.'

Richard managed a small smile. 'I know. I can see you have compassion. But then you're young – in fact, about the same age as Lorna. She knew all about compassion too.'

'I didn't know it was age-related.'

Richard half-turned towards the window. 'Do you know which way this faces?'

Goodhew took a second to get his bearings. 'North-west?'

'It faces towards Shire Hall, and the site of the county jail. Between here and there is Castle Mound – you know it?'

Castle Mound was a large grass-covered hillock which had been part of the original city defences in Roman times, and, like every other person who'd been resident in Cambridge for more than five minutes, he knew it.

'Of course,' he replied.

'You'd be amazed who doesn't.' Richard had become suddenly erect and firm-voiced. 'All right then, do you know what happened in 1855?'

'You got me there.'

'The last public hanging occurred over the gates of the jail. Castle Hill was crowded with spectators, including many women and children. A man and his sister-in-law were executed for poisoning his wife. That's *her* own sister. There were estimates that thirty thousand arrived to watch; they packed the streets. You see, people want to see justice done, and they want to educate their children by having them see it too. My father used to stand at this window and complain at the abolition of the death penalty. He said it allowed people to get away with murder.'

'And you feel the same?'

'I agree with him: it is important to see justice done, and that it's seen to be done. That's what I'm interested in for Lorna. As for compassion, I don't believe I have any left.'

# TWENTY-THREE

Behind him, Richard and his house were gradually fading into the distance. Goodhew knew he hadn't learnt much from his visit, but at the same time he felt enlightened. For the first time, he thought he'd been able to catch a glimpse of what, besides his money and status, had attracted Lorna to this man.

As he walked towards the Excelsior Clinic, he wondered what else he might see in Alice if she were now on her own. As he approached Magdalene Bridge, he realized he was about to find out; he saw her before she saw him.

She strode out of the building purposefully, and he guessed she was heading towards home. She wore a skirt and jacket and low court shoes that had just enough height to accentuate the curve of her calves. He noticed she had well-turned ankles, or so his grandfather would have said.

Her sunglasses were the only outward sign that she might be shielding herself from the world at large. Maybe they were her small guard against the risk of public curiosity. This was, after all, her part of town, and she and Lorna would almost certainly have been familiar faces hereabouts, especially amongst the local business community.

On the other hand, it was a sunny day.

When she was just a few feet away, Goodhew raised his hand in greeting. 'Hi,' he said and smiled.

She smiled back, but blankly at first. Then, as she shifted her glasses up on to the top of her head, she registered who he was. 'Oh, hi. Were you coming to see me?'

'That was my plan. I have a couple more questions. We can sit down somewhere for a few minutes now, if it's convenient.' She looked more attractive without the glasses, and her eye contact helped. She was very good at eye contact. Very, very good. He told himself to curb the smile, as this was supposed to be a serious moment.

'Sure,' she replied and pointed to the nearest tea room. 'Is there OK, or does it need to be more official than that?'

The café was small and almost empty. The tablecloths were blue-and-yellow gingham and a row of brightly painted teapots was displayed on the low windowsill. In fact, it looked like the assembly point for the county's contingent of maiden aunts. 'That looks great,' he said.

They sat at the back, at the table furthest from the door. Alice visited the Ladies while Goodhew ordered a pot of tea, then occupied himself by folding a paper napkin into a square and wedging it under one leg of the table to stop it rocking.

By the time he straightened up again, she had returned. 'Good to know we can still rely on the British police for the important things in life.'

'Like protecting the British cup of tea?'

'Exactly.'

She pulled her chair away from the table and positioned it at almost ninety degrees. She sat very erect with her right leg crossed tightly over her left, the toe of her shoe curled behind her calf. Her skirt draped over her knee and her hands rested in a neat clasp in her lap. Her hair was clipped in place, and a small amount of make-up covered her cheeks. But despite her composed appearance, her voice was drained of the authoritative crispness he'd noticed on each of their previous encounters. Each time she spoke now, it was more softly, and he wondered whether recent events had cowed her voice into submission, or whether the other, sterner, voice was only adopted in the presence of her brother.

The waitress arrived with their tea on a tray, which she balanced on one hand while organizing some space on the table and then unloading its contents with the other. Neither Goodhew nor Alice spoke again until she'd left them.

'How can I help?' Alice asked.

'When I first visited the Excelsior Clinic, both you and your brother carried photographs of Lorna Spence. I realize that she was more than an employee to your brother, but it seems to me that she was more than just an employee to you too?' It was a statement, but he let it sound like a question.

Alice poured the tea. 'Sugar?'

'Just milk, thanks.'

'I met Lorna after I returned to work at the clinic last year. We hit it off, which surprised me because, on the face of it at least, we had absolutely nothing in common. But she was good company. When she started seeing Richard, she behaved as if she was one of the family, not in an imposing way, she was just comfortable with our way of life. At first it felt like we were just friends, but then she began to feel more like a sister-in-law.'

'So you were close?'

'Close?' She tilted her head a little so that her gaze wandered over to the bright rectangle of the window at the front. Almost a minute ticked by before she spoke again. 'I'd never considered that before, but I suppose we were.' She looked down at her hands, resting in her lap, using them as a distraction whilst she reined in her thoughts.

When she looked back up at him, Goodhew noticed that uncertainty had replaced her usual assuredness.

Her voice was now virtually inaudible. 'That's so strange. I've always thought of really close friendships as the ones you read about: best friends since childhood, or the living-in-each-other's-pockets kind; but that's not me. Lorna was probably the closest friend I had, but I never saw it in those terms. She was more gregarious than me, and I'm sure she had plenty of other friends. In fact, for a while, Lorna was very close to another girl working at the clinic. She was called Victoria.'

'But?'

'They fell out.'

Goodhew waited for her to expand on the comment. She didn't. 'Do you know why?'

'It would be best for you to ask Victoria herself, but I think it was over a boyfriend. Apparently, Lorna briefly saw Victoria's ex after Victoria had broken off their relationship. Lorna told me that she was surprised that it bothered Victoria so much, but that's all she said.'

'And this was before Lorna started her relationship with your brother?'

'Of course. As far as I'm aware, Richard began seeing her just before last Christmas.'

'And did that concern you?'

'In what way?'

'In any way.'

'In terms of careers, they were in totally different places, but often that's no bad thing as too much close competition isn't always healthy. And there was an age gap, fourteen or fifteen years, but it didn't affect them, as far as I could tell.'

'But you didn't really approve?'

'You asked me if I had any concerns, and I was only concerned that the gap might cause them some problems because it's the sort of thing that eventually starts to worry Richard.'

'Because?'

She raised her palms towards the ceiling. 'Just because.'

Goodhew had a guess. 'Because he'd worry what other people thought?'

'No.' She sighed. 'Because his glass is always half empty.'

'Ah.' Goodhew got it then. 'Because he might think that the age gap was ultimately going to put her off.'

'It was a possibility, but I myself didn't agree. For example, I would guess that you're the same age as Lorna, or marginally older, and I'm just a couple of years older than Richard. No one that walks in here will know why we're talking, and some may even assume that we're together. We know that's not the case, but I don't think we look ridiculous together, do we?'

She said it in a totally matter-of-fact way, with no hint of flirtation. And, while he couldn't imagine that flirting was her style, he also wouldn't have minded if she'd given it a shot.

'No,' Goodhew agreed.

She glanced down at her hands, then back up again as though she'd had a sudden thought. 'Actually,' she smiled slightly, 'I was worried at first that their relationship might put a strain on my friendship with Lorna. But I was being silly. If anything, Lorna and I grew closer.'

'And how about Richard and Lorna? How would you describe their feelings towards each other?'

'Happy. Not soulmates perhaps, but not far short.'

'What else?'

Alice frowned. 'What exactly are you looking for?'

'Tensions, things they rowed about – not necessarily things that suggest a rift, but perhaps differences in attitude that would tell us more about Lorna.'

Alice refilled her cup, making a small ritual out of the process. Goodhew wondered if she was trying to buy time that way, or just searching for the right words.

'Lorna was quite a liberated type,' she continued. 'It was something that I found at odds with our own upbringing, but it never caused me a problem. Lorna could be very outspoken, openly discussing everything from politics to women's issues. Sometimes Richard found her point of view difficult to comprehend – but I'm sure he's told you that already.

'Lorna and I even talked about sex on several occasions, but sex in general, no specifics. I certainly wouldn't want to know about my brother's sex life. Would you want to know about yours?'

Goodhew shook his head. 'Fair comment.'

For the first time, Alice's attention drifted.

He left her with her thoughts for a few seconds more, then spoke. 'How are you feeling?'

'All right. Shocked. I don't know really.' She tilted her head back, as if trying to think. The muted lighting in the café illuminated one side of her face, where the first hints of crow's feet were traced around her eyes. The effect was strange: in one half of her face he could see how she looked ten years ago, and in the other half how she might look in ten years' time. The twenty-nine-year-old Alice looked a little too earnest, and the forty-nine-year-old a little too melancholy. He liked the current version best.

'Sad for Richard, I suppose,' she sighed finally.

'Not for Lorna?'

'Yes, of course – and for all of us who loved her. But mostly for Richard.'

Goodhew nodded and wondered if her brother was ever far from her thoughts. 'Does the name Emma mean anything to you?'

'No, we've been asked that already.'

'I know, just double-checking. What about dogs? Did she like them?'

Alice thought for a few seconds, then shrugged. 'No idea. I don't remember pets ever coming up in our conversations. Why?'

'We have some dog hair samples that we'd like to identify. They may be nothing, but we need to know if she had any connections to anyone with a dog.'

'I can't say for certain, of course, but I don't think so.'

'I will need to speak to Victoria Nugent, as well. Is she in today?'

'Most probably, although I haven't seen her yet.' A shadow passed across Alice's face. 'Actually, there's something you can do for me, if you don't mind. I've explained why Lorna and Victoria fell out, and it was made more awkward by them working in the same building, but please try to take whatever Victoria says with a pinch of salt. She can seem very . . .' Alice hesitated as she fished for the appropriate word. In the end she settled for '. . . bitter.'

They seemed at the end of their conversation when Goodhew flashed back to the start. 'Earlier you said that you returned to the clinic last year. Where had you been meanwhile?'

'I needed a break.'

'To do what?'

'Nothing, really. We'd had a loss. Our father died and I decided to spend some time sorting out the house.'

'Richard said the house was left to all of you. Does that mean there are other siblings? Or were you and Richard the only two?'

She became very still, as if suddenly not sure which way to go next. He waited, knowing that she had realized she needed to say something. 'No, we weren't,' she said finally. 'There were four of us: myself, Richard, then David and Jackie. David and Jackie were born during my father's second marriage.'

'And did they know Lorna too?'

Alice's eyes widened as if recognizing that was the exact route she had wanted to avoid. Her eyes locked with Goodhew's. He studied her face, gripped by the feeling that there was something more than just the words that she was either attempting to communicate or attempting not to. 'Not David,' she mumbled. 'We lost him years ago.' She rubbed her fingers into her palms, as though they were perspiring. But if anything was bubbling beneath her cool exterior, it wasn't being allowed to break through. 'Jackie's nothing to do with the Excelsior Clinic,' she said. We don't see her often.'

'But she's local?'

Alice nodded. 'Fen Ditton.'

The name made the hairs rise across Goodhew's scalp.

'And Lorna knew her?'

'God, yes. They rode together on several occasions.'

'As in, bikes?'

'Horses. Jackie's the country type. She lives in a cottage.' Alice chewed her bottom lip. 'With a dog.' She stood and brushed down her skirt. It was an abrupt movement, like the urge had come into her head and been translated into movement before her conscious mind had had the chance to be consulted. 'Can I go, now?' she asked.

Goodhew's thoughts were still on Jackie. 'Richard never mentioned any other siblings.'

Alice was staring at the café door now. 'No,' she said quietly, 'I guess he wouldn't.'

# TWENTY-FOUR

Contrary to her prediction, Faith Carver's temping contract hadn't been terminated, and she still occupied the reception desk.

Nevertheless, she didn't look very happy, so Goodhew made sure he sounded positive, just to average things out.

'How are you, Mrs Carver?'

'Fine, thank you. Who would you like to see?'

'Victoria Nugent, if she's in.'

'Yes, she is – but she's just slipped outside.' Faith Carver lowered her voice to a whisper, and gave one of her automatic scowls. 'Cigarette break, I think.'

'OK,' he whispered back. 'Tell me what she looks like.'

Faith stopped whispering and then answered in her usual businesslike voice. 'Tanned and skinny with very shiny black hair streaked with burgundy . . . lowlights, I think they're called.'

'I thought she was a redhead.'

'That was yesterday, but you still won't miss her.' Faith cleared her throat with an awkward cough. 'Have you made much progress?' She rushed the words, clearly unsure whether even asking was the correct thing to do.

'Some, I hope, but it's early days. I don't suppose you've thought of anything else to mention?'

'No. But I only worked with her for one day.'

'That's fine – just thought I'd ask.'

He jogged back down the stairs and, when he reached the pavement, he knew immediately that Faith Carver had been right; Victoria Nugent was impossible to miss. The pavement tables nearby were mostly unoccupied and, sitting with her back to him, was the only woman with black hair. To describe it as shiny had been a gross understatement, it was straight and almost glasslike. The lowlights were in fact half a dozen chunks dyed a pronounced plummy red, incongruous against her white-and-green dental nurse's uniform. The lit cigarette she held in her right hand clashed further. Her elbow rested on the table and the cigarette smouldered close to her ear. The ash was about half an inch long and already threatened to drop on to the pavement. The woman was using her left hand to stir an untouched cappuccino.

Goodhew hesitated. Either spring was in the air, or else Mel's observation that he was a prime candidate for stalker of the year had affected his frame of mind. Firstly he'd found Alice very attractive and he now couldn't help noticing that Victoria had her own unique appeal. In fact, she did for nurses' uniforms what Ann Summers had done for waitresses' uniforms . . . and, well, nurses' uniforms. The stilettos helped.

Goodhew drew a chair up to the table and sat a third of the way round from her. He noticed that her eyes were unnaturally blue, but then her skin was unnaturally tanned, and it was hard to tell if either was genuine. The ash gave up and tumbled on to the cobbles.

'You're a detective, aren't you?' she said. Her lips barely moved as she spoke, but they parted just enough to demonstrate that her teeth were straight and gleaming white.

Goodhew figured that working at the Excelsior Clinic had its perks.

He introduced himself formally. 'DC Gary Goodhew.'

'Whatever.' She shrugged, looked at her cigarette, stubbed it out and reached for another. 'I saw you here when she first went missing. And now I suppose you want to know more about dear Lorna?'

'We all want to know about her.'

Victoria blew a thin plume of smoke in the general direction of her coffee. 'That figures. Men all over the place, even when she's dead.'

'I heard you'd fallen out.'

'Lorna was a bitch.' She gave a bitter laugh. 'I'm supposed to say, "But I didn't want her dead." I can promise you I've frequently wished her dead. I imagined something less attention-grabbing though, quietly rotting away with an untreatable strain of syphilis. You know, something appropriate. Have I shocked you?'

'Did you want to?'

'Don't give a shit. Bet no one else is saying she was a bitch. Well, they wouldn't, would they?'

'Because she's dead?'

Victoria leant towards Goodhew and ran her forefinger along the edge of the table as if feeling the finish. He noticed her nail was pierced, with a small diamond dangling from it. 'No, because they didn't know it. I didn't know myself until we spent just a bit too much time together. She stole my boyfriend – or did you hear that already?'

Goodhew mimicked her body language and leant a little closer to her. 'Yeah, I heard,' he said. 'That's all I heard, though. They suggested I get it straight from the horse's mouth, so to speak.'

'Right, so either Alice told you or Richard did. They don't gossip, not really; they just stick to the facts.'

'How did they know you'd fallen out?'

'Oh, shit. The whole world knew. We weren't exactly subtle about it. Well, *I* wasn't anyway. That was the big difference between us. With Lorna it was all about getting her own way, and if that meant being two-faced, she'd do it. I couldn't do that myself. She'd done the dirty on me and I wanted everyone to find out.

'I'd split up with my boyfriend, and I'm the first to admit that. But she was in there with him, in my bed, within hours. Not days, just hours. Friends don't do that, do they?'

'I don't know. Perhaps he wanted to make you jealous? It happens.'

'Not with him. He screwed around while we were together. That's why I dumped him.'

'But you wanted him back?'

Her hand flew up into the air in irritation, and remained poised by her ear as if she wanted to slap him. 'No I fucking didn't! Wanker.' Goodhew wasn't sure if 'wanker' was directed at himself or the boyfriend. Either way, he decided not to take it personally, and hoped she moved her hand before her nail decoration got tangled in her hair.

Goodhew sighed. 'I don't get it. You dumped him and didn't want him back, so what difference did it make?'

'Do you have a serious gap in your education where women are concerned? She was supposed to be my friend.'

'Oh, I see. You decided he was a bastard and you needed your friend to think so too.'

'No!' she snapped indignantly.

'What, then?'

She sat quietly and thought about it, then corrected herself. 'You put it across in a pretty tactless way but, fair enough, that is one way to look at it. Just not the way *I* see it.'

'Fair enough,' he echoed. 'What was his name?'

'I'm not prepared to say.'

'You can't do that. We need to know. This is a murder investigation.'

'OK, then. It's John.'

'John what?'

'Smith.'

'Seriously?'

She didn't answer, just glared at him in full-throttle disdain. He decided to come back to the name question later. 'And when did you last see him?'

'Don't know.' She thought for a minute. 'I really don't know. Way back, I guess.'

'I'll need to contact him. Can you let me have his address?'

'Sorry, no. Like I say, I haven't seen him since and I lost touch ages ago.'

'No phone number, email address even?'

'That's right. Nothing.'

'And he stopped seeing Lorna?'

'He wasn't seeing her. It was a sex thing. That was Lorna and men, all over. One sex thing after another. By rights she should have been the VD capital of Cambridge.'

'But her relationship with Richard Moran was different?'

'Why? Because it's lasted a few months? Or because he's richer than most? Or perhaps because he was strung out with jealousy and she liked watching the frenzy it sent him into? Have you asked him about the phone yet?'

'What phone?'

'The mobile he bought her. He pays the bill, then gets the calls itemized and sent to his office so he can check on her.'

'How do you know?'

'The clinic's a small place with thin walls; easy to know what's going on if you set out to.' She half closed her eyes and stared at the froth spinning on the top of her untouched coffee. 'Lorna's old phone, the one she lost – it's in Richard's office. You know, I think he's a good bloke, but she just screwed him up. But on the other hand, I'm a shit judge of men.'

He kept his tone casual, hoping the next question would catch her with her guard down. 'And how well do you know Bryn O'Brien?'

Victoria's expression remained unaltered.

'Ah.' She blew out another column of smoke, this time with her head tilted back, sending it straight upwards. 'I suppose it depends on how you categorize what's relevant. I don't know his mother's maiden name or his date of birth, if that's what you mean. But if good sex and superficial conversation qualify, then I'm in. Or, should I say, *he* was.'

'But he'd been seeing Lorna as well.'

'And?'

'Why was Bryn fair game when John wasn't?'

'No one was going out with Bryn, were they? Lorna was seeing Richard, and I was enjoying being single.'

'Now I'm confused.'

Victoria looked unimpressed. 'That, I can imagine. Free-spirited women must be quite an anathema to someone like you.'

'At this moment, you're quite right.' She was grating on him big time now, and he was annoyed with himself for being unable to keep the irritation from his voice. He forced himself to speak more slowly, and he also lowered the volume to make her pay better attention. 'Let me explain why I'm a bit confused. You and Lorna were out with Bryn in January, correct?'

She blinked her eyelashes slowly. 'Yup.'

'But you fell out with her before that, in autumn last year.'

'If you say so.'

'Well, did you, or not?'

'Why not figure it out yourself?'

'Well, if you did, that would imply you patched things up again, yet now she's dead you're happy to admit you hated her. So either you never fell out in the first place, or you fell out for a second time.

And if you really did fall out over this John Smith you've seen him far more recently than "ages ago".'

Victoria ran her tongue across the front of her upper teeth. If it was supposed to look at all sexy, it didn't succeed. Her eyes hardened and she suddenly pointed towards the river. 'Look over there.'

Goodhew did, but saw nothing.

'I think I see your next promotion coming over the horizon.' Victoria stood abruptly, her cappuccino still untouched. 'I know nothing that can help you, so let's just leave it there.'

'What about Colin Willis?'

She looked at him in irritation. 'Who?'

'The bloke you and she and Bryn played pool with.'

'I never even spoke to him.'

Goodhew glanced around to make sure there was still no one within earshot. 'Did Lorna sleep with him?'

Victoria lowered her face closer to his. 'Lorna wanted *something*, but not sex. I know that much.'

'How do you know?'

Victoria straightened. 'Is my tan fake?'

Goodhew didn't answer.

Victoria rolled her eyes. 'It was obvious. But then we've already established that you're a bit retarded on the women front, haven't we?'

# TWENTY-FIVE

The Boat Race stood on the corner of East Road and Burleigh Street and had once been Cambridge's best-known live music pub. But, in the eyes of the planning office, the arrival of major new shops and Burleigh Street's subsequent revamp hadn't left room for such a venue. It was now called The Snug and every trace of its former persona had been eradicated. The place was just a few minutes' walk from Parkside station, and was where Michael Kincaide had suggested they meet for a drink.

Although Goodhew found its new wine-bar guise about as dynamic as a house full of magnolia walls; he still felt a nostalgia for the building itself and tried to superimpose his memories of local bands like the Frigidaires and Jump, Bump and Boogie over the anaemic pop trickling from the new but gutless sound system.

Kincaide had arrived first and already sat near the door with a glass of red wine and a copy of the *Cambridge News*. Goodhew just bought himself a coffee.

He had managed to stay true to his word, and had contacted Marks with each new development as the day went along. His penultimate call, revealing the existence of Jackie Moran, had coincided with Kincaide ending his lengthy interview with Bryn, so it had been Kincaide who'd been assigned to visit her. Goodhew had been disappointed not to go with him, but then again, that had left him with time to see the charming Victoria Nugent.

Hmm.

As Goodhew reached his table, Kincaide held up the front page of the paper. 'Have you seen it?'

Goodhew tilted his head to match the angle of the newspaper, but he didn't really need to: there were only three short words in the headline, easy to read, even upside down: *Who is Emma?*

'I'd like to know how they got it,' Kincaide said and passed it across to him. Goodhew started reading even as he sat down. The story was simple: the paper had been tipped off about the message on Lorna's palms, suggesting that the main line of the police investigation was a theory that Emma was someone known to both Lorna and her killer. Therefore, find Emma and find the murderer. 'Marks went ballistic earlier. I think he wants to slaughter whoever leaked this.'

'It might flush out the answer, though. I mean, if I were called Emma, I'd certainly stop and think about any connection I might have with Lorna Spence.'

'You approve, then?'

'No, I'm just saying that, with some luck, it may work to our advantage, that's all. Any idea who did it?'

Kincaide shook his head. 'Marks said there's been too much anonymity already and it has to stop.'

'Whatever that means.'

'You know what that means. He's going to be flushing out whoever posted him the evidence on the Airport Rapist, and probably demote or sack him over this.'

'Oh, I think he'll calm down.' Goodhew slid the paper back to Kincaide. 'How was Jackie Moran?'

'Not at home, and neither were the immediate neighbours.'

'But the house looked occupied?'

'Oh, yes. And I also checked at the local paper shop. She has *The Times* delivered three times a week and she's bang up to date with paying her bill. I couldn't find out where she works, though, or even if she does. Did you ask Alice about that?'

'Shit, I should have. We could go over now, though – to Jackie's, I mean. More likely to catch her at home in the evening.'

Kincaide checked his watch. 'Haven't you got a life outside work? Tomorrow morning, first thing, will be good enough. We can both go. How was it with Victoria Nugent? Your mate Bryn called her feisty.'

'He's not my mate.'

'OK. But that's what he called her.'

'Well, that's one way to describe her. Personally, I think I'd go for scary. The dates of her falling out with Lorna just don't add up – right in the middle of it they seemed to have patched things up enough for Bryn to think they were still close friends when they all went out together.'

'Unless he's lying.'

Goodhew screwed up his nose. 'Why would he? No, that doesn't make sense, because it means he would have to have concocted the story with Victoria.'

'And?'

'They don't know each other that well.'

'Or so they claim. And the only other two people who were supposedly there that evening are both dead. Then there's this business of Victoria hating Lorna. No one else admits to hating her, but in Richard Moran's own words, he felt jealous because she was a slapper.'

'No, no, he didn't actually say that.'

'OK. He said she wanted a more . . .' Kincaide paused to make little quote signs in the air – '. . . open relationship than he did. What bloke is likely to buy into that one? The only reason he's not going to say anything against her is self-preservation, as we'd be breathing down his throat if he owned up to how he really felt about her. In fact, we *should* be breathing down his throat.'

'So, if it's that simple, how does "Emma" fit in?'

'Let's worry about that tomorrow. We'll start with Jackie Moran first thing.' From within his pocket, Kincaide's mobile bleeped. 'You need a bit of sex to distract you,' he added as he fumbled for his phone.

Goodhew looked down at his coffee. He didn't care for his colleague's phraseology, but had to admit that it was a fair point.

He glanced up in time to see Kincaide unlock his phone, then smirk as he read the message on it. 'And speaking of which,' he said, dropping it back in his pocket, 'I'd better go.'

Somehow Goodhew knew that Kincaide's text hadn't been sent by his wife. He took his time finishing his coffee and he wondered how it was that the Bryns, Kincaides and Victorias of the world seemed to have no qualms about entering into casual liaisons, whereas he couldn't seem to separate the physical from the emotional.

He guessed that those were the signals he gave out too; the women he attracted weren't the one-night-fling kind. And even looking back at school, he could see that the 'Just Say No' anti-drugs campaign had been wasted on him; he oozed so little irresponsibility that, until he was eighteen, he'd never even been offered a cigarette.

Goodhew counted the months back to the last of the half-dozen or so dates he'd shared with Tasha, a gap student from Sydney. More time had passed than he'd realized; no wonder he'd even had a moment of finding Victoria attractive. And the idea of indulging in a quick fling had a certain appeal, but he knew it wouldn't be happening. In fact, he couldn't imagine a time where it would ever be his thing.

On top of that, he couldn't totally grasp the concept of opening up that much to just anyone, so for the time being at least, he knew that any desires he felt were illogically attached to Mel.

He checked his watch and saw it was time to track down his grandmother. Perhaps he could even admonish her for saddling him with a rogue sexual ethics gene.

He dialled her mobile and, as it rang, it occurred to him that she was far more likely to urge him to make the most of still being single. In which case the gene must have come from his granddad, because it certainly didn't come from his mum's side of the family tree.

# TWENTY-SIX

His grandmother lived on the first floor of a two-storey art deco block of eight flats on the Fen Causeway. The building was white with curved windows, sweeping balconies and rooms so large that they would have dwarfed even the bulbous deco furniture they'd been designed to house. Connaught Villas lounged across a plot big enough to accommodate two streets of 'affordable' housing and, although the road outside was often clogged with city-bound cars, the main view was of the lush marshy fields of Newnham Common. This was undoubtedly high-quality city dwelling.

Goodhew arrived there within ten minutes, and having his own key, let himself into her apartment. A small lobby led into the single large reception room.

'Hello, Gran, it's me,' he called out as he entered. The room was warm, feeling slightly humid but not in an unpleasant way. A yucca tree thrived in a large pot halfway between the kitchen door and the french windows, enjoying both the steam from the kitchen and the sun from the south.

He draped his jacket across the back of his favourite armchair and checked the time on the grandfather clock as it clunked through the seconds. It struck the hour with a single dainty chime. As a child he'd wondered why it didn't count out the total hours like every other chiming clock he had encountered, and that began a thought process that led him to wonder why most things in his childhood seemed to be so different to other childhoods.

Then he'd grown up to discover that his best friend was his grandmother, and even if that was unconventional, it really didn't matter.

And, as if on cue, his grandmother appeared in the kitchen doorway with a tray of tea and biscuits. She was still wearing the black cocktail dress that she'd obviously worn that evening to the Felix.

He smiled at her and settled back into the cherry leather wing-chair. 'You're looking well.'

'Good quality meals on wheels,' she joked.

'Really?'

'Yes, my favourite Chinese restaurant has started home deliveries.'

She placed the tray on the coffee table and sat in the chair facing him. She then reached underneath and produced a black box from the magazine shelf. 'Backgammon?'

'Of course.' Goodhew opened out the board and slid the red and black counters into place. He held out the red dice for her, and she opened her hand for him to drop them in. 'Oh, and before I forget . . .' He pulled an envelope from his back pocket. 'Your rent.'

'Thanks,' she said and pulled an expression that he couldn't place, but suspected was in the region of 'You're not going to want to hear this.'

The flat he lived in was hers, in fact the whole building was, and Goodhew guessed that, apart from her own apartment here, it was the last of his grandparents' assets. Paying market rate for renting the flat was something he'd insisted upon, and he assumed that if she ever started to struggle financially, the logical step would be to rent out the vacant floors below his.

'Is it about my flat?' he asked.

'In a roundabout way, yes.' After that she fell silent, and Goodhew guessed there was something that she was waiting for him to say.

'If you need the building back, I can easily move out. I don't mind,' he added, hoping he wasn't the completely useless liar that she claimed he was.

She took one of the dice and twiddled it between her thumb and forefinger. He smiled to himself as he noticed how precisely its colour matched her nail polish; she had a talent for such detail. 'I know,' she said, 'but it's nothing like that. I visited Mason, my solicitor, and I've come away with some documents. I'd like you to look over them.'

'Sure.'

'I'd like us to play first.' She offered him the plate of biscuits.

They fell silent for a few moments, and each picked up a dice and threw them simultaneously. He scored six, she scored one. He moved the pieces, then looked up.

'How's work?' she asked.

'Fine. Why?' A mischievous smile darted on to her face.

He grinned. 'What?'

'I think romance often blooms in the workplace, don't you?'

He shook his head. 'Only when it's mutual. And if anyone ever shows a flicker of mutual interest, I'll be sure to let you know.'

'But you like her?'

'I made something out of nothing,' he sighed. 'I didn't even misread the signals, because there weren't any. And now I don't know what I was thinking. She has a boyfriend, she wouldn't still be with him if she'd had enough of him.'

'Some people just don't leave.'

'She's made it clear she's not interested. Even if that wasn't the case, it's not the way I'd want to start a relationship.'

'So that's that, then?'

'Absolutely,' he replied firmly.

Goodhew leant over and picked up his cup while his grandmother had set hers to one side, preferring to concentrate fully on the game.

'Sometimes,' she said, 'things don't work out the way we want them to.'

He glanced across at her and found her shrewd gaze waiting to meet his. 'We're not still talking about Mel now, are we?'

'No', she said.

He shook his dice on to the board and then took his turn.

She turned over the doubling dice. 'I'm doubling the game,' she announced. She liked raising the stakes.

He waited until his turn before speaking further, and turned the doubling dice again. 'Nothing ventured, nothing gained,' he murmured. 'Your turn.'

'I'm aware of the boundaries you set for yourself, Gary.'

'Such as?'

'The terms on which you're prepared to start a relationship. Or work on your own initiative. Or refuse to pass judgement on Kincaide. The way you push yourself to stay fit. I could go on and on.' He was aware that she watched him as he stretched across the

143

table to move several pieces from her side of the board. 'It is clear to me that you're now ready . . .' She threw her dice and made her move, tapping the pieces on the board as she counted, '. . . to inherit your grandfather's money.' She kept her tone casual, but it was obvious to both of them that her smile was an apologetic one. Without further explanation, she reached behind a cushion and pulled out several sheets of paper, then tried to pass him the top copy. Her voice was hushed. 'I can take you through all the major assets in more detail, but this is a summary.'

Goodhew refused to take at it. 'No,' he said, then realized how sharp his voice had sounded. 'No, thank you,' he said more softly.

'One of your properties is the house in Park Terrace.'

'I own my flat?'

'Yes, and the rest of the building beneath it.'

'This is ridiculous.'

She selected a different sheet and tried to pass it to him. 'This is the current valuation.' She waved the paper. 'I know you're phobic about money, but just read it. Please.'

'I'm not phobic, I just don't want it,' he said quietly.

'It's already yours. And it's part of your grandfather's legacy. Not taking it would be letting him down.'

'What about Debbie?'

'That's your half only. She'll receive a similar settlement when I think she can deal with it.'

'I don't understand. I thought everything was left to Mum and Dad.'

'No, only some of it, otherwise we couldn't be sure that any of it would ever reach you and your sister.'

'Because of my mother?'

'It doesn't matter why.'

Goodhew collected the dice and returned them to the backgammon box. It was obvious that they would not now be completing the game. He fought to overcome the lump in his throat and waited until it felt safe for him to try to speak. 'I interviewed a witness yesterday, his name's Bryn O'Brien and we were at primary school together. As we were talking, I suddenly had this huge flashback. I was in maths class. I loved maths normally, but I couldn't concentrate and I knocked my pen on to the floor. I watched it bounce then roll under the next desk. I went to get it, then looked up and the headmistress was at the classroom door. I knew at once something terrible had happened, and I was sent home because Granddad was ill.'

His grandmother nodded, as if she remembered too. 'And you never went back.'

'Then you went away.'

'It was the best way for me to deal with his death.'

'We understood that. Yesterday reminded me of how much damage that money caused. Once Mum started spending, she stuck us in that school. Debbie and I barely saw each other, and when I did manage to speak to her, she just cried all the time. We were homesick and didn't fit in with the other kids.'

'But that's just it, Gary. It was your mum in combination with the money that caused the problem.'

'We lost touch with all our old friends, then at the end of term we came home to find Dad on the edge of a breakdown, while Mum and the money were getting up to who knows what. I'm sorry, I know this isn't the response you wanted, but I'm very conscious of the parts of my life that are going well and I'm not going to jeopardize them just for money.'

'It doesn't have to change anything,' she said.

But her expression betrayed her, for they both knew that wasn't true. He scratched around for the right words and, in the meantime, heard himself say, 'You hid it from me.' It was a thought he shouldn't have spoken, since he already realized that she knew how he felt and he knew that she was sorry.

She placed one page on the table and left him alone then. Afterwards all he could remember was the clock ticking loudly and his stomach growing tighter and tighter. He rested his elbows on his knees and pressed his face into his cupped hands. He stayed like that for almost a minute, then blew out a long breath, and looked at the paper. As far as he was concerned, money was trouble.

He suddenly remembered Ratty's theory about trouble: *Touch it and it stains you.*

He pushed the paper away, so it slid off the far side of the table and drifted to the floor. He then let himself out of his grandmother's flat and headed back to the station, deciding that right now the only person's trouble he was interested in was Lorna Spence's.

145

# TWENTY-SEVEN

Colin Willis' file had been left on Goodhew's chair, and a sheet of paper lay on the desktop. He dumped the file right next to it and the downdraught he caused sent the page floating towards the desk's edge. He caught it just before it fell. The message was written in marker pen, and the note was headed 'Gary Goodhew', underlined twice.

'10.15 p.m. Faith Carver called from the Exelsior Clinic, wanted to speak to you only. Please call her.' Followed by her phone number.

He glanced at his watch. She was likely to already be asleep, but that was tough luck. Murder was murder.

He took up the cordless handset from his desk and dialled, then flipped open the front of the Willis file, expecting a wait while Mrs Carver stirred. A photograph of the interior of the victim's flat lay on top, looking in a similar state of decay to the body.

Faith Carver, however, answered on the first ring, proceeding in the old-fashioned way with a recitation of her number. Goodhew instantly closed the file and responded. 'It's DC Goodhew here. I'm sorry if I've woken you.'

'No, no, it's perfectly all right. I decided to wait up for you to call me.' Her voice had an official crispness. 'I wanted to speak to you directly because I hate gossip, and what I want to say sounds as if it's exactly that. Also, I'm hoping I can trust you to be discreet if this turns out to be irrelevant.'

'Of course.'

'Good. Victoria Nugent seemed very agitated after you left her today. Obviously I only met her for the first time this week. I know

146

she can be petulant, but she's never seemed the nervous type. So I made a point of keeping an eye on her and after about fifteen minutes she slipped out of the building.'

'Did you see where she went?'

'Yes and no. She walked to the far side of the punting station and stayed there for ten minutes or so. I couldn't actually see her, but she would have had to walk back past me to go anywhere else. When she reappeared, she was closing her mobile phone, so I assume that she'd been making a call.'

'And how did she seem when she returned?'

'Back to normal, I'd say.'

'And that is?'

'Cold and borderline rude.'

'But a moment ago you described her as petulant.'

'I said I know she *can* be. She was like that on Monday. She had a bad atmosphere hanging about her like a robe all day, and she was not the least pleased when I told her that Lorna was late getting in.'

'Do you know what she wanted from her?'

'That's what Lorna asked. She seemed put out when I didn't know the answer. The gist of it was that it was very urgent.'

'And no idea what?'

'None.'

'You said Lorna was late in. How late was that?'

'Just before ten, between quarter to and ten to. I know because I checked the clock.'

'Why?'

'I don't approve of lateness. I believe you can tell the sort of person someone is from their timekeeping. Someone who's consistently five minutes late is quite different from someone who's consistently five minutes early. That may sound like rubbish to you, but it's what I think, and I do like to know the sort of people I work with.'

'OK. And what sort do you think Lorna was?'

'Now she's dead, it seems she had problems . . .'

'But what did you think at the time?'

Faith Carver obviously deliberated for several seconds, long enough for Goodhew to have to enquire if she was still there.

'Yes, I'm here. I was just thinking.' She paused again, this time for longer. Goodhew waited while she patiently gathered her thoughts. 'There are little things I've never considered to mention,' she continued at last. 'Lorna was late that day, as I said, and by the time she'd arrived, several people had been trying to get hold of her. Victoria of course, but Richard and Alice Moran had also both asked for her, something work-related I guessed.'

'Then, when she first arrived, Lorna seemed friendly, but a little tense. Maybe because she was late, I don't know. But she was certainly fairly talkative later on, telling me about the different treatments at the clinic and how much they cost. You know, general chit-chat really.

'On balance, I'd say she was outgoing and popular, though not very professional.'

Goodhew scribbled notes across the original message as he tried to keep up with her. They would need to take a statement from her, too, so Goodhew arranged that for the following morning.

Faith Carver had just finished confirming the arrangement when she suddenly gasped, 'Oh yes, there is something else I forgot to mention. Lorna slipped off to lunch at twelve, and didn't come back until one-thirty but, before she went, I heard her mobile phone receive several text messages.'

Goodhew replaced the handset, unaware that someone else had entered the room, and he jumped when he heard a discreet cough. DI Marks stood in the open doorway. Expressionless.

'Why are you still here?' he demanded.

Goodhew shrugged. 'Nothing decent on TV.' But Marks wasn't about to be moved by flippant comments, so he added, 'I decided to take another look at Colin Willis' file, but I've just been speaking to the Exelsior Clinic receptionist, Faith Carver, instead. How soon will we have Lorna Spence's phone records, do you think?'

'Coincidentally, right now.' Marks held out a wodge of faxes. 'They're the up-to-date listings from all the phones you're checking, from the last bill paid until yesterday and including Lorna's extension at work. Don't stay too late. I'll be in my office, if you need me.'

Goodhew settled down, keen to study the new pile of paper, but he knew he was getting tired as he stared at the lists of numbers and found them totally meaningless. He wandered round to the drinks machine, downed two black coffees in quick succession, then returned to his desk with a slightly clearer mind.

Lorna had made a lot of phone calls and, judging by the variety of numbers, made them to many different people. Then, two weeks and two days before the end of the statement, the calls had suddenly stopped. So that tallied with Victoria Nugent's claim that Lorna had changed her phone, and therefore left him with no way of checking who she'd been texting on the morning of her disappearance.

His extension rang. It was Marks. 'Go home, Gary.' The DI sounded tired, his voice gravelly.

'It looks like Lorna Spence was using a second mobile the day she died. Victoria Nugent said much the same, and reckons the old one is at the Excelsior Clinic. Could the new one still be at her flat?'

'I doubt that; the premises were thoroughly searched.'

'I know, but perhaps it was missed.'

'Read me the number.'

'I don't have it, but I do have a list of mobiles that she was in the habit of texting. We need to know who they belong to, and whether they started texting her on the new number.'

'I'll get that checked. Any other progress?'

'No, apart from that, nothing really. We're visiting the half-sister, Jackie Moran, first thing in the morning.'

'You and Kincaide?'

'Yes.'

'Good. Now go home, get some sleep and start fresh tomorrow.'

# TWENTY-EIGHT

Goodhew managed a fitful doze from just after 3 a.m. until 5.35 a.m., and awoke to the sound of incessant rain and the silence of birds. He lay on top of his bed, bare-chested but still wearing jeans; a slight improvement on a fully clothed crash-out on the settee.

He sat on the edge of the bed until his head cleared, then crossed to the window, wanting to see the downpour. Some days the rain sounded worse than it actually was, amplified by the water gushing through downpipes and dripping from the guttering. But today it was just as wet as it sounded, if not wetter.

The rain fell in sleet-thick sheets, and the sky was bruised and grey, like a battered lead lid nailed down close above the rooftops.

He made the few hundred yards to work much longer by detouring via Parkside pool. But he stopped swimming after only ninety lengths, worried that he might keep Kincaide waiting, and so arrived at his desk promptly on the dot of 7 a.m.

Forty-five minutes after Kincaide was due at the station, there was still no sign of him. No answer on his home phone, and his mobile was diverted to voicemail. Goodhew told himself there was probably a good reason for this and refused the temptation of dropping back into anti-Kincaide mode.

But equally he did not feel like wasting any more time waiting, so he decided to leave without him, and therefore now stood alone on the doorstep of Jackie Moran's cottage. The rain had not abated, and it drove at a forty-five degree angle at the unprotected front of the house. The front garden consisted of one raised stone-bordered bed planted with a couple of dozen petunias and, at the end furthest from the front door, young sweetpea plants growing up the sides of

150

a black wrought-iron obelisk. The garden was hardly ambitious, but both sets of plants were being furiously battered by the weather, and only a few minutes passed before Goodhew himself deteriorated from damp to equally bedraggled.

It was a strong Suffolk accent that snapped him out of his moment of rain-muffled solitary confinement. 'You won't catch Jackie this late.' The voice belonged to the postman, who was approaching him from the property next door. 'She's like clockwork; gone at eight every weekday.'

'To work?'

The postman poked a couple of items of what looked like junk mail through Jackie Moran's letterbox before answering, 'I dunno.'

'Damn,' Goodhew sighed. 'I really needed to speak to her this morning.'

'Well, I can tell you where she'll be – at the stables at Old Mile Farm, just out towards Quy. But I don't know if it's work or not, 'cept I s'pose anything involving horses is work. Worse than kids, they are. Probably why all these females love 'em so much.'

Goodhew had been vaguely aware of seeing the farm's sign along one of the routes leading to Newmarket, but the postman was happy to give him precise directions before waving goodbye.

Newmarket: the home of flat racing, the sport of kings. Many of the racing yards were positioned near the centre of the town itself, tucked just out of sight of the main through roads. Or, more likely in a town where horses had right of way, the roads had been developed afterwards, deliberately planned to avoid disturbing the town's main industry.

Further out from the centre, the surrounding villages remained horse rich, offering acres and acres of pristine post-and-rail heaven.

And it was with that limited amount of local knowledge that Goodhew drew himself a picture of what to expect at Old Mile Farm, while adding in a younger version of Alice Moran to represent Jackie herself.

The sign for the farm was the only thing visible from the road; it was made of wood and nailed to a telegraph pole. The words had been carved out and painted white. He turned down the unmade track alongside it, and immediately wrote himself a mental note against making such assumptions in the future. He was not, in fact, driving towards some smart racing yard, and none of the three horses turned out in the field bore any resemblance to a thorough-bred, instead belonging to the Heinz 57 varieties of the horse world. The two bays, both standing at about fourteen hands, looked like they were at least fifty per cent native breed, while the third was a heavy-set skewbald closer to sixteen hands. One of the bays trotted alongside the fence, its mane and tail sodden and steam rising from its back even as the rain continued to fall. It reached the far corner, then stretched its neck over the top rail, pricked its ears forward and whinnied.

Goodhew drove on past. The track opened out to a small area of uneven hard standing, just big enough to accommodate half a dozen cars. A RAV4 took up one corner, and although his was the only other vehicle, Goodhew still found it hard to park somewhere avoiding the puddles.

In front of him was a fenced-in manège, and facing on to that was a row of ten loose boxes. The air smelt of wet earth and manure from a giant muck heap, while a lone water butt caught the rain as it spurted from a strip of broken guttering on the overhang of roof above the last stable. The butt was already overflowing, with a loud sploshing of water falling into the butt then bouncing out and on to the concrete floor beneath.

A rug hung over the open door to the third loose box, and he headed towards it. 'Hello?' he called.

No reply.

He looked inside but it was empty. He continued along the row and found the seventh stable was the only one occupied. A chestnut gelding, with the name Jester on his head collar, poked his nose over the door. Then, in the distance, Goodhew heard the bay whinny again and was soon able to pick out the sound of hooves. Unlike the others, the horse that was now being ridden into the yard was a thoroughbred. She was a grey and definitely no youngster, walking towards the boxes with the reins hanging loose around her neck. A Border collie trotted alongside, only inches from her hooves.

Her rider wore a crash hat and a wax jacket with its collar turned up, making it impossible for him to catch more than a glimpse of her face.

'Jackie Moran?' he asked doubtfully.

152

'Yes, that's me. Give me one minute to sort Suze out.' She patted the mare's neck, then swung out of the saddle, landing lightly on the balls of her feet. She led the horse into the third box as the collie sat with its back to Goodhew in the middle of the doorway and watched the untacking. Jackie Moran rugged up Suze, then hauled the saddle on to the door and hooked the bridle on a nearby peg. Neither animal attempted to move until the collie was forced to get out of the path of the closing door.

'Which way today, Bridy?' The dog chose the stable and Jackie Moran slid the bolt behind her. 'She's a lazy old girl, sleeps half the day now.'

Goodhew guessed she meant the dog.

'They're both the same,' she added, immediately making his guess irrelevant. 'How can I help you?' Before he had a chance to reply, she corrected herself, and thus drew an end to her initial informality. 'I suppose what I should first find out is who you are and what you want.' She pulled the crash hat from her head and ran her fingers just once through her brown hair, as if that would be enough to unflatten it.

He introduced himself and her expression remained unaltered: cooperative, but not up for having her time wasted. She didn't need to say 'Get on with it', because it was written on her face.

'I'm here about Lorna Spence.'

'Thought you might be,' she said. Perhaps she'd taken stock of him taking stock of her, and she deliberately paused before adding, 'You're very young, aren't you?', like it was the only thing she'd found worth a mention.

He just shrugged in response.

'We can sit in there.' She pointed towards the first stable in the block. 'Will that be OK?' She looked hopeful; whatever was in the horsebox-cum-lounge clearly appealed to her. 'At least it's dry.'

'Fine.' He gave her the 'after you' gesture. 'Go ahead.'

She unbolted both halves of the stable door and he followed her inside. The horsebox-cum-lounge was actually more a horsebox-cum-storeroom with bales of hay and straw, two feed bins and a pile of buckets. She then closed the bottom half of the door – perhaps in the pretence of warmth – and moved two bales so they could sit on them, almost side by side, facing the door.

'I take the tack and grooming kit home each night to reduce the chance of break-ins. When I was a teenager, I used to bring a sleeping bag and camp out in here, so I could get up early and ride, but I'd never do that now.'

They each sat on a bale, Jackie with her feet planted squarely in front of her, and one hand on each knee; she looked like she was bracing herself.

'Lorna Spence?' Goodhew repeated, and let the name hang in the air, hoping she'd conjure up the appropriate question that went with the name. She did.

'We weren't close friends, you know, but I liked her and we seemed to get on OK. She helped me exercise the horses once or twice each week.'

'She rode well?'

'Very riding-school.' He looked puzzled, she explained. 'She'd been taught well, but obviously hadn't ridden enough to be an unconsciously competent horsewoman. I think she would have struggled with Suze, but she was fine on Jester. Suze looks docile right now, but she's smart, and she'd have played up. She always sees through people.'

'Is that a hint?'

A defensive note slipped into her voice. 'I don't hint; I either say it or keep it to myself. Lorna was competent, but not expert. Suze is a retired racehorse; she was highly strung in her day and animals like that are well aware of who they can take advantage of. And that was all I meant.'

'I've spoken to Richard and Alice Moran, so I'm already aware of her connection to the rest of your family.'

Goodhew tried to see behind her defiant look. He had the distinct feeling that she chose to keep her thoughts to herself far more often than she vented them. Reticence was no ugly trait, just one he didn't have the luxury of letting her indulge in right now.

But she seemed to open up a bit whenever she talked about her horse, and if that meant he had to take a metaphorical canter round the paddock to get over each metaphorical hurdle, that was fine by him.

Jackie ran her nail up and down the double-stitched outer seam of her jodhpurs. It was the kind of action that reminded him of a

154

schoolgirl chewing a pencil or twirling her hair. Distracted, and insecure.

'Tell me about Suze,' he asked gently.

Her gaze darted up and directly met his. Her face softened, and for the first time he saw what appeared to be a genuine smile. 'She's really called Souza Symphony – that was her racing name. My dad owned part shares in her, but she only ran a few times. She wasn't quite quick enough. She was fast, actually, but we're talking about a tenth of a second here and there making all the difference. That picture behind you . . .' She pointed to the back of the stable door, where a photocopy of a press clipping was pinned. 'That was the only thing she ever won. Beginner's luck, my mother said.'

There were two people pictured alongside the horse. One was the jockey. Goodhew read the caption: 'Souza Symphony, winner of the 5F Yearling Handicap, pictured with jockey Brendan Quinn and owner Mrs Sarah Moran.' If Jackie Moran had tried to dress up as a grinning *Dynasty* extra, this would undoubtedly have been the result. 'That's her, then?'

'I remember how Mum took us on summer holidays to Bournemouth, then abandoned us at the hotel for the day while she drove to Brighton to watch her run. Dad came down a few days later, and they had this huge row about it.'

'When was that?'

'1982, can't you tell by the clothes? Suze is a real old girl now, and I'm glad Mum went that day. She was thrilled. Suze went on to have a couple of foals, then I talked Dad into letting me keep her. I suppose it's silly to have two horses all to myself, but it's how I like to spend my time.'

'Do you work as well?'

'I inherited this place and the cottage I live in, so there's no rent or mortgage. I'm paid to look after the three horses there in the field and I give riding lessons at the weekend. That's it. I'd love to do this place up properly, but I don't think it'll happen somehow. I'm not one of our family's high-flyers, am I?' Her smile reappeared, but he thought it now looked artificially bright.

'If you spent a lot of time with Lorna, I would have thought you'd have come forward. Why didn't you?' He threw in the question, hoping to catch her more off guard now.

Her eyes narrowed and the smile hardened. 'Time to get down to business, I suppose?'

'Something like that.'

'Well, first off, thanks for letting me chat about Suze, I needed an ice-breaker. I find it hard to talk to most people.' She was quite obviously stalling. 'I suppose that's why I like it out here.' She paused, her stalling stalled. A few more seconds passed before she spoke again. 'I can cope one to one, like this, but not with big groups of people, or in unfamiliar places. It's pathetic, I know.' Jackie said it in such a matter-of-fact way that at first he wondered if there was any truth in what she was saying.

'And secondly?'

'Secondly, I didn't want to give myself stress and waste my time on you lot if you were going to squander it, so I decided to let you find me if you thought it important enough.'

'That could be withholding evidence.'

'That's bollocks.'

'Bollocks?'

'There's nothing to withhold. We rode horses together sometimes, so what's the big deal.'

'How did you meet her – was it through Richard or Alice or the clinic?'

'No way. Lorna found me by accident. She just wanted somewhere to ride, and called in here to ask.'

'A coincidence?'

'In theory, but I don't think so. I'm fairly sure she engineered it. That would be very much like her, you know. Lorna liked to make things happen by chance, if you see what I mean.'

'And you became friends with her?'

'It sounds worse than I'm sure it was, but I think she thought she could bring us all closer together. She hoped to marry Richard, and maybe she was picturing being nice and close to her new "sisters" too.'

'Was it working?'

'It was a non-starter.'

'Why?'

'I guess we're just not that kind of family.'

'Richard and Alice seem very close.'

'Yes, I've always thought they seemed like a healthy example of siblingdom.' She smiled at her own sarcasm, then shook her head and looked away. 'But not my thing.' She changed the subject quickly. 'Do you have brothers or sisters?'

'One sister.'

'And do you live together . . . thought not. They live together *and* work together.'

'I know.'

'And I couldn't imagine either of those two marrying somehow. Wouldn't that just make their status quo wobble too much?' She shifted topic without pausing. 'The stables belonged to my mother. And, as well as the cottage, I was left a third share of the family house. Have you been there yet?'

He nodded. 'Interesting property.'

'It's a monster. My mother never liked it either. Perhaps I'll sell up here, start over somewhere else. It's not like Alice and Richard would miss me. In fact, they'd probably love to buy me out. I know that's what my dad wanted for me. Secretly I think he would have liked it if I'd been more academic, but he let me carry on down here. He'd drop by sometimes, bring a flask with him. When it was raining we'd sit in here, or in his car, and we'd just talk.

'He'd always ask me loads of questions, always checking if I was happy. I knew he was dying, though, even before the others did – ironic when they work in medicine, don't you think?

'He came here last June when it was a perfect summer's day. Warm but breezy, leaves rustling, fluffy clouds – all that shit. In fact, just the way they make England look in tourist adverts. And I looked at him and realized his skin had taken on that horrible greyness, the one people get when they're seriously ill. I had the strong feeling then that it wouldn't be long.'

Goodhew's mobile bleeped and he quickly read the message. 'My colleague DC Kincaide will be here in a minute.'

'Why?'

'Nothing to worry about. We were originally coming together but he's running late.'

'That's overkill.'

'It's just procedure.'

'No, just to talk to one person about a dead acquaintance? That would definitely be overkill. So you want me for more than this, don't you?'

Astute.

Goodhew couldn't decide how to answer, but she didn't seem to be waiting for a reply.

'I don't know who Emma is, by the way,' she said.

'How . . .' He stopped himself there, realizing the answer. 'Last night's paper?'

She nodded.

'Are you sure?' he checked.

'Absolutely.'

She stood and moved to the half-open door, resting her elbow on top of the lower part. She was staring across to the car park. 'So what's your partner like?'

'Why?'

'No, I mean what does he look like? There's a bloke getting out of a dark-blue saloon. He's in a suit.'

'That'll be him.'

'He won't want to sit in here in that neat suit, will he?'

Goodhew rose to his feet and joined her in the doorway. 'Good point.'

She returned to sit on her bale. 'Actually, I'd like to stay in here, if you don't mind.'

He knew that so far, his meeting with Jackie had been casual, unstructured, and nothing like his training recommended. He also felt it had as much potential for proving productive as any other approach.

Goodhew waved out at Kincaide to show him where they were. His colleague carried an A4 document wallet, which he held over his head as he made a dash for the shelter of the stable overhang. He half walked, half ran, trying to avoid getting splashes on his trouser legs. The suggestion that he now sit on a hay bale was going to go down very badly.

Jackie had seemed to relax, and Goodhew didn't want to lose this opportunity to talk to her easily. He guessed with Kincaide's arrival, her earlier stiffness was set to return. There were no more than ten seconds before Kincaide would make it through the door. Goodhew turned to face Jackie, his voice little more than a whisper. 'So, tell me about Colin Willis.'

158

The guard she'd begun to drop flew back into place, but for a split second she looked betrayed. Her whole body had given a sharp and involuntary jolt; if his words were bullets, she'd just been shot.

Kincaide had drawn to a halt right next to the RAV4. He'd driven slowly down the track, trying to avoid mud splashes on his paintwork, only to find the so-called car park was nothing but mud ruts full of silty water. No doubt the air would be hanging heavy with the stench of horse shit.

He soon spotted the manure heap; it was at the far end of the yard, but it was large and steam was rising from it at an unhealthy pace. He opened his door and found that even curling up his nose did not improve the smell. Yep. Definite shit in the air.

One look at this place told him that he'd be adding a dry-cleaning bill to his expenses.

He grabbed an empty plastic folder from the pocket at the back of the passenger seat and used it as a makeshift brolly as he dashed towards the stables. Goodhew waved at him from one of the boxes and, inwardly, Kincaide groaned; what a fucking dump, not even an office.

He just hoped there wasn't a horse in there as well.

There wasn't, thank God. Goodhew and Jackie Moran were sitting together on straw bales and it didn't look like the place even possessed a chair.

In all honesty, neither of them seemed too concerned for his comfort. But Goodhew was still new to the job and might be pissed off with him for arriving late, and if this Moran girl spent most of her time down on the farm, she probably didn't know any better.

She appeared to be one of those women who wasn't basically unattractive, but did absolutely nothing to improve her looks. Her hair was unsightly, Plain Jane brown and unkempt, and why did some women think that make-up wasn't important? No wonder she was single, with just a herd of donkeys for company. Aside from that, though she wasn't in bad shape – petite, but with nicely rounded breasts and an all-over lack of flabbiness that he approved of.

'Everything OK?' Goodhew asked him.

'Yeah, absolutely.' He studied Jackie Moran for a moment or two: she looked sly. Hiding something, no doubt. He made no effort to smile. 'How far have you got, Gary?'

159

'Just idle chit-chat. We thought we'd wait for you. Miss Moran's been telling me about the horses kept here. One of them used to race.'

*Whoopdee fucking doo*. Kincaide made no comment, but couldn't stop his eyes from rolling. There were times when moments of blinding dimness like this made him wonder if Goodhew was just putting on an act. Didn't the bloke have a single ounce of initiative?

Kincaide shook Jackie Moran's hand, making sure he pressed hard enough to assert his authority. 'I'm sure DC Goodhew managed to explain already that we're investigating the murder of Lorna Spence?'

Jackie Moran just nodded and stared him. He cast a glance in Gary's direction, but the younger man was avoiding looking him in the eye. Jackie continued to stare.

'I'd like you to come into Parkside station to make a statement.'

'Is that necessary?' she asked.

He was gratified to see that her eyes widened on cue, and he imagined that the accompanying gulp must have been close to audible.

'I don't think this is a suitable place for an interview as our questioning may take several hours,' he paused, before adding with a flourish, 'We're especially interested to know about your connection with Colin Willis.'

Her expression remained unchanged and, more disappointingly, she didn't even turn pale.

A bit of a let-down. He sniffed. Maybe he'd played that trump card just a bit too early. 'We'll bring you back here for your vehicle once we've finished.'

'I can drive. I can't leave my dog here.'

Kincaide felt his forehead wrinkle involuntarily: he certainly wasn't up for having some scabby old dog in his car. 'OK, follow me. And when we get there, bring the animal in with you. We'd like to take a fur sample while we're at it.'

He smiled: this time she had definitely gone pale.

Three cars drove in convoy back to Parkside station; Kincaide led and Goodhew brought up the rear. Jackie's dog stared at him through the back window of her vehicle, and even though he stared back, his thoughts were really on Kincaide.

In Goodhew's opinion, there was nothing about Jackie Moran that had needed his colleague adopting the aggressive approach.

Bridy finally turned away from the glass and shifted around in a circle before flopping down out of sight. Having said that, if this was the same dog whose choke chain had been used to kill Colin Willis, it might be enough to justify Kincaide's full-on approach.

By the time they arrived at their destination, the rain had stopped and Cambridge was in the process of drying out. The puddles in the car park weren't muddy; they simply lay on the tarmac, reflecting the surrounding glass and concrete. A rainbow of oil floated here and there for the additional urban touch.

Kincaide walked two yards in front, while Jackie Moran followed with her hands in her pockets and her head hung low. And – like owner, like dog – Bridy trotted behind the pair of them, looking as if she was heading for an unwelcome appointment with the vet. Mud caked the dog's legs and similar splatters covered Jackie's jodhpurs and jodhpur boots. Goodhew had already noticed that her hands were grubby. Her hair still lay flat from the pressure of her crash hat.

He lengthened his stride and tapped her on the elbow.

'If you want to take a few minutes to freshen up first, that's fine.'

She nodded gratefully and, once through the main door, he pointed her towards the ladies' toilet. 'I'll wait here for you.'

The spring door creaked shut behind her, making Kincaide turn and scowl. 'What do you think you're doing?'

'She's on edge,' Goodhew said lamely.

'That's good.'

'We're not here to traumatize people.'

'We are if they deserve it.'

'Oh, right, and she's obviously a career criminal, I suppose?'

'She's a potential suspect.'

'How come?'

'Because if it was that dog's chain we found around Colin Willis' neck, then she may have killed once already – and look how the Spence woman died.'

'Drugged and asphyxiated, I recall?'

'Neck, neck. That's a bit of a coincidence.'

'One strangled, one suffocated – yes, I see your point. But until

161

we have proof that she was involved in one, let's just keep an open mind about the other.'

'Yeah, always.'

Goodhew took a breath. 'Look, I just prefer a different approach to you.'

'It's fine. You'll learn, we were all new once.'

Jackie re-emerged with clean hands, tidier hair and surrounded by a strong waft of anti-bacterial soap. She then followed Kincaide to the interview room, her heavy leather boots making loud hollow footsteps and Bridy's claws clicking away like a midget tap dancer doing a warm-up routine. Apart from that, they remained silent.

The only room available was small and chilly. It had one frosted window set up high in the wall; originally, this had been intended as a toilet. Condensation left the glass wet and the entire area smelling like damp paper. Goodhew would have thought that spending long days in the stables would have left Jackie acclimatized to the cold, but nevertheless she began to shiver as soon as she sat down and they settled into the two chairs facing her.

Bridy slunk under the table, circling twice before lying down against her mistress' feet.

Kincaide spoke first. 'Tell us what you know about the death of Colin Willis?'

Again the mention of his name failed to startle her. 'I thought you wanted to ask me about Lorna.'

'Didn't you realize they're connected?'

She shook her head. 'I don't even know who this Colin Willis is.'

'You must remember hearing about an unidentified body being pulled from the Cam back in March?'

'Yes, vaguely.' She blinked slowly, her eyelids swooping gracefully down and up. She still maintained an emotionless expression. 'Was that his name, then?'

Kincaide moved on. 'He was strangled. Did Lorna mention him?'

Goodhew cut in. 'Along with the body we recovered a dog's choke chain. That's why we'd like to take a hair sample from Bridy.'

'Fur,' Kincaide corrected.

'For purposes of elimination?' she asked.

Kincaide spoke again. 'We will be forced to insist if you don't agree to it.'

'Really?' She sighed. The interview was still only in the first twenty minutes, but each time she spoke she sounded increasingly weary. 'On what grounds?'

'Yes, for purposes of elimination,' Kincaide conceded. His response was a deliberate echo of her own question, and that seemed to amuse him. He leant back in his chair as he waited for her to speak further.

She turned her head towards Goodhew, but kept her eyes fixed on Kincaide for a beat longer, before slowly shifting her gaze too. If that was supposed to convey any kind of message, it didn't reach him. As soon as she'd emerged from the ladies' toilet, she'd seemed to switch into a partially catatonic state. Goodhew wondered whether she was inwardly reciting some deep-relaxation mantra, since her calmness was now bordering on the unnatural. She spoke only slowly, showing mild interest and zero anxiety. He wasn't convinced. Either through strict self-control, or as an involuntary reaction to her situation, she had somehow deployed a huge and effective layer of emotional insulation; their questions didn't appear to be making a dent.

Goodhew decided to give her an opening. 'Have you lost a choke chain at any point? Or could someone else have used it?'

Again she blinked before replying. 'I'm perfectly happy for you to take a sample.'

'Thank you, Ms Moran. Colin Willis was a distinctive-looking man, I'd now like to show you a photograph.'

'Of him dead?' she asked bluntly.

'We have a couple of previous shots. I can find one of those.'

'I'd prefer it.'

Goodhew flicked through until he found the two-year-old mug shot, and passed it across. He put the file back on the table, and Kincaide quickly picked it up. 'I'll find the other one,' he explained.

Jackie did the slow blink thing again, before raising the photograph into her line of sight. It was as if it took a couple of seconds before what she was now viewing connected with her brain. The change in her was minuscule: simply a dilation of the pupils. 'He was a criminal, then?'

Before, Goodhew had a chance to respond, Kincaide spoke. 'Have you seen this yet?'

She looked towards him, and so did Goodhew. Kincaide was holding up a morgue photo of Willis' head and torso. It was one of those shots that gave a very good idea of how the morgue must have smelt, and it wasn't pleasant.

# TWENTY-NINE

DI Marks intercepted Goodhew as he walked back from the canteen with a sandwich. It had been the last one that looked vaguely edible: turkey salad, according to the label. The two slices of bread had already begun to curl, no sign of even a lettuce leaf, and the uniformly thin slice of too-pink filling looked more like a play mat for salmonella than anything that had ever boasted feathers.

The sandwich failed to rouse Goodhew from his current vicinity of depressed/embarrassed: depressed because he'd failed to notice that his fledgling relationship, far from being just one-sided, actually didn't exist, and embarrassed because it was now crystal clear to everyone concerned what an idiot he had been.

He gingerly lifted the corner of one slice for further scrutiny. He hadn't eaten since breakfast and, although he didn't feel very hungry, he'd decided that missing lunch reeked too heavily of self-pity. He looked up as soon as he heard Marks' voice.

'Follow me.'

Marks headed towards the stairs, and Goodhew hurried behind, risking a bite of the sandwich. It tasted of . . . bread. He decided to keep eating. Marks led the way down the stairs and across the car park towards his maroon Mazda. He pressed the remote and the doors clicked.

'Are we going somewhere?'

'I can now see how you made it to detective,' Marks replied drily. He slid a folded sheet of paper from his pocket and passed it to Goodhew, who waited until he'd buckled himself into the passenger seat before opening it; the top was inscribed with the name 'Martin

Reed', followed by a Bedford address. The remainder of the page just listed directions for the journey there from Cambridge.

'We're going to Bedford then?'

'Is it your special day for stating the obvious? I thought I'd bring you along in the hope I'd receive some *intelligent* input. Is that going to be too much to ask?'

Goodhew assumed the question was rhetorical, and so kept quiet.

Marks reversed out of the parking space and simultaneously waved a hand in the general direction of the piece of paper. 'That's one of our possible Emma connections.'

Goodhew was aware that some of the other officers working on the investigation had been dredging archives and various databases for any possible explanation of the words written on Lorna's palms.

'So they found something?'

Marks raised one eyebrow slightly, in an are-you-taking-the-piss way, and managed to stop short of saying, 'No, we're off to Bedford just for fun.' 'DC Charles came across it: a missing girl called Joanne Reed, who called herself by her middle name, Emma.'

'Doesn't ring a bell. Was it considered suspicious?'

'You won't remember it because it was 1996. Martin Reed is her father. The nationals ran reports early on, but there were no clues and no sightings so it dropped out of the news pretty quickly.'

'No body?'

'Absolutely nothing.'

'So why are we interested?'

'You've spoken to Jackie Moran, and she claims she doesn't know an Emma, right?'

'Yes.'

'Well, Jackie and this Emma girl were in the same year at Northampton University. Jackie Moran was still a student there when Joanne Reed disappeared.'

Within fifteen minutes they were on the slip-road joining the A14, and Goodhew knew they had a good hour's drive ahead of them. The road was busy and Marks accelerated, then cruised at a steady 65mph. It was fast enough to overtake lorries, but slow enough to be overtaken by almost everyone else. And it gave Goodhew plenty of time to think about Jackie Moran.

* * *

166

Martin Reed's house was the right-hand door of a pair of ex-council semis. The exterior was cream, and saucer-sized bedding plants lined one side of a short driveway at the edge of a tightly cropped lawn. The front of the house had only three windows, two up and one down, made bright white by a set of matching nets. The front door itself was old-style, aluminium-framed with leaf-patterned frosted glass, and it too glinted with obsessive cleanliness.

In normal circumstances Goodhew hated ringing door bells; you press the button and if you can't hear the bell from the outside, you're then left with the dilemma of whether to just wait or whether to knock. If you do knock, it seems almost guaranteed that the door will be opened by someone whose first words are 'OK, OK, what's the rush'. Goodhew pressed the bell once and the door was opened within seconds by a grey-haired woman in her early fifties. She somhow managed to look exasperated and welcoming at the same time.

'Mrs Reed?' Marks asked.

'Yep, but not the first one, so I'm no good to you. It's Martin you really want.' She spoke slowly, as though reluctant to engage them in conversation. 'He's round the back,' she explained. 'Whatever you're here about, I hope it's worth it. He's already gone into one of his moods. I'd rather you stayed away than stir everything up, especially if it's going to be for nothing again.'

They found him standing at the top of a stepladder cleaning the already spotless windows, working a cloth up into the top corners of the glass, making small, dedicated circles.

His hand stopped moving and he turned his head, oh so slowly, to look over his left shoulder. His attention dwelt on Marks for a full thirty seconds and then, with a lethargic blink, he shifted his gaze and set it down again on Goodhew. No one spoke at first, and the effect was like a slo-mo moment in a movie where he read their faces and they read his.

Martin Reed was a giant of a man, at least six four and weighing in the region of twenty stone. His hair had receded, leaving him with just a dark, wavy clump on top. The sides were clipped short, as though he'd once sported a flat-top and had never quite grown out of it. He'd been good-looking when he was younger, and he'd never quite grown out of that either.

He stayed at the top of the ladder, clearly in no rush to invest any of his time in descending. 'How can I help?' His voice was deep but soft.

'We'd like to ask you about Joanne,' Marks replied.

'Well, I realize that.' There was no sarcasm there, just an acceptance that the police would only ever turn up to ask about his daughter. 'You haven't found her, have you?'

'No, I'm sorry, we haven't.'

'OK.' He came down from the ladder then, and led them into the house. They stood in the kitchen and waited while he put the window-cleaning cloths and sprays back in the cupboard under the sink. He put the items away one at a time, folding the chamois and placing it on the shelf, leaving the sponge squarely on top, then straightening the bottles on either side.

Goodhew glanced around the kitchen: every surface was clean and devoid of clutter. The washing-up sponge was precisely located in the middle space between the two taps and a tea towel folded in quarters hung from a drawer. It looked ironed.

A lone pen had been left on the windowsill, but he guessed it didn't count as clutter, because it had been placed exactly parallel to the edge. There were good odds that the rest of the house would match. Martin Reed washed his hands and dried them on the tea towel, then replaced it in precisely the same position. Here the pristine and symmetrical ruled, as the big man struggled to keep control of his surroundings. He reminded Goodhew of a child on best behaviour, trying too hard, concentrating on every small task, and almost imploding with the strain. Instinctively, Goodhew knew that this was a man who rarely left home.

They were led into the front room, where Mr Reed invited them to sit on the settee. 'You met my wife, Mary?'

They nodded.

'She won't be joining us unless you really need her to.'

Marks replied. 'No, that's fine. She said you'd "gone into one of your moods". What did she mean?'

Reed did the slo-mo blinking thing again. 'She knew what I was like when we married. She keeps me sane, I suppose. Even now I get keyed up whenever you turn up. I tell myself not to be disappointed, but I can't help wondering if this time . . . I try to put the thought out of my head, but it still sneaks back in. I kid myself that I have no expectations left, but in the hour before you're due to arrive, I'm counting down the minutes. It would be much easier for me if you could tell me the gist of the news by phone each time. Is that possible?'

'I'm sorry, Mr Reed, but we're now working on a different case. There's a slim possibility of a link, but that's all. Just the name Emma.'

'That's it? The name Emma?' Martin Reed shook his head, sagging as if the fresh disappointment had winded him.

'The case notes state that Joanne was also known as Emma. Is that correct?'

Martin Reed spread out his large hands, palms up. 'It was nothing. She'd always preferred her middle name, and so decided to be known by it while she was at university. But Emma's not a rare name, and it was never a big deal to Jo as far as I could tell. She used it briefly. To my mind, it seemed to be about . . .' He paused to make the quotes sign with his fingers '. . . self-discovery. Some kids go spiky-haired or dabble with drugs. In her case, she changed her name. One of the detectives on the original team wondered if it was a pseudonym she used when undertaking something dodgy. As if. She was a very contented teenager, in fact. We waited for her to become the typical rebel, but it never happened.' It sounded as though his words were practised – that he'd said them over and over in the last ten years – but that made them no less sincere.

Marks plugged on. 'We also have some photographs we'd like to show you. Just let me know if anyone in them looks familiar.' Marks slid the photos from the file, then laid it on the cushion between himself and Goodhew. He handed the pictures to Mr Reed, one at a time.

The five-by-sevens looked tiny in the man's huge hands. At each one he shook his head. 'These are recent?'

'Fairly.'

'So I could be trying to recognize people I last knew ten years ago?'

'Possibly.'

'No one looks familiar – but if I stare at them long enough, they all could. Do you have any idea how many people I've met since Jo vanished?'

Goodhew lifted the front cover of the file. Plenty of sheets of paper inside. Words and more words. But hearing one person's perceptions always had more resonance for him than a whole file of statements.

He was aware that Marks was now mentioning names, and continuing to probe but getting nowhere. He showed signs of drawing their visit to a close, so Goodhew kept his eyes diverted from Marks, knowing that his next words would derail his boss' line of questioning. He placed his hand firmly on Joanne's file, like it was at risk of opening by itself. 'We have all the details here, but would you be prepared to now tell us what happened – just as you remember it?'

Mr Reed looked at him like he'd just noticed him for the very first time. 'Why? This isn't your current case.'

Goodhew didn't have an answer to that. Morbid curiosity or nosiness? Had he just asked an inappropriate question without thinking it through? So far, Joanne appeared to have zero connection to Lorna, and that made his intervention out of line.

He continued to avoid Marks and simply replied honestly: 'Just in case.'

Whatever Martin Reed's reservations, he started talking. 'I used to fear the progression of old age and I was scared of dying. I imagined turning into first my dad, then my granddad, seeing that as the most depressing descent into oblivion. The thought of watching my children turn into adolescents, then adults, then become middle-aged – watching them peak and then decline – I used to feel repulsed by the idea. Now it seems to me like heaven. Joanne would be thirty this year, but I don't do what-ifs about anything except her age. Annie, my first wife, did. She what-iffed until it killed her. She didn't just mourn her daughter; she pined for the wedding Jo might have had, the children and the career, and on and on.'

'Was she an only child?' Marks asked.

'Oh yes.' The happy-sad nerves at the corners of Martin Reed's mouth underwent a flutter of involuntary twitches. 'Imagine having three, four, five kids. You couldn't watch them all, not all the time, but we only had one and we still didn't keep her safe. Logically we knew it wasn't our fault, like logic makes a difference.

'Somewhere between the first and second anniversaries, I accepted she was dead. Not consciously, but I sensed she wasn't in any TV crowds, or in front of me in the check-out queue, or on the other end of a ringing phone. My wife felt differently, though, and to Annie I'd now done the unforgivable: abandoned our child.'

Martin Reed picked up the TV remote from the arm of the chair, licked his thumb, then rubbed at a small area on one side of the control. The silence between them lengthened. Goodhew spoke first.

'Mr Reed?'

Martin Reed snapped back into talk mode. 'The very night before Jo vanished, Annie and I watched a TV documentary about parents who'd lost children. It said how high the resulting divorce rate was, and I couldn't understand it. I thought they'd need each other even more, imagined them clinging together to get through their grief. After all, I assumed the parents would be the only ones who could really understand.

'In reality, I think of it as the last night of our marriage. I don't mean that to sound melodramatic, but until Jo disappeared, we'd lived a charmed life: twenty-odd years of home and family, with nothing more serious happening than in every other household round here.

'You lose a child and you do understand each other's grief at first, but if you get out of step with each other, it's all over. Suddenly each of you is alone; I'd have a good day and Annie would have a bad one. Then she would resent seeing me coping when she couldn't. And vice versa.'

The next time he fell silent, nobody interrupted. Goodhew felt he ought to coax him into continuing, but the only thing he could think to ask Martin Reed was whether he was all right. And very clearly he wasn't, so they just waited out the silence while more imaginary grime was scratched from the remote control.

Suddenly he spoke. 'You can't share any happy memories with your partner any more without feeling like you're deliberately trying to cause them pain. I'd talked to everyone about Jo, pretty much non-stop sometimes – everyone except Annie. Between us, the mention of Jo became the biggest taboo.'

This time, Martin Reed seemed to have definitely finished, but Goodhew waited for a few seconds until he was sure it really was his turn to speak. If there had been a clock in the room, this was the point where it would have ticked loudly. 'From your own point of view, how well has the investigation been handled?'

Reed drew a steady breath and leant back in his chair. He looked up at the ceiling for a while. 'I'm not a bitter man,' he said, 'but I find it painful to accept that whoever is responsible for her death may never be caught. I'm not wishing I could blame anyone. In my heart of hearts, I believe she was dead well before the alarm was even raised. That's because Tanya, her room-mate, rang us on a Wednesday, halfway through *Morse*, saying that Jo hadn't been seen since the previous Friday.'

'Why did she wait so long?'

'Apparently Jo had spent several other nights away, and Tanya just assumed that Jo was seeing someone.'

'But Jo herself never said so?'

'No, but that would be typical. She was very guarded in that way.'

'What about the police?'

'They never found anyone significant. They asked us a few questions about her sex life.' He shook his head, still feeling disbelief. 'She was only twenty, and we were her parents. Do you think we wanted to talk about our child even having a sexual history, never mind any "kinky habits", as one of them put it? Let's just say, we weren't surprised when that turned out to be a dead end.'

'You never thought of anything that wasn't followed up?'

'No, we never felt left in the dark. *Never*. You may not be on Jo's case this time, but I still appreciate your time. I don't stop, you know.'

Goodhew wasn't sure what Reed meant. 'Thinking about her, you mean?'

'No, I mean I don't stop. I don't like going out, I find it easier to stay in and keep busy. But a visit from you gives me hope, lets me unburden a bit too. Even visits like the last one, essentially nothing more than a courtesy call, but it let me know you hadn't forgotten.'

Goodhew flicked open the file and scanned the most recent details. Martin Reed continued to talk, Goodhew kept listening, punctuating the gaps with an appropriate grunt or 'hmm'. Finally, when he was certain that he wasn't making a mistake, he said, 'And the last visit was when exactly?'

They'd made phone calls, checked and double-checked. Whoever had visited Martin Reed had not been a police officer. Mr Reed was vague, remembering him only as a man in his late fifties. But no name, and he said he hadn't asked for ID. But then, he hadn't today either.

They drove away.

Marks shook his head. 'Talking about it obviously helps him.'

'Poor bloke. The best result he's ever going to get will be bad news.'

'You did well, though.'

'Did I?' Goodhew hadn't thought so.

'The mystery visitor was interesting.'

'But possibly irrelevant?'

'We'll see.' Marks pulled out, on to a busier road. 'While I was on the phone, I was briefed on the initial forensics report.' He glanced across, as if checking that Goodhew was listening before continuing. 'As we know, death was by asphyxiation, but she'd also been drugged with GHB. Heard of it?'

Goodhew nodded. 'Gamma hydroxybutyrate, usually in liquid form. Colourless and odourless, but with a slight salty taste. Causes dizziness, confusion and memory loss.'

'Very good. Well, Lorna Spence's was administered to her in coffee. The report estimates that she ingested about four times the amount that would be expected to cause incapacitation. It's a drug often connected with date rape cases.'

Goodhew scanned the report. 'Had she been raped?'

'Semen was present, but nothing else to indicate anything conclusive either way.'

Goodhew thought for a moment, then spoke, 'I'd like to go back to Lorna Spence's flat.'

Marks cast a sharp glance in his direction. 'Why?'

'To search it again.'

'And I assume you have a good reason?'

'Three actually. Firstly and secondly, we've found out about Joanne Reed and Colin Willis only *since* the flat was searched.'

'OK, and thirdly?'

'The search was conducted very quickly, and I think something's been missed.'

'Kincaide would say you're trying to show him up.'

'I'm really not.'

Marks stared at the road in front of him, but far too intently to be concentrating on his driving alone. 'Do I need to know anything about how the "Emma" story was leaked to last night's newspaper?' he said.

'No.'

'You're sure?'

'Absolutely.'

Goodhew had no idea how the two topics could be linked, but his reply seemed to prompt his boss's next decision.

Every hint of warmth had dropped from Marks' voice as he replied, 'I don't want you going anywhere near Lorna Spence's flat, Gary. If there is to be another search, it won't involve you.'

# THIRTY

For the second evening in a row, Goodhew agreed to meet Kincaide at The Snug. They sat at the same seats at the same table, Kincaide with his red wine and Goodhew with coffee. But it didn't feel the same as it had twenty-four hours earlier.

Kincaide was talking, or rather bragging, about his part in the interview with Jackie Moran, and Goodhew had all but stopped listening. One day of working closely with Kincaide had confirmed to him that they had nothing in common. And, more frustratingly, he knew he could have saved himself the trouble of finding out, because Kincaide was just the way he'd struck Goodhew on their first introduction.

He reminded himself that he wasn't the one that needed putting straight, and made the effort to tune back in to what Kincaide was saying.

'Did you see her face when I showed her that photo of the corpse?'

Goodhew tossed his spoon back on to the saucer. 'What was that about?' he snapped. 'You obviously thought it was clever. Did it actually achieve anything? No. Do we look crass, insensitive, stupid? Yes, I think so.'

Kincaide swigged from his wine glass, downing half. 'What's put you in such a shitty mood?' He nevertheless sounded indifferent.

Goodhew lowered his voice again. 'I was embarrassed even to be sitting next to you.'

'But happy to come out for a drink?'

'Maybe I came to tell you how I felt. I thought you were out of line and I can't think of any rational reason for you treating her like that. And now you're sitting here, bragging about bullying a witness.'

Kincaide emptied his glass. 'Jackie Moran is a suspect, and I thought you were being way too soft with her. I was just trying to even things up. If you want to call that bullying, that's up to you.' He stood and glared down at Goodhew. 'This mood you're in is pissing me off.'

The door closed after Kincaide, and Goodhew gave his half-cold coffee another stir. He followed it with a bottle of Stella. The sound system was doling out a cover version of a Ray Charles number; take a great song, then murder it – it had to be a ploy to make punters drink more. He drank his beer and let his annoyance subside, but he still didn't buy Kincaide's excuses.

Twenty minutes later, Goodhew left The Snug and turned down Burleigh Street, and then Fitzroy Street, heading up the middle of the pedestrianized shopping area. There were still plenty of people around, mainly moving in small groups. One group of girls waited for their friend as she used an ATM. Two more had their heads together, giggling as they read a text message. A young couple walked by, holding each other around the waist. One girl walked alone. It seemed so safe, yet he wished she wouldn't do it. She glanced away as she saw him look at her. Once she was beyond him he guessed she may have looked back again to double-check that he wouldn't turn and follow; even when people swore they were safe their actions contradicted them.

He had always been in the habit of checking doorways and alleys as he passed them. Even front gardens sometimes. And it was his automatic custom of checking in all directions that led him to look far down a side street and spot a Vauxhall that he recognized.

It was parked sideways on, with its passenger door facing him, but too far along the side road for him to see the registration. But he'd long known that identifying cars can be like identifying people. A person can be spotted by their gait, or stance, or distinctive dress style, a car by the way its suspension sags, or its aerial sways, or even the unique fingerprint of stickers in the back window. This one he was certain he knew simply from the combination of flashy non-factory alloys and the suit jacket hanging just inside of the rear door. This wasn't Kincaide's usual part of town, but it almost certainly was his car.

* * *

176

Hanging around in a bar with Gary Goodhew fell well short of Kincaide's idea of a good evening out. He checked his watch, and then double-checked that he'd left his mobile switched on. Goodhew was still banging on about his treatment of Jackie Moran; sometimes he just couldn't fathom the bloke's logic. Yesterday, the nostalgia over some old pub and the urge to track a witness down at eight in the evening. Today he was complaining that the same witness hadn't been treated like their new best friend. As far as Kincaide could see, Goodhew spent far too much time fretting about work. In fact, Goodhew never seemed to think about much else. Kincaide tried to flash back to the time when he'd had that level of commitment to the job.

Again his thoughts returned to his mobile; he wished the text would arrive. While he waited, he decided he'd made a more than adequate job of keeping his side of the conversation flowing. And while he wasn't one for enjoying anticipation, by the time the phone bleeped, he wouldn't have been surprised if just the sound of it had given him a hard on.

He read the new message in his inbox: '10 mins usual place.' Part of him wanted to boast to Goodhew and to own up about what was going on. But another part of him, and arguably the better part, resisted the temptation. Goodhew was still too idealistic to understand how an affair could negate some of the frustrations of marriage.

After leaving The Snug, Kincaide had driven to a convenient parking spot at the rear of the Dreams bed showroom, about halfway between the police station and the pub. It was usually a good spot, a small yard that was deserted once the shops closed for the night and a discreet place for them to meet.

Arriving first, he realized that another car occupied the car park. Its windows were already steamed, he'd need to park up somewhere else. He sat in the driver's seat and waited; within two minutes the passenger door opened and she slipped into the seat beside him. She smelt flowery, like she'd just sprayed herself with one of those cheap body sprays that teenagers use before they discover real perfume. He liked it – a lot – more than enough for him to feel the first stirrings of an erection.

'I got here as soon as I could,' Mel began.

They'd been meeting at least twice a week for over a month. He pointed at the other car. 'We'll need to find somewhere else.'

'We could leave the car here and go for a drink. It would be nice if we could just talk tonight.'

He grinned and reached across, taking her hand and pressing it hard against his crotch. 'Are you kidding? I can't start walking around in this condition.' She tried to slide her hand away, but he held on to it. 'Hey, I'm just teasing, and I *was* listening this morning. We'll park up somewhere else and just talk.'

The ideal spot turned up about half a mile away where part-way along a cul-de-sac, they found a right-hand spur which had been blocked off to through traffic. At most there would be an infrequent passer-by; the alley was a poor shortcut to anywhere apart from accesing the alley behind the terraced houses.

He glanced across at her as they drove. The skirt she was wearing finished a couple of inches above her knees, further up now that she was sitting. Her legs were otherwise bare and catching a glimpse of the soft skin between her thighs was enough to keep him hard. She could always turn him on in a way his frigid wife Janice never had.

'How's your head?' he asked.

Her expression softened. She always appreciated his concern. 'It only feels bruised if I touch it.'

'You know you should press charges.' He knew she wouldn't, but said it anyway. Her boyfriend, Toby, had slapped her around several times before, and he was sure that Mel was already acclimatized to the routine of receiving aggression and offering forgiveness. He'd noticed how some women seemed to have a thirst for abuse. One day Toby would be ready to move on, and it would be typical if Mel then went on to another violent relationship. In the meantime, the issue of his marriage wasn't going to be a problem, so long as she had a psycho boyfriend to keep secrets from.

'If I tried to leave him, he'd come after me.'

'Not if he was under arrest.'

'He'd come after you if he knew about you.'

From the corner of his eye, he could see that she was studying his face and it made him feel as though he was being tested. He kept his voice level. 'And how would he get to know? That sounds like a threat, Mel.'

Nothing else was said until he'd finished parking. Then he looked over and saw that she was fighting back tears. 'All I was going to tell you was that Toby's been hanging around at lunchtimes, and that he's getting suspicious, but your first assumption is that I'm trying to pressurize you. What sort of person do you think I am?'

The evening was morphing into aggravation, so he tried to sound soothing. 'Hey,' he whispered, 'you know I didn't mean to upset you. We're getting very intense, and I thought you were forgetting what we'd agreed.' Her tears didn't recede or increase; they merely sat on hold. 'Sometimes I want to just blurt it out to Jan, but I know I mustn't.'

She bit on her bottom lip and said nothing.

'We both agreed on it, didn't we?' he continued.

She nodded, and he leant forward to kiss her. His timing was obviously right; her lips insantly parted and, after the first tentative moments, he felt her hand cup his upper arm and her thumb gently rub his bicep. He pulled away first, just far enough that there was nowhere else for her to look but into his eyes.

'That's still OK with you, isn't it? I don't want you to be uncomfortable with this.'

She leant forward to kiss him then. It was funny how setting such limits on their relationship invariably seemed to produce results. He guessed it might be one of those contrary truths: tell a needy woman what she can't have, and that's what she'll instantly chase.

He pulled her closer and slipped his tongue between her lips. He found the waistband of her skirt and from there slid his hand up and down her spine, marvelling at the tautness of her soft skin. Her back arched as if to let him know that her breasts were available to him, but instead of undoing her bra he traced his middle finger over the sheer fabric, around her body until he was stroking her right nipple.

Her tongue then dipped into his mouth with more urgency and this time, when he pressed her hand against his trousers, she didn't pull away. He encouraged her fingers to find the zip. Her hands were small but dextrous and, as ever, it took only seconds before she had him in the firm grasp of her delicate fingers. He stroked her hair as they continued to kiss, and he waited until her massaging was rhythmic before beginning to tease their mouths apart and gently nudge her face towards his penis.

He settled back further into the corner between his seat and the door. She ran her tongue along the shaft, then drew him into her mouth. God, she was good at this. He adjusted the rear-view mirror to give him a good view of anyone approaching the driver's side of the car and split his attention between it, the rear of the vehicle and the passenger side.

No other vehicles entered the street and, at first, the only pedestrians visible were those passing at the far end of the road. After a while, he stopped bothering to check the mirrors, but continued to watch, now through lazy, half-closed eyes.

Inadvertently his wife slipped into his thoughts, ensuring that he felt a pang of guilt, but he decided that a small dose of guilt was preferable to a bucketload of her indifference, so he quickly pushed her out of his mind again.

Another minute passed and he ceased to care about whether anyone spotted them. He now only watched the gentle bobbing of Mel's head. He wanted to climax slowly.

It was only a semi-conscious decision that prompted him to walk towards Kincaide's car. Goodhew's feet began heading that way before his brain had time to consider whether there was any good reason to.

He could see that Kincaide was sitting in the driver's seat, partially facing in his direction, but although Goodhew raised his hand in greeting, no acknowledgement came in return. Kincaide was stock-still, perhaps concentrating on a phone call.

Goodhew slowed, feeling suddenly as though he was intruding. But with only a few houses between him and the car, there was nowhere to turn off and doing a 180 degree about-face would look pretty stupid.

He slowed some more. He had picked out something else now, draped over the rear of the passenger seat, and an uneasy feeling began crawling up his spine. In the moment between seeing it and recognizing it as Mel's red mac, he chose to take the about-face option. But somehow in that time, he saw Kincaide look in his direction, then jerk upright. Then the back of Mel's head appeared. She turned towards him even as he turned away from her.

The car slipped out of the edge of his field of vision, and he hurried away, far faster than he'd approached.

# THIRTY-ONE

Goodhew knew as he hurried away that this would be no early night, so he went to the cinema and caught Kirsten Dunst's latest film. He'd never heard of it before he arrived, and by the time it had finished, he had forgotten what it was called. But that didn't matter because, in his opinion, Kirsten was one of the two movie stars who could chuck away their scripts and still deserve Oscars.

Kirsten had stared into a mirror, feeling sorry for herself, then she'd cast Goodhew an empathetic glance. He'd sighed and wondered how he'd allowed himself to be blind to Mel and Kincaide's affair, why he felt so let down by Kincaide, and what gave him even the right to feel hurt. Finally, he realized that, despite wishing things were different, they weren't, and it was really none of his business. He'd left the cinema before the end credits rolled.

When Goodhew let himself back into his flat, it was ten minutes past ten. There were no messages on the answerphone. He stood by the window for the next few minutes, wanting to call his grandmother and hating himself for hurting her, but still unable to ring.

Beyond the shadowy expanse of Parker's Piece the police station lay quiet; there were only a few lights on around the building and just a few officers would be on duty. Marks was right: a fresh start in the morning would be the best thing.

Goodhew padded into the kitchen, a narrow room with all the appliances on the right and the units fitted on the left. Under a small sash window a red drop-leaf table occupied the far wall, on which stood only a portable TV, with a calendar of Hawaiian sunsets propped against it.

Goodhew decided to make himself an omelette. He used his last four eggs and threw in some ham and cheese with a sprinkling of black pepper.

He switched on the portable TV and flicked rapidly through the channels while the olive oil heated in the pan. Sport ... sport ... relationships ... He kept flicking. Cop show ... game show ... black-and-white film. He paused. He recognized Veronica Lake and he didn't switch over.

Veronica and Kirsten on the same night; it should have felt like his lucky day, but seeing Kincaide and Mel had thumped the scales down in the opposite direction.

He turned back to the pan and finished cooking, then he leant against the worktop with plate in one hand and fork in the other, and watched someone else trying to solve a different murder.

But before the second mouthful, he knew that it wasn't enough to keep him at home.

# THIRTY-TWO

It took Goodhew just fifteen minutes to walk from Parkside pool to Rolfe Street, Lorna's little street, where gentrified townhouses squeezed together in neat order, their single front steps like children's feet, lined up and waiting one step back from the kerb.

Midges danced in the glow from the streetlamps, parting only to let him pass as he strode through their light pools. His footsteps beat a crisp rhythm on the pavement. It was late enough for the streets to be empty, but early enough for the sound of him to be masked by the television sets, turned up louder than a normal speaking voice in almost every home.

Except Lorna's, of course.

Her flat remained still and silent, the letterbox sealed from the inside, and the windows strapped with striped police tape.

The flat below hers was silent too, unoccupied and for sale when she died. Now still unoccupied and probably unsaleable, and Goodhew was glad of that. The last thing he needed was an anxious neighbour reporting footsteps overhead.

He reached into his pocket and wrapped his gloved fingers around the key. He rubbed his thumb along the teeth of it and silently prayed that the lock had not been changed. He slid it in and turned it quickly. The door opened, and he sighed with relief. Using the stairs was a far easier prospect than shinning up the drainpipe and across the ground-floor flat roof.

This way there would be no evidence of forced entry.

He closed the door behind him and began to feel his way up the stairs. Dust and mustiness had already invaded, pushing out any lingering breath of Lorna from the air.

He reached the landing and groped around, identifying first the door frame, then the door, then the handle. The door opened silently into a large, all-purpose living area. Enough light trickled through the sash window to pick out the shape of a settee and coffee table, and a circular dining set over to one side.

Both the kitchen and bathroom were at the rear of the flat, overlooked only by houses in a road running parallel to Rolfe Street. Turning the lights on in these two rooms was still a risk but, by his reckoning, one worth taking.

He chose the bathroom first, and made sure to close the door behind him before pulling the light cord. The suite had been changed circa 1978, he guessed. Those days when green toilets, in any shade from lichen to avocado, were considered desirable. This one was sage, with marble-effect tiles, pine fittings and cream walls. It was not attractive, but it was clean and well kept. All the surfaces were now bare. He clicked open the mirrored door of the medicine cabinet: that too was empty. He hoped the kitchen would yield more.

He switched off the bathroom light and proceeded from there across the hall and into the kitchen. Again he shut the door behind him, and this time he twisted the blinds shut before flicking on the overhead strip-light.

First he opened and closed each cupboard for a quick assessment. Plenty had been removed from the kitchen: the wastebin, tea towels, fruit from the bowl and any perishables from the fridge. But plenty had been left: glasses, china, cutlery, unopened jars and tins of food.

The units here were fitted, more modern than in the bathroom, and sported beech veneer with polished granite tops and thin chrome handles. He started by tapping and tugging at the four-inch fascia running around the bottom of the units. It was secure and bore no sign of ever having been disturbed.

Two tall stools were tucked under a tiny breakfast bar; he grabbed one and climbed on it to inspect the tops of the units. He then checked inside each separate appliance, and even in the pots of odds and ends under the sink. He only wished he knew what, if anything, he hoped to find.

It was ten minutes later before he started on the food cupboard. He guessed Lorna had eaten out a lot, or maybe hadn't eaten much at all; her cupboard catered just for breakfast and snacks. One shelf was filled with tins of soup, and not just plain old Heinz Tomato like his own kitchen boasted. There were at least a dozen upmarket varieties, from asparagus to lobster bisque. He lifted and shook each can, and when he was content that each was still unopened, he moved on to the rows of spreads arranged on the shelf below.

Most of the jams were also unopened and stood with their labels neatly facing forwards. The two jars of peanut butter, one crunchy and one smooth, told a different story. Their inner sides were scraped clear, so that only a few spoonfuls remained at the bottom of each. Behind the peanut butter was the familiar fat-cheeked shape of a Marmite jar. People either loved it or hated it, but Lorna must have been in the 'loved it' camp as she had three jars of the stuff on the go. Goodhew picked up the first jar: liquorice-coloured stains streaked the black glass. He unscrewed the yellow plastic lid and glanced inside: just Marmite with a couple of flecks of butter.

He replaced the lid and noticed the seal was gone from one of the other two jars. He felt a kick of excitement as he snatched up the used jar at the rear, which was altogether too clean looking. He unscrewed it quickly, noticing it felt light enough to be almost empty. Under the lid was jammed a ball of cotton wool.

When he was a kid, his mum had kept cotton wool in the top of vitamin bottles. He had never understood why, but now he sensed he'd find tablets in this jar too.

There weren't many of them, he estimated about twenty. And they weren't all the same, but a mix of red capsules and torpedo-shaped pills. He replaced the cotton wool and returned the jar to its place at the back of the shelf.

He ran his gaze along the shelf below. The lid of a vinegar bottle protruded from behind a coffee jar. He pulled it out and immediately saw the liquid was clear. He removed his glove and dripped a splash on to his finger. As soon as it hit his tongue he smiled. Jackpot.

Later on, he'd wonder how different things would have been if he'd just replaced the bottle and left. But he couldn't have done that.

Not really. Not when the rest of the flat beckoned him. He checked the bedroom curtains, making sure the heavy red velvet overlapped to seal in the light. Then he used his torch to search the room. Her wrought-iron bedstead had been stripped of its sheets. Her stereo stood beside the bed, accompanied by a stack of a dozen CDs. He ran the beam of torchlight down their spines. The last one was *The Best of Blondie*; the rest were modern chart compilations.

He moved his torch around the room and went over to Lorna's wardrobe. The door creaked as he opened it. He stopped and listened. Had he heard something else too? No, he'd just been in the house too long. Time to leave.

'In a minute, in a minute,' he whispered to himself, and shone his torch into the cupboard.

Most of her clothes still hung from the rail, though some had fallen off. He knelt to check the bottom of the wardrobe. Then froze. He heard a creak on the stairs, then a whisper. Shit. There was only one option; he clicked off his torch and felt his way into the cupboard. From somewhere near the landing a woman's voice hissed, 'I'll start in the bedroom.'

Goodhew pulled both doors to within an inch of shutting. Above his head, clothes swayed and the hangers click-clacked against each other. Footsteps entered the room and he froze.

'You do the kitchen.' This time she spoke clearly and he recognized the voice as Victoria Nugent's.

'OK,' a man replied.

Goodhew could now see nothing, so he half closed his eyes and just listened. She was wearing stilettos and she moved with short steps that echoed on the bare boards. He heard the curtains open and shafts of moonlight slipped into the wardrobe. Not good. Then her shadow fell across the crack between the doors and he knew she was about to open them.

Victoria had spent a giddy afternoon riding on an adrenalin surge. She had made a mistake – no – it had been an oversight. But now she had a plan. In her mind's eye she'd visualized every move. Especially the finale.

As they entered Lorna's flat, she realized she was rushing up the stairs too quickly and checked herself. She had to be convincing. She would fail if she let her motives become transparent.

He followed, more heavy-footed, less enthusiastic. But that would change.

'Where will it be?' he asked.

'I don't know.' She led the way across the living room; she knew the route, even in the dark. She made straight for the bedroom, but turned back to him at the doorway. 'I'll start in the bedroom.'

He stopped in his tracks, not sure what she was expecting him to do.

'You do the kitchen.'

Her heart thumped, but she didn't allow herself to think about how dangerous it all was. It was good that he seemed more nervous than her, even though she had no doubt that she could easily lead him where he didn't want to go.

She crossed to the window, the curtains rasping as they were hauled back on their tracks. That was better, she could see the room properly now, without turning on the light.

She knew she still had at least a few minutes while he poked around in the kitchen units.

Directly across from her was the room's only wardrobe, which would be the logical place to start. She opened the doors simultaneously, then, without even a glance inside she made a point of slamming them. Then she equally loudly opened and closed the chest of drawers.

Finally, she retrieved a tissue from her sleeve and lay down on one side of the bed. She kept the tissue pressed to her lips and did her best to feign emotional exhaustion. She was no great actress, but firmly believed that people noticed only what they chose to.

It didn't take him more than a few minutes to search the kitchen, then he came to find her. He stopped in the doorway and nodded towards the open curtains. 'Someone may see us,' he said. Then he looked at her. 'What's wrong?'

'You didn't find it, did you?' Her voice was thick with emotion. 'It's not here either.'

He stepped further into the room, but stopped halfway towards the bed. 'Where will it be?' he demanded.

'I don't know. Most of her stuff has gone.'

'Perhaps the police have it then?'

This was good. 'Do you think I hadn't considered that?' She raised her voice just enough to threaten hysteria, then sighed and raised both hands with a 'just hang on' gesture. 'I'm sorry, I know it's not your fault. But, Bryn, I don't know what I'd do if anyone saw it.'

'Why would that be so bad?'

She bit back the urge to scream. He was so thick. Even this simple fictitious scenario was beyond him. If she'd really lost her private diary in Lorna's flat, why would she need to spell out that she didn't want every Tom, Dick and Plod poring over its steamy pages?

Did Bryn really think she was that brazen regarding her personal life?

Her voice trembled with irritation as she spoke, but she was sure he would merely interpret it as raw emotion. 'If they found out, I just don't know what I'd do.'

Her body sagged and she buried her face in her hands. He was quick to sit down beside her. 'It'll be OK,' he whispered. She reached out and found his hand, then pulled him nearer. She felt his arm slip round her shoulder and she nestled closer still. She shivered and her skin tingled against the silky fabric of her blouse.

A minute of silence passed.

'I bet you miss her,' she said.

'I didn't really know her.'

'But you were sleeping with her.'

'You've got it wrong; it was very casual. We weren't having a relationship.'

She turned her face up to his, and kissed him tentatively. He jerked his head away, but she could already tell that there was no way he was about to bolt.

'What are you doing?' he asked.

He started to say something else, but she pressed her fingertips to his lips. 'Shhh.' She kissed him again, and slid her hand around to cup his neck and keep him close to her. The kiss lingered and became deeper as she teased his tongue into her mouth. Her lips were soft and her mouth tasted of spearmint. He wasn't a bad kisser, just a little too eager, too adolescent. But maybe that was a good thing.

With her free hand she started to unbutton her blouse. Pulling the buttons apart, letting him think their kissing had reawakened the sexual chemistry between them. She knew the exact moment when his focus on her became total, and then she pulled back. He looked surprised. She ran her hand across his lap, pretending it was a casual touch – but they both knew it wasn't.

She stood up in front of him. Her nerves had now calmed, she'd stopped shivering, and suddenly the room felt much warmer. She dropped her blouse to the floor and watched his intense gaze fall on to her cleavage.

Her stare was unwavering as she pushed her bra down and cupped her breasts, massaging the nipples with her thumbs.

She saw him rub the palm of his hand on the hip of his trousers, and she knew she was making progress.

'Why not?' she asked lightly and let her skirt drop to the floor.

She unhooked her bra and let it fall, then stepped back and pirouetted slowly in just her black G-string and high heels. Her skin was tanned and taut, and she knew her body was better than Lorna's.

'You look good,' he said.

Her lips parted and she ran her tongue across her teeth and smiled.

'But we're not doing it here,' he added.

She knew she was committed now, and held his gaze. 'Why not? You're hard, aren't you?' She reached down, took his hand and guided it between her legs. 'It's what I really need right now.'

'But not here.'

'Why not?'

'What if we're caught?'

'We won't be, but it's the risk of it that's turning me on. I don't even think I'd mind if someone were watching.' She bent forward and kissed him again. His fingers travelled upwards, across her stomach to her breasts. Her skin was warm, her nipples erect. She tilted her head back, encouraging his lips to caress her neck. 'Come on,' she breathed. 'Come on.' She pushed his hand back down to her G-string. 'Pull it off,' she gasped.

Obediently he tugged it a couple of times. On the second attempt the flimsy elastic snapped. He paused to mutter, 'I'm sorry.'

'It doesn't matter.' She rolled backwards on to the mattress, using all her weight to pull him with her. His left hand tugged at the zip of his trousers. His legs pressed themselves between hers, his hips pushing them apart.

She squeezed his arm with her fingers and wriggled as if trying to escape, but in his ear she breathed, 'Come on then, fuck me.'

He was heavy and enthusiastic; it felt like being humped by an eighteen-month-old Labrador. His mouth moved to her neck, and he sucked at the skin over her jugular, his hips pushing her legs even further apart. She wrapped her ankles around his thighs. He penetrated her and pushed himself in deep. Her neck began burning as blood rushed to the surface, her lower body throbbing as his body ground against hers. Credit where it was due: he was more Dobermann than Labrador.

Even so, she gritted her teeth and stared into the gloom of the ceiling, patiently counting his thrusts, just for something to do. There were always three hundred or so, she reckoned. Blokes: it was the monotony of them that got to her.

As the wardrobe doors had opened, Goodhew braced himself for instant discovery, only to see the doors bounce back at him in the same instant. For two or three seconds, he was in total darkness, then, as though the wardrobe suddenly relented, the doors popped back open by a good inch and a half. He hoped he wasn't as visible as he felt.

He watched Victoria positioning herself on Lorna's bed and realized what she had planned long before the other guy had a clue. Goodhew wished silence wasn't obligatory at that moment, having a major urge to groan. Why hadn't he just left when he had the chance?

Then he recognized Bryn's voice and knew his only real option was to sit tight and wait for this situation's inevitable climax.

Goodhew leant back and stared upwards into the darkest part of the confined space, probably straight up the skirt of one of Lorna's little black dresses. The bed springs kept creaking along in the key of F, and he didn't dare look out through the gap in the door.

When he and Bryn had been sitting in the same class and the teachers asked the children what they thought they'd be doing in fifteen years' time, he hadn't pictured this. Strange really.

After about another five minutes, the creaking ceased and he sneaked a glance. He was just in time to see Victoria climbing astride Bryn and off they went again. The springs changed key and picked up in tempo. A few seconds later, they were moving faster and faster still; it was starting to remind him of the end of 'Come On, Eileen'. Goodhew closed his eyes till he judged it was safe to take another look.

Bryn was lying on his back with his trousers tangled around his calves, but Victoria had slid off the bed and was reaching for her skirt.

'I'm cold now,' she explained quietly, but Bryn stared at her and didn't move. She picked up her underwear. She slipped her feet into her shoes and began buttoning her blouse.

He watched, unblinking.

'That certainly lived up to expectations,' she remarked coldly.

'What do you mean?'

'I got what I expected. Mediocre.' Bryn didn't move. 'I'd stick with the cars,' Victoria continued, 'you've probably got some talent for *tinkering* with them.'

Bryn stiffened. 'What are you on about?'

'Lorna.'

'What about her?'

Victoria stood and faced him full on. 'To think I fell out with her over you. But now I've proved she never mattered to you. For your information, I was so over you when we did this.'

'Bollocks.'

'I'm sorry?'

'It's bollocks. You must think I'm stupid. Lorna wasn't interested in me, any more than you were. So what's the big deal about proving you can shag me on Lorna's bed?'

Bryn had only gone as far as rolling on to his side and raising himself on one elbow. If she had expected him to be irate, she would have been disappointed.

'What's the real reason then?' he insisted.

When she turned her head away from Bryn, Goodhew knew he was now in her line of sight, and could only pray that her attention remained elsewhere.

'Believe what you want, but I'm telling you, she was jealous about us two. And I'm glad we did it in here, because in the end I hated her.'

'There wasn't any diary, was there?'

'So now I'm a liar? You're sick.'

'I'm sick? You got me in here with the sole idea of trashing Lorna, even though she's dead, and *I'm* sick?'

'Like you weren't up for it,' she sneered.

This time Bryn reacted like she'd gone too far. 'Enough.' He growled and began to pull up his trousers. 'I admit it, I was up for it. You offered, and I accepted. But you – you're in a whole other league.'

'You slept with Lorna, and felt jealous,' Victoria goaded. 'Then I slept with you, and she was the jealous one. Looking at you now, no, I don't understand it, but that's how it was. I like to settle scores, Bryn.' She hitched her skirt up a few inches with one hand, and rubbed the other between her legs until it was wet and shiny with his semen, then she smeared it across the mattress.

'What the hell are you doing?' Bryn spluttered.

Victoria now had her back to him, facing the wardrobe, and appeared to be staring straight at Goodhew. Suddenly her hand flew towards the twin doors and slammed them shut. 'That was a message just for Lorna and you.' Her voice was sharp enough to penetrate the plywood doors. 'A fuck-off message, if you like.'

Goodhew heard her hurrying away, heading off through the unlit flat and down into the street.

Goodhew listened carefully; he'd only heard Victoria leave. Was he alone yet? His legs were seizing up with cramp and his right arm was turning numb. He was desperate to move, but emerging to find himself face to face with Bryn O'Brien didn't appeal either.

Victoria had made a good job closing both doors before she left. Goodhew pressed his hand against one of them, testing how tightly it fitted, and realized that opening it silently would be difficult. He dug the tips of his fingers into the join and pressed gently, then harder. It creaked slightly as the doors parted by quarter of an inch, and just as Bryn was dragging the curtains half shut.

Goodhew put his eye close to the opening. The only illumination came from the streetlamp outside, still drizzling just about enough light into the room to leave Bryn O'Brien bathed in anaemia. Bryn was too busy frowning down into the street beyond to sense he was being observed.

He buckled his belt, brushed down the front of his shirt, then stepped into the dark interior of the flat.

Goodhew didn't dare move, just listened as Bryn moved slowly through the sitting room, feeling his way from door frame to chair, and from chair to wall. It was slow but uneventful until he reached the landing. A stumble. A clatter.

'Oh, fuck. What the hell is that?'

Bryn must have kicked something, for wood cracked as an object bounced on the stairs. He ran down after it, then the street door opened and slammed shut.

Goodhew scrambled from the wardrobe and staggered to the window as fast as his numb legs would carry him. He was just in time to see Bryn stride out of sight, but there was no way of telling where he was heading. Goodhew sighed in disappointment, but what did he expect? Bryn wasn't going to park outside, was he?

Goodhew used his torch again to light his way across the flat, aware of the risk that someone outside might see the light dancing on the walls.

The narrow beam caught something shiny on the landing. He knelt down beside it, directing the torchlight down the stairs. Bryn had tripped over a side table, then sent it crashing down to the hall below.

And, before it had fallen, it had been home to a small pile of junk mail: brochures for holiday parks, lawnmowers and orthopaedic mattresses, still in their cellophane envelopes. There were four of them altogether, inconspicuous and easily overlooked. But none read 'L. Spence'; they were each addressed to other people.

The first two names he recognized: 'V. Nugent' and 'J. Moran'. The other two were new to him: 'Miss H. Sellars' and 'W. Thompson-Stark'.

They'd all been carefully opened, cut open with nail scissors by the look of the neat seams.

He rescued the table from the foot of the stairs, leaving it propped up against the landing wall to hide its newly broken leg. He scribbled the four names and addresses on a scrap of paper, replaced the brochures, then left to vanish into the night.

Suddenly he had much to do.

# THIRTY-THREE

Victoria scuttled from Lorna's flat on to the street. She ran, clattering along the pavement as fast as her spiked heels could carry her. Everyone thought she was tough but her brittle coat of bravado had just chipped and shattered.

Yes, she'd played the scene out pretty much as she planned, but Bryn wasn't the pushover she'd expected him to be. Instead of recoiling at her big finale, he'd become infused with rage, the room had filled with it. She suddenly wondered if she'd been terribly wrong about him. She hadn't finished their encounter with an arrogant flounce out of the door, instead she'd bolted.

Now she didn't care if anyone saw her, since the only thing on her mind was fear of being caught. Fear of Bryn.

She clutched the small handbag containing her phone, keys, money and cigarettes, none of which she could afford to lose. She darted through a back alley and was out of sight of Lorna's flat before the door reopened. Ahead of her was a dark tunnel of unlit back fences and high gates, but at the end she knew she'd find a narrow gap taking her out on to the footpath running alongside the Cam.

She was furious with herself, having been so excited by the prospect of humiliating him that she'd been too vague in considering the details of what might happen afterwards. She had already planned this route, but only thought about it as it looked in daylight. She'd accepted that it might be muddy, but now she couldn't even see the thick puddles underfoot. Silty water slopped into her left shoe.

There'd been another oversight too; she'd arrived in Bryn's car and now she was cold, with no underwear and no jacket but, more importantly, he could still drive and she had no hope of reaching her flat first.

As the moon vanished behind a shifting cloud, she could only inch her way forward until it reappeared. She needed to run, but not wearing these shoes, and not in the pitch black.

She finally emerged on the path beside the river and then hurried towards the illuminated restaurants on Magdalene Bridge, wondering whether she should hail a taxi. But the lights were only on while staff cleaned up, and the customers were long gone. She glanced up and down the street in case a cab was parked up, waiting there for a job from its dispatcher. Nothing but an already occupied car, whose driver and passengers all stared at her as they rolled past.

She glanced down at her deliberately tarty skirt and mud-caked shoes, and imagined what they must be thinking. She hurried away from the kerb, realizing that any cab driver would be disgusted at taking her such a short distance and, anyway, the wait itself looked as if it would be longer than the journey.

As she moved away from the centre towards home, she kept to the inner side of the pavement, checking regularly over her shoulder and ducking into doorways as soon as she saw the beams of car headlights.

Victoria rented a small flat in the annexe of a large Edwardian house. The approach to it was therefore impressive, even if her flat itself wasn't. A waist-high wall enclosed the gardens, like an immovable girdle keeping the conifers pinned up against the house. Movement sensors controlled security lighting, and she could now see its familiar glare from a hundred yards away. She kept low and close to the wall, peering over it between the low straggling branches.

Bryn's old Ford waited in the driveway. Lights off. Engine silent. Victoria hugged herself and waited. A passing taxi flashed its lights on to her, but then drove on. She wondered whether someone would think she was loitering and perhaps call the police.

Five minutes later, she heard the Zodiac's engine start up. But it didn't move and, several minutes on, she heard the fan running, kicking warm air into the interior and clearing the windows. Bryn was planning to wait.

She lit a cigarette, not a conscious decision, just one instinctively made by her agitated fingers. She drew a couple of quick breaths, with her eyes shut, and opened them again just as the taxi returned. This time he slowed to a stop and rolled down his electric window.

'All right, miss?'

'Yeah,' she nodded. 'Just waiting for someone.'

'You don't want a lift then?'

'No.' She shook her head firmly, and he pulled away. Before he'd travelled fifty yards, she wished she'd said yes. She watched the taxi's tail lights shrink to dots. And she desperately wanted to be somewhere else.

She felt in her bag, to check for her purse and phone. Both there. What the hell, she had the money, and it made sense to spend the night in a hotel.

Fuck Bryn, she thought, and she pictured getting warm and clean in the bath, then sliding between smooth cotton hotel sheets and drifting off to sleep, while he was condemned to sleep upright in that aging piece of scrap.

She turned and strode back towards the city centre, intending to check in at the Doubletree Hotel. She'd stayed there once after being taken to Grantchester and back by punt. Before Bryn and Lorna, and all of this mess. She'd had a romantic night, they'd ordered dinner in their room and watched the last punts return just before sunset. Then they'd cuddled in bed and watched *Sleepless in Seattle* on the TV.

A night of escapism was what she needed now. Just forget about Bryn and Lorna, and all but one of the Morans.

She reached the traffic lights on the junction of Castle Hill and Magdalene Street and she hurried back towards the bridge. This time it was a welcome sight. She had a plan, and she didn't care what any late-night bystanders thought of her.

On her right was a row of matching shops, painted a sombre battleship grey, with the window and door frames picked out in black.

On her left, the soot-covered wall of Benson Hall rose high and dark. It was sooted and glassless, with bricked panels in stone window frames. In daylight it simply appeared old and genteel, and never seemed the slightest bit threatening.

So Victoria continued down the dark conduit that whisked her towards the centre.

The lights were mostly out on Magdalene Bridge, but two lofty streetlamps still operated, diffusing light across its span. Shops and restaurants left small courtesy lights glowing, but nothing more. The last diners and drinkers had long since dispersed and the only sounds were the rippling of the Cam as it slithered beneath her, and her heels clacking on the pavement.

She didn't realize that she had stopped shivering; her next small victory was in sight and all her thoughts were by now on the hotel, not on the chilly night air licking at her bare ankles, or her fingers stiffening with cold.

And, worst of all, she hadn't felt the goosebumps climbing her scalp, trying to tell her she was being watched. Ahead the road narrowed and a shadow moved. But Victoria didn't notice.

# THIRTY-FOUR

The Round Church stood at the top of Trinity Street, like a sentry marking the next precinct of the city. As she hurried towards it, a nervous little butterfly darted around in her stomach. For the first time she noticed how the gateposts were topped with stone figures of eagles with books under their feet. She glanced up at them, and they glared back down, looking ready to fly off and scatter loose pages into the streets of Cambridge.

The walk seemed further through these empty streets than it did during the average hectic lunch hour. She wished again that she'd stopped that cab, but she wouldn't find one now in this deserted pedestrian quarter. She followed the parameter of grounds of St John's round to the right, before turning into Trinity Street.

Somewhere close by, running footsteps suddenly echoed.

Victoria hurried on, skipping into a trot every few paces, past the lower levels of St John's College Chapel. The way in front of her darkened and she struggled to remind herself of the same street in daytime. The ornate railings were just as pretty. The blackened stone-work was just as old. She drifted towards the kerbside, narrowly side-stepping a low bollard. What a stupid decision to paint them black.

Another entrance to St John's College came and went, and for a fleeting moment she considered finding the porter's lodge and demanding assistance. But she didn't need the night to continue any longer and, in just another five minutes, she'd reach the safety of the hotel.

Ahead of her, her route became darker still. As she passed a little park, for a few yards the only illumination came from the moon and the eerie glow it cast on the white blossom of the chestnut trees. Their branches waved at her from over the railings.

She passed Trinity College next, and forced herself not to look up at its medieval elevations, remembering all the gargoyles and grotesque stonework. Instead, she fixed her sights further ahead at where all the shops commenced, and began to feel relief that she was soon getting back into safer territory.

The street now made a slow curve to the right. A cashpoint machine flashed, winking at the pink-and-blue display in Jaeger's window opposite. Even in the dark, the shops here were designed to appeal. But the diversion they offered her was to be short-lived.

She slowed again when she saw a figure ahead: a shadow slipping out of a doorway. Seeing one person was worse than seeing none. But she kept walking, because she had no choice. There was nowhere else to run.

She was feet from passing by, when she risked a glance, and instantly her sense of apprehension vanished.

'Oh, hi,' she beamed.

'Victoria?'

She exhaled in relief. 'Yes.'

'Why are you walking around on your own?'

'I've just had a row with a boyfriend, and I don't want to go home, so I was walking to the Doubletree to spend the night there. To be honest, I was getting a bit spooked out here in the dark. I'm so glad it's you.' She knew she'd never been this friendly before, but suddenly hoped it sounded genuine. 'And what are you doing here?'

'I just needed to get out for some fresh air. Is he still hanging around your flat?'

Victoria lit another cigarette. 'Waiting outside.'

'I didn't know you had a boyfriend.'

'It's a casual thing.'

'Still not ready for anything more serious?'

'Something like that.'

'But it's been several months since . . .' The sentence died and they both gave it a moment's silence to be laid to rest. 'Do you want me to go back with you?'

Victoria puffed out a thin stream of smoke as she reflected on that. Then she sighed and tried to sound weary. 'I can't face him right now.'

She made a few half-hearted steps in the direction of the hotel. 'He scares me,' she moaned.

'Scares you? How? He's only sitting outside your flat. He can't do anything from there.'

Victoria lowered her voice, like she was confiding a secret.

'He's really angry with me. He's convinced I'm coming back tonight and he's waiting for me.'

'But you're leaving him to rot there just to teach him a lesson?'

'That was the idea,' she said, 'but I've gone off it now.'

'Well, I think you should. I'll help you.'

Victoria shrugged. 'I'm not sure.'

'You have your mobile, don't you?'

Victoria reached in her bag, pulled out her phone and unlocked the keypad.

'But he'll know it's my phone.'

'Yes, but he won't know the text is from me, and I know how to make him squirm. Remember it's because of him that you're stuck out here, cold and vulnerable.'

Victoria nodded. 'OK.'

'So it's a good idea?'

Victoria shrugged, then nodded again. 'Why not?'

'Text this . . .' The words were recited slowly to give her enough time to spell them properly. '"You'll be sorry in the morning and . . ."'

Victoria prodded the keypad with both thumbs. 'And what?'

'That's it.'

'Send?'

'Yes.'

She pressed the send button and watched until the message icon had flown from the screen. 'Do I send him the next bit later?'

'Why not?'

'And how's that going to work?'

Her companion sighed and stared skywards, and Victoria looked up too. The moon was a cold yellow, and the small clouds were racing by fast enough to give the impression that the chimney tops themselves were moving. A few yards further down Trinity Street, a building stood on the corner of Trinity Lane, with carvings protruding from both sides of the roofline. They appeared to be ships' figureheads, sticking out about two feet under the guttering, and gave the impression of tugging the main structure in two different directions at once.

'Why will that message scare him?' she persisted.

Her companion sighed, exhaling breath in a deep hiss of theatrical exasperation, then looking down again, gaze dropping in a straight line, like it had fallen from the roof. 'When I first found out you were seeing our father I felt a bit uncomfortable, but I didn't begrudge him some company. After all, we all know what it's like to be lonely. You weren't what I expected, at first, but you deserve our thanks for sticking with him right until the end. In fact, I thought it showed a kind and generous side to your nature.'

They began walking again, slowly this time, but within yards they'd stopped once more. Victoria shifted her weight from foot to foot, feeling the cold more accutely, and the conversation had slid into more difficult territory. It was uncomfortable to stand still, but neither was it the right time to walk away. 'I wanted to be with him,' she said.

'I'm surprised he didn't leave you something, a token of his thanks perhaps.'

'I didn't expect anything.'

'Oh, come on. If he'd lived, you would have been enjoying his money, so why not once he's dead?' There was a pause. 'Or did you assume one of us would look after you?'

And it was the following pause that made Victoria hesitate. In that three-second silence there was a shift, a mutation in the mood between them that told her finding the correct answer had just become imperative. But she couldn't think of anything appropriate to say.

She felt a hand grab at her sleeve and, in bewilderment, she pulled her arm away, but not enough to break free. The fingers gripped too tightly.

She looked from left to right, hoping for even one pedestrian to come by. In one direction there were rows of chained-up, riderless bikes, and in the other, windowless walls and a solitary glowing lamp in the shape of a barber's pole. But no people, now that she needed them.

Her eyes widened, she still wanted to be mistaken. 'No, I didn't, and I don't know why you're getting angry with me . . .'

201

'I'm angry with myself because I didn't see it sooner. You took something from my father.'

'I didn't.'

'You took something from my father,' the voice repeated.

'It wasn't *about* you.' Victoria gasped as her back slammed against the damp stone wall, her body feeling weightless, swimming nowhere against the sudden pain.

The hands released her, and she staggered forwards, trying to regain her balance. She stumbled four or five steps, hoping she was free to go.

She felt a hand on her shoulder and shrugged it away, but it wasn't there to spin her round, just to loop something around her neck. She was then hauled back in, like a toy mouse on the end of a string.

Her shoulders hunched and she threw herself from side to side, snapping her nails on the webbing belt savaging her skin. Her bag hit the footpath, spilling its contents in all directions. Her feet flailed, fighting for purchase. Her left foot landed on a spiralling lipstick and her ankle rolled, pitching her weight against the ligature.

And in response to her struggle, it merely tightened. She felt her mouth gaping and her tongue arching as it gagged her tonsils. No one came running to save her, and the last thing she did was piss herself.

The final thing she felt was it overtaking the semen already trickling down her cold bare thighs.

Victoria slumped to the ground and, after a couple of seconds, her leg kicked once, like a dreaming dog's. But that was all.

There was no attempt to retrieve either her handbag or its contents, but the phone was slipped into a pocket.

Above her body, a square bay window protruded from the corner of the building. Under the windowsill a man's head was carved, about ten feet above the ground. He was black with pollution, except for the dome of his bare head, where the untarnished cream stone looked like his skull.

Victoria's features were distorted, but her face was still intact. It didn't look right. So she was rolled on to her front. Fingers twisted into her hair and held tightly. Then her head was lifted and her face slammed against the ground. Again and again. Pummelled against the stone pavement until it grated tracks into her skin.

The killer walked away towards the river, still carrying Victoria's phone. It was time for Bryn to receive another text.

# THIRTY-FIVE

Bryn glared at the message. 'What the fuck's that supposed to mean?' He threw the phone on to the passenger seat. He knew one thing: there was no point waiting for her.

The drive was big enough to turn the Zodiac without reversing, but even so he backed up closer to her door before flooring the accelerator. The car seemed to crouch there before leaping forward, its fat tyres spitting flint chips at her windows.

He shot out through the gateway on to the deserted road beyond, leaving just the growl of the engine and quickly dispersed vapour trails billowing in the disturbed air. He felt satisfied that he would at least have annoyed someone.

Instead of heading directly home, he took the road out of town. Normally, he needed thinking time and the best way to achieve that was to drive. He rested his right hand on the top of the steering wheel, and his left on the gearstick.

His speed crept steadily up, passing forty in the thirty zone, then nudging fifty a few seconds after that. He was touching sixty as he swung around the last bend before reaching the motorway when he suddenly remembered the speed camera. He touched his brakes too hard, the back end of the vehicle wobbled and then straightened, just as a familiar flash exploded in front of his eyes.

'Shit,' he snapped. This was all he needed: everything was going from bad to worse. He just hoped there was no film in the camera, but looking at the way the day was already turning out, he doubted luck was with him, and it wasn't like he could afford many more speeding convictions. 'Shit,' he repeated and now kept just under the speed limit as he coasted down the slip road leading on to the M11.

The traffic was thicker here, with overnight lorries heading to the South Coast docks and late-night businessmen heading for London. Even so, he kept carefully to the speed limit and let them thunder past. Above all else, he needed to calm down. Let it go.

He'd always known he wasn't Victoria's type, not in anything other than a casual way. But, hey, at first it had been fun. Now, though, she was playing a game, and he didn't understand what it meant. Gary had asked if Lorna had been jealous, but he felt sure there was no way. Even if Victoria pretended there was. So what was her motive? His brain meandered around the issue.

And soon his speed was drifting downwards, and the same aggressive wide tyres that had churned up Victoria's gravel were stroking the tarmac as they floated towards the edge of the lane.

Bryn started, jerking his eyes open as the car shuddered on the ridged white line separating him from the hard shoulder. He didn't think he'd been dozing. Or perhaps he had. What time was it anyway? Twenty to two. Fucked for work tomorrow, that was certain. He could always sleep in the car, of course . . . But not now. Absolutely not now.

He opened the quarter-light, turning it backwards so that the cool air gushed into his face. He took several deep breaths and blinked rapidly to clear his vision, then he leant across and opened the glove box. Keeping hold of the wheel with his other hand, his fingers groped around, locating first an A to Z, then a pair of sunglasses, some mints and, finally, the packet of cigarettes. He tried to grip it with the tips of two fingers, but instead only managed to flip it to the back of the glove box, somewhere behind the ring-bound spine of the road atlas. He could do without this.

Bryn pulled over on to the hard shoulder, taking the car out of gear, but leaving the engine running, then he stretched across and retrieved the cigerette packet. He slid one out and pushed the dashboard lighter in and waited. But he rarely smoked in the car and wasn't even sure the lighter worked. After a few seconds it clicked and popped back out, glowing; at least something was finally going right.

He lit up, then tossed the packet back, slamming the glove box shut. He knew he was tired and wished he'd never decided to drive. He would double back at the next junction, get home, think again in the morning.

He kept the window open but, just to be certain, he shuffled his backside back until he was sitting sharply to attention, put the car in first and signalled. One pair of headlights appeared in the rear-view mirror, and he waited for them to pass.

He used the hard shoulder to gain some speed, and was doing forty by the time the other vehicle, an articulated lorry, caught him. Bryn's car wavered as it was buffeted in the slipstream.

He pulled out into the first lane, but the horn bellowed and he swerved back off the road again, just as a second lorry thundered by. How the fuck had he missed something that big?

He checked behind him once again, and this time made doubly sure that the road was empty. He levelled his speed at seventy-five; no one got speeding tickets for travelling less than ten per cent over the limit. Well, he didn't think so anyway and, with thirty-plus miles until home, he didn't want it to take a minute longer than it had to.

With twenty-eight miles to go, he turned up the heater. Just a little. No point in freezing, he reckoned.

Twenty-five miles to go, as tail lights suddenly appeared two car lengths in front of him. He swung out into the second lane, round the other car dawdling at sixty. Twenty-three miles to go. He was still in the middle lane and, by now, Victoria didn't matter. Getting home was all that mattered. Sinking into bed. Drifting into sleep.

Twenty-two miles to go. The tyres sounded like a ticket machine as they bumped over the cat's eyes between the middle lane and the slow lane. New ticket . . . new ticket . . . new ticket.

Then, like knuckles rubbing on a washboard, the tyres rumbled again on the raised white line between the slow lane and the hard shoulder. First the passenger side tyres, then the driver's side. All at a perfectly uniform seventy-five miles per hour.

One hand lay in his lap. His eyes were closed and staying closed, not seeing the bridge support rising from the verge ahead. And his other hand rested on the wheel, doing nothing to stop the car's gentle trickle away from the road.

The bridge dealt the car a glancing blow. Buckling the corner of the front bumper, twisting the front wing inwards. The headlamp shattered, the surrounding chrome bezel springing from its mounting and smacking the windscreen. The car bounced away, back towards the carriageway.

But only for a second. Bryn jerked awake. He heard the crash. And opened his eyes enough to see the road slewing under him. He felt the car careering right. He slammed on the brakes and yanked the wheel left.

The Zodiac left the motorway, front nearside first. It slid on a narrow strip of mud, then bounced through the furrows and deep grass further off road, coming to rest at an unnatural tilt.

Bryn yanked on the inside door handle and stumbled out on to the verge. His shaking hands gripped his mobile and he managed to dial 999. He walked around his car once, then decided he'd seen enough. He sat back inside it and knew he was going to cry. He also knew that it was entirely his own fault.

When his phone beeped and he saw Victoria's name on the incoming message, he had absolutely no desire to read it. He'd been dragged into more trouble by her than he'd experienced in a lifetime. So he never saw the three little words which said 'PS I'M DEAD'.

# THIRTY-SIX

Mel sat in an armchair in the front room of her flat. Its upholstery was decidedly tired, but she'd been sitting in the same position for hours and the sagging cushions seemed to have wrapped themselves around her. She was warm and feeling cosy here; a comforting place in a worrying home.

Toby was out somewhere. Probably at Mickey Flynn's, potting Aftershock faster than pool balls.

Her mobile silently vibrated on the arm of her chair: she checked the number rather than simply answering. It was Michael Kincaide. She pressed 'end', then switched it off.

It was now time to think, not time to talk.

Kincaide switched off his mobile. He pulled off his tie and plodded upstairs towards his bedroom. His wife was already in bed, either asleep or pretending she was.

'Jan?' he whispered. No reaction.

He brushed his teeth, undressed and slipped in beside her. 'Jan?' He nudged her between the shoulder blades.

'What?'

'Roll over.'

She sighed and turned to face him. 'I've had a long day, Mike. I really don't feel like anything.'

'It's been ages.'

'Ages since the weekend? Don't be pathetic,' she grumbled and turned away again. 'And next time try something more creative than "Roll over."'

Marks couldn't sleep. He was drinking coffee and staring across Parkers Piece at the unlit windows of Goodhew's flat, just as DC Charles brought in an envelope.

'Sorry to bother you, sir, but this has just been delivered and I thought you'd like it straight away.'

Marks stared at it before taking it from the detective. He already knew what it was, just not what it said. 'I don't suppose you know if Goodhew's currently in the building?'

Charles gave a tut. 'You've just missed him, sir. He was looking up some stuff on the computer till about ten minutes ago.'

'And he's definately gone?'

'Yep. I saw him get into a taxi out the front.'

Once Charles had gone, Marks finally opened the envelope. He wouldn't even bother with fingerprinting it. Firstly, he knew there'd be no point. Secondly, if by a fluke there was a point, then he didn't want to find it. He'd given up debating the ethics of accepting these anonymous tip-offs; he preferred instead to treat them with due suspicion, but follow them up anyway.

The words were typed in the usual way, vertically centred on a sheet of A4.

What did Lorna Spence keep hidden in a Marmite jar and a vinegar bottle?

Why does she receive other people's junk mail?

Ask Victoria Nugent why she visited Lorna's flat tonight.

Had Marks gone looking for Goodhew half an hour earlier, he would have found him with one hand resting on the open pages of the telephone directory and the other on his mouse, directing the flow of data scrolling up on his PC screen.

Goodhew was watching for the name 'Sellars'. There were a few already, but none with the initial H., and in the phone book there were too many, at least too many to phone up at this unsocial hour.

He moved on to 'W. Thompson-Stark'. He guessed with a name like that, any match might be the only one.

He typed 'Thompson*' first, in case the Stark had been added later. The screen immediately filled with Thompsons, so he started at the bottom and there, one entry below Z. Thompson (Shoplifting), was W. Thompson-Stark (Sexual Assault).

He double-clicked the entry and waited a painfully slow one and a half seconds for the data to appear on the screen.

The W., he discovered, stood for Wayne, who was now twenty-six years old. And the case dated back six years.

Goodhew's gaze scanned the information. Rape charge brought. Reduced to sexual assault. Assault occurred on 9th July, reported after five days. No forensic evidence. Defendant denied charges, but was sentenced to three years, released after two.

Goodhew flicked on to the next screen to continue. Two words jumped out at once. 'Lorna Spence.'

He let go of his mouse like it was hot.

He held his breath, reading the details slowly, making sure he read them correctly. His heart pounded. He printed the details and called a taxi.

Wayne Thompson-Stark lived in Cutter's Path in Ely, a pretty development of townhouses running from the river back towards the cathedral. The cab dropped Goodhew at the edge of the estate.

'I'll drive you round if you want,' the driver offered. 'I just don't know which road it'll be, not with it being too new for the maps an' all.'

Goodhew shook his head. 'Don't worry.' He preferred to find it on foot.

The houses were actually too new for most of them to even display numbers yet, and it took several minutes for him firstly to find an entrance to Cutter's Path, and secondly to work out which direction to head for number 71.

The 'path' part of the name was appropriate; the cul-de-sac end of the road opened out on to a mock village green, complete with winding footpath. Cobbles, of course, and lit by faux Victorian lamp posts. Goodhew guessed it might stay looking pretty, until too many new owners began improving with white plastic doors, or adding porches and innovative garden features.

Number 71 was the last house on the left and, like most of the others, its lights were out.

Tough on Wayne, then, as murder and sleeping comfortably didn't belong together.

From outside the front door, there was little to be seen of the inside: just one distorted pane directing his gaze up towards a black blur of darkness beyond. He gave the bell a firm press, and heard it chiming from the hallway. An upstairs light was switched on within a second, so he knew he hadn't woken anyone.

The little pane of rippled glass revealed a view of a white handrail rising towards the top of the stairs. A man stepped into view. He stood on the landing while he felt his way into some sort of dressing gown. He was big built, and when he finally banged down the stairs it was as if he let gravity do all the work.

The man opened the door to halfway, not bothering with the chain, so perhaps pre-dawn callers didn't worry him. The light shone from behind him, making it hard to see his face, and Goodhew caught sight of a shadow moving upstairs. The man didn't speak.

Goodhew flipped out his ID. 'DC Goodhew. Sorry to disturb you. I expect you've heard of a recent murder in Cambridge . . .'

His sentence trailed away to nothing, as the word 'murder' finally opened the door.

Wayne Thompson-Stark was at least six two and broad, like a rugby player but with a straighter nose.

'Who else is in the house, Mr Thompson-Stark?'

'The name's just Thompson. My girlfriend, she'll be down in a minute. Gone to the bathroom.'

'You weren't asleep?'

Thompson shook his head as though the bags under his eyes hadn't already answered for him. It looked like he probably hadn't slept well for days. He spoke in a gruff voice, which made him sound older. But then he looked considerably older than twenty-six. 'Come through, and sit down.' He patted his towelling robe. 'You don't mind if I stay like this?'

The front door opened directly into the sitting room, but Thompson led the way through to a narrow dining area at the back of the house and they chose chairs on opposite sides of a Formica-covered drop-leaf table.

Upstairs, a door creaked and footsteps padded across carpet. Goodhew lowered his voice, 'You realize I need to ask you some questions about Lorna Spence?'

Thompson looked surprised. 'You don't need to whisper. Do you think she wouldn't know?'

211

Goodhew shrugged. 'Can't assume.'

Thompson reached over to his left and pulled a chair alongside his own, ready for his girlfriend.

'We don't have any secrets,' confirmed a woman's voice.

She stood a few feet back from the door, as if weighing up the situation before deciding whether to step into it. Her hair was gathered up in bunches and she wore pyjamas, pink winceyette covered in a jumble of numbered sheep. The fabric stretched tight across her belly and she looked about eight months' pregnant. She turned towards Thompson and he held out his hand for her to join them.

'This is DC Goodhew.'

She nodded and sat in the empty seat.

Goodhew waited for her to be introduced, then realized they had no intention of bothering. 'What's your name?' he asked.

This time it was her turn to look startled. 'Hayley,' she said.

'Sellars?' Goodhew supplied and she nodded.

Thompson laughed. It was short and humourless. 'I thought you already knew. Like you said though, you can't assume.'

Hayley reached out her hand and slipped it into Thompson's. He gave it a squeeze.

Goodhew's gaze wandered across to the clock, already ticking towards 3 a.m., then it drifted back to the couple facing him.

Thompson didn't look at all aggressive; Hayley looked neither scared for Thompson, nor scared of him. But they both looked sorry. For what though?

Goodhew wiped his eyes. Something was clouding his vision and he needed to push it away. 'I'll be honest,' he sighed. 'Hayley, I don't know what connection you had with Lorna Spence, but I know there was one. And, Mr Thompson, I need to know about your relationship with her too, about the assault and your conviction.' He sighed again. 'I know it's now the middle of the night, but if you could explain it to me I'd be very grateful.'

Their entwined fingers seemed their only means of communication. She wanted him to speak first and he knew it.

'It was the week I was twenty and I only had a vague idea who Lorna was. I'd seen her and her mate Vicky around, but I just knew their first names, that kind of thing. I was out with some old school

212

mates, having a few drinks, playing pool, and I noticed her having a row with her boyfriend. This was early that evening, not much after seven, and the next time I looked round, she was on her own. She looked really choked up by then.

'Later on, she came and stood near the pool table, and asked if one of us would let her play. My mate played her and, between shots, I got talking to her. She'd split with her boyfriend, or that's what she said. She seemed all right, so I had no reason to think she was lying.'

Hayley was staring at her hands and chewing her lip. Goodhew wondered whether she was listening or had drifted somewhere else. Thompson released her hand and wrapped his arm around her instead. 'By about ten, we were getting on fine and, when the others moved on, we decided to stay and talk for longer. I remember the bell rang for last orders, then she asked if I could take her home. I didn't even own a car, so I walked her back, and before her house we started kissing. I honestly don't remember whose idea that was, we just had one of those moments when we both paused and knew it was about to happen.

'We were there for a while, and she was pressed up against me, and knew, I s'pose, that I was turned on.' He paused to shrug in apology. 'I'd just turned twenty, that's what I spent most of my time thinking about.'

He paused again.

'And then you had sex?' asked Goodhew.

Thompson nodded. 'Not sex like I expected. Not that I'd ever expected it. What I mean is, she had weird ideas. We went into the kitchen because she said everyone else would be in bed and no one would hear if we did it there. And it started off OK, just basic messing around. But then she took my hand and wanted me to shove it inside her, saying she wanted it to hurt.'

Hayley kept silent, her eyes turned away, but cheeks turning red.

'I didn't like it, so I wouldn't do it, but when we started having sex she wanted me to fight her for it and pretend that I was raping her.

'Now, when I say it, it sounds too weird, and it's obvious I should've stopped then. But she made it seem like I was being dull, so we did do it, and it was rough, but that was what she wanted. Oh, fuck it. I don't mean that because she wanted it rough, it was OK.

213

I just mean it wasn't rape, or assault, or anything done against her will.'

'So why do you think she pressed charges?'

'Because . . .' Thompson's voice was replaced by Hayley's.

'Because Lorna liked to make everyone suffer.' She looked up at Goodhew and tears brimmed in her eyes. 'When we heard she'd been murdered, I wondered whether Wayne had done it, and he even wondered whether it was me. That's how much she still affects us.' She sniffed and pressed away the tears with the heel of her hand. 'I wrote to Wayne when he was in prison, and I asked him to let me visit him. And he said yes. That's how we met.'

'But you knew Lorna?'

'Oh, yes. I was on my lunch break one day, and decided to go down town and grab a sandwich. I swallowed it the wrong way and stood outside Marks and Spencer's having a coughing fit. Next thing I knew, she was banging me on the back and sorting out a glass of water. We agreed to meet for lunch a couple of days later, and before long, she'd become my best friend. We went everywhere together, told each other everything, too. She told me about the rape, the trauma she'd been through with examinations and the court case, and the fear she felt at the thought of Wayne being released. And I believed it all one hundred per cent.'

'We went out one night, though, and somehow I ended up drunk, much too drunk for what I'd ordered. It didn't even occur to me that I'd been drugged, and I stood at the bar happily leaning on some guy. Probably telling Lorna how lovely he was, for all I can remember. Well, that's what she said I said anyway. She said she felt really hurt at being ignored, then went home.'

Hayley drew a deep breath, and new tears appeared and slipped silently on to her cheeks. 'He broke my nose and four fingers, I had six stitches, an Aids test, a tetanus shot and a dose of the clap. And they never caught him. And as for Lorna . . .'

Her voice trailed off as her face screwed up with the pain. Thompson held her closer and he kissed her hair.

Goodhew wasn't sure what to do now. 'I can arrange for you to talk to a female officer if you prefer.'

Thompson gave his head a small shake; it didn't just mean 'No' but 'Be quiet, wait.'

'No,' she whispered. 'It isn't the man that bothers me. Lorna was racked with guilt afterwards, distraught that she'd left me alone with him. She kept me company, helped me deal with the police and cope with the medical problems.

'The drug I'd been slipped left me with only bits of memory, and every day I tried to recall more about the attack. I had a vague picture of an alley littered with beer crates. Oil stains on the tarmac, grit and sludge in the puddles. And not looking at him, but turning my head away towards the narrow end of the alley, where it's only wide enough for a bicycle, like I was pleading for someone to come and save me.

'Every time I thought about it, I remembered looking towards that narrow end of the alley, not the other end where people actually might pass by. Why would I do that?' She didn't wait for an answer. 'I'll tell you, it was because I knew someone else was in that alley.

'Then, after that thought, I couldn't get the idea out of my head that Lorna had been there. Hidden. Watching. And that's been the greatest battle – having that idea in my head and not being able to get it out again.

'I didn't even know if I'd just invented that part, but I stewed on it. I had no proof and told myself I was being hysterical. But I couldn't dismiss it. The feeling of those eyes on me . . . In the end, I accused her. She was outraged, of course, but she would have been, wouldn't she? I didn't see her again after that.'

'So you had no real proof?'

She shook her head. 'None. Women's intuition, maybe.'

'But why would she do it?'

'Why would anyone want to watch their friend being raped? I don't know, but it makes her worse than him. Can you imagine what this has done to my friendships since? I couldn't get over this feeling that I was raped by her too, then I remembered everything she'd told me about her own rape. That's when I started to wonder whether she'd made that up as well.'

It wasn't anything to go on so far, and perhaps Thompson understood what Goodhew was thinking. 'It may not sound much in the way of evidence, but when Hayley came to see me, I'd also spent months trying to grasp what had happened to me. I then realized she'd come with the answer.'

'Where were you when Lorna died?'

'Here at home, with Hayley.'

'Just the two of you?'

'You're asking all the wrong questions. What you need to know is Lorna's objective. What was she chasing, and who was she prepared to damage to get it?' Thompson leant closer to Goodhew. 'Lorna only did things for Lorna. She was the centre of her own universe. Everybody else just spun around her, and she made sure it happened that way.'

Thompson fell silent and the pair of them looked across at Goodhew. He didn't know what he might have expected, but it definately hadn't been this. Maybe they were lying, concocting it all to cover for whichever one had killed her, but he threw out that idea at once. Instead he saw the truth of the situation: a light had been shone into the dark corners of Lorna's life, and there she stood, quietly manipulating all the people around her. The drugs found at Lorna's flat fitted the picture. Lorna had already sent one man to prison and manipulated a social situation until a young woman had been brutally raped. How much further had her game-playing needed to go before it had become an extreme and deadly sport?

The only sound now came from the hand-me-down fridge freezer which gurgled and hummed from its cubby hole behind the door.

Goodhew suddenly shuddered.

'Are you OK?' Hayley looked genuinely concerned.

'Just tired,' he answered and stood up hastily, keen to leave behind the sense of foreboding which had just draped its leaden arm across his shoulders.

# THIRTY-SEVEN

Goodhew had lost all track of time, and he had no idea how long he'd been awake. He wasn't even sure when dawn was due, although he could see from the light seeping into the sky from the east that it was on its way.

The taxi hurried from Ely, past flat farmlands, and eventually into the fringes of Cambridge. There was one thing Goodhew had known earlier: he was too tired to drive.

As the cab approached his flat he realized that his attention had drifted towards Parkside station. At the last moment, he directed the driver away and, several minutes later, he arrived on the doorstep of his grandmother's apartment.

She took what seemed an age to open the door, and when he saw her he wondered whether she'd paused to apply make-up or if she slept with it on every night. Her housecoat looked newly ironed, too, and he felt more dog-eared than ever.

He frowned and she didn't look too happy either. 'You look like shit,' she said.

'You swore.'

She held open the door for him to step inside. 'It's called communicating with the younger generation,' she said drily. 'I was making a valid point.'

'Oh, I see.'

'Besides, at 4.30 a.m. I'm entitled to swear.' But she didn't sound at all tired, was clearly more awake than he was. 'What's up? And why didn't you use your own key?'

'Sorry, I left it at home. Look, I can't sleep, I need to talk.'

He slumped into his favourite chair, and she perched on the edge of the chair facing his.

'Well, well, I never thought I'd hear that coming from you, Gary. Not that I'm surprised, since you've pushed yourself to the limits to make detective in record time and now, correct me if I'm wrong, you seem to pressure yourself with far too much responsibility for every serious crime you touch.' She paused. 'I'm right, aren't I?'

'Not exactly.'

'No? Look, you have yet to master the art of leaving work at work – it seems to follow you round all the time as if it's hiding in your back pocket.'

Goodhew shrugged. 'Yeah, well, actually it's the murder I want to talk about,' he said.

'Explain it to me.'

'The case? Sure.' He settled back in the chair, and she did the same.

She listened without interruption.

'I feel,' he said finally, 'as if we just don't know anything. It's too random, just a fog of possibilities and no clear direction through it.'

'Of course there will be.'

'Go on then, infect me with optimism.'

'Of course, you know crucial pointers already, the problem is you have hoarded too many little gems of information and you can't distinguish the ones that matter.' She beamed at him.

'Case closed then,' he muttered.

'Gary. Just pull in the slack.'

'I'm sorry?'

'All these little gems – perhaps they're all actually threaded on to the same bracelet. Pull in the slack and you'll see how they all sit together.'

'Oh God, optimism and analogy combined. Sorry, but I really am too tired for that.'

But she was on a roll. 'What do your instincts tell you?'

'Nothing. That's why I came to see you. I haven't got a clue any more.'

She gave the chair's armrest a decisive thump. 'I'm putting the kettle on. If you were ten years younger, I'd say you were over-tired and send you to bed.' His grandmother retreated and Goodhew closed his eyes until he heard the kettle start to boil, then followed her into the kitchen.

'I thought getting it off my chest might help.'

His grandmother raised an eyebrow. 'Does that mean you're turning over a new leaf?'

Goodhew laughed, but without humour. 'No, just a one-off.'

'You know the bracelet analogy? Maybe the gems are just in the wrong order.'

'And I suppose you already worked out what the right order is?' He took three tea bags from the canister and dropped them into the pot.

'No, I haven't the foggiest.' She pulled out a tray and he loaded it with the milk, sugar and two mugs. But she wasn't about to drop the matter either. 'If Lorna's death was planned, why do it in such an open place? Even at 1 a.m., there must've been a good chance of someone seeing them.'

'Someone put the GHB in Lorna's coffee, but how quickly it took effect wasn't entirely in the killer's hands. Perhaps the original plan was to kill her down one of the footpaths.'

He paused, aware that his grandmother's train of thought had started to wander down an obscure footpath of its own.

'Was she notably promiscuous?'

'Possibly no more so than many single people. But what I am discovering is that she was a manipulator. She pulled strings in several people's lives, then was there to pick up the pieces. I found some post at her flat, junk mail really, but it was all addressed to people she was connected to.'

'Who?'

He listed them: 'Jackie, Victoria, then two I've just visited; Hayley Sellars and Wayne Thompson. I now wonder if the killer sent them to her as some kind of reminder. Maybe Lorna had done something to hurt all four of them.'

'Does that put them on your list of suspects?' she asked.

'I don't think so,' he mused. 'The killer would hardly include themselves in the mail shot.'

'Who knows?' she replied. 'They say the best place to hide is in a crowd.

'And what's it got to do with what was written on her palms?'

'Lorna probably wrote the words herself, you know?

'Maybe,' he muttered, as he abruptly found himself heading down another stagnant backwater. 'That's the problem: too many pissing maybes.' He carried the tray through to the sitting room and his grandmother followed.

'Now *you're* swearing,' she observed.

He sank into the chair again, and his tiredness returned. He smiled wearily. 'I'm entitled to, it's a belated attempt at misspent youth.'

She changed the subject. 'Could that man Bryn have killed her?'

'Definitely not.'

'Why not?' she persisted.

Goodhew shrugged. 'Gut feeling.'

She pressed him. 'You're adamant?'

'Absolutely.'

She beamed. 'And ten minutes ago I thought you were banging on my door because you didn't know whether you could trust your own judgement any longer.'

Goodhew smiled tiredly. 'Touché.'

His mind wandered and she left him uninterrupted with his thoughts. Ten minutes later, his grandmother left the room, although he barely noticed. In his mind he was reading the labels of the junk mail envelopes, flicking through them one by one.

*Jackie Moran.*

*Victoria Nugent.*

*Hayley Sellars.*

*Wayne Thompson-Stark.*

He added more envelopes, one for Richard Moran, another for Alice Moran and a third for Bryn O'Brien. That made seven.

He knew the police would soon be swarming all over Hayley and Wayne's lives, dragging up all their worst memories. Hayley's words drifted back to him; spoken in a quiet but determined voice. *Lorna made everyone suffer.* Her words rang with such certainty. Perhaps she was wrong, but she believed it.

He flicked through the imaginary envelopes again, but now there were ten. Colin Willis had one this time, so did Kincaide, and the tenth was for Mel.

Shit, it was like a Rubik's cube, coming neatly together on one side, only to be jumbled up on another. Jumbled and blurred.

He shut his eyes and pictured the cube gently levitating and unravelling.

\* \* \*

In the kitchen, Goodhew's grandmother stared into the eye-level grill where the bread lay face up like a row of sunbathers catching the afternoon rays. She loved seeing the golden tan creep across the white slices. When the toast was uniformly brown, she stacked it on a plate, before stealing a glance into the sitting room. She watched until she was sure he really was asleep, then poured his tea down the sink and took her own mug into her bedroom.

She turned on the bedside radio, just loud enough to pick out the banter from the Heart FM DJ; at 5.55 a.m. there was no chance she was going to get back to sleep.

She glanced over at her late husband's photo, then at the photo of Gary with his sister. What did he want to prove anyway? But she knew his trouble; he had inherited a little too much of his grandfather's conscience. He had to learn to let go of the things that he couldn't put right.

On hearing the jingle for the start of the news, she carefully turned up the volume.

'A woman's body has been found in the centre of Cambridge in what looks like a shocking repeat of the recent Midsummer Common murder of Lorna Spence. A student made the grim discovery in the early hours of this morning, and early unofficial reports are are not ruling out the possibility that the deaths may be connected.'

She swung her legs back off the bed and muttered under her breath, 'So much for your sleep, Gary.'

# THIRTY-EIGHT

As Marks spoke to the coroner's office on his mobile, he turned away from the murder scene and found himself facing the window of a gift shop. A teddy dressed as a Beefeater smiled back at him. Marks wandered out of the bear's line of vision and instead stood at the end of Rose Crescent, his favourite street in the city. Such a shame for him that for some considerable time, he'd be picturing Victoria Nugent's crumpled body at the end of it.

Marks hung up just as Gary Goodhew came into view. He glared, but his subordinate was too busy staring past him towards the cordon surrounding the body for his reproachful gaze to have any effect.

Marks held on to most of the dirty look and managed to sound caustic. 'Oh, it's you, Gary. There's definitely a problem when I find it easier to identify murder victims than to recognize a member of my own team.' He immediately felt a stab of guilt, knowing that Goodhew wore responsibility like a second skin. He lived with it day in, day out, and Marks doubted that he could shake it off it he tried. If Goodhew wasn't always around, it certainly wouldn't be because he was shirking.

'Who?' Goodhew asked.

'Victoria Nugent.' Marks saw no surprise in Goodhew's eyes, just a final, almost apologetic glance in the dead girl's direction. 'Preliminaries say between eleven thirty last night and two thirty this morning.'

Goodhew looked for a second as though he was working on some kind of mental arithmetic, but all he said was, 'How?'

'Beaten and strangled. Actually, it might be the other way around. The killer pummelled her face into the ground, there's not much

222

blood, but what there is concentrated in one spot, like she wasn't capable of struggling by then.'

'Bryn?' Goodhew didn't often dabble with one-word sentences, but he was struggling to collate his thoughts. He hadn't expected another death, and he was kicking himself because the one thing his limited experience should have taught him, was to always expect the unexpected.

Marks looked quizzical.

Goodhew rephrased it into something more comprehensible. 'Has anyone spoken to him?'

'Spoken to who?' Marks still looked puzzled.

'Bryn O'Brien.'

'Where the hell did you get that from?'

'Must've mentioned it. He was the guy that dated Lorna Spence a while back.'

'I know that, and he made a statement after her death, remember? I still don't remember anything about a relationship between him and Victoria Nugent.'

Goodhew shrugged. 'Might be worth cross-checking the semen . . . if there is any, I mean.'

'You irritate me—' Marks began, then broke off mid-sentence.

After a moment, Goodhew asked another question to fill the awkward silence. 'Did the murderer leave any message?'

Marks held up a hand in protest. 'You irritate me,' he repeated, sounding more matter-of-fact, 'because I need you to be available as part of the team. Instead you resort to your disappearing skills, you shoot off like a bullet once an investigation starts, ricocheting around the case until you hit a target. I only know—' He stopped abruptly as PC Kelly Wilkes hurried over with a folded sheet of A4. 'What's this?'

'Sorry to interrupt, sir, but we've found the dead woman's mobile phone. It was handed in to PC Jerram, who's working on nights, and he's been trying to get hold of you. It appears to be registered to the dead woman, and he had a play around with it, says she was texting another mobile early this morning. He's checked that number and it is registered to a Mr O'Brien. I said I'd ask you to ring Sheen as soon as possible.'

Marks' eyes narrowed as they studied first the note, then

Goodhew's impenetrable expression. Finally he sighed. 'I was going to say next that I only know where you've been by the sound of the ricochet.' He held up the sheet and flicked it with his finger. It gave a sharp crack. 'That's today's ricochet, isn't it?'

# THIRTY-NINE

Ignoring his boss was not a deliberate ploy, and Goodhew was well aware that Marks had a point. But even so, just as Marks was making it, Goodhew stopped listening to him. Instead, his attention focused about two hundred yards further towards the city centre, as he watched a familiar figure turn and walk away from the police cordon.

'I'm sorry, sir, I'll only be a minute,' Goodhew said, and ran towards the cordon before Marks could order him to stop.

A couple of heads turned as he passed and he thought he heard Marks shout his name, but he was only interested in catching up with the man he'd just spotted. He made it past the barricade, and on to the market square beyond just in time to see Bryn O'Brien vanish behind the striped canvas awning of the organic fruit and veg stand.

Goodhew kept running along between the rows of stalls as Bryn headed along a parallel path of the adjoining street, along the perimeter of the market. He didn't try to hurry, and never looked back, but when Goodhew emerged suddenly from a gap to his right, O'Brien didn't seem surprised either.

He stopped squarely in front of Goodhew. Bryn's smart clothes were gone now, and the scuffed boots were back, but this time teamed with jeans instead of overalls. That gave him two deep front pockets, ideal for stuffing his hands into, which was what he immediately did. 'What do you want?' he demanded.

Goodhew turned and began to walk away, only speaking when Bryn caught up with him. 'You came to find me,' he pointed out. 'So what do you want?'

'I wanted to know who's dead.'

Goodhew kept walking, looking straight ahead, forcing Bryn to make all the effort. 'Don't you already know?' he asked coolly.

'Why would I?' And what sounded like indignation in Bryn's voice could have been panic.

Goodhew slowed his pace slightly. 'What are you afraid of, Bryn?'

'The only person you knew connected to Lorna was Victoria Nugent. So—' Goodhew halted abruptly and spun round to face Bryn. 'Are you afraid that she's the victim or afraid of having the police on your back?'

'It is Victoria then?'

'That's right.' Breaking news of a death should have prompted more sympathy, but Goodhew felt strangely detached. 'But why were you looking for me?'

'I told you.'

'No, why me? Why not call the station, or ask the PC at the cordon or, come to that, wait for the *Cambridge News* like the rest of the general public?

Bryn scowled. 'I just thought you'd tell me.'

'So you thought I'd treat you differently?'

'Gary, what's your problem?' Bryn held up his hands in a gesture of surrender. 'I'm sorry you've got a bit of an issue here. The bottom line is, you did tell me, so you did treat me differently.'

This time it was Bryn who started walking away. Goodhew watched him tramp towards the corner before catching up. He launched straight in. 'Including Colin Willis, we now have three deaths and, as far as I can tell, you are the only person who knew all of them, so you're right in the middle of this.'

'I'm not in the middle,' Bryn argued. 'I just look like I am.'

'OK, so when did you last see Victoria Nugent?'

'I don't know.'

'Don't know? Not last night then?'

Bryn shook his head.

Goodhew persisted. 'Did you see her last night?'

'No.' It sounded as though Bryn was testing out the word at first, and he must have thought that it sounded all right, because he immediately repeated it again with more confidence. 'I didn't see her,' he added for good measure.

Anger surged through Goodhew. All at once, it punched him squarely in the gut. He grabbed at Bryn's shoulder, spinning him around into a shop entrance. 'Do I have gullible stamped on my forehead or something?' he growled.

Bryn paled. 'What are you on about?'

'You're a liar.'

'I didn't see her.'

'I know, for a fact, you were the last person to be with her.' There was no way they were about to debate this and he rammed it home with a prod of his finger. 'I *know* you were with her at Lorna's flat, too. Do you really think that we wouldn't have the place under surveillance?'

Bryn groaned. 'Who else knows?'

'Let's just say that depends on how soon the swab results come back from the forensics lab.'

Bryn took a couple of seconds to digest this comment, acknowledging its impact by groaning again. Goodhew reached forward and hauled him out of the doorway. Bryn half walked and was half dragged around the corner into Petty Cury's pedestrianized arcade and through the newly unlocked doors of a sandwich shop. A surly woman in a cheerful gingham apron was too busy wiping the work surfaces to even look in their direction. The long glass counter was still empty, so it was just as well that they had no desire to place an order.

Apart from the counter, the place had a token table and two chairs. They both sat down on opposite sides. Bryn spoke first. 'What happens now?' he whispered.

'I need to take you in, and you have to make a statement.'

'So why are we here?'

'I want to ask you some questions of my own.'

'Off the record?'

'You're just telling me first. And I wouldn't be economical with the truth if I were you, it has a way of coming out in the end.'

'That's what my mother always says.'

'Yeah, well, that's what I think too.'

Bryn shrugged. 'OK then.'

'You made out you barely knew Victoria, and said there was nothing going on between you and Lorna. Why lie?'

'I didn't.'

'You had sex with both of them.'

'But there wasn't anything else going on.'

Goodhew rapped the table with his knuckles. 'Hello! Most people call that more than nothing.'

'Why? If we'd only gone to the same gym or restaurant, now and again, then it would be fine to say there was nothing important. We just happened to . . . you know . . . that was all.'

'Just happened to? And how did you just happen to break and enter into Lorna Spence's flat?'

'Victoria had a key, and she said she'd lost something.'

'The diary?'

Bryn shook his head in dismay. 'What don't you know, eh?'

'At the moment, I'd say everything that matters. She called you first, I assume?'

Bryn nodded. 'Yeah, she phoned me yesterday, said she wanted to meet up. I didn't mind, actually.' Bryn pulled an apologetic face. 'I did fancy her, she looked just like August off last year's calendar. It was still pinned up by the kettle until recently.'

'Then you met her and threw it out?' Goodhew replied sarcastically.

'No, I met her and moved it next to the phone.'

'This is a murder.'

'I know, I know, and I'm sorry but I was just being honest.'

Goodhew interrupted him. 'OK. When did you decide to go to Lorna's?'

'Victoria suggested it as soon as I saw her again. She said she had a key and we'd be in and out in a minute. I didn't like it, but she argued that it wasn't a crime scene any more, and we weren't breaking in. I thought that made sense, until we got there. Then I knew, straight away, that we were doing something we shouldn't.'

With only minor prompting, Bryn described everything Goodhew already knew.

'So,' Bryn concluded, 'even I can see that the diary was invented, which means she wanted me there for some other reason.'

'And?'

'I don't know the answer.'

'It's common knowledge that Lorna and Victoria fell out, but supposedly over a man. You're the only one I can find who has slept with both of them, but you are also the only person who disputes this theory.'

'So?'

'So, it's my theory that, whatever they fought over, it wasn't a lover. I think Victoria tried to make you think there was jealousy between them, after all, as a diversion from the real reason.'

'Hey!' The voice belonged to the surly woman with the gingham apron. They both looked up. She had her hands on her hips. 'This isn't a bus shelter. Are you ordering or not?'

It was a not, Goodhew decided. He jerked his head towards the door. 'I'm going to walk you to Parkside station.'

Bryn liked to think he could take things in his stride – tackle new obstacles running – roll with the punches. Fine in theory, but the last twenty-four hours had demonstrated that his everyday life hadn't, up until now, been very challenging. It had been hours since his Zodiac had ground to a halt, but it was only as he and Gary stepped back out into Petty Cury that his world finally stopped spinning. And it felt better that way.

'I'm sorry I lied,' he said and retrieved his mobile from his pocket. He hoped that sharing it with Gary might keep the brakes fully engaged. 'I had a text from her last night.'

'From Victoria?'

'It arrived while I was waiting to be towed, but I was too pissed off to look at it until I'd got the car safely back.' Bryn opened the message, but couldn't bring himself to read it again.

He passed the phone to Gary.

'You didn't take it seriously?' Gary asked.

'I didn't know what to make of it. I never thought it really meant she was, you know . . .'

'Dead?'

'Yep.' Bryn tried to push the thought away. He wanted to ask how she'd died but, at the same time, he guessed he didn't really want to find out. So he shoved his hands into his pockets and stayed quiet.

'I suppose your trip down the M11 is your only alibi?'

'Won't that do?'

'It depends on the precise timings.'

Bryn felt his stomach make an uneasy shift. 'I wouldn't hurt anyone.'

'I want to believe you.' Gary smiled, but Bryn wasn't too blind to see the melancholy behind it.

'Sure, and I want you to. And I also want the patron saint of panel-beaters to pop the dent out of my Zodiac's wing, but things like that only happen when you make them.'

'You mean, you make your own luck?'

'Exactly.' Bryn said it with more bravado than he felt.

Gary seemed to be thinking things over. 'What was supposed to be in Victoria's diary?'

'She called it "intimate" and said it would be humiliating if anyone else read it.'

'And you believed her?'

'Why not? She wasn't very inhibited, I'm sure she did some wild stuff in the past.'

'But she didn't seem the apologetic type. I can't imagine her feeling humiliated by exposure.'

They were within a couple of hundred yards of the police station and Bryn was aware that he was now walking more slowly. He didn't want to sit in some soulless interview room sharing the details of his last twenty-four hours with a complete stranger.

'Anyway,' Gary pointed ahead, 'we're here now and it doesn't matter about the diary. I was more interested in your reasons for believing her. And I think you've been very gullible.'

That comment stung and Bryn suddenly felt indignant. 'No, remember she worked with Richard and Alice Moran on a day-to-day basis. I can understand she would have felt humiliated if it had all come out. Most normal people would find that situation pretty kinky.'

Gary scowled. 'What are you on about?' Just then his mobile rang, but he made no move to answer it.

Bryn hesitated, then replied, just as Gary reached into his jacket after all.

# FORTY

Bryn's most recent words echoed something else Goodhew had heard, but he just couldn't place what it was. He struggled to retrieve the memory, but it was wedged on the edge of his subconscious.

And his mobile was still ringing. He wanted to ignore it, but knew he would find it too distracting. He finally answered, planning to promise to ring the caller back. But the voice at the other end was Mel's, and his intended words caught in his throat just long enough for her to start to deliver the message.

She sounded awkward, or maybe he imagined she did. 'You have an urgent message from a woman. It's personal, she said, and made me promise to pass it on straight away.' She paused. 'OK?'

'Uh-huh.'

'She wants you to ring her on her mobile about a horse called Suze.'

He waited for more, but there wasn't any. 'That's it?'

'What else were you expecting, something about a boy named Sue?'

'What?'

'The song? Oh, never mind.' She sounded embarrassed now. 'I was being silly. Sorry.'

'OK, fine. I'll call her.' He knew he sounded brusque, but he couldn't help it. 'I'm just about to drop off Bryn O'Brien at the station. Ring DI Marks immediately and let him know.'

He slipped the phone back into his pocket and concentrated on Bryn. 'Did you just say something about "Victoria and the dad"?'

Bryn managed a combination of shrugging, nodding and looking apprehensive. 'Victoria was going out with old man Moran till he died. You didn't know?'

231

'No one mentioned it. So what else do you know about them?'

'Nothing except that he was rich and she was gorgeous. I think it was what's called mutually beneficial.'

'Right. You sure?'

'Ask the Morans.'

Goodhew nodded, still fighting for that elusive memory. 'And what did you say just before that?'

'No idea.'

'Come on, I said you'd been pretty gullible, and you said . . .'

'Oh yeah, yeah, I was just saying that working with the Morans would make any sexy stuff between her and the dad more embarrassing, especially as her best mate was shagging his son.'

Goodhew snapped his fingers as he finally got it. 'No, you didn't say "sexy". You said "kinky".'

'And?'

Goodhew tapped Bryn's arm. 'And we've been loitering outside for too long. Time to get in and help us with our enquiries.'

# FORTY-ONE

Goodhew accompanied Bryn as far as the main entrance, confident that Bryn wasn't stupid enough to abscond through the rear door.

He then rang Mel again. 'One more thing,' he said without preamble. 'Marks has the Joanne Reed case notes in his office. I'll be back shortly, so please get them ready and I'll grab them on my way past.'

'OK,' she said.

'It's urgent,' he added.

'Fine,' she replied, probably thinking he was lazy for not doing it himself. He thought he probably was. He had nothing else to add, so he just hung up. Now he'd be arrogant, as well as lazy.

He was still standing at the top of the steps leading into Parkside station as he rang Jackie Moran's mobile. Looking towards the city centre as he put the phone to his ear, he noticed that her RAV4 was parked in the nearest of the metered bays to his right. He could make out the shape of someone sitting in the driver's seat, but he couldn't tell if it was Jackie Moran herself. But then, as the phone began to ring, he saw her step on to the pavement in the same instant as he heard her voice. 'Thanks for phoning me,' she said.

'Stay there,' he said and hung up.

Today she was wearing navy-blue jodhpurs and a dark-green pullover, making him wonder how often she dressed for anywhere but a visit to the stables. She had a large manila envelope pressed to her chest with her arms wrapped around it, like high school girls held their books in 1950s teen movies.

Two things had altered, though. Firstly she was dogless and secondly, even from a distance, he could see a marked change in her

233

body language. She stood on the path with feet planted squarely and, as he came closer, he saw she had a resolute expression to match her stance.

'Why the coded message?' he asked.

'I didn't want to be fobbed off with anyone else,' she replied.

'Look, it all depends what you're going to say, but I can't promise that I will be allowed to deal with it.'

'I've made a decision, and now all I want is some moral support. I think I can trust you?'

'Sure, but . . .'

She took a deep breath. 'Don't spoil it. I want support, not an accomplice.'

'All I was about to say is that my authority is practically zero. I'm still a junior officer.'

'Determination outranks rank, you know.'

Goodhew gave a short laugh. 'Everyone's a philosopher today. Let's sit down somewhere, and you can show me what's in the envelope, and then I'll either take a statement or stay with you while you repeat it to my superior. Is that suitably supportive?'

'Absolutely.' She started to walk towards Parkside station. 'I think I may as well talk to you inside, as I don't think this will be quick.'

Mel must have seen him arrive because she was already waiting with Joanne Reed's case notes. She silently passed them over and he thanked her. He tried to make eye contact, too, but she just turned away again.

Two rooms further along the corridor from Mel's desk was an unoccupied office containing nothing but two chairs and a small desk, but with a large window overlooking the rear car park. Goodhew decided that it was the ideal place and the window clinched it.

The rear of the desk was set against the wall and they sat along the other side, facing each other. 'Before we go any further,' Goodhew began, 'I need to know something about Joanne Reed.'

Jackie looked towards the ceiling as if trying to recall where she'd heard that name. 'The girl that disappeared from university?' She was trying to sound vague or surprised, or both. In fact, she managed neither.

'Did you know her?' Goodhew asked.

'No.' The answer was of the not-up-for-debate-definitely-not type. He didn't believe her, but decided to move on. His folder lay on his lap, Jackie's envelope tantalizingly close to him on the desktop.

'OK then,' he said. 'Fire away.'

'I've heard about the new murder.'

'What do you know, exactly?'

'That there's a connection to Lorna.' Colour briefly flushed her cheeks, and then was gone. 'Is it Victoria?'

Goodhew gave a small nod. 'Yes.'

'I'm sorry. I didn't know her too well, but . . .' Her sentence drifted into silence. 'I've realized it's time to talk to you, because I killed Colin Willis.' She put her hand on the envelope, not to pass it over, more to hold on to it. 'Your tests would have shown that the dog fur was Bridy's in any case.'

'So why not tell us at the time?'

Jackie turned her face away, and seemed to be frowning at the desktop. Her expression remained unchanged through several minutes, even when she looked up again. 'I was still trying to understand it all,' she said. 'I thought it was over, so I didn't realize that there was any urgency. Then, with this other death, I knew I was wrong.'

Goodhew suspected that her earlier show of confidence had been brought on by nothing more than the decision to act. Since entering the room, her skin had lost its former colour and her expression had changed into the sluggishness of perpetual shock. He wanted her to keep talking so that her resolve to tell all didn't diminish. 'How well did you know Willis?'

'I didn't. I'd seen him hanging around on the footpath beside the river several times. I only noticed him in the first place because his presence there made me feel slightly uncomfortable. But you know, by the time he attacked me, I'd convinced myself that I was being paranoid. I walked past him and he suddenly grabbed my throat.' As if to illustrate it, she put her hand to her own throat. She closed her eyes as she recounted the attack. By the time she had described Colin Willis' body disappearing into the Cam, she was still clenching her own neck and breathing hard.

Goodhew reached forward and gently pulled her hand away. She opened her eyes and gulped in just enough air to calm herself. When she spoke again she sounded hoarse. 'I'm not sorry I killed him, because I don't think I had any choice. But I'm sorry I didn't call for help. I know I should have made a statement at the time. I still have nightmares about it. I have nightmares about everything. And I've regretted it so many times. I know I should have told you at the time you took those fur samples from Bridy.'

'Why didn't you?'

'For the same reason I slid his body into the river.'

'I thought that was on impulse?'

'It was . . . when I saw the knife I realized that he'd been planning to kill me. It didn't seem at all random, then, but like someone had put him up to it, and that's what I couldn't deal with. And I thought if I came forward, no one would believe me. In that moment I thought that, just by getting rid of him, I wouldn't have to face up to the truth that someone, probably someone I know, actually wanted me dead.'

'Like who?'

'I don't know.' Jackie bit one side of her bottom lip and stared at him.

Goodhew felt as though she was weighing him up, having second thoughts about telling him this. 'But you have some information, you say?'

Her gaze moved away from him and fixed itself on the envelope. For the first time, tears welled in her eyes. 'I've had it for weeks.' She passed him the envelope. 'But I didn't know it would lead to all of this.'

'You had it before Lorna died?'

She nodded.

'And when she was murdered, you still didn't think you needed to come forward?'

Again colour rose in her cheeks but, this time, spread with enough intensity to reach her temples. 'I didn't think there was a connection. I just thought . . . oh, I don't know, maybe that she was the victim of a random attack.'

'Until you heard that there had been another death?' He slid his hand into the envelope. It was the kind that had gusseted sides and had been slightly puffed out, and looked fat enough to contain a sheaf of papers, so he was surprised to find only one sheet.

She nodded again and rubbed her face with the heel of her hand. 'I'm sorry.'

He laid the page on to the table in front of him. It was A5 size, and made from a flimsy cream paper, the sort that can sound like a crisp hundred decibels when it's the only sound in an empty room. It had been written on by a dark-blue ball-point pen. The handwriting was angular and erratic, and had been applied with sufficient force to cause the imprint of the words subsequently written on the back of the page to interfere with reading the words on the front.

'Do you recognize the writing?'

'Read it,' she whispered. 'You'll see.'

It started mid-sentence:

*so drained. All these successive entries of 'nothing to note, nothing to note'. I watched the hare and ignored the tortoise.*

*Alice was full of anger today. It is the same cold temper that she's always had, but today was the first time I've noticed it directed at her own sister. I should have known, her love for Richard . . . Jealousy is a dark and irrational beast.*

*I have been obsessively documenting one scenario, thinking that I can contain the problem when, in reality, I may have given free rein to the genuine demon. Only circumstance, and not my intervention, has stopped further deaths occurring.*

*When I face God, I hope he forgives me, I have been so selfish.*

Then there was a small gap before the writing continued.

*Despite yesterday's low, I have made the decision to continue this journal. I love them all, regardless of any flaws. I believe I have been right, and wrong, in equal measures.*

*Of course, I'm just as scared for Jackie as I've always been, but I will speak to Alice, because I'm sure she would never harm her own sister.*

Goodhew read it twice. There were no dates and no clue to the author's identity. 'Your father?' he guessed.

She nodded. 'He was a compulsive list scribbler, one of those people that seemed unable to think without a pen in his hand.'

'And this was the only page you've seen?'

'Yes. I don't know what it was torn out of either.'

'How did you get it?'

'I found it at the farm the day Colin Willis tried to kill me. I suppose I was in shock, but I still had to go over and see to the horses. It was in the stable, the one with the bales where we sat. I took Suze out for a couple of hours, and found it when I returned.'

'You think someone deliberately left it while you were out with her?'

Jackie's left elbow was resting on the table, and her left palm was propping up her head at the temple. He wondered whether her brain was starting to hurt. His certainly was.

'It may have been there already, I really don't know.'

'What does he mean by further deaths? It implies someone had already died.'

She blew out a long, slow sigh. 'I don't understand that bit.'

'OK. Are you saying that you think Alice may have hired Colin Willis?'

She dropped her hand away from her face and sounded surprised. 'No, of course not. That's not what I meant. The note implies that she hates me, and it's true we're not close, but I think it was just left there to frame her. If I *had* been killed, it would have been found there, and she would have been investigated, wouldn't she?'

'Undoubtedly, so the next question is who could have taken it from your father?'

Her eyes opened wider. 'I don't know about any casual visitors, but I'd say the main suspects would have been the three of us—'

'You, Richard and Alice?'

'Yes, and Victoria.'

'So you knew that your father dated Victoria?'

'Of course. It was common knowledge.' He saw a glint of amusement spring on to her face. 'They even went out together *in public.*'

'You never mentioned Victoria and your father.'

'Because you were investigating Lorna's background then – why would I?'

238

'So how did you feel about her?'

'In what way?'

'She was only about your age and having an affair with your dad, wasn't that weird?'

'No, I barely knew her. In any case, my father would just have told me to mind my own business.'

'And what about Richard and Alice? They actually worked with her.'

She shrugged. 'I doubt they were much bothered – but even if they were, Richard's never had my father's ear so he couldn't have influenced anything, and Alice would have kept her thoughts to herself.

'It's only because I was so much younger than them that it was different for me. They've always had each other, so they wouldn't care about what he was doing. It affected me the most, but Dad made the rules in our house and we stuck to them.'

# FORTY-TWO

Grey areas were always the most difficult to navigate, and as soon as Goodhew had finished talking to Jackie Moran, he found himself in the middle of one, because he didn't know what to do with her next. He wasn't about to sit with her until Marks returned, but he didn't want to leave her alone either. Arresting her didn't seem appropriate, but considering that she'd just admitted to killing a man, perhaps it was. In the end, he spotted PC Kelly Wilkes arriving back in the car park. As soon as she'd locked her vehicle he tapped loudly on the glass, and when she saw him at the window she pointed at him and signalled to him to stay. By the time she arrived in the corridor, she had her mobile phone in her hand and was brandishing it in his direction like it was on stun mode. Meanwhile, she sliced her other hand backwards and forwards across her throat.

'You're dead,' she whispered, then spoke louder: 'DI Marks is on the phone.' She slapped the phone into his palm.

Goodhew guided her through the door to Jackie. 'Look after her till I get back,' he said, then shut the door behind him and tentatively raised the phone to his ear. 'Sir?'

'You deliberately walked away from me. You were openly insubordinate in front of my team and in public.' His voice was icy. 'Furthermore, you then refuse to respond to your mobile.'

'It was turned off.' Goodhew bit his lip; there was no point in saying anything to excuse himself, he knew from Marks' tone that he'd gone far too far this time.

'Go back to your desk, sit there and don't move a muscle until I arrive. I might not get back for quite some time. Do you understand?'

'Yes, sir.'

'Good, because if those ants in your pants take you anywhere at all, I'm going to be treating it as gross misconduct. Where's Wilkes?'

'With Jackie Moran, sir. I was just about to ring you.' Goodhew brought his boss fully up to date, and only hoped that news of the progress made with her and Bryn O'Brien would defuse the worst of his anger.

Goodhew apologized to PC Wilkes for having her keep Jackie Moran company, then returned to his desk with a coffee in one hand and Joanne Reed's case notes in the other. Even with the challenge of sitting still, he had plenty to do and began searching for the reference to anything that could be construed as 'kinky'. It didn't take him long, and in fact he wondered how he'd missed it the first time round, but on the second page of the inventory of items found at her flat were listed the contents of her wardrobe. Item 6 – S and M whip.

One person's kinky was another person's bland, but to him there was nothing else on the list that seemed any racier than her lacy knickers. Whoever had picked that description for the item had clearly enjoyed one lad's mag too many the night before.

He switched on his PC, then drained his coffee cup and wandered off for a refill. When Marks had ordered him not to move a muscle he was sure that he hadn't meant it literally.

By the time he returned, it had completed booting up, and the hard disk was now silent after chugging through its endless stream of security programs. It always seemed so much more efficient when he didn't watch it: if only Marks would accept the same excuse from him. Goodhew went straight on to the Internet, ignoring his new emails, and to Google where he typed in *Dr Moran Cambridge.* The usual long list appeared, headed by a link to eBay, where it seemed items on both 'doctors' and Cambridge were popular. One day he would investigate an effective way to use a search engine, but for now expert scrollbar control was his limit. At the bottom of the first page, the word 'obituary' jumped out. He double-clicked and in milliseconds he was viewing a recent photograph of Dr Alex Moran, Cambridge – physician, father, and founder of the Excelsior Clinic.

Goodhew stared thoughtfully at the photo, and the face in the photo stared back enigmatically. It would be fair, Goodhew decided, to describe him as a man in his late fifties. He right-clicked the photo and selected copy, then pasted the picture into a newly created email. He added only his own mobile number, and the words 'Call me if this is the man.'

On his phone he arrowed 'up' through the list of last dialled numbers until he recognized Martin Reed's, then he pressed 'dial'.

Mrs Reed answered with just 'Hello'.

'This is DC Goodhew,' he replied. 'Is Mr Reed there, please?'

He'd gone for a walk and she didn't expect him home for another hour. She began to fish for the reason for Goodhew's call.

'I'm sorry, there's still no news of Joanne, but I do need to send him an email. Do you have a computer?' They did, and Goodhew sat and gazed at the screen long after the 'sent' message had disappeared.

Mel had entered Marks' office, almost certain that it would be empty. It was, but that left her with a dilemma. She turned the envelope over and over in her hand. The DC who had brought it in had insisted that it must be given to Marks, not kept for him in admin; and no way was it to be left sitting on his desk. As far as she could see, that now meant hanging round until Marks returned.

Then she saw a second option: hand it to another detective working on the same investigation. And so what if the only one in the building was Goodhew; wasn't it time they cleared the air?

She found him sitting at his desk, seemingly oblivious to everything apart from his PC screen. 'Just the person,' she began.

'Jump to the front of the queue.'

'What queue?'

'Never mind, go for it.' He sat back in his chair. There was no urgency in his expression and she sensed his interest in her had evaporated.

'Kincaide and I . . .' She stumbled over the words, took a breath and began again. 'Look, I know you saw us and it's obvious you don't approve.'

'It's none of my business.'

'Well, actually, that's my point. You don't have the right to take it out on me. I'm sorry if you feel personally affected by my relationships but—'

242

'I don't. I was surprised . . .' He paused, then corrected himself. 'More than surprised, actually. When you were crying the other morning, I thought it was because of Toby, and I thought that was the mess you were trying to untangle yourself from, not a relationship with Kincaide.'

There was something in the way Goodhew worded things that made them sound far less complicated than they were, like unmessing her life could be as easy as pressing a button marked 'reverse'. She flopped into the nearest vacant chair, and they spent the next couple of minutes in a strangely amicable silence.

In the end it was Goodhew who spoke first, 'I had no right to be upset with you, and I'm sorry if you feel I've been sort of stalking you.'

'Stalking?'

'The whole transparent thing.'

Mel smiled for what felt like the first time in days. 'That's not how I meant it, and I've decided it's good to know someone who can see the real you.'

'Is it?'

'What's the point otherwise?' She held out the envelope. 'This is for Marks, and I'm not supposed to leave it lying around, would you pass it to him personally when you next see him?'

'Sure, what is it?'

'Some sort of book, but I don't know exactly, only that it came from Victoria Nugent's place. DI Marks phoned the team on charge there and asked them to look for it, and they found it almost immediately.'

Once he was alone again, Goodhew opened the envelope. If his guess was correct, he was about to set eyes on the book from which Jackie Moran's page had been torn.

The best lies, the most convincing ones, are grounded in truth. When Victoria took Bryn O'Brien to Lorna's flat she pretended that she had lost a diary. There were countless other stories she could have concocted, but she chose one she could easily remember. One that was connected with something true.

All this was obvious now Marks had worked it out. At some point in the morning he had called the team investigating Victoria's flat and asked asking them to make a special search for anything resembling Alex Moran's journal, and bingo.

Goodhew slid it out on to his desk. It had a navy-blue hard-back cover, a red linen spine, and looked like it had once been part of the stationery supplies of a government department circa 1972. The pages were sewn in place rather than glued, and Goodhew immediately saw that the cream paper matched the loose sheet. The book itself was just over a quarter of an inch thick. He opened it at the back and thumbed forward until he located the last used page. The book was almost empty, and he continued to flick forward, turning a total of eleven pages before he reached the front.

A date and the number '56' were inscribed on the inside cover. Did that mean there had been another fifty-five of them? Moran had started on this one a couple of months before he died, so fifty-five of them would probably take him back at least twenty years.

There were no dates, but it seemed as though he'd written something in it every day, commenting that there was 'nothing to note', or in some cases abbreviating this to 'ntn', rather than skipping a day. His style was rambling, and initially it was difficult to grasp his purpose. He frequently mentioned his daughter Jackie. He felt she had been in some kind of danger, and just as he had on the torn-out sheet, he wrote that he was scared for her. As Goodhew turned each new page, it was her name that constantly jumped out, but the purpose of the journal only hit him as he reached the end of the fifth page.

*I have always thought that two things keep me from handing her over, namely my fears for her safety and the slimmest doubt that I am mistaken. But now I think I have been kidding myself. There will be no one left to monitor Jackie once I am gone. I don't know whether I can ask Richard and Alice, since they have isolated themselves from her; it is as if they know. I only ever know on a day-by-day basis that all is well, but I cannot be sure she won't do something again. I made excuses for her when David died, but she isn't a child now. It may be better that she languishes in an institution rather than risk having another innocent family suffer. I think I must visit Martin Reed.*

244

Goodhew's stomach lurched. The one seperated page had appeared to point to Alice, but the rest of this journal was her father's documentation of his younger daughter's guilt. He turned to the sixth page and scanned the words, looking for any reference to the proposed visit to Martin Reed. He spotted it on the opposite page, and he traced the words with his index finger to prevent himself from rushing ahead too quickly:

*Why did I visit him in the first place? Did I think that I could learn to sidestep the occasional waves of guilt that swamp me even at this late stage? I know my own shortcomings, and loving Jackie as I do has made me a victim of her.*

*I think he is a braver man than me, since he wants to face the truth and, despite my intentions to do so, I am incapable of making myself break it to him. Instead, I prefer to think that I am being kinder by keeping the rotten truth from him. If her body turned out to be somewhere else I would have made things worse again, although in my heart of hearts I know I am correct. There are only so many good places to hide a decaying corpse.*

By the time Marks returned to the building, the journal was back in its newly sealed envelope, and photocopies of the eleven pages were safely hidden in Goodhew's inside jacket pocket.

# FORTY-THREE

'My office,' Marks growled, 'Now.' He didn't wait for a response before he strode off. Goodhew grabbed his phone, the sealed envelope and Joanne Reed's case notes and darted after his boss.

Marks sat down at his desk, but with no paperwork in front of him. In fact, all that was in front of him were his crossed arms. Body-language experts claimed that folded arms were a sign of ill ease, but from where Goodhew was standing, it looked like Marks' folded arms might be the only things preventing him from exploding.

Goodhew approached the visitor's chair. 'Is it OK if I sit, sir?'

His backside had barely touched the seat before Marks began. 'When I saw you this morning, I had the distinct impression that you were not taking your responsibilities seriously.' His voice wasn't raised, but he spat out the words in succinct volleys and it didn't sound as though attempting to interrupt or answer would be wise.

'You,' he continued, 'are the youngest DC we have ever had working in this department. You may think you are merely acting on your own initiative, but you have nowhere near enough experience of life, never mind the police force, to even begin to comprehend what genuine initiative is and how to employ it effectively. I need people who follow orders, people who follow protocol and, most of all, who follow things through. You may be bright and talented, but I thought I'd made it clear that I wouldn't hesitate in getting shot of you if you kept pissing me around. Do you really think that I have somehow given you a mandate to do whatever the hell you like?'

Marks glared. Goodhew said nothing.

'In case you're confused, that was not one of my rhetorical questions, Gary.'

Goodhew shook his head then. 'No, sir, I don't.'

'I have a technique I apply when I want to get a really clear picture of how an individual is affecting my team. I imagine that the team consists entirely of clones of that same person. When I visualize a team consisting only of Gary Goodhews, it is anarchic, inappropriate and intolerable. I will concede that you do have moments of brilliance, but you made your own choice. When I said those anonymous notes had to stop, I was serious.'

Goodhew tried to interrupt, but Marks carried on over him. 'Yes, you're right, I can't prove a thing. But I *know*.' He tapped his forehead just above the left eyebrow. 'I tell the team that we now have DNA from the so-called Airport Rapist; next thing I get sent the match I need. Lorna Spence's flat was searched within hours of me ordering you not to. And what the hell was the idea of tipping off the newspaper with the "I'm like Emma" connection?'

That caught him out. 'I didn't,' he protested, but Marks was already rolling on.

'It was not information that the papers should have received at that stage, and though earlier I considered turning a blind eye to all of this, such unauthorized pow-wowing with the press, combined with your erratic behaviour today, has finally forced my hand. Do you have anything to say to me?'

'I didn't contact the newspaper.'

'Wrong answer.' There was a long pause before Marks spoke again. 'The fact is, I am not prepared to work with you any longer, Goodhew.'

Goodhew nodded to himself. Hadn't he asked for just that?

His mobile rang, its relatively sober ring tone sounding like a crass interruption. He glanced at Marks, who nodded for him to answer it.

The call took less than thirty seconds, and he subsequently relayed its contents to his boss in the hope that he would salvage at least something from this meeting. 'That was Martin Reed, sir. He rang to confirm that the man who visited him, posing as a detective, was in fact Dr Alex Moran.'

'How . . .?'

'I emailed him a photograph.'

'So what's your theory on the page now?'

'I don't know.' Goodhew bit his lip.

'No, not good enough. You had enough insight to show him the picture, so tell me more.'

'It was just the mention of "further deaths". I think he knew he was dying and went to see Martin Reed in an attempt to "put things in order". I don't know what connection he had with Joanne Reed. He sounds as though he was feeling guilty when he wrote that page, so perhaps he thought seeing Martin Reed would clear his conscience.'

Marks raised his eyebrows. 'Like I said, moments of brilliance, but that's just not enough.'

Goodhew took a deep breath. 'What happens now?'

Marks' tone was cool and final. 'Go home, take leave for the rest of the week. By Monday, you'll be assigned to another department.'

# FORTY-FOUR

Kincaide had already spent the best part of the day working through Jackie Moran's statement with her. She'd made it transparently clear that she didn't like him much, or at all in fact, and he reckoned this was probably because he wasn't letting her prattle on about her flock of animals. She showed more concern for them than any of the people she mentioned, particularly the one she'd strangled. At this rate, he'd be stuck with her for a few more hours yet.

He glanced at his watch and wondered whether he could engineer enough of a break to sort out the Mel situation. He didn't like the way she'd cooled off, and had no idea what had caused it, but neither did he think that she'd need much coaxing. With her type, a little attention went a long way.

He suddenly realized Jackie Moran was staring at him.

'You didn't write anything down,' she said. 'If you've finished, I'd like to go, because I need to see to the horses.'

'Sorry.' He smiled as he said it, and decided in that moment that he'd definitely take a break, even if it achieved nothing more than delay her departure.

But, before he could say anything, the door opened, Marks appeared and beckoned him into the corridor.

'How's it going?

Kincaide shrugged. 'I don't buy that self-defence argument of hers.'

'But she's sticking to it?'

'Not budging.'

'Might be worth picking it up again in the morning. Arrange for her to come back here first thing.'

Kincaide wasn't about to argue, and made a swift exit. As he walked towards the stairs, he thought of Mel again and grinned. Now there'd be plenty of time to get her back on track. With any luck, he'd still be home in time to remind Jan that their own weekly routine had slipped by a few days. Perfunctory it might be, but it was still worth doing.

# FORTY-FIVE

It was almost 9 p.m. before Goodhew met up with his grandmother.

'So is that a suspension or not?' she asked.

'One step short. I don't think Marks would want to try to explain why he never took an official line on those anonymous notes, especially if he actually suspected they were an internal issue. He's not happy though.'

Goodhew had finished explaining the current situation to his grandmother, and they were seated by the window in the Galleria, a small Italian restaurant by the river. Goodhew had chosen it himself, and it was no coincidence that it was within sight of the unlit Excelsior Clinic. The waiter returned to their table with the pepper mill and ground some on his bolognese. His grandmother had ordered salad and he had no doubt that her pale blouse would stay unblemished; his white shirt wouldn't be so lucky.

He waited until they were alone again before he continued. 'But to be honest, it's not as bad as I thought.'

Her fork hesitated a couple of inches from her mouth, and then descended. 'I thought you'd be devastated.'

'Of course I'm upset, but on the other hand, what's really changed? As long as I'm in the building, I'll still have access to information on various cases, so I can still do things in my own time.'

'Gary, that's the part of your behaviour you're suppose to curb. You've had a lucky escape, so imagine if you were caught.'

'I'm learning, but I just need to be more careful, and I'm proud of the things I've achieved. The one misdemeanor that's got me into more hot water with Marks than anything else is the one I didn't do.'

'I'm confused now. Which one didn't you do?'

'I never tipped off the local papers.'

'You didn't? I thought you were bluffing.'

'If I'm such a useless liar, why can't you work out when I'm telling the truth?' Goodhew frowned and twirled some spaghetti on to his fork then said, 'Marks assumed I'd done it. That's why he never asked anyone to look into it. We need to know who really did tip off the papers and, more importantly, why.'

'We? Does that mean you and me or you and your colleagues?'

'Either – does it matter who comes up with the answer?'

'With you it's just one big rush for the truth, isn't it? Doesn't matter who gets there first, just as long as it gets uncovered.'

'And what's wrong with that?'

'You watch too many old movies. What's it going to take to tuck you safely back under Marks' wing?'

If she'd seen the finality in Marks' dismissal of him, she wouldn't have even bothered asking that question. In truth, he knew how bad he'd feel if he was left to follow the rest of this case via press reports and snippets of canteen chat.

For the last couple of hours he'd been bloody-minded and unrealistically upbeat about it all, and that had suited him fine, but now, as he stared across towards the Excelsior Clinic, he knew he had to face the reality of his situation. It would take much more than his grandmother's sympathetic ear or the agreeable diversion of their surroundings to buffer him from the sick and empty feeling currently hollowing out the pit of his stomach.

Once they had finished eating, he excused himself and left. He needed to be alone now, just like he was alone with the mess he'd created for himself. He walked towards the centre of the city, knowing that the hollow feeling wasn't going to disappear, but somehow hoping that walking past the places where Victoria Nugent and Lorna Spence had died would numb it.

In the end, when he was no closer to achieving any peace with himself, he gave in to the illogical compulsion to hail a cab and drive past every other address connected with the case he was now excluded from.

He sat directly behind the driver, and firmly chose not to engage in any conversation. The roads were almost empty, and the car made unhampered progress back and forth across town, slowing past one destination before transporting him towards the next.

If the driver thought this job was a strange one, he didn't comment.

Both of the dead women's flats were pitch black, but numerous lights were on in Richard and Alice Moran's large house. A security light illuminated the hard standing outside Bryn O'Brien's workshop, and a single light shone from Jackie Moran's hallway.

This time the 'where next?' question was the easiest to answer. Jackie's RAV4 hadn't been parked anywhere near her house, and unless there had been a major new development, Goodhew doubted she was still making her statement. They drove by Parkside station on the off-chance and, once he was certain that her car was nowhere on site, he instructed the driver to head for Old Mile Farm.

# FORTY-SIX

Goodhew paid the driver and asked to be dropped at the roadside by the gateway to the farm. The track down to the stables was unlit, but he wanted to walk into the yard unannounced. The moonlight was just sufficient for him to be able to pick out the shape of the post and rails fencing running alongside him, but it still took him several minutes before he came within sight of the parking area.

A tree marked the end of the track and he stopped there while he was still under its shadow. Jackie Moran's car was parked in the same spot as the last time he'd visited. From where he stood, it looked empty. There was no sign of life from the stables either; not even the sound of horses shuffling their feet.

As he crept across the yard, he paused long enough at her vehicle to confirm that it really was empty, then quietly made for the stable where they'd sat before. Both halves of the door were closed. He felt his way over the bolts, checking that both were locked from the outside. They were, and he was about to check the other loose boxes when he heard her voice behind him. 'I'm here.'

He spun around but couldn't see her. She sounded about fifty feet away from him.

'Put on the floodlights,' she called.

'Where?'

'In the corner, to your right.'

He felt his way to where the shorter side of the L-shaped stable block met the long side and found three switches.

'It's the middle one,' she added, as if she had seen him hesitate.

He turned towards her voice as he flicked it on. Four halogen lamps burst into life, drenching the menage in cold white light.

Jackie lay on a travelling rug spread out in the middle of the arena, supported on her left hand, holding a mug in the other. Gone was her usual stable girl look; instead she wore strappy sandals, jeans and a baggy green-and-white cotton shirt.

'What are you doing?' he asked, puzzled.

'Come here,' she instructed.

He climbed the railing, jumped down on to the sawdust and walked towards her. It was like a scene from an arty photo shoot; her clothes looked far too flimsy for nighttime, her cheeks were unusually red, her lips damson and glossy. She didn't look at all cold, and her smile was unnaturally luminescent.

'Would you like to talk to me?' she asked.

'That's not why I came. I just wondered where you'd gone.'

'No, I mean, please talk to me.'

'Sure.' Goodhew sat down beside her. 'Are you warm enough there?'

'Yep.'

She lowered her voice. 'I'm a bit drunk.'

'I can tell.'

'Really? I'd offer you some too, but I've only got what's left in the mug.' She swigged another mouthful. 'Do you know that point when you're so unhappy that you're not scared any more?'

'Scared of what?'

'Of anything, because if it's going to get you, so what? What can it do to you when a bullet in the brain would actually be a relief. That's what I've been doing, lying here and thinking, "So what?" So what. So fucking *what*!'

'What is "it"?'

'It. You know, the "it" that comes into your room when you're a kid, that makes you scared to open the wardrobe or look under the bed.'

'The "it" that might jump out and get you?'

'Yes, that's the one. But not just might, because it will.'

Goodhew reached out and wrapped his fingers around the mug. He gave it a gentle tug and she let go.

'Your father knew about Joanne Reed, so why did you pretend you didn't?'

'You're not at work now, surely, Mr Detective.' She reached for the mug but he held it away from her.

'Why not tell me? I know you knew her,' he persisted. 'What really scares you, Jackie?'

'Nothing.' She glared at him, but the woolliness of too much drink left her unable to remain intractable. She leant forwards, breathing out brandy fumes and wafting something that smelt like Paco Rabanne. She touched his cheek, then ran her hand down and inside the breast of his jacket. 'My father didn't allow Richard to bring women home, so he and Joanne came here for sex.'

'Richard told you?'

'No, I saw them.'

'How often?'

'They came here several times but I only saw it once.'

Goodhew thought he'd misheard, but Jackie laughed.

'They were in the end stable and I watched them through the window, both stark naked, not the tiniest bit aware that they could be seen.'

Goodhew looked across to the dust-covered window and pictured Jackie watching her brother and his girlfriend, possibly even standing on the edge of the muck heap to gain a better view. Jackie's fingers began fiddling with the top button of Goodhew's shirt; he pressed his hand on top of hers to keep it still.

'Is that true?' he said.

'My father said I should say nothing . . .' She paused and tilted her head towards the stables. 'We could . . . you know, I could show you what I saw.'

He ignored the suggestion. 'Your father thought he knew what happened to Joanne Reed. What did he tell you?'

'Not much. He drove down here one lunchtime, jumped out of his car and started shouting at me. He kept saying, "What happened? Tell me what happened to her. You should know by now that I'm not stupid." I had no idea what he meant. He stomped round the place for about ten minutes, ranting to himself. Finally he said, "Very clever", and just drove out again.'

Goodhew thought about her father's journal and its account of his search of Old Mile Farm. After a minute he lifted Jackie's hand away from his shirt and up to his lips. He kissed her fingers. 'Thank you for telling me. Now, I'm going to drive you home.'

'Then pull me in, in the morning?'

'I'd prefer it if you just showed up.'

'Why not take me straight there now?'

'Go home and sober up. You can't go on like this.'

'Stay with me, then.'

'No.' He stood and pulled her to her feet, but didn't release his hold on her hands. 'Why were you here tonight?'

'Honestly? I missed Alex.'

'Oh yes, your father who knew you so well.' He felt her tense.

'What's that supposed to mean?'

'What did he mean when he wrote in his journal that he made excuses for you when David died?' Jackie tried to pull away from him but he wouldn't let go. 'Did he think you were responsible for killing your baby brother?'

He knew she was going to cry even before the tears began, but he could also see that it wasn't sadness that made her cry. Frustration maybe, or more likely anger. She still squirmed in his grasp and Goodhew still refused to release her. He tried again. 'Jackie. Is that really what he thought? Is it?'

'Is it? Is it?' she mimicked. 'Did you put the pillow on his face? You can tell me, Jackie. Is that what you did? Is it? Is it? All right, I'll tell you what scares me, the "it", the fucking "it" that's controlled everything I've done every fucking day of my life.'

A breeze ruffled the sawdust and puffed out the fabric of her shirt. Suddenly Goodhew realized that the scent wasn't just like Paco Rabanne aftershave: it *was* Paco Rabanne, impregnated in a man's unwashed shirt. Her heightened sexuality hadn't been solely the result of alcohol, and Goodhew suddenly understood a whole lot more than just where Joanne Reed's body was buried.

# FORTY-SEVEN

Goodhew arrived home in the early hours, but didn't bother kidding himself that trying to sleep would be anything but a wasted journey to the bedroom. He switched on the jukebox, and selected what he guessed would be enough tracks to keep him company until Marks arrived at the station for the coming day's work. He turned the volume up high, amplifying every hiss and scratch on the old 45s, filling the room with obscure fifties doo-wop.

He made some coffee, then settled by the loft window and watched Parkside police station, until eventually he saw his boss arrive. He stopped to unplug the Bel Ami, then hurried out from the building and across Parker's Piece, only slowing as he approached Marks' office door. Inside, a phone rang twice before it was answered. Goodhew knocked anyway, then stepped away from the door to wait. It was almost five minutes later when he heard his boss telling him to enter.

Marks leant forward with both elbows resting on the desk. He didn't smile, but he didn't look angry either.

Goodhew stepped just far enough into the office to give himself space to close the door. 'I'm not ignoring your instructions, sir, but I do need five minutes with you.'

'Being in this building at all is already ignoring them.'

'OK, I'm ignoring them slightly, but I totally respect the spirit in which they were made.'

'For pity's sake,' Marks sighed, 'just get on with it.'

'I think I know where Joanne Reed's body is hidden.'

It was easy to see he'd grabbed Marks' interest but, even so, his boss remained cautious. 'Go on.'

'That's why I need five minutes with you.'

Marks gestured towards the nearest chair. 'Make it good.'

'When you called me insubordinate earlier, you were right. There have been times when you've placed your trust in me, and I value that. I didn't tip off the *Cambridge News*, so someone else must have had a motive for doing that.

'What I did do, though, was to sneak a look at Alex Moran's journal while I was waiting for you to return yesterday afternoon, and I think he'd guessed where the body was hidden, because he talks of the "rotten truth" and there being "only so many good places to hide a decaying corpse".'

'So where's the body?' Marks growled, seemingly overlooking the admission of prying.

Goodhew gave him a slightly diluted version of the previous night's events.

'So now Jackie Moran admits seeing Joanne Reed there with her brother, and you think the body's where?'

Goodhew told him.

Marks looked sceptical. 'And that's based on the Moran father having a quick look round, then saying, "Very clever"? He must have been talking about something else, because I don't believe you pat your kids on the head and say, "Well done for hiding a corpse."'

'Not in normal families,' Goodhew conceded.

'But she only offers this information when we've pretty much worked things out for ourselves. All I see here is a woman who's constantly covering her own back.'

'I don't agree.'

'I see,' Marks said, letting the words settle for several seconds. When he spoke again, his first question surprised Goodhew. 'In that case, do you know what motive Jackie Moran might have had for killing Lorna Spence?'

'None that I know of. I don't think she did.'

'And that's your unbiased opinion?'

'Absolutely.'

Marks frowned. 'Personally? In her position I would have gone for help rather than dumping Colin Willis' body in the river. I suspect that anyone who kills, then covers it up, is deliberately hiding something. But go on, tell me the rest of your theories.'

259

Goodhew had some, of course; plenty in fact. They'd only been a jumble of seedling ideas until this last hour, but talking to Marks had stimulated his thoughts and some of the ideas had since flourished; they'd sprouted tentacles and now seemed to be intertwining quite effectively. The next step would be to try voicing them out loud. He took a deep breath, then jumped in. 'Firstly,' he began, 'we know that Colin Willis had already had dealings with Lorna Spence and Victoria Nugent, therefore it seems too much of a coincidence that he just happened to target Jackie Moran for a random attack. Either he picked on her as a result of something Victoria or Lorna said, or he was hired to kill her by one of these two women.'

'Which one?'

'Lorna, I reckon. From what Bryn O'Brien said, it was Lorna who spent some time alone with Colin Willis, whilst Victoria wasn't interested.'

'So why would she want Jackie dead?'

'Perhaps she didn't. Maybe she hired Colin Willis on behalf of someone else. Once it was obvious that the plan had failed, disposing of Lorna would have broken the link between Colin Willis and whoever wanted to see Jackie Moran dead.'

'So the diary page left at the stables was just planted to throw suspicion on her sister, Alice.'

'And we only know it was planted because Jackie Moran survived, otherwise it might have looked like she'd had it in her possession all along.'

'Actually,' Marks corrected, 'we only know it was planted because Jackie Moran told us so.'

Goodhew didn't like the implication. 'Even if it didn't turn up as she said it did, I'm still sure it's genuine.'

'OK, so if it was deliberately planted, that would be by Lorna?'

'But ultimately for the benefit of whoever it was who hired Willis as a killer.'

'Who then goes on to kill Lorna when Jackie survives?'

'I guess so.'

'And this same person will be Victoria Nugent's killer, too?'

Goodhew nodded but suddenly felt his ideas drifting off course – or wilting, to use his earlier analogy.

'So you're saying,' Marks was hitting his stride now, 'that behind all of this is a very determined killer who has murdered both Lorna Spence and Victoria Nugent, yet felt it necessary to go through a third party to hire an amateur like Willis in a half-hearted attempt to kill Jackie Moran? And when the first attempt on Jackie Moran failed, why wasn't there a second? So why the "I'm like Emma" message? And who sent Lorna that junk mail?'

Goodhew couldn't answer.

'You see, Gary, ideas are all fine and good, but they need to hold water. If you spend too much time working on your own, you'll lose sight of the real objectives.'

Goodhew nodded dumbly. Marks was right, of course, and he felt stupid for letting himself colour the facts so carelessly, even if he hadn't realized he was doing so.

'Do you want another chance in this department?' his superior asked suddenly.

'Yes please, sir.'

Marks sent him to get coffee and, on his return, Goodhew found his boss sitting with Alex Moran's journal in one hand and his phone in the other. His attention seemed primarily with the phone, however. After another minute, he replaced the receiver and took the coffee he was being offered.

'Do you know what leads are like?' he said.

This was one where Goodhew knew the answer. 'Buses?'

'Exactly. Right now I've got a bundle of them.'

'Not a fleet?'

'In the hours before Lorna's death she'd had intercourse with two men; Bryn O'Brien and Richard Moran. It was easy to determine who Victoria Nugent had recently had intercourse with because up pops our friend Bryn O'Brien again. And due to the chaotic nature of the subsequent attack on her, there are hair and fibre samples in abundance. Luckily for Mr O'Brien, it seems she died at just about the same time as he was flashed by a speed camera out near the M11.'

Marks sipped his coffee thoughtfully, then turned his attention back to the journal, flicking slowly through its pages. 'Imagine having to wade through fifty-six volumes of this stuff, he's cryptic beyond belief. And obsessive. And I worry about someone who can't at least be honest in their own private diary.'

'Perhaps *he's* the unstable one?'

'But somehow I doubt he killed those two women from beyond the grave,' Marks replied drily.

They still didn't know nearly enough about Lorna Spence, but it had become obvious to Goodhew that the people who liked her the least would inevitably turn out to be the ones who knew her best. He remembered a comment that seemed to sum her up, and realized that it led them towards a different line of thinking. 'Lorna only did things for Lorna – *that's* what Wayne Thompson-Stark and Hayley Sellars said.'

'And what are *you* saying?'

'If that's the case, Lorna didn't hire Colin Willis on anyone's behalf except her own.'

'And if Jackie Moran knew that, it would be sufficient motive for revenge.'

Goodhew stiffened, because he hadn't intended to throw greater suspicion on Jackie Moran. He reined in his feelings. Just because he hoped she was innocent didn't mean that she was. 'That's not exactly what I meant but, yes, you're right.'

He closed his eyes to help him concentrate. Eventually Marks prodded him in the arm. 'Are you feeling all right?'

Goodhew opened them. 'If I come up with another possible scenario, sir, will you shoot it down in flames again?'

'Only if it's crap, Gary. What are you thinking?'

'We know that Lorna had a history of playing games with people's lives, being an arch manipulator. Say Lorna hired Colin Willis after becoming aware of the contents of that journal. If she could successfully frame Alice, then, with Jackie gone, she would have had brother Richard and his money all to herself. Lorna nicked the crucial page from her friend Victoria, who'd been having a relationship with Alex Moran, and that's what they fell out over – not some boyfriend. Wayne said Lorna's friend back then was called Vicky – if that's Victoria Nugent, it would have been her that sent all the junk mail because she was the only one who had known Lorna long enough to know about Wayne and Hayley.'

'Apart from Wayne and Hayley themselves.'

'Yes, I suppose so,' Goodhew admitted.

'OK,' Marks continued slowly, 'it makes sense so far. You're saying that, after Jackie Moran survived the attack, she would have realized that Lorna – and therefore Victoria – had access to Alex Moran's files. You realize your scenario still makes Jackie the prime suspect?'

Goodhew pulled a face. 'I know that, but I just can't imagine her killing anyone.'

'Apart from Colin Willis, of course?' Marks shut the journal. 'I'm not quite as trusting as you, Gary, so I've sent a car to bring her in. You have half an hour to plan your interview, then we'll speak to her together.'

# FORTY-EIGHT

Marks deliberately arrived at the interview room fifteen minutes before Goodhew appeared. He'd wanted a few minutes alone to assess Jackie Moran.

She seemed very withdrawn and she reminded him of certain children he'd interviewed in the past, the ones whose lids were so tightly sprung that they stayed snapped shut. A crowbar might prise them open, but it was only patience that ever budged them without causing permanent damage.

He wondered what was going on inside her head, but she kept it all secret, except for a response he'd noticed when she'd heard Goodhew's name. Just a quick blink. A move of the hand. Two signs that let him know that he'd been wise to have Gary back.

He and Jackie Moran sat in virtual silence for the remaining ten minutes it took for Goodhew to join them. After a while, Marks didn't even try to guess what was going on in her head; he was too busy trying to corral his own thoughts. He knew he'd behaved inconsistently: throwing Goodhew out of his team and then having him back within hours made no sense. And formally disciplining him would have been the right thing to do, not treating him as if the normal rules hadn't been written to include him. Police work was a science, and therefore Goodhew could not be allowed to run around working to his own agenda. And Marks realized that failing to control him would ultimately be no one's responsibility but his own.

And yet.

And yet.

And yet.

Marks knew that what Goodhew possessed was a talent, a gift for people and truth and logic that didn't come with any amount of training. Marks knew he'd be a fool to condone it, but trying to extinguish it ultimately seemed the greater crime. In those long ten minutes he knew it was now time to decide.

# FORTY-NINE

Goodhew reached the interview room door and took a deep breath before pushing it open. Meanwhile, he silently thanked Marks for giving him another chance and, equally silently, promised not to mess it up.

Marks didn't even acknowledge his arrival, but Jackie Moran wriggled slightly in her chair when she saw him, not in a restless way but with a shift of weight that made it look like she was settling down, ready for a long interview.

He didn't wait for Marks to speak. 'How are you?' he asked her.

'Tired,' she replied.

'Can I make a suggestion?'

'Go on.'

But Marks interrupted. 'Wait,' he said quietly, then stood up and rested his hand on Goodhew's shoulder. The touch was brief but handed him every opportunity he'd hoped for. 'Carry on without me,' the DI added, unnecessarily.

When the door closed behind Marks, Goodhew began again. 'I'm sorry I made you cry.'

'Don't worry about it.'

'Can we start by clearing the air – and putting all the other times we've spoken to one side. I now understand why you didn't tell me about Colin Willis, or about knowing Joanne Reed. Whatever you've said so far doesn't matter.'

'But you know things about me.'

'Just tell me your version.'

'What, about my father's journal?' She tried to look defiant, but there was the slightest quake in her voice, and he wanted that to be the real Jackie Moran.

'No, forget your father just for now. You don't have to live under the shadow of everything he wrote, especially when he was mistaken. Imagine nothing had happened to your little brother or to Joanne Martin. Imagine you could have the freedom to do whatever you wanted with the rest of your life, what would you do?'

'That's a stupid question.'

'Why?'

'Because . . .' She tried to leave it there, but he waited in silence longer than she could. 'Because, that's not where I am.'

'You're wrong, it's exactly where you are. How old are you?'

'Thirty, but you already know that.'

'Thirty? Well, in ten years' time, when you're forty, and in the same place you were at thirty, which was the same as at twenty, you may as well assume the pattern's been set for the rest of your life.'

She looked unimpressed. 'If you were at least forty, I might buy that, but you're younger than me, so I'm sitting here thinking: what do you know?'

Goodhew had a flash of clarity, the kind that he knew from playing chess, one where he could read the board and mentally jump three or four moves ahead. It largely depended on how well you knew your opponent and understood their game plan.

Jackie now wavered between looking stubborn and depressed. As far as Goodhew was concerned, that amounted to one hundred per cent defensive play. 'What if I come up with a really good answer?' As she thought him so young, he thought he'd try a burst of boyish charm and managed a cheeky flicker of the right eye that stopped just short of a wink.

She snorted briefly and one corner of her mouth twitched. 'Go on, then.'

Good, that was move one achieved: a sudden release of excess tension.

'OK, I know this is very important, so I'll need a minute to think. What do *I* know?' he pondered. He watched her watching him as he was pretending to concentrate. Once their eyes were locked like that it was easy for them to keep on staring at one another and he let the moment stretch out until it began to feel silly. Then he said, 'Can you give me a clue?'

Perhaps it was involuntary, perhaps it was just a burst of nerves but, as he'd hoped, she giggled.

Make her laugh: move two completed, and straight into move three. 'If I can't convince you about being forty, try this,' he said quietly. Their eyes were still locked. 'If no one believed me when I told the truth, I'd be pretty upset. But if I was six and it was my parents who didn't believe me, I'd devastated. And it wasn't as if they were remote people, I reckon. You loved and admired your father.' Jackie's face reddened, but she didn't look away; he guessed she wanted to, but it was like she was witnessing a car crash and she couldn't. 'If that was me and he died still thinking the worst of me, I'd be heartbroken. I wouldn't expect anyone else to believe me, not when my parents didn't.'

Jackie opened her mouth to speak, but nothing came. Still she watched him.

'You should have told us about Willis and Joanne Reed, but it hurts too much when everyone assumes you're lying, doesn't it?'

This time she finally tore her gaze away from him. She hid her nose and mouth behind her hands, and tried to hide the tears forming in her eyes.

'It hurts, doesn't it?' he pressed, knowing he was at the point where he couldn't afford to continue taking no answer as any sort of reply.

But he didn't need to ask her again. Her hands didn't move, making the 'Yes' sound more like a muffled grunt, but they both knew what she'd said. She opened her eyes and tears fell on to her cheeks; they trickled down in twin tracks, pausing at her jawline and vanishing into the mesh of her jersey.

'I'm not trying to catch you out,' he said.

'I know,' she said finally. The stubbornness had left her face – so, strangely, had her depressed expression – and in its place was acceptance. 'I haven't lied to you, just kept things back until I knew you'd believe me.'

'And I do, so no more now, OK?'

'OK.' She spent a single minute collecting herself, though it felt more like the entire afternoon. 'My father wasn't just educated,' she explained at last, 'he was by far the most intelligent and inspiring man I've ever met. And yet he spent nearly all of his life thinking that I killed my own brother. If he could be so wrong, how could I ever be sure of anything? I actually *know* nothing.'

'But you think you do,' Goodhew persisted.

She opened her mouth to speak, but he could see the tears threatening again. She blinked them away and took deep breaths until she seemed to feel confident that they weren't going to choke the words she was about to speak. 'I *know* I saw Richard with David that afternoon . . .' She paused. 'He was in David's room, sitting on the floor at the foot of the cot. I wasn't very old, of course, but I remember thinking that was odd.' She frowned. 'Maybe it was later that I thought it was odd. I don't know now.'

'What was odd?'

'Odd that Richard was in the room at all when he had never shown any interest in the baby. No interest whatsoever. He had a pillow on the floor beside him . . . and there was poor little David. Lying in his cot. Looking all wrong. Not even like a baby somehow. I could tell it was all wrong, he was like a toy. Like alabaster. Richard said nothing, just stood up, then walked right past me and through the door. I didn't go any closer, but I couldn't leave either. I don't know how long it was before my mother came and found me there. She said something to me, but I don't know what, and when she saw David she began to scream, but I can't remember any sounds, just a huge silence. I only know she was screaming because of her face. She was holding him, and he was completely limp, and I remember thinking that it looked like there weren't any bones left in his body. Then there were people everywhere. My dad, of course, but I don't know who else. They were in and out of the house, and they took his body away, and my dad kept asking me what had happened.'

'What did you tell him?'

'Nothing.'

'You didn't tell him about Richard?'

'I tried to talk to my sister Alice, but she said I was wrong, called it a stupid story, so I never told anyone else.'

'Why not?'

'Oh God!' She shook her head. 'I've asked myself that so many times. My dad kept asking me what had happened. Over and over. By the time I realized he thought I'd killed David, telling the truth would have sounded like a lie.'

'And he really thought you'd done it?'

'Absolutely. He even explained to me, later, how children can create false memories. To be honest, there are times when I've even doubted myself.' Jackie dug a tissue from her pocket and blew her nose. 'As he pointed out, I was just a small child, I might have been taken into care, and that would have finished my mother off. But she drank herself to death in any case, so I'm not sure what difference it would have made. I regret I didn't push things further, because it could have saved Emma.'

'Emma, not Joanne?'

'I didn't know her well but, yes, I knew her as Emma. We had what you could call a fledgling friendship. A group of us had gone to watch the racing at Newmarket, and Emma and I seemed to hit it off. We talked about spending a whole day with the horses ... We were enjoying ourselves until she met Richard. He spotted us and made a beeline for Emma and I didn't see much of her for the rest of that evening. I don't even know what went on between them. In fact, I didn't realize that anything was going on at all. Until I caught them having sex together ... A few weeks later she disappeared.'

'You never came forward.'

'To say what, exactly? I would never have thought anything of it if it hadn't been for what had happened with David, so I spoke to Alice again. You know they're really close – you've seen it. Alice was furious with me, said I had to promise to keep quiet, that it was too late to stir things up again about David, and far too cruel to my parents. She promised she'd deal with Richard, and said it was my duty to show some loyalty to them both.'

'So you are saying that you think your brother was responsible for Joanne Reed's disappearance?'

'I think so. It's his jealousy. He gets these rages, till he kind of burns up with them. If there had been any proof that Emma was dead, I might have come forward.'

'And when "I'm like Emma" appeared in the papers? Did you consider that it might be intended as a message for you?'

'I didn't know what to think, but I'd never thought Lorna was in any danger.'

'Did it scare you? Wasn't it like a threat?'

'What do you mean?'

'You told me about your father turning up at the farm and shouting, "Tell me what happened to her." Who was he talking about?'

'Emma.'

'And what was he looking for?'

When Jackie hesitated, Goodhew cut in, 'Don't make me tease it out of you one sentence at a time, Jackie. You know where this is going.'

She nodded. 'He never told me what he meant by "very clever", but I walked everywhere that I'd seen him go. There was only one place that could have hidden Emma's body and that was the manure heap, which, if you think about it, is pretty cunning. I assumed then that he said "very clever" to me because he thought it was all my doing. I didn't even try to convince him that it wasn't me. I thought about digging it over just to see for myself, but I never did.'

'In fact, you never did anything.'

'No, I didn't.'

# FIFTY

When Goodhew stepped outside the interview room, he wasn't surprised to find someone waiting in the corridor. It was PC Kelly Wilkes.

'I'll go in with her now,' she said. 'DI Marks is next door.'

That made sense. Goodhew had deliberately ignored the camera in the corner of the room because he didn't want to be put off by it, but at the back of his mind he'd been certain Marks was in the adjoining room, and with him for every second of the interview.

Marks himself opened the door from the inside before Goodhew was even close. 'She agreed to the search then?'

'Yes, sir.'

'I've requested to see everything that's available on David Moran's death. Richard and Alice Moran are already on their way. We're picking them up together, because we don't want to raise his suspicions until he's interviewed on his own. I'm going to keep out of the way, let him think it's all low-key, then I'll join you at the appropriate moment.'

'*I'm* going to interview him?'

'Why not? Your interview with his sister made very good TV.'

For the nine-to-fivers in the city of Cambridge, the day had only just begun. Schools were ringing their bells for morning break and the traffic had settled down after the rush hour. Goodhew glanced out of the nearest window and saw heavy clouds were heading in their direction; he guessed that meant another wet twenty-four hours. Already he wished the day was over. He was fuzzy with tiredness and had spent the first few hours of the morning reviving his brain with a succession of cups of coffee. He'd reused each polystyrene cup until it cracked, but even so was about to ditch the third of the morning. He took his latest half-drunk cup along with him to Interview Room 3, where Alice and Richard Moran sat side by side.

Alice was looking slightly tidier than immaculate. Whereas on previous occasions her appearance had been A-grade faultless, today she deserved an added star for extra endeavour. Richard, on the other hand, had crumpled even further, and now looked as though he were the shorter of the two. The combined effect gave the impression that they shared the same reserves of energy and emotional strength and just passed them back and forth by osmosis.

As Marks held up the journal, Richard's gaze did a skittish jig from one person to the next, whereas Alice just said, 'Oh.'

'Do you know what this item is?' Marks asked.

Richard nodded and Alice said, 'Yes, of course. My father kept journals for as long as we can remember: the burgundy ones were for work and the dark-blue ones were about our . . .' She took a breath, 'our family.'

'I see, and why didn't you tell us that one of them was missing?'

'I didn't know.' She turned to Richard. 'Did you, Richard?'

'No.' He shook his head. 'They were packed away with the rest of his possessions.' He looked down into his hands. 'Jackie's here, isn't she?'

'She's been making a statement. But this diary was found at Victoria Nugent's house.'

'Is Jackie under arrest?' Richard asked. Alice was watching him closely, but didn't seem unhappy that he'd decided to do the talking.

'Not yet,' Goodhew replied. 'Tell me about your half-brother, David.'

Richard's gaze then met his sister's, and from his imploring expression Goodhew guessed it was some kind of SOS.

It was Alice who replied, 'Because of what my father wrote?'

'I can't comment.'

She scowled. 'Well, it wouldn't have come from anywhere else. David was the youngest of us – I think I told you that before – and he died. He was a small baby, but not ever ill, as far as I can remember. Our stepmother had put him down for an afternoon nap and she found him dead a couple of hours later – a cot death, the doctors said.' She looked towards her brother. 'Except our father couldn't accept that, could he?'

Richard shook his head and picked up the story, the handover seamless. 'Our stepmother wasn't a healthy woman, she suffered from severe post-natal depression after Jackie was born, and by the time David arrived, she'd started drinking heavily too.'

'And your father blamed her?'

'No, no, he felt he needed to protect her. You see, he thought Jackie had killed David because she was jealous of him. But she was only six at the time and he felt that she wouldn't have understood what she'd done. If she'd been taken away, our stepmother would have been devastated, Jackie was all she had.'

'Apart from you two?'

Richard shrugged. 'She was only our stepmother. In any case, who would hand over their six-year-old child, even in that situation? She probably would have been institutionalized, and for what purpose? I can quite understand why our father kept quiet.'

Alice took over again. 'But that's when he started keeping his notes on Jackie. He told us much later that he wanted to be sure he had a record of her behaviour in case she showed signs of doing something like that again.'

'And you all knew about this?'

'We knew he made all these notes, but we had no idea of the contents,' Alice said. 'He kept it entirely to himself until near his own death, and it was only then that he told us what he had suspected.'

'And you both thought it best to keep that secret from this investigation?'

'Our father wanted it kept in the family.'

'Even if there was another murder?'

Alice stiffened. 'You misunderstand us. We think our father's suspicions were wrong. He was a complex and intelligent man, but not infallible. He was devastated when David died and, for some reason that we'll never know, he directed the blame on to our sister. He was obsessed with his notes, but why would we connect those to Lorna's murder?'

Goodhew ignored the question. 'In his notes he also mentions Joanne Reed. Did you both know her?'

Alice shook her head, but Richard nodded, and Goodhew found the sight of them responding independently of one another slightly startling.

'I met her,' Richard said, 'through Jackie. I saw her twice, or maybe three times, I don't remember now for sure. Dad knew, only because I'd told him, and after she disappeared he asked me about her and Jackie, and what they'd done together.'

Goodhew spoke without realizing he'd planned to, and his voice sounded sharp. 'What did he mean by that?'

'How do I know? Joanne was uncomfortable about Jackie hanging round at the stables, and Dad asked me if I'd seen Joanne the weekend she disappeared.' Goodhew studied Richard closely, though he didn't seem to enjoy the attention, and quickly added, 'But I hadn't, I swear.'

'Then why not tell us all of this before?'

'We told you, we promised our father that we'd look after her.' There was an audible trembling in his voice.

'Yes, and Alice has just told me that you both considered your father's suspicions unfounded. Do you share that opinion with her or not?'

Richard wavered, then replied, 'Yes.'

Perhaps he realized that it was the wrong answer, or maybe he'd been distracted by an unexpected thought but, as Goodhew waited, Richard simply stared at him, his eyes unnaturally focused on the bridge of Goodhew's nose. When he spoke again, his voice was low and ponderous, as though he was articulating unfamiliar thoughts. 'But now I think about it, my life was perfect until she arrived.'

'DC Goodhew?' It was Alice who'd cut in, sounding calmer than ever, thus supporting Goodhew's theory of osmosis. 'What can we do to help Jackie?'

His initial response to Alice's interruption was relief; her simple question had redirected her brother into a calmer state, possibly saving them all from another emotional eruption.

Then Goodhew rethought his strategy and decided to move Alice to another room.

By the time he returned, PC Wilkes was waiting for him in the corridor again.

'This is becoming a habit,' she announced, and handed him a single sheet of paper. 'That's all we've come up with so far. I've got a mate in the County Records Office and she scanned it for me. Lucky we got anything at all, I guess.'

The copy was pale and Goodhew had to turn it to the light before he saw it was the death certificate for David Joseph Moran. He glanced at the dates: born in August, just after Goodhew's first birthday, and dead before Goodhew's second. The verdict: 'natural causes'.

It was the mention of the County Records Office, housed on the site of the former jail, which reminded Goodhew – that, and the word justice . . .

He had left Richard Moran alone for, what he hoped was, enough time to make him wonder whether he'd been abandoned. He folded the copy of baby David's death certificate in half and returned to the interview room with it tucked in his inside pocket. He sat back down, this time pulling his chair much closer.

'We were talking about Joanne Reed. Where did you actually meet her?'

Richard slid one hand under each thigh, which reminded Goodhew of school teachers yelling, 'If you can't keep your hands still, sit on them,' but he'd never seen anyone over the age of about eight actually doing so. 'Newmarket . . .' Richard began, falteringly, then started the sentence again more clearly. 'Newmarket races. Dad and I went to watch the racing, and Jackie was there with some other girls, and one of them was Joanne Reed.'

'Who else was there?'

'Just Dad and myself.'

'Not Alice?'

'No, she didn't feel well that day.'

'How can you still remember this after ten years?'

'I just do.'

'And you saw Joanne again after that?'

'No, not really.' It was obvious to Goodhew that Richard was lying.

'But you liked her?'

'From what little I saw of her, yes.'

'Did you want to see her again?'

'I thought it might happen, but nothing was ever arranged.'

'Did you ask her?'

He hesitated, then, 'No.'

Goodhew paused.

Richard took a deep breath. 'I asked her that day if she'd like to come racing again and she said yes, but it wasn't a specific invite. I gave her my number, and she called the following week and we met for a drink.'

'Where?'

'The Eagle, Cambridge.'

'Then what?'

Richard pulled the sort of awkward expression that Goodhew guessed was supposed to convey a mix of discretion and candour.

Goodhew decided to fill in the gap. 'So you went somewhere private?'

Richard nodded.

'For sex?' Goodhew waited for another nod, then continued. 'If you were already in Cambridge, why go to Old Mile Farm? Why not just go home?'

'I took her out to the stables on the pretext of seeing the horses, in the hope that things would progress once we were there.'

'I see. So you didn't meet there for sex just because your father wouldn't let you bring any women home?'

Richard hesitated. 'Well, there was that too,' he admitted.

'We now know of two women with whom you've had a sexual relationship; one is dead and the other has been missing for a decade. Doesn't make you catch of the week, does it?' Richard looked away, and Goodhew changed direction. 'A few minutes ago, the word "justice" came up, and it made me recall that conversation we had earlier in the week.'

Richard looked curious, but said nothing.

'You told me that you thought it was important to see justice done, and that it's also seen to be done. You said that's what you wanted for Lorna.'

'That's right.'

'Did you mean Lorna as the innocent victim, or Lorna as the condemned?'

Richard leant back in his chair and crossed his legs. 'Now you've lost me.'

'Her death was carefully orchestrated. She'd had plenty of experience controlling other people, but she went too far with you. You weren't going to let her walk away; you needed to punish her. There was a risk you'd be caught, but it had to be out in the open like that, otherwise it wouldn't have felt like she'd been given a public execution.'

'And what was her unforgivable crime, exactly?' Richard said, sitting up straight again. There wasn't much more fidgeting he could do without breaking into a sweat but, there again, he looked pretty close to breaking into a sweat in any case. Goodhew could see he wasn't scared, though. The nervousness was just the bubbling by-product of a rage that was nearing boiling point. Richard Moran still had the lid on it, but it was rattling loudly.

'Perhaps she found out you killed Joanne Reed. Was she trying to blackmail you?'

'I never killed Joanne.'

'Come on, you admit you have a problem with jealousy. And a temper, too. What happens when you lose control? Did Joanne end up like Victoria, with her skull caved in? You didn't have a chance to hide Victoria. And we're looking for Joanne's body right now.'

The first visible bead of sweat appeared at Richard's hairline. It reminded Goodhew of condensation running down the inside of a saucepan. The man wiped it away, and Goodhew kept pushing. 'She's buried at the farm, isn't she, Richard?'

'Don't.' Richard hissed.

Goodhew smirked. 'Don't what?' he said coolly.

'Don't.' Richard said it like it was a threat, but Goodhew remained unmoved, refusing to let it grow beyond the impotent, orphaned word it really was. Without warning, Richard pushed his chair back, the metal feet squealing in protest. 'Don't try to trick me.' He pointed his finger at Goodhew, prodding the air as if to emphasize a point he was about to make, but the words would not come. Then he realized his hand was shaking and he dropped it back into his lap, clasping it with the other hand to keep it still. 'You don't know anything. You're just playing games.'

'No, you're wrong. Your sister's making a statement even as we speak.'

The colour drained from Richard's face and he slumped backwards. 'You're lying. She wouldn't do that to me.'

'Why not?' As far as Goodhew was concerned, Jackie Moran should have made one years ago. Goodhew stood up and reached into his pocket. He held the baby's death certificate close to Richard's face. 'Jackie says it was you who killed David.'

Richard gasped and his expression altered, travelling from disbelief to dismay, with a brief but unmissable stop-off at did-anyone-notice? 'I see,' he said, trying for finality, desperate to make them the last two words of the interview.

For Goodhew it was more than illuminating. He'd accidentally tripped the switch that activated the floodlights, and Richard Moran was the only one basking in the glare.

# FIFTY-ONE

The first revelation had been so blinding that Goodhew was almost too dazzled to see the second.

Marks was already out in the corridor, but talking urgently on his mobile. He made the 'one minute' sign and turned away so he could concentrate. Goodhew didn't want to wait: this was the wrong moment for him to slow down, the right moment to barge into the room at the other end of the corridor. It was as if Marks could sense his impatience, because he turned back briefly and repeated the gesture.

OK, OK, Goodhew thought. He leant back against the wall, then slid down it until he was squatting. He refolded the death certificate and fanned his face, then unfolded it and held it like a wobble board, rippling it up and down, hoping the noise would irritate Marks enough to make him hang up.

It didn't.

The only person's attention it succeeded in grabbing was his own. He stopped agitating it as the significance of baby David's date of birth suddenly hit home.

'Shit,' Goodhew muttered, and rushed away from his boss towards the nearest photocopier. It took three attempts before key details on the next-generation copy were clear enough to read.

He grabbed his mobile and rang Mel's extension. 'Have you left your desk in the last half-hour?'

'No.'

'Marks told me he sent someone out to Old Mile Farm – have you any idea who?'

'Kincaide and Charles.'

'Thanks.'

Goodhew rang DC Charles, hurrying towards his own desk even as he spoke. 'Are you there yet? Good. One of the loose boxes has a press clipping pinned on the wall – could you photograph it with your phone and text it over? Make sure the picture and the date are both clear.'

His fatigue had fled, replaced by renewed vigour and clarity. He still had only a single purpose, but now at least he knew where his efforts were converging. He booted up his PC, plugged a USB cable into his mobile, and waited for the double-beep that announced each new message.

It arrived without a hitch. He enlarged the image and sent it straight to the laser printer. It was still warm when he slapped it on to the desk in the interview room in front of Jackie Moran.

'That's the newspaper clipping from your stable.' It wasn't a question and she didn't have to nod. He followed it with the photocopy. 'And that is David's death certificate. If I can put the two of them together and see it, so will any jury.'

She opened her mouth to speak, but Goodhew held up his hand. 'Enough, because this very minute I'm not listening, especially to people who think I buy every lie and half-truth that's thrown at me.'

He almost left the room without saying any more, but turned back just before reaching for the door handle. 'Think about it before I get back. I am getting this close,' he held the tips of his thumb and forefinger a millimetre apart, 'and this investigation is finishing *today*.'

# FIFTY-TWO

Fifteen minutes earlier, Marks had been in the viewing room next door, sitting in front of a PC. The individual CCTV screens were on an adjacent desk, but Marks was watching via his monitor, where the various real-time images were running in separate windows on his desktop.

Alice Moran leaning forward with her elbows on the table.

Richard Moran leaning back with his hands cupping his neck.

Jackie Moran staring into the camera.

Marks had a fourth window open: a paused image of Goodhew's earlier interview alone with Richard. Marks had played it twice before he began seeing what had rattled Goodhew, and he would have replayed it again but, before he had a chance, his young DC reappeared in Jackie Moran's room, this time shoving a couple of photocopies in front of her.

Marks leant closer to the screen.

Goodhew's demeanour had changed; he seemed cold, every movement measured, his conversation terse and his exit from the room equally abrupt. Jackie Moran stared at the back of the door for several seconds after it closed, then she placed the two sheets of A4 side by side and perfectly symmetrically in the centre of the desk. She sat so still that it looked like the shot had been freeze-framed.

Marks continued to watch her until he heard his own door open. At first glance he thought Goodhew was enraged; his jaw was set, his eyes bright and unusually intense. Goodhew looked at the paused footage of Richard Moran and then stared at Marks.

Marks sensed he was being challenged, then he understood. Goodhew was angry but, more than that, he was brooding with intense determination. He had seen the way to the end of this investigation and he felt compelled to follow it through. The challenge now was not to put the brakes on Goodhew, but to give him the keys and let him drive.

Marks reached forward and tweaked the two sheets of paper out of Goodhew's hand. 'Are these what you just gave Jackie Moran?'

'Yes, look.' Goodhew pointed to the dates.

Marks studied both pages, his gaze pacing around each image, then flicking back and forth between the two. He noticed the closeness of the dates almost at once; the subsequent deduction came more slowly.

Then it dawned on him. 'Oh, I see,' he said thougthfully. 'And how do you suggest we proceed from here?'

# FIFTY-THREE

There was no room for compassion now. Any that Goodhew had felt, or might have felt in a less heated moment, had been displaced by his rising fury. He threw open the door. She was standing at the window and turned to look at him.

She was just as good at eye contact, but now he wondered how he'd ever found her attractive.

'I know who killed Lorna Spence.' He left it as a blank statement of fact. No futher discussion. Neither was he going to be drawn into any prolonged gazing. He sat on one of the two chairs and motioned for her to sit on the other.

'I'm fine standing,' she said.

'Suit yourself, just don't expect to intimidate me with any of that "I'm higher than you" body-language crap.'

She pulled the chair back. 'It's no big deal, I can sit down if it bothers you that much.'

'What do you know about murderers who kill in teams?'

'Nothing.'

'Teams can include pairs.'

'Like I said, nothing.'

So many thoughts were raging through his head that it would have been easy to open his mouth and release a disjointed battery of accusations. In fact, the words which came were as dispassionate and steel-edged as any he'd ever spoken.

'Team killers follow common patterns. They are strongly attracted to one another, sometimes even related, and one is dominant, making decisions and controlling their partner. The submissive one feels guilt and fear and the dominant one's temperament may include aggressive outbursts. The dominant one decides what they do next. Does any of this sound familiar?'

'Frankly, no.'

'That's the best thing about killing teams,' Goodhew said. 'Mostly it's the submissive one that controls the final outcome – like now. It seems illogical, since you'd think it was the dominant one that steered it all the way, but no, sooner or later, when they've had enough, the weaker partner will take drastic steps in order to escape.'

Jackie Moran opened her eyes. The papers were still laid out on the desk, and she was still in the interview room. On the face of it, nothing had changed, but for the first time she could see the world, or more specifically, her world, for what it was.

In front of her was proof of a lie. It was proof that it wasn't the first lie she'd been told, and proof of the many other lies that had rained down on her ever since. Here was conclusive evidence, the gas and canary test whose verdict found all of her relationships to be tiny, featherless corpses.

She recalled one of Goodhew's questions: imagine you could have the freedom to do whatever you wanted with the rest of your life, what would you do?

It was no longer a stupid question; in fact, it was the only little bird that still hopped and sang. Its voice was clear and insistent. All she had to do was open the cage.

She knocked on the door until he came to see what she wanted. He held it a few inches ajar and spoke through the gap. 'What?'

'I know what I was afraid of,' she said.

His eyes were at their most vivid, concentrating on her, looking for subtext. He said nothing and the space between her and Goodhew became hot and airless, slowing the seconds and constricting her chest.

She drew a deep breath and spoke first, 'Finding out it was all lies, and then facing up to it.'

'And?'

'I've no choice now.'

He gave a half nod and she saw his expression soften. 'What do you want to do?' he asked her.

She looked beyond him to the interview room along the corridor. 'Go in there.'

'One to one?'

'No, along with you.'

Goodhew opened the interview room door and let Jackie walk through first. Part of her wanted to hang back and make him take the first step, but the rest of her knew this was the right way to do it.

'Jackie has been cleared of any involvement,' he announced, 'and she wants to talk to you. I said you'd already expressed the desire to help her in any way possible.'

Jackie picked up a chair and placed it directly across from her sister. She sat down and took her time to study Alice, whose expressions were always hard to read and, in the end, Jackie categorized this one as an attempt at indifference. But she could also see that Alice was trying much too hard.

Goodhew had moved his own chair three or four feet back from the table. This was the only time he had seen them together, and Jackie considered it from his point of view. There was certainly a family resemblance, but Alice was taller and wiry, more self-assured, and they both knew she was the smarter of the two. Jackie stared at her big sister, and could still feel the lingering residue of childhood awe. She hoped Goodhew wouldn't intervene, and also hoped he wouldn't need to.

Jackie wanted to broach the first question, but her thoughts wouldn't crystallize into an opening line. She hesitated too long and finally Alice spoke, looking only at Jackie. 'What are you are doing?'

'I need some answers.'

'What answers?' Alice frowned, the skin between her eyebrows drawing into two deep vertical creases.

'Ones that will make everything add up.' Jackie heard the defensive note in her voice, and knew she needed to stop and regroup.

'What are you talking about?' Alice persisted. So far she'd been the only one who'd ever asked any questions.

Jackie let Alice's words hang in the air until it was clear that she had no intention of answering.

Goodhew watched her, steady and calm. He was the true strength in this room now, not Alice.

And when Jackie spoke, it was with all the authority that she'd been hoping her voice could find. 'You have manipulated me and you have all but ruined my life. I came to you for help and you dismissed everything I said, and I thought it was all because you truly believed I had killed David. Then later, when Emma disappeared, I thought you were blindly protecting Richard. You are such a liar.'

Alice said nothing, and Jackie continued.

'My God, you really don't get it. I see through you now, and you can't fob me off. When Colin Willis attacked me, I came to you to warn you. You have completely betrayed me.'

Alice looked away, but Jackie jumped to her feet and forced herself back into her sister's line of sight.

'I need to know what I ever did to you, Alice. Why do you hate me so much? Why let me be the one that my whole family has believed is a killer? Why, Alice? I thought we were close once? Don't I deserve the truth from you? Don't I deserve to know why I've spent my whole life being terrified?'

A cold smile touched Alice's lips. 'No, you don't.'

Jackie settled back into her seat. Did Alice really think she had anything to negotiate with? 'Remember how it was me who comforted you each time you miscarried . . .' She saw her sister's surprise. 'That's right, Alice, how many times? Four? Five?'

Alice was quick to answer, her voice hushed. 'Five.'

Jackie heard her own voice change. '*All we want is our own baby, Jackie.*' She had repeated the words she'd heard her sister say so many times over the years, but a cruel and sarcastic note distorted her impression. 'But you had him and you let Richard kill him. You never cried about that on my shoulder, did you?'

'Jackie!' Alice snapped out the name, expecting it to produce instant silence.

'Alice!' Jackie mimicked. 'My mum was photographed the week before he was born, and she was as thin as a rake. David was *your* baby, then Richard killed him and you let him get away with it. You never gave a shit.'

'Jackie, I'm warning you.'

'No, Alice, you have nothing more to threaten me with. Every-one lied to me. I was the only one who thought that David was my brother. It wasn't post-natal depression that my mother was suffering, it was the burden of covering up your pregnancy and your affair with Richard. You weren't even her children, yet she was still trying to protect you. And Alex was protecting you both too.

'But me, I've been cheated out of my whole family. Because of you, my own parents thought I'd smothered the baby.'

Something changed in Alice, less than a muscle move, an invisible nuance that made Jackie suddenly react. 'What's funny?'

Alice shook her head. 'You really are laughable. Do you honestly think Alex would have grieved over a child that wasn't his? Alex was creeping into my room regularly and your precious mother was too busy drinking herself stupid to notice.'

'But you and Richard . . .' Icy shock flushed Jackie's veins, flooded her brain, orphaned her thoughts and left them staggering in numb circles.

'Alex always knew you never killed David. Did you really think I chose to have a relationship with my own brother? I only turned to Richard because of Alex.'

Jackie heard herself make a sound, half gasp, half cry. But no words came.

'Come on, Jackie, we both know we are the products of a disturbed home.' Alice reached forward and stroked Jackie's hand. 'No point shaking your head like that. Your mother died and I had Richard, leaving our father with no one. You weren't special, Jackie, you were just there. It was inevitable that Alex would want sex with you, too. He never loved Richard, but he always loved his girls. You deluded yourself into thinking he felt something for you, and in return you loved him in that first-big-romance way of yours. You were never enough for him, though. Never. He saw other women, like Victoria, and all he had to do then was make sure you stayed quiet. That's why he kept his journals, that's why he pretended you had killed David, and Joanne Reed. They were a means of potentially discrediting you.'

Jackie's voice was barely audible. 'No, he loved me.'

Alice leant closer. 'No, he didn't. He was perverted and corrupting. He abused you and you have twisted it around in your head into something it never was. It suited him to have you all to himself. It was also convenient for him to make you the scapegoat for David.'

The shock seemed to leave Jackie as quickly as it arrived. She knew that Goodhew was still in her corner, ever patient, never judging. He saw her as more than just a string of sordid revelations. She would come to terms with those later.

Right now all that mattered was Alice and the verbal grenades she was hurling at her. Jackie levelled her stare at her sister, then took her best shot. 'But not for Joanne Reed.'

Alice stumbled, tried to rewind the conversation, but couldn't quite make sense of Jackie's comment. 'What do you mean?'

Jackie spelt it out, her voice quiet but dogged. 'If Alex knew I'd never killed David, then he never believed I killed Joanne Reed either. He would not have kept up that pretence just for Richard. You said yourself Dad never loved him, so even as an adult Richard could never step out of line. Richard had nothing to negotiate with, but you had everything.'

'No,' said Alice quietly.

'Why not? Surely you're not really saying it was Richard who killed Joanne Reed?'

Alice began to shake her head, then stopped.

Jackie seized the moment. 'Now you're stuck, aren't you? It's you or him, Alice. I went to the races at Newmarket, and that's when Richard met Emma. You weren't there because you'd just had another miscarriage. Then, a few days later, I saw Richard and Emma having sex up at Old Mile Farm. When she disappeared, I thought Richard was behind it. And I warned you about him, but I thought you just wouldn't listen. You killed Emma, then told me to keep my distance so you could play me and Richard off against each other. You made him think I'd killed Joanne Reed, knowing that I would stay away and convince him that I'd done it.

'Then what about Lorna Spence? You introduced her to Richard because you wanted them together. Lorna told me how you encouraged her to get pregnant, and you told me last summer that you'd lost hope of having a successful pregnancy. It must really have knotted you up, hearing them at it in the next bedroom. Would you have killed her once she'd had the child? She never wanted one though, did she? When I told you about Colin Willis, you realized that Lorna wanted both of us out of the way to get to Richard, and then it turned into a classic battle of two women chasing one man. Or did Richard kill her because he found out she was sleeping around?

'And what was Victoria? Just an impulse kill by Richard, or an opportunity to tie up your loose ends?' Jackie stopped abruptly and sat back in her seat. 'It's you or him now, so just tell the truth.'

Alice ran the tip of her tongue over her teeth and narrowed her eyes. It was a look that Jackie recognized from as far back as she could remember: it preceded one of her sister's most calculated game plays, and appeared just as she contemplated making any key move. In this instance, there was only one move available.

'OK,' she sighed, 'it was Richard, he killed them all.'

Jackie smiled. 'Jealous, was he?'

'Irrationally jealous. I tried to reason with him, but he's not well.'

'I don't believe you.'

'Neither do I,' Goodhew said, then added, 'Just wait,' with no further explanation.

Five minutes passed and Jackie was beginning to wonder whether something had gone awry. Then the door opened, and a female officer stepped through, accompanied by Richard. 'I want to speak to Jackie,' he said, seemingly oblivious to everyone else there, even Alice.

Jackie nodded. 'OK.'

'You're wrong about Alice.'

Jackie blinked. 'How?'

'She didn't make me think you'd killed Joanne because she told me she'd done it herself. I killed David all those years ago to give us a fresh start, but it left me in an impossible situation. From then on, we were in it together. I did realize she had killed Lorna, it was only Victoria's murder that I knew nothing about. I've agreed to make a confession, but I just wanted to tell you first.'

He was many things she despised, and so many things Jackie recognized in herself. And some that were both. He left the interview room and Goodhew ushered her out too. At the last second, she turned back to find Alice white-faced and staring after them.

Goodhew spoke. 'We can't just let you leave, you'll be facing charges for—'

'Colin Willis, I understand. I want it all out in the open now.'

Goodhew stopped Jackie in the hallway. 'Will you be all right?'

'Yes, I think so.' Jackie thought there ought to be something deeper she could add, something more profound. But the only words that flashed through her mind were too forward and inappropriate to utter. In the end she shook his hand, and all she said was, 'Thank you.'


Marks studied the TV, having just finished watching the tapes of Richard and Alice Moran for a second time. Finally, he turned his attention back to Goodhew. 'That was impressive,' he said.

'Thank you, sir.'

'And that's the sort of inspired chaos I'm missing when I don't keep you fully occupied?'

'Possibly, sir.'

'Heaven help us with you in the department.'

'I don't have to stay.'

'Yes you do, even if keeping you here turns out to be the only reckless thing I do before I retire. But here's the deal: I keep you challenged, you keep me informed. Anything else is on your own head. I will never cover up for you. Understand?'

'Thank you, sir.'

'Never.'

'I know.'

'Right. I expect you've heard they've started a search at Old Mile Farm.'

Goodhew nodded and imagined the forensics team swinging into action, taking measurements and planning their assault on that mountain of manure. The tactic would be a slow and thorough sift through the site, but it wasn't an occasion to use the term 'fingertip search'. 'Can I go along?' he asked.

Marks shook his head. 'Not this time. It could take days and your paperwork needs you. I'll let you know as soon as anything turns up there. If it ever does.'

'It will.'

# FIFTY-FOUR

It was now two days since Alice and Richard Moran had been formally charged. It was early afternoon and Goodhew had a call to make. The receiver was ready in his hand, but he hesitated and looked across Parker's Piece from his quiet corner on the third floor.

Ratty had finally come in and made a statement. It contained nothing new, but involved supplying him with three hot drinks and a plate of sandwiches. Goodhew sat and watched Ratty walk away, back into his life of sleeping rough.

Just beyond Ratty's departing figure, Mel was returning from lunch; the two passed within feet of one another. While Mel continued to choose dangerous relationships, he wondered whether her life was much safer than Ratty's. He hoped so, but he also knew that caring about someone wasn't enough to keep them safe; after all, there was nothing Martin Reed could have done to save his daughter.

He dialled the number from memory. For the first time in many weeks, Goodhew had woken up after a decent night's sleep, reborn in a mood of quiet reflection. The calm after the storm had finally arrived and this was like the last gust blowing its way out of his life and into someone else's.

Goodhew's call to Martin Reed was short. The phone rang only twice before it was answered.

'Mr Reed? This is DC Goodhew.'

'I know, I recognized your voice.'

Goodhew wouldn't have recognized Martin Reed's. It was taut, hoarse even.

'We wanted you to be aware that we've recovered an unidentified body.' He was careful to stress the word 'unidentified'. 'We will be conducting tests and as soon as—'

'But it could be Jo?'

Goodhew hesitated. 'It could, yes.'

'And you'll ring.'

'Yes, as soon as we can.'

'I'll just wait then,' he said and immediately put down the phone.

Murder was a very big stain to leave on the world. He guessed it marked even those on the periphery, like the clinic receptionist Faith Carver and Bryn O'Brien. He knew that both Martin Reed and Jackie Moran would definitely be scrubbing away at it for years to come.

The pile of typing on Mel's desk had grown to about three inches thick, most of it urgent and illegible. She didn't mind. She'd just shared a sandwich and a packet of crisps in the pub with Toby, and though neither of them had spoken much, the silence had lacked any trace of bad atmosphere and surely that was progress.

On the way back to the station she'd glanced up at the third floor, knowing where Goodhew liked to sit. She couldn't see him up there, but she almost waved, just in case. She hoped they'd get a chance to talk properly soon, but she wasn't going to push that one either. She wanted to thank him for helping her find the gear that would reverse her out of the mess she was in, but first she had to be sure she could use it.

She snapped off another row of squares from her half-eaten bar of Dairy Milk. Thank God for chocolate.

Behind her the door opened and she knew, without looking, that the footsteps belonged to Michael Kincaide. She'd avoided him for two days and had hoped that if she ignored him sufficiently, he'd go away, but now she felt him sneak up on her. He planted a ticklish kiss on the bare skin at the back of her neck, making goosebumps.

She swung her chair around and stared up at him. He was wearing a suit which made him look all of his twenty-seven years. Was that an age gap big enough for him to be a father figure?

His aftershave was Calvin Klein, and it used to smell good to her, just a splash too strong, but still good. She wasn't sure when she'd gone off it.

'I'm sorry if I've upset you, Mel. I've really missed you,' he said. 'Why not meet me later and we can talk?' He was so sincere that he was starting to remind her of the double-glazing salesman who had persuaded her mum to replace a perfectly good set of windows.

'I've grown out of you, Michael. Go and find someone else.' She sounded more assertive than she felt, and was pleased when he didn't hang around to argue. Off he went, banging the door open with the heel of his hand.

It was caught by Goodhew coming the other way. 'Have you upset him?' he enquired.

'I've ended my date-a-married-man phase.'

'Oh, I see. And how about Toby?'

'I'll see.' She changed the subject. 'Where are you going?'

'Early finish today, I'm meeting someone at the pub.'

Then it was her turn to say, 'Oh, I see.'

He left through the back door of the station and she watched him until he disappeared from view.

Bryn O'Brien sat on the bench seat in his workshop making a pointless examination of the end of his five-eighths spanner.

For a while he had felt he was in the direct path of the police investigation. It had been like a juggernaut thundering towards him, headlights blazing, horn blaring. And he had been transfixed, seemingly unable to step out of the route that lined up with its front grille. But now it had passed him. It had thrown up dust and confusion and buffeted him with its slipstream, before he realized that he was back in his usual quiet spot at the side of the road. He guessed he'd hear it rumble on for some time yet as it manoeuvred across town.

The whole experience had introduced him to the unfamiliar territory of deep thought, definitely not somewhere he wanted to linger for long, but he gave a few minutes to Willis and Lorna and Victoria. Death had never touched him before, and now, as if to prove things came in threes, they'd all died in the space of weeks.

He didn't know how he was supposed to feel. He'd had an experience of passing closeness to each of them but, in reality, he knew less than nothing about any of them. And that was kind of how it was with everyone he knew. Therefore his deep thought for the day was really to ask himself if that was enough.

He wondered then about Gary Goodhew. Perhaps just the knowledge that they'd been classmates gave them something of a bond, or maybe he'd only imagined that they'd been, to some extent, on the same wavelength.

Bryn gave a small chuckle. He was hardly going to track Gary down and ask if they could be friends. What next, swapping football cards? Besides, a mate in the police force – it didn't seem likely.

But, even so . . .

Bryn threw the spanner back in the toolbox and grabbed his jacket. It wouldn't hurt to ask Gary to meet him for a drink, then they'd see.

There was one more thing that Goodhew knew he needed to do before the end of the day. The Avery pub stood on Parker's Piece, at the opposite end to Parkside police station, and a few hundred yards from his own flat.

Inside the pub his grandmother was waiting for him with two halves of lager. 'I thought champagne would be inappropriate for the occasion – besides, I don't like it much.'

'What are we celebrating?' he asked, then before she could reply he continued. 'Tell me that in a minute. First, though, I am really sorry I gave you a hard time over the inheritance. I know it's not your fault, and in normal circumstances it would be much appreciated.'

'Gary, I understand, though I doubt most of the rest of the western world would . . . It shouldn't be considered a crime to hate the thought of inheriting money. Just do your best.'

'I will.' He smiled. 'You make it sound like a spelling test.'

'It's probably not quite that bad.'

'So what are we celebrating?'

'End of the case.'

They clinked glasses. 'End of the case,' he repeated.

'And you weren't fired. I was very proud. After working with him, did you sort out why you don't like Kincaide?'

'Oh, he's just sexist, racist, big-headed, narrow-minded, spiteful and arrogant, but beyond that . . . a really good bloke.'

'Mel?'

'Who knows? We'll see.'

'And Bryn O'Brien?'

'Gut feeling? I guess I think he's OK. Why?'

'He's standing outside your house right now.'

They both watched the big man in the distance for a second. 'Do you want to meet him?' Goodhew asked.

His grandmother smiled. 'Yes, actually, I'd love to.'

# AUTHOR'S NOTE

One of the pleasures of completing a book is looking back at the list of people who have helped in some way, many of whom I have only met through the book itself. Among the people I will always associate with *Cambridge Blue* are DI Neil Constable, Kimberly Jackson, Laura Watson, Christine Bartram and Barry Crowther, Paul Johnston, Mark Billingham, Simon Kernick, Imogen Olsen and Peter Lavery, and Lisa Williams and Laura Clift at Cherry Bomb Rock Photography.

I would also like to make a special point of acknowledging Richard Reynolds and Roger Ellory, who have both been generous with their time and expertise. Thank you to Sarah and Graham Fraser at Graham Fraser Productions for their support and help in producing 'Emma's Theme', the trailer for *Cambridge Blue*.

Thank you to Krystyna Green and all the staff at Constable & Robinson. I may be biased, but this book looks fantastic.

Finally, I've seen lots of authors thank their agents and I now have first-hand experience of what a special role an agent plays and how much they deserve appreciation. Thank you, Broo.

A.B.

# THE SOUNDTRACK FOR
## *CAMBRIDGE BLUE*

When I write a book, I find there are songs that 'keep me company' at various points. By the time I finish I have a playlist that belongs to that book alone. Maybe the concept of a book having a soundtrack seems a little odd, but that's how it works for me.

*Back to Black* – Amy Winehouse

*Better than Nothing* – Restless

*Come On Eileen* – Dexy's Midnight Runners

*Dreaming* – Blondie

*Lovers' Lane* – Jacen Bruce

*Miserlou* – Dick Dale

*School Days* – Chuck Berry

*Summer of '69* – Bowling for Soup

*Tonight, Tonight* – The Mello-Kings

*Torn* – Natalie Imbruglia

*Tornado* – The Jiants

*Wild Saxophone* – The Stray Cats

For more information please visit www.alisonbruce.com